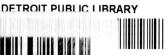
DIGGING
UP LOVE

DIGGING UP LOVE

Chandra Blumberg

This is a work of fiction. Names, characters, organizations, places, events, and incidents are either products of the author's imagination or are used fictitiously.

Published by Montlake, Seattle

www.apub.com

Amazon, the Amazon logo, and Montlake are trademarks of Amazon.com, Inc., or its affiliates.

ISBN-13: 9781542033909
ISBN-10: 154203390X

Cover design and illustration by Liz Casal

Printed in the United States of America

To Peter, my always and forever love

CHAPTER 1

ALISHA

Alisha's car wouldn't start—again. She growled and hit the steering wheel with the heel of her hand. Why was she surprised? Every penny she earned went straight to her bakery fund, not upkeep on her rundown ride. But she did *not* have time for this tonight, not when she needed every second to get ready to share her big news.

Before she could head back inside to ask for a jump, her phone lit up. FaceTime with her little sister could either brighten her mood or send it spiraling south—Simone did nothing by halves, and resisting her whirlwind was as futile as taking a stroll in a hurricane. But Alisha never dodged her sister's calls, even on her busiest days.

"Hey, sis!" Simone puffed out the greeting. Her shoulders swung in a steady rhythm under a strappy sports bra as she jogged, a dark halo of kinky curls making her already-delicate features even more feline. Rows of elliptical machines were visible behind her. "Please tell me you decided to come this weekend."

Alisha pantomimed a grimace and pulled out her go-to response. "I dunno, Sim. A whole weekend away is a lot."

In reality, a whole lifetime in Chicago would never be enough. The tiny town of Hawksburg suffocated her like the washed-out confines of a tintype photo. Dull and monochrome. Trips to visit her sister in the city infused her with enough oxygen to survive the in-betweens. But keeping Simone in the dark about her discontent had become second nature.

"Are you serious?" Simone dragged her forearm across her brow. "I knew you were going to try to wriggle out of your visit. And here I was about to tell you my plan to help you end your self-imposed man-drought before you hit middle age this fall."

"In what world is thirty considered middle aged?"

"Good point. I should have said 'old age.'"

"Humph." Alisha wrenched her keys out of the ignition. "Can we talk about this later? I gotta get home and help Granny with dinner."

"See this?" Simone jabbed a finger at the screen midstride. "This right here is why you need to get out of there every once in a while. Lord knows Gran's perfectly capable of making her own dinner. I bet they'd love to have you out of their hair for a weekend." Simone bounced her eyebrows.

"Gross, Sim."

"Whatever, I'm messing." Simone waved a hand, breezy even when drenched in sweat. "You know I appreciate you watching out for them. And I don't want to pull you out of your beloved Hawksburg—"

A harrumph escaped Alisha's lips, but she covered it with a cough.

Simone puffed on, seemingly unaware. "But will you come, please? Ask your bestie, Margaret, to check in on them. You know she loves a chance to feel useful."

"She doesn't need to spend her weekend running errands with Granny." Not that her best friend wasn't capable—she taught teenagers every day, so taking one elderly woman to the store would be a cinch—but Granny and Grandpa were Alisha's responsibility. "Meg has a life of her own."

"Debatable. And you're only proving my point. You have a life, too, or at least you could if you got out of there more than a couple times a year. C'mon, sis. We'll go dancing, and there's this amazing new tapas place I found . . . plenty of great photo ops for your legion of Insta-stalkers."

"They're followers, not stalkers." And all that sounded amazing. Still, she waited a few seconds before answering, schooling her face into reluctance. "If I say yes, will you agree to nix the man-hunting plan?"

"Lame." A beep signaled the treadmill's slowing down. "But fine, if it gets you out of Hawksburg city limits, then yes. I promise not to try to set you up with a hot, eligible, wildly successful Chicago guy." Simone's sly half grin belied her words.

"Sim, I mean it . . ."

"Ope, sorry, girl." On screen, she came to a halt and flipped the towel over her shoulder with fingers tipped in lilac nail polish. "My boss is calling. She's been riding me like crazy to finish this pitch, so I'd better go. Text me before you hit the road tomorrow. And don't you dare bail on me again!"

"Wouldn't dream of it." But Simone had clicked off the connection. Gone in a flash, as usual.

Fighting the exhaustion of a long day spent balancing the books for her grandfather's barbecue restaurant, Alisha looped her scarf around her neck and trudged through the back door into a kitchen permeated with the scent of caramelizing onions. Grandpa hovered over a sizzling steel pot, laughing with his good friend and longtime cook, Hank Murphy.

Hank locked eyes with her over Wayne's head and frowned. "Thought you were done for the day, Ali."

"I did too." Feet aching, she leaned against the metal counter, and her hip bumped into a plastic package filled with an assortment of green-colored desserts—Rice Krispies treats dusted with green crystals, mini cupcakes topped with clover sprinkles, and perfectly uniform sugar cookies. Prepackaged baked goods were as out of place in her corner of the kitchen as kale greens in Grandpa's smoker.

"Who brought these in?" She prodded the package with a finger through the pocket of her coat. "You guys know I'm always happy to whip up extra batches for the crew."

Grandpa wouldn't let her change up the dessert menu for the holiday, even though there'd be a rush of customers after the Saint Patrick's Day parade tomorrow. But she'd fulfilled several orders of green treats for her own customers, sneaking in the work in the predawn hours before her shifts at the restaurant.

"That's what I keep tellin' your granddaddy Wayne." Hank grinned, round face red and shiny with sweat. "We don't need none of those supermarket treats when we've got our very own master baker in residence!"

In residence, as if Honey and Hickory were a Michelin-starred bistro, not a repurposed general store kitty-corner to the lone stoplight on Main. Wide plank floors and ornate crown molding lent a weathered, rustic charm. Office break room taupe plastered the dining room walls on the other side of the pass-through door. Rolls of paper towels held court on the center of Formica tables, with bottles of barbecue sauce and sticky salt and pepper shakers flanking them like knockoff pawns and bishops. A menu scrawled in chalk hung above the beadboard counter, low enough for cashiers to erase sold-out items.

But what Honey and Hickory lacked in ambiance, it made up for in flavor. Meat and potatoes, hearty and addictive, drenched in their signature smoky-sweet sauce. Which meant no one had room for dessert after filling up on Grandpa's award-winning ribs and brisket. People stopped in for finger-lickin' barbecue, not a sugar fix.

Wayne added a handful of chopped bacon to the heavy-bottomed pot in front of him, blue eyes obscured behind foggy glasses, another pair perched on his thinning white comb-over, a sharp contrast to Alisha's thick black curls, which defied gravity. "And I keep tellin' both of you: dessert is not the focus of our brand."

Alisha mouthed the phrase along with him, and Hank caught her eye and grinned. Well, soon enough Grandpa wouldn't have to worry about *his* brand. She bounced on her toes, full of nerves at the prospect of sharing her dreams aloud. *Soon—just a couple of hours now.*

"Now, what brought you back in, Ali girl?" He shook a generous handful of salt into the pan.

Rubbing at the spot on her chest that always burned with stress after voicing her opinions, she said, "Sorry to bother you, but my battery's dead."

A crinkling smile overtook his frown. "It's no bother. Matter of fact, it'll save me from sittin' through another one of Hank's tall tales." He chuffed his friend on the shoulder, dislodging the glasses perched atop his head in the process. Alisha grabbed for them so they wouldn't hit the floor, then slid the frames into her purse for when evening rolled around and his other pair went missing. She snagged his ancient bomber jacket off a hook and passed it to him before tromping back out into the cold.

"You know, you oughta get rid of that hunk a junk." He popped the hood on his brown Suburban while she fetched the cables. "I don't like the idea of you driving around in somethin' so unreliable. 'Specially in the winter." He sucked breath through his teeth, shooting her a scowl.

"You're one to talk, Grandpa." She lifted her brows at his rust bucket. "And I drive all of twenty miles a week, if that." Other than occasional trips to Chicago to visit Simone and weekly excursions with Granny to stock up at Walmart, life in the one-stoplight town of Hawksburg didn't require much time behind the wheel. "My car should be fine for another year or two."

Though she hadn't told him where her savings were going, Grandpa approved of her thriftiness. Or had in the past. What had changed?

"But if you're so worried, you could always give me a raise." She winked at him, but instead of the chuckle she expected, he rubbed the stubble on his chin, leaning back against the mismatched door of his Chevy.

"I wasn't gonna tell you this yet, baby girl. But a raise might be comin' your way."

She cocked her head. "Grandpa, I was kidding. You pay me plenty. Plus room and board." She forced a laugh at their old joke.

Wayne waved her off. "I know we pay you well. Fair," he amended with a sniff. "But I was thinkin' more in the way of a new title and a raise to match. What you said in there about the treats . . . I know I been a stick in the mud about it, but what if I gave you more freedom with the dessert case?" He spat into a patch of gritty slush in the gravel. "Loosen up the reins, so to speak."

Her grandpa crossed his arms, the cracked leather of his coat squeaking with the motion. "Whaddya say to head pastry chef?"

She barked out a laugh, but Grandpa didn't join in. "Wait, you're serious?"

Head pastry chef? Head of whom? Besides herself and Hank, the crew consisted of a few part-time cooks and a revolving door of dishwashers. She spent most of her time at the stove stirring barbecue sauce, not crème anglaise.

What did she say to a promotion in name only?

How about "Thanks, but no thanks"? No way, no how would she put down roots in the boonies of western Illinois. Never mind she'd already spent over half her life here.

Alisha's eyes flicked to the passenger seat of her car, where commercial real estate printouts and apartment listings lay on full display. She'd planned to tell her grandparents about her business plan tonight. Okay, so originally she'd circled a date back in December, but the frenzy of the holidays had taken over. And last month she'd gathered her courage to speak up, but then a cook quit and the timing felt off.

Point being, tonight was the night. No more hesitation. Pick a path, and leap.

After all, she'd set these plans in motion years ago. Now Grandpa tossed head pastry chef toward her like a half-gnawed bone in front of a kennel gate. One bite and she'd find herself locked inside without a key. Her freedom in sight, obligations now yanked her back once more on a tight leash.

She'd focused most of her energy on looking out for Granny, but maybe Grandpa needed her more than he let on. She tugged aside the lapel of her jacket to run a finger under the collar of her black Honey and Hickory tee, searching his face for a sign.

But he just squinted at her. "Don't look so opposed, Ali. It's pretty much what you've been doing, just more of it. I know you can handle it."

Of course she could handle it! Anyone with a brain in their head could run a restaurant they'd worked at since they were old enough to bus a table. A restaurant where the menu was a twentieth-century relic. Choice of meat on a toasted roll. Shells and cheese. Shoestring fries. Apple pie à la mode, and brownies, also à la mode, courtesy of a big plop of store-bought ice cream. Bottled chocolate syrup on request. The creativity and innovation she'd worked hard to cultivate after college in pastry school didn't do her a lick of good here.

A shadow passed across her grandfather's face, pinching his nostrils and tightening his lips. Alisha dropped her hand from her collar and shoved it in her pocket. She'd never once let her grandparents down and wasn't about to start now. Of course she'd say yes.

Slowing her breathing into a calming rhythm, she forced herself to find the positives . . .

More money in her pocket.

A chance for better fixtures and equipment in her bakery.

She'd play along for a season, sleuthing out what had brought on this change. If it turned out Grandpa needed her here, well, then good thing she hadn't spoken up tonight. And if not, at least she could leave town knowing she'd upped the dessert game at Honey and Hickory.

"When do I start?"

Her grandpa grinned, then walked to the engine to hook up the cables. Head between his arms, he spoke, muffled but stern. "You might not have as much time for your cookie stuff. The restaurant comes first."

Cookie stuff. "I know how to budget my time, Grandpa. And haven't I always put Honey and Hickory first?"

"Mm-hmm, sure have, Ali girl." He grunted and ducked out from under the hood, brushing his hands on his wrinkled khakis. "Just wanna make sure you're ready to put your hobbies aside and make a commitment."

Wow.

Commitment? Like coming back to Hawksburg halfway through senior year of undergrad to pick up the slack at the restaurant and take the pressure off her kid sister? Like putting her bakery dreams on hold to help run Honey and Hickory for *seven years*?

And whatever he said, this pastry-chef gig wasn't a bigger commitment. Just a title. Plus an extended sentence. But what else did she deserve? She leveled a straight stare in his direction. "Pretty sure I can manage."

He nodded once, azure eyes locked on hers, clear and unwavering despite the folds of wrinkles around them. "Good. That's good to hear, Ali. Now let's get this clunker of yours started."

A frustrated sigh hit the back of her clenched teeth, and she bit down harder to contain it. After settling onto the ripped seat behind the steering wheel, she slid her key into the ignition, and the printouts caught her eye. Her ticket out of this claustrophobic little town.

An hour ago, moving seemed like the right choice. Now her certainty swung back to doubt, the ground beneath her feet dipping and rising like a plane in turbulence. Except she hadn't even boarded yet. She stood planted in the concourse, staring at dueling escalators, torn.

Up, down. Stay, go.

Rat-a-tat-tat sounded on the window. Alisha snatched out her hand and flipped the papers over. Grandpa bent double, peering at her through the glass. She pushed off the floorboards and reached over to crank down the passenger window. Cold wind gusted in.

"You planning to start the car or sit there pondering the meaning of life?"

"Sorry."

He shook his head, muttering something about youths, and she cranked the engine. Once, twice, then it wheezed.

"Give her some gas!"

She did, and the engine rumbled to life.

"Good, good."

He took the cables off her car, then his. She climbed out to grab them from him, and he wrapped her in a back-thumping hug. "Knew you'd say yes, Ali girl. This'll be a great new direction for Honey and Hickory. What would we do without you?" He planted a kiss on her forehead, breath smelling of spearmint, then released her. "Tell your granny I'll be home late—don't wait up."

Nodding, Alisha got back into the Geo. A few new recipes. A few months in the new role. Then, if everything went smoothly—she crossed her fingers for luck before shifting into drive—her grandparents would rubber-stamp her plans to move out of Hawksburg, and her future could finally begin.

CHAPTER 2

QUENTIN

"Harris, it's your lucky day."

Quentin dragged his attention away from the CT scans on his computer but pasted a bland smile on his face. Dr. Lawrence Yates, chair of the Earth Sciences Department, was known for taking it out on the staff if he got a whiff of dissent. "Oh?"

The aging professor remained silent as he stood in the office doorway, so Quentin closed his laptop in deference.

"Got a little field trip for you." Lawrence's chuckle turned into a cough. Decades of lunch break cigarettes had racked him, and not just his lungs. Wrinkles etched like erosion lines into his lips, his skin stretched dry and papery over an angular face.

Coughing bout over, he regarded Quentin through watery, bloodshot eyes. "Someone from downstate called about finding a bone on their land. Said, and I quote, 'It's a big 'un.' Emailed a photo. As *proof*." Lawrence snorted—whether to dismiss the claim, the homeowner's intelligence, or humanity at large remained unclear. "Like no one has access to Photoshop these days."

Quentin opened his mouth, but Lawrence cut him off with another dry cough. He pressed a palm to his rumpled denim shirt, clearing his throat like a rusty garbage disposal. "Check your email." Already half-way out the door, he paused. "You can head down there Monday and get it over with. Ask Reid to cover your classes." He left the door open on his way out, the stale scent of tobacco lingering.

Crossing himself—you could never be too careful—Quentin walked over and peeked out into the hallway.

One of the geologists in the department, his best friend, Dr. Tremaine Edwards, leaned out of his office two doors down. "Is the coast clear?" Not waiting for an answer, Tre jogged over on tiptoe. He muscled his way in and plopped down in a faded blue chair next to a shelf crammed with books and loose papers, the chair's rusty wheels squeaking in protest.

Quentin shut the door and leaned back against it. "Think so, but better safe than sorry."

A bone had turned up on someone's land? Odd. He went back to his laptop, opened it, and clicked through to his university email.

"Just glad that old fool didn't darken my doorway today," said Tre. "What's he got for you? An extra freshman course this fall? Night class? Wait, don't tell me. A tour for prospective students. Shoot, brother, what is it?"

Barely registering his friend's questions, Quentin was captivated by the contents of the attachment he'd just opened. His hand drifted to his mouth as he looked at a huge bone sticking out from the side of a pit dug in a grassy field. Mammoth was his first guess, or mastodon.

Definitely not a dinosaur, not in Illinois. No dinosaurs had ever been discovered in the entire state, owing to a lack of Mesozoic rock. He clicked and squinted closer at the enlarged photo. *Maybe . . .* but no. It couldn't be. No way. And Lawrence didn't think so, either, or he wouldn't have pawned this off on him, right?

"Whose dig is that, Q?" Tre had appeared over his shoulder.

"Quit breathing down my neck, man!" Quentin shot out an elbow reflexively and covered his neck where Tre's warm, Funyun-scented breath had hit it. "It's no one's dig. Someone from western Illinois called in a find. Apparently this is in their backyard."

Tre squatted down next to him and peered at the screen. He lifted a meaty finger to the image. "Do you see those layers of shale, just above the clay there? You don't think . . ."

"A dinosaur? No way, man. No way. Right?" Against his better judgment, Quentin's interest was piqued. Dinosaurs used to roam Illinois, Michigan, Wisconsin, and Ohio; of that there was no debate. But glaciers had obliterated any trace.

Although . . . Quentin snapped his fingers and spun toward Tre, knocking his friend off balance with his knees. "Remember how I told you about that hadrosaur find in Missouri? From the forties? They're still excavating the site, finding theropod teeth, claws . . ."

Tre dusted off his hands where he'd caught himself on the tile. He nodded, bushy brows tugging together. "This photo was taken in the western part of the state, you said? If it's near the Baylis Formation, there's a chance. A small one. But don't get your hopes up, Q." Still, he came back to stand behind him, and both men scrutinized the image in silence.

Without permission, Quentin's mind raced. A dinosaur in Illinois? Unprecedented. And a huge boost to his career if they could excavate. A chance to get his father off his case, prove paleo was a legitimate career choice.

Thoughts reeling, he leaned back, forgetting as always the springs were broken. The chair dipped low, and he threw out his arms and legs for balance like a turtle flipped onto its shell. His knees bumped the underside of the desk and knocked a picture frame facedown.

"Watch it!" Tre scooted out of range this time, covering his crotch. "Are you trying to sabotage my chances for a Tre Junior?" He edged around the desk, overcautious. "Not that I would mind a free vasectomy, come to think of it." He smirked. "But Radhika would probably have my useless balls cut off out of spite."

"Jeez, man. Enough with your balls," said Quentin. "And your reproductive life in general, just—"

"Interrupting something, am I?"

Both men flinched. A ghost of cigarette smoke drifted into the room, and Quentin fought back a sneeze. He could almost see it framing Dr. Yates in a sinister halo.

Their department chair eyed Tre with faint disgust. "Edwards," he said with a dismissive nod. Then his pale-blue eyes drilled into Quentin's. "Forgot to mention, Harris, although this should go without saying—if this claim does turn out to be anything, do not discuss it with anyone besides the homeowner. We don't need a circus down there. Understood?"

At a nod from Quentin, Lawrence backed out. Mouth twisted into a frown, he shut the door with a sarcastic flourish.

Tre collapsed into the chair again, head in his hands. He peered out through his fingers. "How does he do it?"

"You mean how does he reduce humanity to dust?" Quentin resisted the urge to fling a pencil at the now-closed door. "I'll let you know when I find out. In the meantime, I need to go talk to Bridget about a favor."

Tre perked up. "Ooo-ooh—"

Quentin cut his friend's childish chant short. "Don't start with me."

"Okay, but it's been more than a *year*, man. Mercedes found someone new months ago."

A new boyfriend? Quentin righted the picture frame to reveal his twin nieces wearing matching pajamas and not-quite-identical smiles in front of a fireplace on what should've been his and Mercedes's second Christmas as a family . . .

"Radhika's still her friend on Facebook," said Tre, tugging at his wiry goatee with a wince. "Ridiculous, I know. But she says it's purely for intel purposes." He continued, softer. "I know you loved her. But there are other women out there. Good women. *Better* women."

Quentin kept his mouth shut, but Tre pushed on. "Mercedes wasn't your future—she was your fallback. The safe option."

Where was this coming from? A four-year relationship culminating in an almost-wedding seemed like the real deal to him, but who was he to argue? Only his life, after all.

But as usual, Tre plowed on, heedless of his friend's reaction. "When's the last time you went out on a date? Or said hi to a female outside work?"

Wow, really? "Sorry not all of us are willing to get married in Vegas on a whim."

"I didn't go through with that and you know it, so you can stop bringing it up." Tre shifted in the chair. "Also, Radhika and I are celebrating three years this June, in case you'd forgotten."

He sure hadn't. Somehow his playboy friend had fallen into marriage before him. It would've been funny if it didn't hurt so much.

Tre stood, hitching up his khakis under the beginnings of a paunch. "All right, that's me out, before this conversation hits *rock* bottom," he said, brown eyes alight with mirth.

Quentin let his head fall sideways and blinked once, refusing to encourage his friend's nonstop geology dad jokes.

Undeterred, Tre grinned and dropped his voice. "Just remember, if Bridget does you a favor, the least you could do for her is a favor of your own." He waggled bushy eyebrows.

This time Quentin caved into the temptation to hurl his pencil. It bounced off Tre's shoulders on his way out. His friend's laughter echoed down the hallway.

Tre could joke all he wanted, but no way would Quentin ask out a colleague. After Mercedes had toppled the foundation of his future, the university was all he had left. He wouldn't jeopardize his career just to get back into the dating game.

His ex-fiancée's specter pushed the mysterious bone out of his mind. He pivoted on his rickety chair until he faced the long rectangular window. Broken blinds slatted his view of the campus, the gray sky and still-bare branches a mirror of his darkening mood. Throwing himself into work and running countless miles hadn't let him escape the truth that Mercedes had canceled their wedding via *text*. Obliterated their future in 160 characters.

Love of his life? Gone.

Newfound family unit? Gone.

Hope for kids? Gone.

Quentin's eyes pricked with tears, and he banished them by dragging a hand impatiently across his face. Stupid Harris curse. Tears flowed freely for men in his family, and for the hundredth time, he wished for the hardened exterior that seemed to come so easily to most men.

Yet lately he wasn't sure what he was mourning: Mercedes, or the dream they'd built?

The echo of Tre's words pelted like sleet against his mind, dumping an unwelcome shower of cold reality on his persistent state of suspended animation. Of course there were other women out there.

But he remembered their long runs on the Lakefront Trail, trivia night at their favorite bar . . . a good, solid relationship. And their future shone bright. Until she snuffed it out in an instant, abandoning him for her dream job in Spain. Didn't even ask him if he would join, or be up for long distance. She skipped town without a backward glance. The custom engagement ring he'd spent four months and six visits to the jewelers designing became just another jettisoned piece of baggage.

Stupid ring. Mercedes's returning it like an overdue library book had dealt the crushing blow. The next morning he'd almost pawned the now-meaningless piece of jewelry. But part of him—okay, all of him, all the time, for a long time—hoped she'd fly back over the ocean into his arms.

She hadn't.

Maybe he ought to take Tre's advice and rip off the relationship Band-Aid. Jump back into the dating game before life passed him by.

What was the other option? Give up on love at the ripe old age of thirty-three and invest in a tweed jacket with elbow patches and a pair of wire-framed reading glasses?

One corner of his mouth lifted at the irony, Quentin took off his round tortoiseshell glasses and rubbed the lenses clean on his polo shirt, then scanned the email again. *Hawksburg, Illinois.* He Google Mapped the route: four hours, eleven minutes. *Oh-kay.* No wonder Dr. Yates had pawned it off on him.

But he leaned forward, chin on his hand, and zoomed in on the photo again. The bone jutted out of the dirt like a wish, or a promise. His pulse sped up.

Maybe . . .

A tendril of hope wound its way into the long-barren soil of his heart, taking root. Who knew what the future held? For once, uncertainty was his ally.

Now on to the tricky part . . . finding a way to get there.

CHAPTER 3

QUENTIN

Quentin took the train to his brother's auto shop. Sidewalks slick with half-melted ice slowed his steps on the brief walk from the station. Cars hissed through a sheen of water on the pavement, and a CTA bus lurched to a halt by the curb as he rounded the last corner.

Head down, hands in his pockets, he kicked aside the grimy remains of a snowbank outside the open garage doors and ducked into the glassed-out office. Blinds slapped back when he shut the door, muffling the zings from electric wrenches. Dueling smells of engine oil and exhaust permeated the room, even with the door closed.

Reggaeton thumped out from a boxy stereo on Hector's desk. His brother sat scowling at an old desktop computer, glasses perched on his nose. Looking up, he snatched the frames off and tossed them into an open drawer. "Hey, little bro!"

Quentin grinned. "Hey, old man. See you finally listened to your wife and started wearing your glasses."

Hector slammed the drawer closed with a matching smirk. "Must be seeing things, Q." Hooking an ankle over his knee, he tipped back in his chair. "What brings you into the trenches today? Need some extra cash to beef up that crappy paycheck you get for teaching entitled college kids? I could always use an extra hand."

"Ha. You know I got no time to spare." And if he did, he wouldn't spend it here. He'd clocked enough penitential hours under the hood during his teen years to atone for a multitude of sins. If he never saw the underside of a car again, it'd be too soon.

He took a seat on the black vinyl chair opposite the desk, toeing at a ripple in the carpet. Asking favors never came easy for him. He chose the roundabout route.

"We're hosting a fossil fair at the museum. Thought maybe I could take the girls." He tugged a pale-green flyer out of his back pocket and unfolded it onto the desk. Hector picked it up, eyes drifting over to the drawer.

"It's next Saturday at noon." Quentin chuckled—his brother was too proud to retrieve his glasses.

"Sorry, I'm sure they'd love that. Kids and dinosaurs." Hector dropped the paper onto the desk. "But they got gymnastics Saturdays."

"Oh. Can't they miss, just the once?"

Deep-brown eyes met his, serious now. "If you saw the bill, you wouldn't ask me that. No way am I paying up the nose for them to skip it."

The door banged open, and at the sight of the tall Black man in the doorway, Quentin snatched the flyer off the desk. Hector slapped a hand on the stereo, and a weighted silence reigned.

Surprise registered on his father's face, but he covered up by addressing him in a booming voice better fitted for an auditorium than the small office. "Quentin! What brings you down from the ivory tower?" His words were teasing, but his voice glinted like sharpened steel at the edges.

"Oh, you know . . ." He pressed a palm to his knee, which had started to jitter, hoping his dad wouldn't notice the crumpled paper in his hand. The last thing he needed was another lecture on his chosen profession.

"He stopped in to invite the twins—"

"I came by to see if I could borrow one of the loaners on Monday." Quentin flashed Hector a WTF look and cleared his throat. "For a work thing."

"A work thing? You mean a dinosaur thing." His dad leaned against the dinged-up metal desk, and it creaked under his bulk.

"That is my field, yes." His dad and brother both sniffed, nostrils twitching in unison.

Forget this. He could find another way to get to Hawksburg. "Never mind about the car. I'll figure something out."

A mechanic in coveralls poked his head in, blinking at the full office. "Uh, could I get you to take a look at the BMW, Hector?"

Nodding, he sprang out of his chair and practically jogged out of the room. *Coward.*

His father blew out a breath and walked around the desk. He fished a can of Coke out of the mini fridge in the corner and flipped the top. Raised a brow at Quentin, who shook his head. Last thing he needed right now was caffeine to add to his jitters.

His dad took a sip, then bared his teeth in a hiss. "I just don't see why you insist on keeping your nose buried in the past when you could be out there on top of it all, making a difference." He raised his can, gesturing toward a mythical reality where his youngest son hadn't turned out to be a disappointment.

"Again with this, Dad? All my research reframes the way we see the world. I'm studying extinct creatures to impact the future. It's the very definition of making a difference!" Quentin shoved his fists into his armpits. "What's your problem? Just because I'm not doing it from a law office, is that it?"

"Lawyer, MD, engineer—you name it, Q! Here you are, a grown man, asking to bum a ride."

"And there it is. It's not about changing the world. Everything always comes back to money with you." And not owning a car was a conscious choice, not a budget issue.

"What if it does? You moan all the time about wanting a family. Well, what happens when you get your wish? How're you going to provide for kids if you can barely make ends meet?" The dagger hit in a soft spot, and a spark of ire ignited under his sternum.

"I make ends meet just fine, Dad. And there's more to life than money." Like assistant professor at one of the top paleontology departments in the world, with a great shot at tenure. But then again, his dad hadn't cared enough to ask about his position at work in years, and he'd long since quit volunteering news.

His dad squeezed the Coke can hard enough for the tin to dent. "That so. Hmm." Unflinching, he said, "Excuse me for not falling over myself to praise my grown son for chasing some childhood fantasy."

His dad's cold retort doused the inferno in Quentin's chest. Three degrees and fifteen years after disappointing his father by choosing a career in a field Dad insisted was on its way to extinction, Quentin yearned for a return to their old bond. But the harsh words wedged between them had created an impenetrable wall, mortared with a mix of venom and contention.

The door banged open, blinds flying, and Hector came back in, wiping his greasy fingers on a rag. He stopped short, splitting a look between Quentin and Reggie. "Uh, DeMarcus wanted a word when you're through, Dad."

Their father took one last swig from the almost-full can and dropped it in the trash. "You can take my truck, Q. Loaners are for paying customers." He pushed off the desk and strode out the door without a backward glance.

Hector ran a hand up over his hair, ruffling the strands. He'd inherited their mom's straight black hair, though Isabel's had begun to gray. Quentin got his dad's coarse curls and his mother's light eyes.

Abandoning the pretense, Hector fished his glasses out of the drawer. He slid them over his nose, then flipped through the filing cabinet and dragged out a folder.

Eyes trained on the sheaf of papers in his hands, he said, "You know he doesn't talk like that when you're not around."

"And that's supposed to make it better?"

"It should." His brother tossed the file on the desk and sank into his chair, broad shoulders hunched. Another contrast. Quentin had his dad's height, but Hector had his brawn. "He leans into you because he expects a lot of you. Not because he doesn't care."

"I know. But you'd think after all my hard work, he'd see my career is worthwhile. Maybe the one worthwhile thing I've got."

Emotion clogged his throat, unwelcome but not unexpected. Hector's eyebrows tugged up and inward over his brown eyes. Quentin hated being the object of that hangdog expression. He stood, shouldering his messenger bag. "I'm out. See ya Sunday."

Before he could turn, Hector stood and grabbed his palm, pulling him in for a hug. "Take care, Q."

CHAPTER 4

ALISHA

Bzzz. Bzzz. Bzzz. Thwap!

Alisha's phone vibrated itself off the metal prep table and hit the floor. Whisk in hand, she stooped to retrieve it with a jaw-cracking yawn, exhausted from rising before dawn for the long drive home. Janet Snyder. *Jeepers, what now?*

"Hello?"

"Hiya, girlie! Glad I caught ya. Ellie told me you were at your sister's for the weekend." Alisha didn't bat an eyelash. Granny and Mrs. Snyder had been best friends for almost sixty years and kept no secrets from each other. "Yeah, I was. Just got back into town." She blinked blearily at the bowl of flour on the counter. Had she added baking soda yet?

"Oh, so you're already home, then." A soft *scritch* came through the phone, and Alisha imagined the curtain sliding open to reveal Mrs. Snyder's bulbous nose pressed to the glass pane of her living room window. "Don't see your car."

Busybody. She crooked the phone into her shoulder and stood on tiptoes to pull down the cocoa powder. "Not home yet."

Almost there. Another inch . . . and the canister tumbled off the shelf and into the bowl of flour, dumping its contents. Great. "Figured I'd get a jump on the week's baking so I could take Granny to the store later." And maybe actually devote the rest of her day off to her cookie business for once. A girl could dream, right?

"Oh, don't got to worry about that, dear. I had Steve take us both on Saturday. He likes to stay busy, get out of the house every day." She bet he did. "But that's neither here nor there. The reason I called is . . ." Mrs. Snyder's voice dropped, and Alisha palmed the phone to see if she'd lost the call, but the connection was intact.

Bringing her cell back to her ear, she said, "Sorry, lost you for a minute."

Mrs. Snyder tsked. "I said, your granny's got a situation on her hands. She didn't want you to know, but you really ought to be in the loop."

Alisha stopped listening. Blood pulsed in her ears. *Granny.* Her cancer had relapsed.

No, no, no, no. Her hands shook, and she set the phone on the counter, activating the speaker button on her second try. Blackness crept into the edges of her vision. She never should've accepted Simone's invitation. Granny needed her here, not hundreds of miles away.

Guilt welled up in her chest. All this time, she'd been contemplating deserting her grandparents to start up a bakery in Chicago . . . stupid. Selfish.

"Are you listening, Ali? It's Steve. He dug up a dinosaur."

If Alisha hadn't been a panicked mess, she would've burst out laughing. Relief cascaded over her, immediate and overwhelming. False alarm. Just the latest in Mrs. S's absurd snippets of gossip, passed on with all the credibility of a sleepover game of telephone.

She lifted the empty cocoa tub out of the bowl and dusted it off, not even bothered about the new batch she'd have to start. She'd bake a thousand trays of plain brownies, as long as Granny stayed safe and healthy.

But a dinosaur bone . . . what in the world? She brushed her hands on her apron, trying to connect the dots. Her grandparents had enlisted Mrs. Snyder's husband, Steve, to use his backhoe to dig them a pool. He'd planned to break ground this weekend. Another reason her reluctance to leave town hadn't been all show, but Granny had practically packed her bag for her.

"Are you hearing me, Ali? Steve discovered a real live *T. rex* right on your property!"

"A *live* one, huh?" Retreating adrenaline left her on the verge of laughter, but Mrs. S went on, oblivious.

"On Friday, Steve took the tractor over. Your granny and I went on out to supervise, since your granddad's out of town. Shame, you both abandoning your grandmother on the same weekend. Lucky Steve and I are around to look after her."

The barb hit its mark, and Alisha rubbed a thumb at her breastbone.

Perhaps sensing her guilt trip had landed, Mrs. S let it lie. "Anyhoo, Steve's out there digging. And when he's 'bout finished, up comes this almighty scrape. I run over, waving my arms for him to stop. Lucky he saw me 'fore he shattered the bone. Thought sure we'd uncovered a murder."

Not a big leap for a woman who spent her afternoons bingeing serial-killer documentaries on Netflix.

"But lo and behold, the bone was bigger than any human had rights to. Any *animal* neither. So your granny just went ahead and made a few calls. See, you might not know this, but our Bobby went to Chicago Northern for his microbiology degree."

Of course Alisha knew that: it was all the Snyders talked about for years after their grandson had gotten into the prestigious program.

"So I advised her to call the university, on account we had the connection, and before we know it, we hear back from the folks at

CNU, who say they're sending someone down to investigate. Can you believe it?"

She *couldn't* believe it, actually. But Mrs. Snyder wasn't looking for an answer. "So we'll see you soon!"

"Excuse me?" Had she missed something?

"You sure haven't heard a word I said, else you'd be halfway here by now. You got a man there with ya?" Innuendo dripped like bacon grease off Mrs. Snyder's words, and Alisha held the phone away from her ear, gagging.

"At the restaurant? C'mon now, Mrs. S. Just throwing some brownies together, like I said."

"Mm-hmm." Mrs. Snyder drew out the sound, and Alisha banged her forehead silently against the walk-in fridge. "Well, get your little heinie back home. This here could be the most exciting thing to happen in Hawksburg ever. Best get here before the scientist does."

She rubbed her brow, where a headache was fast forming, and not from the fridge. "What scientist?"

"The pro-fe-ssor. From Chicago Northern University?" Mrs. S annunciated each word like an American tourist asking for directions to the Louvre. "Told your grandma he'd drive down this morning to check out the claim. Sounded very professional on the phone, she said."

Had Granny shared that tidbit, or did Mrs. Snyder have their landline bugged? Chances were fifty-fifty.

Still, she should get home before Mrs. S lost her mind. Alisha tossed the cocoa container and lid into recycling, then washed up the bowl so Hank wouldn't walk into a mess. The brownies could wait, since technically Monday was her day off.

Her car sat under a dusting of unusual spring snow, so Alisha pulled her sleeve down over her hand to clean off the windows. Once the windshield was snow-free, she hip-bumped against the driver's side door, lifting the handle at the same time. The door caved open with a thud, and she stumbled back but quickly righted herself, used to the routine.

After falling into her seat, Alisha cranked up the ignition with a muttered Hail Mary. After a heart-stopping second, the engine turned over. Ignoring Grandpa's oft-repeated warning to let the car warm up a minute first, she pulled out into the deserted street.

Who had time for that? From the sound of things, Hawksburg would be crawling with news crews any minute now. Alisha giggled, but she did wonder just what kind of bones Steve had dug up. A few years ago, she remembered hearing about a farmer who'd discovered a wooly mammoth in Michigan. Were there mammoths in Illinois? She had absolutely no idea. Probably a rotten deer carcass.

The gossip chain liked to make a mountain out of a molehill, and Granny and Mrs. S were the ringleaders. Nothing else to do in Hawksburg. If she stayed here for almost three-quarters of a century, no doubt she'd get invested in small-town tomfoolery too. But that wouldn't happen. *Couldn't happen.* Besides, Granny's last checkup went great. And no red flags from Grandpa since the "promotion."

At the blinking red stoplight leading out of town, she clicked on her blinker needlessly, then rubbed a sleeve against the inside of the windshield to bail out the feeble defrost. Fallow fields stretched to the horizon, an endless brown sea with dirt-clod and cornstalk flotsam and jetsam. She contemplated running the light. But like always, piece of gum working restlessly in her jaw, she waited.

Goody-goody, her inner critic scolded in a singsong voice that sounded a lot like her little sister's. No traffic in sight, she accelerated, gritting her teeth at the stark reality that returning home hadn't been the blip she'd expected. Seven years since she'd planned to put Hawksburg in her rearview for good, she remained stuck at its epicenter, rooted like the ancient oak in her grandparents' front yard.

Fields gave way to pastureland dotted with cows gave way to more fields. Pothole-riddled pavement turned to dirt. The Geo bottomed out in a moon-size crater, and Alisha's gum hit the back of her throat. She coughed it out and shoved it onto the lid of an empty coffee cup on the passenger seat to focus. Snow was blowing across the road, and she didn't want to hit a stray deer, or worse yet, a cow.

She passed the Snyders' well-kept brick farmhouse on the left and pulled into her grandparents' driveway a quarter mile down. A couple of bare maples and a brown-leafed oak sheltered the two-story white farmhouse. The peeling porch pillars were wrapped in cheery multi-colored Christmas lights Granny might take down by Memorial Day, maybe.

A pickup truck sat in the gravel driveway. The paleontologist? Alisha killed the engine with her usual prayer that the Geo wouldn't sink into its final rest, heaved the door open, then popped the trunk to retrieve her bag.

Schlepping her duffel past the truck, she had to restrain herself from caressing its sleek black side. Though she'd stubbornly resisted most facets of farm life, she wasn't immune to the purr of a diesel engine and the allure of an extended cab. Nothing quite like a man sitting behind the wheel of a big truck to set her heart aflutter.

But she had a mental picture of the paleontologist, and it didn't match the sexy pickup. Pushing fifty, craggy faced, with sun-bleached blond hair. Dressed in head-to-toe khaki. A brown leather fedora the hokey cherry on top.

Not like appearances mattered. She would help Granny deal with the situation and send him—or her, she thought, correcting another assumption—on their merry way, hopefully with no hard feelings for a wasted trip. She headed into the house, the sagging porch steps creaking under her feet.

Dropping her duffel at the foot of the staircase, she called out into the quiet house. "Granny?"

No answer.

"Mrs. S?" Surely she'd zoomed over to watch the show as fast as her motorized scooter could carry her the moment she'd finished her illicit phone call.

Still nothing. Must be out back. Alisha clomped down the shotgun hallway in her boots, risking a tongue-lashing from Granny.

Her phone chimed, and she dug it out of her pocket.

Meg:
Home yet?

Alisha:
Yes, and apparently there's a T-rex waiting for me in the backyard.

Meg:
Is that some kind of code?

Alisha:
I wish. I'll call you later, but right now I have to run a fossil-hunter off our property.

Meg:
WHAT??

Grinning at her friend's consternation, she pocketed her phone and pushed out the back door. About forty yards behind the house, Mrs. S sat on her trusty motorized steed. Granny stood next to her, the top of her blonde bob a good foot shy of the reflective orange safety flag jutting up out of the back of the seat.

Opposite the women, a backhoe perched motionless on the edge of the crater like a mechanical gargoyle, motor silent. Granny was holding a whispered conference with Mrs. Snyder, doused in her trademark rose-scented perfume so strong it could penetrate a gas mask.

Alisha slunk up to the women like an uninvited guest at a funeral. She couldn't help but address them in a hushed tone. "Hi, ladies."

Mrs. Snyder let out an almighty yelp and revved her engine. The scooter lurched forward toward the edge of the hole. Alisha dived for the kill switch, and Granny wrapped both arms around her friend's ample waist, the heels of her Wellington boots making furrows in the grass. The scooter skidded to a halt like a clown car dumping its occupants at center stage.

Alisha collapsed onto her knees, panting. "So sorry, Mrs. S!"

"Janet." Fanning her flushed face, she leveled a beady gaze at Alisha. "If I've told you once, I told you a thousand times. Call me Janet." She adjusted one of her clip-on earrings, blue-veined hand trembling. "'Mrs. S' makes me feel about a thousand years old."

Alisha nodded just to pacify her. The switch would be impossible. Mrs. Snyder was Hawksburg's answer to Mr. Feeny: a seventh-grade math teacher, religious ed catechist, and, after retirement, a high school substitute teacher. No sense in arguing, though.

She pushed off the freezing ground and turned to Granny. "What's this I hear about a skeleton in our new swimming pool?"

Pulling the sides of her coat around herself, her grandma said, "I was gonna tell you when you got home, sweetie. But you never get much time to yourself. I didn't want to interrupt your visit with Simone. And I doubt it's anything. Janet just said we should be sure."

Surprise, surprise. Mrs. Snyder had called in the professionals, not Granny.

"I'm sure we'll have this whole thing resolved today." Granny patted her arm in reassurance.

Alisha relaxed a bit at her grandma's touch. The Blake women looked nothing alike. Her grandma was a fine-boned peroxide blonde and fair as winter moonlight. But temperament-wise, they were a match. If Granny wasn't fussed, everything would be fine. But still . . .

"So there *is* a bone?"

Granny nodded. "A big one. See for yourself."

Obediently, Alisha took a step forward to peer down into the pit. The man—and it *was* a man, after all—crouched in the mud, squinting against a battered digital camera, and wasn't wearing the khaki uniform she'd expected.

Instead, a dark-gray zip-up hoodie showed the curve of strong biceps and wide shoulders. He sat on his haunches in worn-in jeans and brown work boots. A cobalt-blue beanie was pulled down over his ears, accentuating the line of a straight, clean-shaven jaw. Definitely not middle aged either.

This was fine. Totally fine. Well, *he* was fine, that much was certain. *Keep it together, Alisha.*

No worries. She tugged at her cropped leather jacket. She was perfectly capable of sending a fit young scientist packing.

Just then, he rested the camera on his thigh and looked up at them through the snow, his gaze as dazzling as a burst of sunshine after a storm.

Alisha's knees almost gave way. Up until this moment, she would've put weak knees right up there with Bigfoot in the realm of myth. But the man's electric gray-green eyes short-circuited her nerve endings and left her legs wobbly as Bambi's.

He pulled his full lips to the side, gaze unfocused, clearly deep in thought. Then he dropped those striking eyes to the ground and stood up, rubbing a hand absently along his chiseled jaw. Her stomach turned itself inside out. It wasn't every day she encountered a man who looked like her fantasies incarnate. But the biting wind and snowflakes swirling through the air hit her like a bucket of ice water. Not a daydream, then. Which begged the question, What to do now?

The textbook definition of a sexy scientist stood a few feet away, smack-dab in the middle of her grandparents' future swimming pool. Chills that had nothing to do with the freezing temps collided with the heated flush of a heart gone into hyperdrive. A magnetic tug drew her a step closer, vying with a hysterical urge to turn tail and run.

Heavens to Betsy, cool it, Blake.

Without another thought, Alisha took a breath and jumped into the deep end.

CHAPTER 5

QUENTIN

Quentin's fingers twitched with the impulse to pick up the four-inch curved claw in his viewfinder, but he snapped a photo instead, making sure to capture the measuring tape stretched out next to the fossil. He lowered the battered digital camera to his thigh, rubbing his jaw.

Besides the partially exposed limb bone off to his right, a little digging with a hand trowel had revealed several fragments of vertebrae, along with a conical tooth he'd bet good money was ceratopsian. A triceratops tooth would never be found alongside Ice Age remains, and the claw all but sealed the deal. Evidence was mounting that the giant bone wasn't a wooly mammoth after all.

Quentin stood, rubbing his hand along his jaw. Could this be a prank? A dinosaur femur, and the claw and tooth less than a meter away? Too good to be true. The whole thing reeked of a ruse. He scanned the area for a clue the situation was rigged. A quick glance up at the rim reassured him neither of the elderly women had a phone out to film the situation. But any minute now, the rug would be pulled out from under him.

"Alisha, wait!"

A shower of loose rocks snapped him out of his reverie. He turned his head just as a woman dropped into the pit, landing with a thud.

Annnd there went the rug.

She straightened and squinted up at him through the softly falling snow, looking wholly unconcerned about disturbing fossils millennia in the making. In fact . . . there, sticking out from under her boot. His fists clenched of their own accord. "Do you mind?"

In response, she arched one dark brow. Her face was framed with long braids spilling out of a winter hat topped by one of those little fluffy balls. Women always looked so cute in those.

But *this* woman—Ayesha, was it?—looked more amused than adorable. *Nuh-uh.* She didn't get to grin at him like that, Little Miss Rain on His Parade.

She stuck her hands into her pockets and rocked up on her toes, grinding the fragment into the muck.

"Seriously, could you please step back?"

Her grin disappeared. "Could you?"

What the heck? No, he could not blindly step back. And who was she anyway? If he were prone to daydreams, a beautiful stranger materializing out of thin air at a dig might've ranked high on the list. But that woman would be treading lightly, not trampling fossils like a *T. rex* at a tea party.

Plus, she wore a black leather jacket and jeans tucked into boots to combat the cold, and his fantasyland was a tropical island. A fictional Cuban tropical island. Okay, so his fantasyland was Isla Nublar, sans a power outage—

"Are you going to clue me in?"

Blinking fast, he bit back the first three retorts that sprang to mind. The sheer nerve of a random civilian hopping into a field site like she owned the place. Here he was, out in middle-of-nowhere Illinois, amid dinosaur bones where they had no business being, and now he had to contend with an entitled interloper.

Who was she, anyway? A nosy neighbor? Friend of the family?

Dr. Yates's voice rang in his mind, an unnecessary reminder. Press around a dig, especially at this stage, could spiral out of control, attracting rubberneckers and looters. Shutting down this trespasser had become top priority.

Quentin crossed his arms. The woman shifted her feet to mirror his wide stance. She took her hands out of her pockets and set them on her waist, and her jacket rode up just enough to expose a peek of skin below her belly button. Not that he noticed.

He also didn't notice when a single crystal snowflake landed on the tip of her nose. Or the plump curve of her lips before she pressed them together, almost like she was trying to hide a smile. He pulled his own mouth into a straight line and narrowed his eyes.

Could she be from another university? No way. He discarded the hypothesis as soon as it sprang to mind. No self-respecting paleontologist would leap feetfirst into an unmapped dig. He held his ground and tightened his jaw, refusing to speak first, lest he give something away.

So they stood frozen, toe to booted toe, breath mingling in plumes of vapor, gazes locked. A minute passed, two. During their stalemate, the snowflakes picked up, drifting between them. She must be cold, with only a thin jacket on. He regarded her narrowly through the white flakes.

A slight tremor ran through the woman, and she crossed her arms. Cold, for sure. Her jacket rode up higher. His eyes tracked the movement, then snapped back up.

Must. Not. Be. Distracted. By. Her. Sexiness.

Too late. Now all he could think about was the glimpse he'd had of her thick legs in those skintight jeans. *Stop it!* Think of your career, Quentin. And not getting screwed over on the biggest find of your life because you got distracted by a pretty face. Her nostrils flared, and her molten brown eyes ignited. Not just a pretty face—a stunning one. He sucked in a breath to match hers and tipped up his chin.

"For goodness' sakes, Ali. Either invite the man in for coffee or get out of his way so he can finish up 'fore he catches his death of cold."

The voice came from the top of the pit. He'd forgotten they had an audience.

The intruder dropped her confident pose in a snap. "Right, sorry. I'll just . . ." She bit her lip and dropped her eyes to the ground, casting about.

Interesting. She knew the owner of the property well enough to take orders from her at the drop of a hat. The woman pivoted and took a step, stumbling back when she came face to face with the femur. He caught himself just before his fingertips grazed her arms. Her shoulder blades hit his chest, and she spun away.

"Um, is that what I think it is?" Her eyes hadn't left the bone.

"That depends," said Quentin levelly.

"On . . ."

"On what you think it is." He hitched a shoulder.

Meeting his eyes, she groaned. "Are you being cagey for a reason?"

"Come again? You're the one who dropped in on me, with no explanation."

"Well, since this is my grandparents' yard, I feel like I deserve to know what's going on here."

Her *grandparents'* yard? He lifted his eyes to where the two elderly women hovered at the pit's edge, but they'd disappeared. Great. Alone with the troublemaker.

Wait a minute. His flustered mind translated the implications of what she'd just said. The homeowners' granddaughter?

Oh no. Please, no. Why had he iced her out like that? Quentin took a deep breath through his nose, thumb and index finger pinching his forehead. This was bad. Very bad. He might've screwed the university's chances. If the owners of the property wouldn't let them excavate because he'd pissed off their grandkid, he was done for.

He dropped his arm and produced a polite smile. "Look, I'm very sorry, Aliyah . . . ," he started.

"Alisha."

Shoot, he'd called her the wrong name? Worse and worse.

"*Alisha*, right. I'm so sorry, I didn't realize you were . . ."

"Related to a white woman? Yeah, I get that a lot."

"Actually, I was more worried about this." He bent to retrieve the fossil from her boot imprint. And yeah, he hadn't expected a gorgeous Black woman to drop in on him out of the sky out here in Farmville.

She leaned forward to inspect the fragment in his hands, and he hissed. "Sorry. I just—" He slipped the fossil into a plastic bag from his pocket. "Sorry. But can I j-just ask you to please . . ." As he stammered, a slight smile played across her lips. Did she enjoy seeing him squirm?

"Stop stomping around your fossils?"

"Yes." He breathed out the word in relief, and her grin widened.

"Got it." She glanced around. "It's just hard to believe our backyard is some sort of point of interest." *Our* backyard? So she lived here too. Quentin filed that information away. "Didn't catch your name, by the way?"

Good manners finally returned to him, and he extended a hand. "Quentin Harris, associate professor of vertebrate paleontology at Chicago Northern."

She gripped his hand, her fingers chilly. "Nice to officially meet you. And now I'll let you get back to work." Letting go, her feet remained planted. "Uh, which way?"

Realizing she didn't want to disrupt the site, he angled a real smile her way for the first time. Respect for fossils earned brownie points with him. He turned slightly to indicate the side of the pit behind him. So far he hadn't seen any evidence of exposed fossils in that section. She moved past him, boots sticking in the mud like in wet cement.

"Do you need a hand?"

She waved him off. "No thanks, I'm good." Another step, and she face-planted. He reached her side in a single stride and knelt next to her. The cold muck seeped into his jeans.

Alisha pushed herself to hands and knees, and a glop of mud fell off her chest. "Ugh."

"It's just mud."

"Says the man who digs in the dirt for a living."

"Actually, the digs I usually excavate are in deserts. Dust and rocks, not mud. This dirt is very different from where fossils are normally found. In fact, these bones might not even be fossiliz—"

She sat back on her heels and cut him off with a look. Mud coated her chest like an apron. Only the white pom-pom on top of her hat remained unscathed. Other than that, she was drenched in muck like Augustus Gloop after his swim in the chocolate river. He pressed his lips together to keep in his laugh, but at her squinty glare, a deep chuckle rose up from his belly. He held an arm over his mouth.

"'Just mud,' huh?" A dimple appeared in her right cheek, though the rest of her face remained impassive under mud specks that dotted her cheeks like freckles.

"I'm sorry." He gasped out the words, short on breath with the effort of holding in his laughter. He'd already done enough damage with his obstinate silence earlier. "But your braids . . ." He sobered. "Are they ruined?" His cousins were always complaining about how long it took to get braids put in.

Alisha bit her lip and gingerly lifted a braid between two muddy fingers. "Gosh, I hope not. But I think I'll be able to wash out the mud, as long as I'm patient." Her lips twisted in a rueful expression, and he guessed patience wasn't her strong suit.

"If you don't mind me asking, what was your endgame, jumping in here?"

"Um, reconnaissance?" A laugh bubbled up out of her, and he couldn't help but join in this time. She rubbed a finger under her nose, leaving a trail of mud snaking across her upper lip, and then cringed. "Whoops. Just gave myself a killer 'stache, didn't I?"

Quentin rolled his lips together to contain a smile. "Do you want me to—"

She nodded before he could finish. He swiped his thumb along her soft skin, and a tremor went through his hand. His finger slipped and he brushed her lip. Her lush cupid's bow sent a jolt through his fingertip straight to the base of his spine, propelling him to his feet.

"You're good." His words came out rough and scratchy, his cheeks hot. Shoving his sleeves up on his forearms, he offered her help to stand, but she just stared at his outstretched arms.

He tucked his chin, bending to catch her eyes. "I don't mind the mud, remember?"

With a nod, she grabbed hold and pulled herself up. Dropping his hands, she clucked her tongue, maybe at all the dirt. To show he really didn't mind, he wiped his palms down the front of his hoodie, leaving smears of mud. "Now we're both a mess."

Her white teeth flashed against her light-brown skin in a quick smile, and his stomach dipped.

Then she turned and scrabbled out of the hole. Or tried to. He watched her for a minute, not minding the view, before he spoke up. "At the risk of sounding like a broken record, do you need any help getting out?"

Head craned back, she said, "Turns out today pride actually did go before the fall. So yes, I could definitely use a hand out of this pit of humiliation."

"Well, in that case . . ." He stopped, because his first impulse, grabbing her butt and boosting her over? Yeah, that was *not* happening. Instead, he hauled himself out and knelt down on the edge of the sod. He grasped her arm just below the elbow and tugged gently. She dug her toes in and threw herself over the edge.

Tucking her knees under herself, she said, "You seem to always be helping me up."

"I can't help if you're always falling down around me," Quentin countered with a smile.

Alisha cocked her head. "Yeah, well, when I woke up this morning, I wasn't prepared to go swimming with dinosaurs."

"Swimming?"

"My grandparents want an in-ground pool. Hence the La Brea Tar Pit situation."

"Ah, right." Quentin's mind chose that particular moment to alert him to the fact that he and Alisha were sitting intimately close, knees pressed together. He cleared his throat and pushed himself up off the snow-dusted grass. "So Eleanor Blake is your grandmother?"

"I guess you didn't notice the family resemblance?" Her eyes twinkled.

"Not so much, but now that you mention it, it's the hair." He gave a half smile. "You're just not what I expected when I drove out here today."

Alisha stood up and shuffled toward the house. "That makes two of us." They stopped outside the large screened-in porch. "When I heard there was a paleontologist headed to my grandparents' house, you're not exactly what I pictured."

"Oh? What did you picture?"

"I dunno." She looked at him from under thick lashes, then gestured with mud-coated fingers. "Older. Rounder. More khaki."

He tipped his head back and laughed. "Indiana Jones with a dad bod?"

She chuckled and shrugged.

"Sorry to disappoint," he said.

"Oh no, I'll take the lack of khaki . . ." She trailed off, gaze dropping down his body. Then her eyes shot away, and she fiddled with the zipper of her coat.

Heat pricked his cheeks. Suddenly he didn't know what to do with his hands, or his face.

"To be fair, Indiana Jones wasn't a paleontologist; he was an archaeologist." Oh gosh, flashing his awkward-teacher badge. Once a nerd, always a nerd.

But she met his eyes again with a smirk, still working at the zipper. "Are we certain that's what Indiana Jones was? Seems like 'Tomb Raider' would be more apt."

Quentin laughed. "True. I doubt any scientific discipline wants to claim him. At least not nowadays." He shifted on the yellowed grass, nearly turning his ankle. "Speaking of claiming . . ."

Alisha had gotten the zipper down and was trying to worm her way out of her jacket, without much success. He raised an eyebrow at her, and she nodded. He went around behind her and pulled at the leather collar while she shimmied. The sweet, cheerful scent of citrus wafted up from her nape, scrumptious as orange sherbet, and Quentin swallowed.

"The thing is, any dinosaur bones found on private land belong to the property owner. There's no onus to turn the fossils over to science." He spoke into the frosty air above her head, the pom-pom tickling his chin. "Your grandparents could sell them for a profit." The words stuck in Quentin's throat like silt in a sieve, but it needed to be said.

He finally peeled the coat all the way off Alisha's shoulders and gulped. Underneath, she wore a plain white tee, nothing racy, but something about helping a woman undress felt, well, like helping a woman undress.

Cheeks aflame, he ducked his head and came around in front of her again, holding the coat at arm's length. No sense making it look like the two of them had been mud wrestling when he went in to talk to her *grandmother*. Although . . .

He looked down at the muddy streaks on his hoodie, and his cheeks burned hotter.

If she noticed his embarrassment, she gave no sign. "So lemme get this straight. Mr. Snyder actually *did* dig up dinosaur bones in our backyard, and now you're asking me if, in light of that fact, my grandparents would rather go on eBay and auction them off than donate them to you guys?"

"More or less." Just because her grandma called in the find didn't mean she wouldn't change her mind when she found out what lay beneath the winter-brown grass in their backyard.

Alisha sat on the concrete steps and hunched over to undo the mud-encrusted laces on her boots. "I can promise you my grandparents have no plans to get into the fossil trade. They're in their seventies, and that sounds like a giant hassle. I'm guessing they just want to be rid of the bones, since right now the swimming pool looks like a prehistoric crime scene." She tugged off one boot, then the other, stripping off her socks to reveal toes painted a glossy orange. Another detail about her he most definitely *did not* notice.

"Whether or not they want you and your cronies trampling all over the yard is another story," Alisha said. "If I were you, I'd turn on the charm in there when you plead your case. Oh, and leave those out here, or you're dead in the water." She pointed to his mud-caked boots.

He squatted down to untie his laces while she opened the screen door and waddled, legs wide, dodging white wicker furniture, to the back door. She turned the knob and pushed a shoulder against the glass pane. "Granny?"

"In the kitchen, sweetie!"

The scent of fresh coffee and cinnamon drifted out the doorway, inviting. Legs splayed, Alisha rotated toward him. "Kitchen's down the hall to the right. I'd say good luck, but I heard you cackling just now, Dr. Harris." One corner of her mouth lifted, belying her stern tone and sparking her eyes again.

Backlit by warm light spilling out of the house, with muddy braids and dirt-splattered jeans, she was beauty incarnate. A warrior princess.

The laugh dried in his throat, replaced with a deep and pleasant ache below his breastbone.

Then she resumed her bowlegged march toward the stairs, and his laughter returned.

"Heard that!"

Quentin stepped out of his boots and shook his head. *Unbelievable.* Against all odds, Lawrence had been right. *Lucky day, indeed.* This dig could provide endless research opportunities, not to mention the kind of renown that would make his father sit up and take notice. Here's hoping his luck held out and the Blakes signed off on the excavation.

CHAPTER 6

ALISHA

"You're telling me you had a real-life Owen Grady in your backyard today?"

Alisha brought her hand up to shield the side of her face, darting a glance toward the crowded bar. "Shh, keep your voice down!"

She'd met up with her friend Meg to play darts and debrief about the dino situation at the Back Forty, the only place in town able to boast anything remotely resembling a nightlife, thanks to a liquor license and spotty satellite service broadcasting sports on four wide-screens. Shellacked, knot-ridden wood paneling lined the walls, and classic rock wailed from a jukebox to give the outdated decor a run for its money. Like most of Hawksburg, the bar's ambiance chafed like a piece of gravel stuck in her shoe.

"And no. I'm pretty sure there's no such thing as a real-life *Velociraptor* trainer." She shook her head at Meg, who looked runway-model gorgeous as always, despite coming straight off a long week teaching social studies at the local high school. Meg's wavy dark-brown hair fell across her shoulders to brush the top of the table, her creamy skin flawless even without the aid of concealer.

"Well, if you ever meet one, step aside. I'd be all over that." Meg spoke around a mouthful of mozzarella stick.

Alisha raised her brows at her friend. "Is that"—she gestured to the string of cheese dangling from her friend's chin—"part of your seduction technique? Because if so, I think I'm safe." She grinned, then closed one eye and cast a dart. It hit the wall a good four feet away from the target.

"Anyways, he's less Chris Pratt and more of a . . ." She paused, bottle halfway to her lips, inadvertently reliving the moment Quentin had leaned down to help her up and she'd gotten a front-row view of his lean, corded forearms . . .

Was it hot in here? It was definitely hot in here. She knocked back a swig of hard cider, the crisp taste not cooling her desire one bit.

Meg pushed the cardboard tray of mozzarella sticks aside and leaned on the wobbly high-top table to peer into her eyes. "Okay, missy. This is as close to flustered as I've ever seen you. What aren't you telling me? He's less of a Chris Pratt and more of a *who*?"

Alisha slid off the barstool and went to fetch her misaimed dart, hoping she wouldn't get a staph infection from the gritty carpet. She didn't feel like dishing about the whole mud-drenched, embarrassing encounter. Not until she'd had time to digest it herself. As for Quentin's out-of-this-world looks . . .

"He's . . . cute," she hedged, and then scooted her hips back up onto the stool.

"Uh-uh. Nope. You can either give me more than that, or I can just google him." Meg's Disney princess–size green eyes lit up at her own suggestion, and she pawed through her purse.

Steeling herself for the inevitable outburst, Alisha took another bite of freezer-burned mozzarella stick to fortify herself. But the impending interrogation made the cheese congeal in her throat and plop into her stomach with a heavy thud.

"What did you say his name was?" Meg's eager face glowed in the light emitting from the screen. "Oh. Ne-*ver*-mind." Her words may as well have been a catcall.

Of course she'd already found him. After years of online-dating disasters, Meg could teach a course in cyberstalking. She slammed her phone faceup onto the table, and Alisha almost choked on her mouthful of cider.

Dr. Quentin Harris, PhD, stared back at her from the homepage of the Earth Sciences Department at Chicago Northern University. Man, but he was fine. No one had any right to look that flawless in a faculty photo.

A white button-down set off his deep-brown skin, his prominent Adam's apple on display above an open collar. His lips looked soft—kissable was her first thought, before she stamped it out like a spark in a dry forest—and those stormy seafoam-gray eyes she'd never forget crinkled at the edges from a wide smile. His curls were cropped close to his head in a fade that accentuated his angular cheekbones and strong jawline. Alisha gulped before drool hit the screen.

"You mean to tell me this Steph Curry look-alike is the dino guy?" Her friend's voice came out as a squeak, and for once Alisha didn't have to worry about the whole town hearing. *Thank heavens for small mercies.*

"Steph Curry's not quite accurate . . ." She trailed off, eyes glued to the phone.

"All I can say is: Why didn't you lead off with 'The paleontologist I met today is a certified hottie'?" Meg's voice ricocheted back up to its typical decibel level again, and Alisha snapped from her Quentin-induced trance. Finger to her lips, she shushed a warning and flipped the phone over.

Just then her own cell lit up with a text from an unknown number. She snatched it before Meg could.

Unknown:

Hi Alisha, this is Indiana Jones.

She giggled, and Meg's eyes slit into suspicion. Alisha pasted on a bland face as another text popped up.

Unknown:

Your grandmother gave me your number. Said I should have it to contact you in case they weren't home.

Subtle, Granny.

Also, did her grandma think she was that desperate? Her current relationship status didn't mean she was incapable of scoring dates on her own.

Unknown:

Any chance you've seen a digital camera at your house? I can't find the one I brought today.

She frowned at the screen, thumbnail working its way between her teeth, unable to recall seeing a camera anywhere other than pressed against Quentin's mouthwatering face. *Not helpful.*

Alisha:

Any idea where you left it?

Unknown:

Maybe in the kitchen?

Meg came around to snoop over her shoulder, but she ignored her and sent a reply.

Alisha:
I'll look around when I get home and let you know.

Unknown:
Thanks.

"Sparks fly," said Meg dryly.

"I told you there's nothing going on."

She sighed and leaned her chin on Alisha's shoulder. "Is it so wrong that I want a man for my best friend?"

"It is when you put it that way, yes. And also disturbing." But she tipped her head down to rest on Meg's. They sat that way for a moment, with the buzz of basketball in the background, food and drink forgotten in all the almosts and what-ifs they'd consoled each other through over the years.

Line Quentin right up along with the rest. Right guy, right place, wrong girl.

"How long do you think the dig will take—all summer?" Meg broke the embrace and walked back to her stool.

Alisha dipped another mozzarella stick into the marinara. "Gosh, I hope not. Grandpa spent all afternoon complaining about strangers running rampant on our property. Maybe I should've just told Dr. Harris the dig was a no-go, instead of letting him plead his case."

When she'd reemerged from soaking the mud out of her braids, Grandpa was home, talking to Quentin in the backyard. She'd cracked her attic window and caught the words, "All right. Save me digging them up myself." The dig was a go.

Meg shook her head. "Stop. Your grandpa always has to make a stink. It's in his nature. I bet deep down he's thrilled."

"I don't doubt it. But what about Granny?" She discarded the uneaten mozzarella stick on her napkin. "I don't love the idea of a bunch of strangers out back when I'm not around to watch out for her."

"It's not your grandma you should be worried about." Meg waggled her expertly microbladed brows.

"I'm serious." She flicked a balled-up napkin toward her friend. "Next thing you know, she'll be trying to serve them breakfast, lunch, and dinner. Cleaning the house at all hours of the day on the off chance they pop in for a drink. I know her. She doesn't need that kind of stress. No way I can leave for Chicago until this dig wraps up."

"Does that mean you told your grandparents about moving?" Meg pillowed her cheek against clasped hands.

And this is why she hadn't let anyone else in on the plan. The constant prodding. Didn't Meg get it? Her grandparents came first. Shifting her eyes to a sticky coaster on the table, Alisha hedged, "Uh, not yet."

"Hmm, shocking." Out of nowhere, Meg slapped the table with flat palms. Someone over at the bar hollered in response, but she didn't even bat an eyelash, keeping her gaze trained on her friend. "Alisha Marianne Blake, when are you going to pull the trigger?"

With a groan, Alisha slumped onto her elbows, shoulders round. She poured ranch into the marinara and mixed them into a Pepto-Bismol pink. "I dunno. Maybe on a night when a dinosaur doesn't turn up in our swimming pool?"

Pushing Alisha's hand away from the dipping-sauce slop, Meg said, "Ali, there's always going to be a dinosaur."

"Umm—"

"Shut up, you know what I mean. I'll give you a few weeks; then you leave me no choice but to say something in front of Mrs. S—then we'll see how long your secret stays safe."

"Empty threats," said Alisha, rolling a dart along the sloping tabletop. "And why is my best friend so intent on getting rid of me? Way to make a girl feel cherished."

"Because your best friend wants you to be happy, and you hate it here."

"I don't hate it . . ."

"Okay, and I don't hate brussels sprouts. I just despise it when people waste bacon and butter on something that tastes like it was harvested in a swamp."

"I like Hawksburg more than you like brussels sprouts."

"Barely." Meg stopped the dart with a fingertip. "I already miss you, and you haven't even left yet. But you're not happy here, girl. I'd rather only see you a few times a year and know you're fulfilled than see you unhappy every day."

"I could be happy." Or at least content. Didn't she owe it to her grandparents to keep trying?

"You're just going to miraculously love it here? Stop. Tell your grandparents. Tell that snarky sister of yours." Meg grinned. Alisha was certain they got some kind of sick joy out of ragging on each other. Couple of weirdos. "At least get your family's opinion before you talk yourself out of moving."

She glared at Meg. "Don't get your panties in a wad. I'm not talking myself out of anything. And you know, if you're going to miss me, you could always join me."

"Hard pass. Skyscrapers and traffic is your thing. Besides, we both know you'll be back here every few weeks to check in on your grandparents. We'll see each other plenty."

"We'll see each other every day if I decide to stay put and open up a cookie shop here."

Meg's emerald eyes narrowed to slits. "Woman . . ."

"Kidding! I'm kidding." She wasn't. But this battle of wills had gone on long enough. "I'll tell them soon so I'm ready to go when the right listing pops up."

"All right, girl, I trust you." The wrinkles bunching Meg's porcelain forehead said otherwise, but she started yanking her darts out of the board, and Alisha blew out a relieved breath. Unfortunately, on her inhale, a miasma of cologne enveloped her, accompanied by a tug on one of her braids.

"I see Bob Marley's back in town."

Alisha winced and extracted her hair from Greg McAllister's clutches. She shifted to give him a withering look. "And I see too much time breathing in fertilizer has gotten to your head."

Greg laughed. *Ick.* You'd think after fifteen years he might come up with new material.

Freshman year she'd shown up after Christmas break with micro-braids. She'd flounced into homeroom, floating on a cloud of oil sheen and ready to debut the intricate braids that reached nearly to her waist, ending in glossy curls. Greg had taken one look at her and climbed up onto his chair, his pointed index finger the exclamation point to the shouted words still ringing in her ears. "Look, guys, it's Bob Marley!"

No disrespect to the late, great reggae artist—the blatant stereotyping is what had pricked her skin like an assault from a thousand tiny needles. What would he say if she ever decided to get her hair loc'd? Probably not even know the difference, was what.

She sighed. Yet another reason she didn't love Hawksburg. Because she was Black. Or mixed, or biracial. Whatever people felt like labeling her at the moment, regardless of her preference. She'd even been called "colored" once, during a class on US history. The teacher hadn't said anything.

Growing up in the Chicago suburbs, she'd gone to school with a diverse group of kids. Then she'd moved here and discovered she and Simone stuck out like black sheep in a white flock.

But not everyone was Greg McAllister. Meg, for one. When a girl at a sleepover said Alisha's mom must've tricked her father into getting her pregnant, Meg drew a line in the sand—or shag carpet, in this case— and stood up for her with red-faced indignation, when Alisha would've waved it off. That zero-tolerance policy and a shared obsession with the *Jurassic Park* franchise had cemented their friendship from day one.

"I could really use a latte." The safe word she and Meg had created for bad dates snapped Alisha back to reality. Meg aimed a rictus smile at Greg where he'd cornered her by the dartboard, no doubt fumigating her with the Old Spice he applied by the gallon like pest spray. Her wide eyes begged for rescue.

"On my way," Alisha mouthed, but across the bar, at the entrance to the billiards room, Shawn Ingram hailed her with a wave and scooted his muscular frame around the stools toward her, pool stick in hand.

Lifting his mesh trucker cap, he raked his fingers through his sandy-blond hair. "Don't tell me—Greg's pestering you about why you don't speak Ebonics again." He wrapped her in a hug, then stepped back, a gleam of mischief in his glacier-blue eyes. "Idiot."

She shrugged. Living among people who'd known her since childhood but still held a deep-seated belief that the color of her skin set her apart as "other" wasn't always comfortable. But being on a first-name basis with only one person who wasn't white? Must've made it hard to get it right. At least Shawn made an effort.

"We missed you this weekend at the Saint Patrick's Day festival," he said.

Since she wasn't interested in succumbing to insanity brought on by one too many town parades, her weekend escape to Chicago had provided the perfect excuse to skip out on the whole production.

He laughed at the face she pulled. "Word on the street is you ditched us for Simone. How is she?"

"Doing good. Headed for a promotion, looks like." Her sister might've been a workaholic, but Alisha's chest swelled at her success. At least one Blake sister was living the dream. "Lately she's been talking about getting her MBA. You know Simone, always looking for what's next."

Shawn leaned on his pool stick with an easy smile. "Sounds like the Sim I remember. Glad the city hasn't changed her. Any idea when she'll be home next?"

"Not sure, her schedule is crazy right now." If he still held a torch for her sister, good luck—not only was Chicago a world away, but

Simone had no time for a boyfriend these days. But that little detail wouldn't stop her from stirring the pot. "You could always call her up yourself, you know." She grinned. "Or FaceTime her. Whatever it is you youngsters are doing these days."

The flush that spread up his neck confirmed her hunch, but Greg stalked up from behind and choked him in a one-sided dude hug. *Saved by the bro.*

They started up another round of darts. Alisha begged off, claiming exhaustion after a long morning on the road. From the grin on Meg's face, she'd guessed Alisha's real reason for skipping out early—to text Quentin. But if her friend wanted to think there was something going on, fine. At least it would keep her off Alisha's back about dating for now. The sooner she resolved the camera issue and put Quentin out of mind, the better.

By some twist of fate, Mrs. Snyder's half-baked prophesy had become manifest. The dinosaur dig *would* be the biggest thing to happen in Hawksburg, maybe ever. How cool to see a *National Geographic* centerfold come to life. But the hot professor running point? A speed bump she couldn't let knock her off course. Alisha needed to do everything in her power to keep her life on track, and that included steering clear of Dr. Harris.

CHAPTER 7

QUENTIN

Miles of blank highway stretched in front of Quentin, dotted with only the occasional pickup or eighteen-wheeler. Now that he'd crossed over the Illinois River, he had about an hour's worth of driving before traffic picked up around Springfield.

He switched on the radio, searching the static for a song while his thoughts ping-ponged between the dig and Alisha Blake.

Dinosaur bones, right here in Illinois! Incredible. This dig would go down in history books. Well, maybe not history books, but definitely scholarly journals. A Wikipedia article for him to religiously fact-check. Imagine the papers he could author. Maybe there'd even be a documentary. *Take that, Dad.*

He tapped a staccato rhythm on the steering wheel. His grad students were going to lose their minds over this find. Excavating here would be very different from their usual digs in the deserts out west. How would working with packed clay compare to chipping bones out of rock? Limitless questions unfolded in his mind like trails on a map, and he couldn't wait to follow where they led.

But as for the beautiful woman who lived at the dig site? Their conversation had lit a spark in him, the first one since Mercedes. A spark he absolutely needed to smother before it burst into flames. In a close-knit workplace, rumors spread like unchecked wildfire, and he didn't need his handling of the find called into question.

Paleontology had always been a safe haven. He couldn't afford to blur the lines between work and his personal life, not with so much at stake. Losing the chance to excavate the find of a lifetime? Unthinkable. He took a swig of sugary gas station cappuccino to chase down the acid burning his throat.

A semi cut him off, and Quentin squeezed the cup so hard the lid popped off. Sticky liquid sloshed onto his thighs. With a growl, he dropped it into the cup holder and laid on his horn. Reaching blindly, he snatched up a fleece jacket from the passenger seat. Reggie was embroidered in red letters on the front. He used it to mop the coffee off the center console with a smirk.

Quentin's ringtone eclipsed the speakers. Caught out, he flinched and hurled the jacket onto the passenger floor mat. But a quick glance toward the caller ID had him relaxing back against the headrest. He clicked on the Bluetooth. "Hey, Hector."

"Wow, you answered your phone for once. I planned on leaving a voice mail."

"That's what texting's for."

A piercing shriek came across the other end, and Hector yelled, "Careful!"

Quentin chuckled. Which twin was wreaking havoc this time?

"Say again, Q?"

"You heard me." Quentin flicked on his blinker, passing yet another semi. "No one under eighty leaves voice mails anymore."

Hector snorted. "You sound like Ma."

"What does that say about you, brother? Our baby boomer mom has embraced technology more than you have."

"*Any*way," Hector said, dragging out the syllables, "I called cuz Vanessa's been on me to invite you to the twins' birthday party. It's Saturday."

Leave it to his brother to tell him the week of. Lucky he had a wide-open social calendar these days. Lack of a love life would do that for a guy.

"Of course I'll be there." But presents would be involved, yes? He scratched at his jaw. Seeing his nieces every Sunday since their birth didn't mean he could keep up with their interests. Last year, he'd been the stooge who'd showed up at the party with a pair of Little Tykes hoops, basketballs, and a bin of sidewalk chalk to draw a court on the driveway, only to find out the girls had traded in their Jordans for soccer cleats. "What are they into these days?"

"You mean besides destroying everything?"

Quentin laughed.

"I'm not kidding!" Hector's voice climbed a few octaves. "The other day I caught them pumping hand soap into my shoes. Every single pair I own, Q. Said they were stinky. Although, they weren't wrong." He chuckled. "Man, whoever said girls aren't a force to be reckoned with obviously never raised one. They're a constant blur."

Another crash, and Hector shouted, "I'll be off in a sec!" To Quentin he said, "What do my babies like these days besides making mayhem? Hang on."

There was a rustling sound, then Hector's voice came again, muffled now.

Was he hiding out in the closet?

"Let's see . . . *Frozen. Frozen II*, actually. Apparently there's a difference. The princesses get pants or something. I dunno. But if you buy them something that makes noise again, I swear to God I'll find Lily a new godfather."

The loud toys were payback for years of gut punches and brotherly warfare. He had no plans to stop using his biggest advantage.

Hector spoke away from the phone, and Quentin heard an answering giggle. "Yep, you sure did, you found Daddy." He grunted, and Quentin pictured him making room for one of the twins. "Lauryn, say hi to your least favorite uncle."

"Hi, Uncle Q."

"Hey, girl. I'll see you this weekend, okay?"

More rustling, then Hector chuckled. "She's gone already." Warmth radiated in his voice. His brother adored those tiny terrors, and so did Quentin. His throat closed up a bit. *Harris family curse.*

"Listen, Hector, I gotta go. I'm on the road."

"Oh yeah, the secret dino mission. Guess reducing your carbon footprint isn't always practical, huh?" The sneer in his words stretched across the airwaves.

"I know a car-free existence is mind-boggling for you, but I live two blocks from campus. And even if you don't care about our planet, what about the fortune I've saved in parking tickets?"

"Yeah, yeah. Are you really not going to tell me where you went today?"

No way would his clueless brother be the first to hear the biggest news of his career.

"Nope. But thanks for the invite. See you Saturday." He ended the call before Hector could grill him any further.

His dad and brother had always set him up to be the one in the family who would "make it." They couldn't wrap their brains around his fascination with the bones of animals that had vanished into extinction millions of years ago. Or the years of work for tenure that may or may not materialize, despite his best efforts. Still, in Quentin's mind, he *did* have it made, career-wise.

Relationship-wise, well . . .

His growling stomach interrupted his thoughts, just as he passed a sign announcing fast food. A miracle, considering the last ten or so exits had marked country roads going nowhere. He pulled into a parking spot at McDonald's, and his phone chimed with a text.

Not his brother this time. Alisha.

Heart thudding, he opened the message. A photo of the missing camera filled the screen. He let out his breath in a whoosh. What had he been expecting?

Another text pinged through.

Alisha:
I believe this belongs to you? Will accept 1,000,000 euros as ransom.

He laughed out loud.

Quentin:
I'm fresh out of euros. Will you accept yen?

Alisha:
Works for me. Deposit the funds in my Swiss bank account by 12:00 CST and the camera is yours.

Quentin:
This is starting to feel like a budget Bond film.

Alisha:
Lol. I can mail it out tomorrow. No worries.

Quentin:
Whew. I'm not very liquid right now.

He sent her his office address, then climbed down out of the cab, shuddering against the frigid night air. His phone beeped in the middle of paying for his meal, and he jerked his card out of the reader, dropping his wallet in a flurry of coins in his haste to pull his cell out of his pocket. Slick.

Alisha:
Got it. I'll take it to the post office tomorrow.

Quentin:
Thanks! I owe you one, and of course I'll pay you back for the postage.

A grin tugged up the corner of his mouth, and he paused in picking up the change to key out another text.

Quentin:
In dollars. 😏

Absently, he put his wallet back into his pocket. Why did he add an emoji? Weird, right? It felt weird. He fetched his cup off the counter and buzzed it full of Sprite, trying to relax. But still, the emoji taunted him. His phone pinged again, and sweat broke out under his arms. He forced himself to put a lid on the cup and shove in a straw before he read the text.

Alisha:
No worries.

No exclamation points, no answering emoji.

He put the phone on silent.

"Order three fifty-eight?" Two employees hovered by the registers with matching smiles. Another woman materialized next to them and leaned her hip against the counter. "Hey there. Want a McFlurry? On the house."

He frowned, mind still on the texts, and her smile wavered. "We, uh . . ." She looked at the woman next to her, who gave a quick shake of her head. The first woman narrowed her eyes at her coworker, then upped the wattage on her smile. "We made it on accident. For a drive-through customer."

The guy cooking fries muttered something under his breath.

Never one to turn down free food, Quentin accepted the cup with a murmur of thanks. The women's eyes bored into him while he pumped out three ketchups. But when he looked up, the cashier stood alone behind the register. She tucked her chin and offered a waist-high wave.

Huh. He slid onto a sticky white bench.

Winky face? Smooth. You just met her today, Quentin. Smooth as crunchy peanut butter, more like, and every bit as gagworthy. But he made himself take a bite of the burger, and the savory taste of pepper and pickles reminded him how starving he was.

Somehow the knot in his belly left room for the entire burger, a large order of fries, and the free McFlurry. Not even a misguided attempt at flirting could ruin a Big Mac. And the tangle of nerves slackened when he reminded himself—pretty woman notwithstanding—that a dinosaur in Illinois could change the trajectory of his career.

Wouldn't hurt to check his phone again, though . . .

Alisha:

Goodnight, Indy.

He crinkled the yellow wrapper in his fist and dunked it into the paper bag.

The sappy smile still hadn't left his face when he merged onto the interstate. Maybe he could try going with the flow for once. Yes, she lived in rural Illinois, across an ocean of back roads and cornfields—a big, glaring obstacle, especially for someone in the business of spotting tiny details.

But look at Tre—he'd been enjoying wedded bliss for three years after meeting Radhika on a sunset booze cruise on Lake Michigan. Maybe Alisha's proximity to the dig was serendipity, not a cosmic joke. After all, fate had certainly played a hand in the improbable dinosaur discovery today. He'd have to be careful not to let his focus stray, but why not indulge in a little harmless flirtation, see what developed?

Besides, ignoring Alisha's liquid brown eyes and luscious curves all summer?

Impossible.

CHAPTER 8

ALISHA

Fog hung thick in the air, muting the clink of metal as Alisha and Quentin maneuvered an aluminum ladder into the pit. The close embrace of vapor made it feel like they were the only two people in the world, and for a breathless second, she wished it were true. No obligations, no uncertainty, no tangled past.

Her grip slipped in the condensation, and she caught Quentin's eye over her shoulder. "You always seem to bring atmospheric weather when you come. Snow last time. Now this."

"Are you comparing me to Thor?" He lowered the ladder, hand over hand. "Not that I'm going to turn my nose up at Avenger status, but I'm definitely partial to T'Challa."

Thor? No, ostentatious thunder and lightning didn't hit the mark. His presence affected her like a breath of wind in the doldrums at sea. Though the air clung to her, close and still, Alisha's lungs expanded in a full inhale, and she imagined a weather vane shifting.

"More like the day Mary Poppins flew in." She grinned, head down.

"Ouch. A burn already?"

"Nah, I'm just saying all this is a whole lot of new." The ladder hit the dirt below, and she stepped back in an attempt to pull herself out of Quentin's orbit.

"I get it." He locked eyes with her, and she swallowed. "I'm not big on new either. Explains my fixation on fossils, I guess. They've stuck around for a few hundred million years. Not going anywhere anytime soon." He rubbed a hand up his arm, rumpling the fabric of his long-sleeved tee. "All I can say is, I really appreciate your family allowing us this opportunity. It means so much to be able to work on a project of this magnitude."

"Okay, okay." She waved him off. "Save it for the Oscars."

His dimples appeared. "Sure thing." He swung one boot onto the ladder, and she gripped the rails to steady it. "See, if I were Mary Poppins"—he descended another rung—"I could float down in a snap. What with my magical umbrella and all."

She clucked her tongue, secretly loving his cheesiness. "You sure you teach college students and not third graders?"

Stepping down into the mud, he flashed a smile up at her, and her heart skitter-leaped.

"I've done a school visit or two in my time. Dinos are a big hit with the twelve-and-under crowd."

"I can imagine." She bit back the urge to admit her own dino obsession. There was a fine line between interested onlooker and *Jurassic Park* megafan, and he didn't need to know where she stood on that particular continuum. "Anyway, I'll get out of your hair, unless you need a hand?"

"No, thank you. You've done more than enough."

She narrowed her eyes. "Is that a reference to my first performance down there?"

He laughed. "It's not, I promise. I may have overreacted."

"I don't blame you. I'd freak out if someone just stormed into my kitchen in the middle of a bake, and my desserts aren't even irreplaceable relics."

"Again, I feel like you have me confused with Dr. Jones."

Alisha grinned. "What can I say? He made an impression on me as a kid." In fact, between Indiana Jones and Alan Grant, she was belatedly realizing "hunky scientist" just might be her type. But cracking the lid on that can of worms could only lead to abject embarrassment.

"Well, if you do need a hand, I'll be in the house. I kind of figured you'd show up with an assistant or something."

Quentin unzipped the bag and pulled out a wrinkled tarp. "Yeah, if this all pans out, I'll be coming back with a team. But everyone deserted me for Cabo." He squinted up at her. "Spring break."

"Ah, gotcha. No beaches for you?"

"Oh no, I love the beach. But resort vacations cater to couples, you know?" He paused, hinting at his lack of a girlfriend? Fishing for her relationship status? Why did the idea of a single Dr. Harris give her the sudden urge to revisit her vow of singlehood? Probably the same reason she was lingering here like a fan with a backstage pass.

When Alisha didn't volunteer an answer, he shrugged. "Besides, I wanted to get a better idea of what we're working with. This could be an even bigger deal if it turns out to be a new species."

A new species? It started to sink in that this dig was going to blow her timetable to smithereens.

"Do you think it is?"

"No way to know at this stage. And I doubt it, but then again, I never in my life thought I'd be excavating dinosaur fossils in Illinois, yet here we are." Trowel in hand, he rested one arm on his knee and smiled up at her, his features in soft focus from the fog.

Here they were indeed. "Well, if you need a break or a drink or anything, the back door will be open."

"Thanks. I'll stop in on my way out."

"Cool." Alisha rocked back on her heels. Oh, she was staring. And smiling. And officially earning herself creeper status. "See you in a bit, then."

Alisha hit the upload button and stood, arching her back. Editing the video had wound up taking longer than expected because she'd fielded three phone calls from one of the part-timers about the new point-of-sale system and submitted an order to their produce vendor Grandpa had forgotten to send out.

The post wasn't as cohesive as she'd like because all the interruptions had zapped her concentration, but better than skipping a day. Blogging and social media offered a baked-in clientele for when it came time to launch her cookie shop, and consistently sharing fresh content and unique flavor profiles had earned her a loyal following.

Ever since she'd hit thirty thousand followers last year, she'd allowed herself to dream. But the leap from dreaming to doing was proving harder. She needed to bridge the gap from small-town home-based bakery to trendy urban cookie shop without letting her family fall by the wayside, and juggling Honey and Hickory responsibilities didn't make the balancing act any easier.

Her phone buzzed with a calendar notification. Shoot. She'd forgotten about the lollipop cookies for her friend Laney's baby shower, a super simple but tedious bake. She raced down both flights of stairs to the kitchen and grabbed her apron. Flinging open cupboards and drawers, she gathered her ingredients with chaotic precision.

Twenty minutes later, she was kneading gel food color into a portion of the dough when she heard the back door open. *Be cool, be cool.*

"Alisha?"

"In the kitchen. You can come on through." Knuckle-deep in crimson, she said, "Caught red-hand—" She looked up and froze. Quentin stood at the entrance to the kitchen. His shirt clung to his torso like a second skin, sleeves bunched up around his elbows in a gratuitous display of mud-streaked forearms. Raindrops glistened in his curls like dew.

"So, it's raining," he said.

She glanced behind her out the window above the sink into a yard obscured by curtains of rain. A crack of lightning punctuated the downpour thundering on the roof. How had she not noticed? Turning back, she caught Quentin in the act of plucking his sopping shirt away from his chest. "Yeah, I see that now."

Oh yes, she could see. A lot. The white shirt clung to him like body paint, highlighting his broad chest and narrow waist, outlining the ridges of his abs. She discreetly rested the inside of her wrist on the cool granite in lieu of fanning her face.

"I've got an extra hoodie in the truck, but first, is there a, uh, bathroom I could use?" He lifted his muddy arms by his face like a scrubbed-up surgeon, and Alisha gripped the counter edge.

"Just down the hall. Can't miss it."

"Thanks." He padded away, and she sunk down onto one elbow, back of her wrist to her forehead. *Get it together, woman. Four more months of this. Can't be swooning every time he comes in to wash up.*

By the time he reappeared, looking cozy in a thick forest-green-and-gold CNU hoodie, she'd colored another portion of dough and knocked back an entire glass of ice water.

"Whoa, it's like a burst of sunshine in here," he said, eyeing the five mounds of dough, each a different color. She had to agree, but for a totally different reason. Quentin upped the temperature in the room like solar rays under a magnifying glass.

"I'm making sugar cookies for a candy shop–themed baby shower. They'll end up looking like old-school lollipops."

"So this is what you meant about 'baking projects.'" He stepped closer, and she caught a hint of spicy cologne. Nothing strong, just enough to smell, well, yummy. "Is this what you do for a living?"

She shook her head. "Just a side hustle. My real job is making the desserts for my grandpa's barbecue restaurant."

"Best of both worlds."

"Sometimes." Her tone hit a notch just below neutral, but something kept her from autocorrecting.

A flicker of awareness passed over his features. "My dad and brother have a family business, so I know how that goes." Quentin leaned one hip against the island, at ease, like chatting with her was an everyday occurrence.

"My dad is a mechanic, and my brother followed in his footsteps. Opened up his own custom shop a couple years ago. But I was never supposed to work with cars. Dad had other plans for me." He hooked a thumb on the counter. "I'm not sure whether that makes me lucky or not."

"Lucky." Alisha dropped the word like a rock, then winced at the ripples she'd caused in the conversation. "I mean, you're doing what you want. That's good, right?"

He palmed the back of his neck, and the hoodie rode up, exposing a line of taut brown skin. She dipped her chin and only ended up checking him out under her lashes. Worse than outright ogling. *Snap out of it, Alisha.*

"Sort of. But the fact that I didn't become a mechanic didn't stop him from mapping my whole future. He decided early on I was going to be the one who did big things." He impersonated a deep, reverberating intonation, then switched into his normal register, tone wry. "Only it turned out my idea of big things were extinct creatures."

Alisha offered a smile in solidarity. "Really, really big things."

Quentin let out a laugh. "True. I sometimes wonder if being roped into the family business would've been easier."

"Easier? Than the chance to follow your dreams?" The note of sarcasm had crept into her words uninvited.

"No, I meant easier than winding up a disappointment, I guess." He traced the swirls of granite with a fingertip. "But this dig might be a chance to show my dad my career is viable."

Alisha nodded to cover the mix of emotions in the pit of her stomach. She knew what it was like to feel squashed under the weight of family obligations, wanted this chance for Quentin. But what would it mean for her own family if the dig turned out to be big news? Sure, Grandpa would love the sensationalism, but Granny didn't need that kind of upheaval.

"Anyway," Quentin said, pushing off the island, "I just came in for some water. Didn't mean to interrupt."

"Oh, no worries. Glasses are in the cupboard to the right of the sink." She rolled out the dough on a piece of parchment, forcing herself not to track his movements.

The cabinet squeaked open; then a rush of water filled the sudden quiet. A warm presence at her elbow signaled Quentin's return. Her nerve endings tightened and burst into tiny tingles of sensation at his closeness.

"How do you manage a baking business with a full-time job?" He took a gulp of water, and she tried not to watch the dip and bob of his Adam's apple. Failed.

She turned back to the dough, scoring the surface in a grid. "Coffee. No sleep. And I schedule most of my social media posts ahead of time."

"Wait, you're an influencer too?"

"Hardly. It's for my baking."

"Alisha, that's super impressive. I have a hard enough time just holding it together with my day job."

"Which involves research, teaching, fieldwork, authoring papers . . ." She nudged him, tingling when her shoulder brushed against his solid chest. "I'd say we're pretty even in the busyness department."

"Maybe, but I've got grad students who do some of the heavy lifting. Who helps you?"

She grinned. "Are you offering?"

He leaned back to set the cup on the counter behind them. "Sure."

"Quentin, I was kidding."

"Why? You think I'm not up for it?" He raised an eyebrow in challenge.

She shook her head. "It's not that. But I got this."

"Are you saying that because you really don't want my help, or because you don't want to accept my help?"

"What's the difference?"

"The difference is, one way I'm getting in your way, and the other, I'm taking a burden off you." His gray gaze met hers. "So which is it?"

She chewed her lip. Pulled open the drawer in front of her and withdrew another rolling pin. "Aprons are hanging in the pantry. And wash your hands again."

The grin he sent her way spread warmth from the roots of her hair to the polish on her toes. "Yes, Chef."

Quentin hovered at eye level with the counter, tongue poking out the side of his mouth. Flour dusted the backs of his hands, and bits of blue dough clung to his nail beds. He'd donned a sunflower apron, probably just to mess with her. "You said a quarter of an inch?"

"Give or take. And then we'll cut it into twenty roughly two-inch squares."

"Um . . ." He flicked his eyes up to hers, doubt creasing his brow.

Grinning, she took pity on him. "Here." She passed him a ruler, and their fingers touched, sending tingles up her arms.

"Now we're talking." He tapped the ruler against the counter and stood. The apron looked doll-size on his tall frame, which somehow only added to his charm. "Tools make everything better." His eyes widened. "Not everything. Every job. You know what? I'm just gonna shut up now. Please pretend I didn't just reference sex toys in your grandparents' kitchen."

Alisha smothered a laugh. "Too late. But it'll stay between us. That I can promise."

"Speaking of grandparents," Quentin started, and she groaned. "I'm sorry, I know, terrible segue. But I'm just curious—have you always lived here? Or is this sort of a temporary arrangement?"

"Is that your way of asking if this is a *Failure to Launch* situation?"

"I could pretend I didn't know what movie you were talking about and save my street cred, but I think that already went out the window." He gestured to his apron. "I'm just kind of curious. Usually it's the children that take care of their parents. I think it's really cool that you're stepping up." Quentin ran a mini pizza cutter along the edge of the ruler.

"I am their kid. Kinda. My grandparents raised me. After my mom . . ." She stopped, unscrewed the lid on a container of lollipop sticks. Pushed the words out. "After she passed away. Breast cancer," she said, to forestall the inevitable question, and hoped he wouldn't ask about her father.

"Alisha, I'm so sorry." Quentin set down the ruler, his gray eyes soft as misty clouds. "How devastating."

Devastating. Inconceivable. Even after all these years, she sometimes woke up expecting Mom to be in the front room with a cup of coffee, robe tucked around her knees, NPR on the radio. "It's fine, old news."

Not fine at all.

But Quentin didn't take the out. Instead, he waited, silent.

What if she told him the truth? How losing her parents had left her holding too tightly on to everything else around her, gripping until her hands were calloused and bruised, and still feeling like it all might slip away in an instant?

The fear that usually strangled her tongue loosened its hold. "Senior year of college, my grandma received the same diagnosis. Breast cancer." She scooped up a square of dough, rolled it in her palms, placed it next to the others. "And I knew I had to do everything in my power to keep her here. So here I am." A diluted version of the truth that still left her feeling exposed, naked to her bones, a bare skeleton displayed behind museum glass.

What would he think of these fractured pieces of herself?

"You must love her so much."

He'd listened. He'd heard.

"I do. Her and Grandpa, and my sister, Simone—they're my whole family. Mom and my father were only children. My mom's parents passed when I was young." Snatches of memory slipped, hazy, to her consciousness. The smell of damp soil and rosebuds. Grandpa arranging cut stems in a porcelain vase. Grandma spreading thick, sweet frosting on a cake.

Memories of love and wholeness from a time before Momma was sick. Before Alisha's family was shattered and shaken to the core. She'd been left straddling boundary lines and navigating a new life that felt so perilous. Fractured, fragile. Desperate to hold on to those who remained. Simone. Granny. Grandpa. "And I just . . ."

"Want to keep them around?"

"Yes. More than anything."

"I get that." Quentin blinked down at the countertop, the muscles in his jaw clenched. "Not that I've lost a family member. But loss is hell."

Hell on earth. Exactly. She rubbed her palms down her apron with a quick nod, swallowed hard. "Anyway, looks like you're ready to roll."

Quentin swept a searching gaze over her face, then nodded. He made a show of cracking his neck and shaking out his shoulders, shuffling in place. "I was born ready."

A giggle bubbled up out of her despite the thickness in her throat. "Remember Play-Doh time in kindergarten?"

He nodded. "Fondly."

She snorted at his earnestness. "Same deal. Roll a ball, then make a snake. We'll end up twisting up all the colors together." Laying six ropes of dough side by side, she rolled them into a single log. "Then we wind it in on itself." She swirled the rope into a flat circle. "Like a giant lollipop. See?"

Nodding, he got to work, his fingers deftly rolling the dough with a light touch, not leaving any imprints or blending the colors. She grinned up at him. "You're a pro."

"No, you're the pro. I'm just the sidekick."

She placed a lollipop stick on the sheet tray and pressed the cookie on top.

Watching her, he did the same, but the swirl came apart in his hands. "You make this look way easier than it is." He unwound it and tried again. "Have you ever thought about opening your own bakery? Separate from the restaurant?"

His eyes never left the dough, giving her the space to breathe, to consider.

This could be the perfect, low-stakes trial run. He'd be in her life for the summer, then gone. This whole afternoon had been a sort of suspended unreality. A cathartic confessional. What could it hurt? She inhaled a big breath, held it in, then released it in a rush of air.

"Actually, yes. I have thought about it. A lot."

Key in the lock, she turned it, opening the door on her dreams and letting Quentin in. "At the end of the summer, I'm going to move to Chicago. I have enough saved to open my own bakery in the city."

CHAPTER 9

ALISHA

Turns out hot professors were her kryptonite. What else explained why she'd opened up to Quentin like a long-lost friend? She quartered a potato and dropped it into a pot of salted water. A week had passed since his last visit, and things had settled back into normalcy at home, their sugar-cookie interlude in the kitchen fading to a hazy memory.

Why had she told him about her bakery dream? About Mom? Maybe it was the humid embrace of the vanilla-scented kitchen. Or perhaps the calm, quiet way Quentin listened had peeled back the disordered scraps of armor she'd pieced together to shield her heart.

She eyed the pile of potato peels in the sink like a reality check. Or maybe too many years of single life had her overanalyzing common kindness. Her phone rang, and she glanced at the screen. Speak of the handsome devil . . .

"Hello?" Heart beating triple time, Alisha slid the pot of potatoes to the back burner. Water sloshed onto the flame with a hiss. She clicked off the gas and tiptoed down the hall, double-timing when she passed the french doors of the den, the blue light of the evening news reflecting off the glass.

"Hey, Alisha. Is this a good time?"

Her chin nearly hit her collarbones in an overzealous nod. *He can't see you, loser.* "Yeah." She twisted the knob and slipped outside, then latched the door behind her. Goose bumps ran up her exposed arms, but too late to go back in for a coat. "Yeah, now's a great time. What's up?" Gosh, she sounded winded.

In the fading glow of sunset, she stealth-jogged around to the side yard and stopped on the far side of the maple tree. She peeked around the thick trunk toward the house, checking for the telltale stir of curtains. No denying the perks to grandparent roomies, like a freezer perpetually stocked with ice cream and companions to binge *Downton Abbey* with. But privacy? Ha.

"Hey, actually, can you give me a sec?" Not waiting for an answer, she tossed the phone up into the crook of the tree, then wrapped both hands around the lowest branch and swung a leg up—a move she'd perfected on childhood trips to Hawksburg, when she'd hide in the sheltering branches to escape Simone, who used to toddle everywhere after her like a menace, Momma shouting to let her big sister be.

After hoisting herself up, she settled into the hollow. Almost-thirty-year-old knees objected to the pretzel pose, and she groaned, shifting her butt on the damp, chilly bark.

"Sorry, I'm back," she said, even more breathless than before, if that was possible.

"No problem. How are you?"

"Good." She slid her phone down to her chin and took a deep breath to calm her erratic pulse. "What's up?"

"I called to let you know we're a go for the dig on our end."

Her heart leaped, but her mind jumped in and clipped the wings of exhilaration before it took flight. So what if Quentin would be spending a few months in her backyard? Nothing would happen. Nothing *could* happen.

"I also wanted to tell you we need to keep a low profile," Quentin said, all business. A total switch from their last conversation, when he'd gushed over her bakery plans. "Otherwise we could contend with looting, among other things. It's best if no one knows about the fossils until we're finished excavating. Do you think that's possible?"

Possible? Heck, if she had her way, no one besides the crew would ever find out. This dig could turn her grandparents' life upside down. Bring the paparazzi down on Hawksburg like *Notting Hill*, post–Anna Scott revelation. So far the only other people who knew about the dinosaur bones were the Snyders and Meg, who would keep the secret to her grave. And Mr. Snyder hadn't strung more than two words together in all the years she'd known him.

But Mrs. Snyder? If loose lips sunk ships, Alisha wouldn't even trust that woman on a rowboat in a kiddie pool. Still, Granny had all but extracted a blood oath from Mrs. S that she'd keep the dino bones a secret, though her friend had called dibs on breaking the news at bunco when it was all over.

"We'll do our part," she told Quentin. "I never imagined getting a front-row seat to something like this. Not that I'll be in your way or anything," she hastened to add.

Quentin chuckled. "I'm not worried about that. I love it when people take an interest. We'll start in May, after spring semester ends. And if your grandparents are okay with it, stay through July."

"Oh, they're fine with it." Alisha shot the words out, wincing at her eagerness. "As long as you guys don't mess up the place." A flash of Quentin's muddy forearms in the kitchen last week sprung to mind, and she squeezed her eyes shut.

"That's kind of the definition of a dig." He laughed. "But I know what you mean. We'll be on our best behavior. I'll make sure of it."

Alisha tipped forward and pulled her braids over her shoulder before settling back against the tree trunk. "You won't have to worry about my grandma. She talks a good game, but she's a softie." Not entirely true, but since he'd never have to undergo the ordeal of an Ellie Blake cross-examination, a white lie wouldn't hurt.

"Noted. And your grandpa?"

She kicked restless legs out, putting her soles up against an opposite branch. "Grandpa's definitely not a pushover. But he's fair. He really won't mind you guys working, and both he and my grandma will be over the moon for more people to feed." Alisha paused, realizing this sounded weird out of context. "Grandpa is the restaurateur in the family, but Granny is a true midwesterner. Feeding people is her religion."

"Sounds like my mom." Quentin chuckled. "She cooks enough every Sunday to feed the whole block and then some. Not that anyone ever turns down her enchiladas."

"I think I'd like your mom." Good food was the gateway to her heart. But the thought of meeting his mom left her tongue-tied. "Speaking of food, I'd better get back to cooking dinner."

"Of course." His tone shifted, a return to formality. "Sorry to keep you."

Phone pressed to her cheek, she breathed out in tune with his exhale. "No worries, it was good to chat."

"Yeah?"

"Yeah." Really good.

"See you soon, Alisha." The deep vibrations of his words struck a chord inside her, and she sucked in her bottom lip. His voice was velvet, and close, so close, like he was sitting next to her in the enveloping privacy of the branches.

"See you soon, Quentin."

🐾

Hours later, Alisha lay on the couch, blinking away yawns and replying to comments on her latest Instagram post. She couldn't afford to slack off now, even with her timeline up in the air. Her growing online presence would help boost sales while she earned a name for herself in the Chicago foodie scene.

Finally caught up on all eighty-four replies—she'd used just about every version of smiley face that existed and laid on cheery emojis like buttercream—she exited out and flicked through to Quentin's contact, ignoring the voice that told her she was playing with fire.

Alisha:

I know it's hush-hush and everything, but any idea what 🦴 is lurking in our yard?

Nerves ravaged her instantly. Why couldn't she leave well enough alone? She wasn't even interested in a boyfriend, *couldn't* be interested in a boyfriend. And she'd never once let a hot guy derail her resolve in the past. What made Quentin different? He listened without an agenda, for one. He didn't twist her words into what he wanted to hear, or leap to conclusions.

And the way he looked at her . . . not like he was sizing her up, or trying to poke holes in her existence, deflate her just enough to stuff her into a box. Around him she got a reprieve from the exhausting performance art her life had become ever since moving back home. Ever since moving to Hawksburg, period.

She swung her legs off the couch, clicked off the lamp and TV, and double-checked the locks before heading upstairs to bed.

Halfway through brushing her teeth, her phone chimed. A GIF of Rex from *Toy Story* appeared on her screen.

Quentin:

Not this kind.

Alisha laughed, spraying toothpaste foam all over the mirror. *Dang it.* She swiped at the splatter with the hand towel.

> **Alisha:**
> Bummer. But I win the bet with Mrs. Snyder. Her money was on Rexy.

She spat and rinsed, then found a GIF of Barney.

> **Alisha:**
> This one?

> **Quentin:**
> Lol, not quite.
>
> Maybe one of these. [GIF of *The Land Before Time*]

> **Alisha:**
> Lol, loved those movies as a kid.

> **Quentin:**
> All 50 of them?

> **Alisha:**
> 😄 I think there were only like a dozen.

> **Quentin:**
> "Only." 😄

> **Alisha:**
> I guess that means you weren't a fan?

No reply came, so she wrapped a scarf over the braids she'd pinned up, patting her head to ease the itchiness. Her mouth twisted in a rueful smile. If only she could banish thoughts of Quentin so easily—with a good hard whack upside her head. She was supposed to be blocking him out, not finding ways to keep their conversation going.

But that was just it. She wasn't grinding gears, pushing the relationship along. They'd tumbled into the stream and been swept away together, and for once she wondered if it would be so wrong to let go of the reservations weighing her down and just float.

CHAPTER 10

QUENTIN AND ALISHA

April 12

Quentin:

All I'm saying is, why have there been multiple seasons of The American Singer? It's called THE American Singer. Not American SingerS.

Alisha:

Ok, hard agree. It should've ended after one season. But I see your loathing of The American Singer and raise you The Singer with No Face.

Quentin:

Do I want to know?

Alisha:

You don't, but you must. Put on channel 12 right now.

Quentin:

Holy crap, Alisha. You watch this? I may have to revise my opinion of you.

Alisha:

Stop. It's my grandma. She loves this show.

Quentin:

Does she even know who these celebrity contestants are?

Alisha:

She does not. But honestly, does anyone?

(I have no idea why she loves it but I lied and said I liked it the first time and now I have to sit through this mania every Wednesday at 7. Help me!)

Quentin:

LOL

Alisha:

I know you really are laughing, and I hate you for it. 😏

Quentin:

Whoa, strong words.

Alisha:

You could make it up to me by watching this with me.

Quentin:
You'd owe me.

Alisha:
I'm okay with that.

Quentin:
Alright then.

. . .

Make it stop!

What is with their voices? It's like Alvin and the Chipmunks on LSD.

Alisha:
LOL

April 15

Quentin:
One of my students doubted my ability to do the floss.

Alisha:
Please tell me you didn't try to prove them wrong.

Quentin:
There was no trying.

I DID prove them wrong.

Alisha:

💀 But really, you flossed in front of your whole class? Is there a YouTube video?

"Paleontology Professor Gets Lit"?

Quentin:

Oh no! What if there is??

Alisha:

There isn't, I checked right when you told me.

Quentin:

Lol, of course you did, you villain.

April 23

Alisha:

I need you to talk me off a sourdough ledge.

Quentin:

What??

Alisha:

No judgment, deal?

Quentin:

Never.

Alisha:

Ok, picture it . . .

Sourdough sugar cookies.

Quentin:

Alisha:

That felt like a lot of judgment.

Quentin:

Oh. Did it show? Sorry.

Alisha:

Lol. It's a bad idea, right?

Quentin:

I mean, yes. But then again, you are an amazing baker.

Alisha:

You're making me blush.

Quentin:

Picture?

Alisha:

[IMAGE of a jar overflowing with beige foam]

Quentin:

What in the ever-loving heck is that?

Alisha:
Sourdough starter.

Quentin:
I rescind my endorsement.

Alisha:
Too late.

Quentin:
Also, that's not the kind of picture I meant.

Alisha:
I know. 😏

May 4

Quentin:
Less than a week now. <smiley face emoji>

Alisha:
Are you guys gathering supplies? Drawing up plans on a whiteboard? Modifying your vehicles?

Quentin:
This is paleontology we're talking about, not a heist movie.

Alisha:
Bummer.

Quentin:
But there will be tools.

Alisha:
I'm listening.

Quentin:
Shovels, pickaxes, jackhammers . . .

Alisha:
Keep going.

Quentin:
Toothbrushes, spoons.

Alisha:
You were on such a good run.

Quentin:
😬

Alisha:
Does your crew look like this? [GIF of the Wolf Pack from *The Hangover*]

Quentin:
OH MY GOSH ALISHA HOW DID YOU KNOW?

May 7

> **Alisha:**
> What about fossilized biscotti?

> **Quentin:**
> I feel like you're going to tell me the dig inspired you and I don't want to be held responsible.

> **Alisha:**
> But it did!

> **Quentin:**
> Alisha, that sounds terrible.

> **Alisha:**
> Lol, right?? You know I only share my bad ideas with you.

> **Quentin:**
> I do know. Because you're trying to hide your brilliance.
>
> Also, I can't wait to taste more of your cookies, but I swear to God, if you give me a sourdough cookie . . .

> **Alisha:**
> I'll save those for your grad students. 😊

CHAPTER 11

ALISHA

Curlicues of yellow lemon peel floated down into the sugar. Aromatherapy.

Some people might turn to the homey flavors of vanilla and cinnamon to chase away nerves, but citrus calmed Alisha's soul. She tapped the zester on the bowl's edge and checked the clock. Plenty of time to get this batch of lemon curd made and cooling for the pistachio tartlets she planned to debut this week in place of apple pie. Nailing this recipe had meant turning down three cookie orders, but Honey and Hickory—family—took priority.

After slicing the lemons, she put half of one in a juicer and squeezed tight. The paleontologists were due to arrive sometime this afternoon. An entire crew was headed down to work for the summer: Quentin, three grad students, and another assistant professor.

All good in theory, except the idea of seeing Quentin again lit up Alisha's nerves like downtown at midnight. She cracked an egg on the rim of a ramekin, cradling the yolk while the white ran through her fingers, and willed her tension to follow suit.

Despite her resolve to avoid getting involved with him back in March, they'd been texting ever since. When her bite-size berry pavlova recipe failed in gruesomely spectacular fashion, she'd caved to the urge to reach out and sent him a photo of the aftermath. He returned the favor with an anecdote about a technology mishap during class. They bonded over cringeworthy network TV and people's poor decisions on social media.

Turned out he was fluent in GIF, which pretty much cemented his spot in her heart—if she had a spot in her heart for a man. Which she didn't.

A pinch of salt, and then she placed the bowl atop a panful of simmering water, whisking so the eggs wouldn't scramble. Strictly speaking, texting Quentin didn't violate her "no boyfriends" policy. But comparing their conversations to chats with her guy friends? May as well compare a supernova to a bottle rocket.

And though she'd deny it to her grave, connecting with him marked the best part of her day. In a few moments of weakness—okay, more than a few—her finger had hovered over the call button, but each time she'd chickened out. And once, a few weeks ago, Quentin had called her, but she'd stared at her phone in panic and let it go to voice mail. He hadn't tried again, and she told herself not to be disappointed.

Now he would be here in a matter of hours, and if anything, her attraction to his personality, to his quirks, to the memory of his beautiful storm-gray eyes continued to grow. If she couldn't pull away with hundreds of miles between them, how would she fight the draw with him in her backyard all summer?

She picked up a wooden spoon and dragged it through the bowl. A satin layer of lemon curd coated the back of the spoon. Perfect. She took it off the heat and dropped slices of butter on top, stirring until they melted away. If only her worries could dissolve so easily.

Baking wasn't working its usual magic on her stress level. Time to bring out the big guns.

Spring warmth mingled with damp air to steep a muggy brew even the blasting fan couldn't touch. Weight lifting equipment surrounded Alisha in the last bay of a three-car garage, where she bent over a barbell in concentration.

Blue skies had morphed into a gentle rain misting down outside the open garage doors, and Alisha couldn't help but grin over the change in weather. Good thing she'd left her phone inside, or she might've done something stupid, like text Quentin an Avenger GIF.

A trickle of sweat ran down her face, and she wrinkled her nose against the itch, then pressed the soles of her teal Chucks into the ground and pulled up on the roughened steel bar. The barbell bent slightly, resisting, then gave with a gratifying lift.

Flexing her glutes, she stood tall and dropped the bar, letting the weight bounce down to the pads with a dull thud. Bruno Mars sang out through a speaker on the dusty windowsill, and Alisha joined in with breathless karaoke, hitting her watch to start her rest timer before the next set of dead lifts. She dropped down into a low squat, rocking side to side to loosen tight hips.

Why had she let a pseudorelationship progress this far? He was a mistake waiting to happen. Torn between regret and something suspiciously like excitement, she straightened up and tightened her lifting belt, the leather that helped brace her core. If only she had a similar brace for her emotions.

She bent and wrapped both hands around the barbell again, thumbs hooked under her first two fingers for grip. Planted her feet and shuffled her heels in her readiness ritual. She worked through another set of three dead lifts, blocking out the mental noise, then dropped the barbell and stepped back after the last rep with a satisfied nod.

Too bad she couldn't whip her heart into shape like her other muscles. She'd lifted weights for years now, and whenever she added resistance, her muscles rose to the challenge. After a few weeks, the new weight felt light, and she could tackle heavier lifts with success.

Yet after years spent building up an immunity against her desire for a relationship, she succumbed to a handsome face and shared sense of humor like a weakling.

Gasping, she loosened her belt so it hung down around her lower abs and tossed her wrists up on her head, sucking air. What was wrong with her? She should be focused on her business, on anticipating her family's needs, not sitting here heart-eyes over a guy she had no future with. She was officially done mooning over Quentin and ready to fast-forward through this roadblock of a summer.

The unmistakable crunch of tires on gravel hit Alisha's ears, and she whirled around. Headlights shone through the gray drizzle. She crossed over to the speaker and turned down the volume, looking around for her hoodie.

A car pulled to a halt in front of the garage, and the driver's side door opened. A woman got out, then leaned in to say something to the passenger. No one Alisha recognized. Abnormal, in a town where she could draw everyone's family tree from memory. Her search for the hoodie turned frantic.

The driver jogged over and stopped just under the garage overhang. "Good morning," she chirped.

One of the paleontologists? If so, she was a good hour and a half early. *Awesome.*

"Hi," said Alisha, spectacularly. She resisted the urge to tug down her booty shorts, noting the other woman's thigh gap with an internal groan.

The stranger was immaculate in a navy raincoat and tall Hunter boots over formfitting jeans, her golden-brown hair tumbling out from under her hood and cascading down in shimmering waves. "I'm Bridget Reid, from Chicago Northern. You must be Alisha."

Hunch confirmed, she nodded. Feeling like the Hulk next to Captain Marvel, pre–pixie cut, she busied herself with contriving a way to hide all her exposed skin. But covering up when she wore only a sports bra, spandex shorts, and neoprene knee sleeves was like fighting a forest fire with a squirt gun. She ended up hugging her middle like a hospital patient awaiting an appendectomy, hyperconscious of the liberal dusting of white chalk across her thighs.

"That's me. Alisha." She undid her weight lifting belt and instantly regretted the reddened indents and surplus bare skin it revealed. Couldn't well put it back on now, though. "Sorry, we weren't expecting you this soon."

Bridget smiled an apology. "Yeah, I know. I just couldn't wait any longer to get down here and see the site. Too bad this rain started up." She spoke with a slight twang—nothing jarring, just a soft rounding of her vowels.

Out on the road, Alisha spied a black pickup slow down, then turn into the driveway. Quentin.

Ohmygoshohmygoshohmygosh . . .

Where the heck was her sweatshirt?

Water rushed out of the gutter, and Bridget ducked, stepping deeper into the garage. She slipped off her hood and shook out her hair in slow motion like in a shampoo ad. Alisha stood mesmerized, a wildebeest trapped in the hypnotic gaze of a lioness.

"I hope this doesn't inconvenience you, us showing up early." Bridget's lips pressed into an expectant smile. Delicate perfume wafted toward her, and Alisha fought the urge to clamp down her arms. Had she even put on deodorant this morning? *Unlikely.*

She ran her tongue along her unbrushed teeth before answering. "No, no. Of course not. And from here on out, you're welcome anytime." She made a mental note to keep the garage door shut for every workout from now on, no matter the temperature. And to lift in an old pair of knee-length basketball shorts. And a shirt—definitely a shirt.

Maybe she could flee for cover inside the house. Locate some clothes and salvage the shreds of her dignity. A burst of rain sheeted down in denial of her unspoken wish, chasing Bridget all the way into the garage.

She cast a glance around at the squat rack and weights. "This setup is so neat! Are you, like, a bodybuilder?"

"Powerlifter."

"Neat!" Bridget repeated, and then wrapped her arms around her small frame, shivering. "I did CrossFit for a while. In undergrad. But then I was getting too big. Y'know, bulky?" She spread her fingers and flung out her hands in a clawing motion. Then she dropped her eyes to Alisha's arms and blushed. "Now I mostly stick with barre workouts and Pilates."

Of course she did.

Aloud, Alisha said in a clipped tone, "Heard great things about those."

"Oh yeah, you should give it a try sometime! Your muscles will be jelly afterward!" She spoke without a trace of irony.

With great effort, Alisha pulled her lips into a scant curve she hoped passed for a polite smile. Her roving eyes finally snagged on her hoodie, underneath the bench. While Bridget inspected the rainbow-hued assortment of elastic bands that hung from the pull-up bar, Alisha dived for her sweatshirt and scrambled to put it on.

But when she pulled the hoodie over her head, it loosened her ponytail holder. Half her twists tumbled over her face, and the other half hung absurdly to the side, still trapped in the hair tie, an eighties music video gone wrong.

Someone cleared their throat, and Alisha emerged like Punxsutawney Phil from the neck of her hoodie to find Quentin about a foot in front of her. He wore an olive-green utility jacket and jeans, a battered tool bag rucked over his shoulder, and those same leather work boots she remembered all too well. The cover model for *GQ*, Hunks of Academia edition.

Words escaped Alisha. All of them. Instead of greeting him, she yanked at her hair tie in a last-ditch effort to regain her composure. But jeez Louise, the hair band remained tangled in her twists, and she spun in a slow and tragic circle trying to free it, like a pony being tugged by its bridle. *Wonderful.*

"Here, let me help you." Bridget's golden eyes swam into view, and she stepped around to pull off the hood. She gently freed Alisha's twists, then handed her the ponytail holder. Her eyes said, *Been there,* but Alisha couldn't picture a world where that was true.

Dredging up gratitude, she muttered, "Thanks."

Quentin, who watched this whole performance with an expression somewhere between confusion, pity, and—screw him—amusement, now spoke up. "Sorry to drop in on you like this; we expected more traffic." He chewed his lip, telegraphing an apology with his eyes, whether for her pride or their arrival ahead of schedule, she wasn't sure.

"Oh no, it's fine." Alisha's voice came out a few octaves higher than normal. She forgot to breathe for a second, rolling the hair tie in her fingers. "You must be dying to get out there and see the dinosaur. Er, the fossils. The bones." She slipped the hair tie onto her wrist and wrestled a smile onto her face. "In the backyard, I mean. Unless the rain is an issue?"

Too late, she fisted her hands in her hoodie pocket, lifting up the baggy fabric so her shorts were visible. Naked weight lifting wasn't a skill set she wanted on her résumé.

"I think we can handle a little rain, right, Quentin?" Bridget blinked up at him, maybe wondering why he'd gone silent.

Held under his colleague's gaze, Quentin opened his mouth, then closed it again. He ran a hand under the strap of the tool bag and shuffled his feet. The women waited.

"Yeah, looks like it's letting up," he finally said.

They all squinted out into the gray mist for a few seconds, motionless. The dam of awkwardness filled to the brim and overflowed right along with the gutters. Alisha couldn't remember a time in her life when she'd wished harder for the power of teleportation. Or time travel, to go back and erase the past ten minutes.

Since no DeLorean or portkey materialized, she crossed one ankle over the other. In this unstable position, with muscles wobbly from exertion, she nearly toppled over when Quentin turned her way again.

His gaze flicked down to her body, once. He turned toward his colleague. "How about I show you and Cait the field site now, in case this rain gets worse. Then, once the guys arrive, we'll come in to do introductions. Is that okay?" He addressed the last question to Alisha, not quite meeting her eyes.

That tragic, huh? She let her shoulders fall and rubbed chalky palms down her thighs. "Sure. I'll go let my grandparents know you're here."

The paleontologists nodded at her, then headed back out. As he cast a glance over his shoulder, Quentin tripped over a kettlebell, but he recovered in a snap and half jogged out into the drizzle.

Well. That could've gone worse. She could've set the kitchen on fire.

CHAPTER 12

ALISHA

Alisha ladled sauce into the last plastic cup. At the cooktop, Hank shook shredded Gruyère into the pot of macaroni and cheese.

Meg emerged from the walk-in fridge with a jug of coleslaw and kicked the door closed with her heel. "Ready to charm the pants off Hottie Harris, PhD?"

The tiny tub of barbecue sauce went pinballing across the counter and ricocheted off the wall, splattering sauce all over her apron. She shot a glare at Meg and jerked her chin in Hank's direction. He shoved the sleeves of his checkered shirt farther up over his elbows and started humming. Loudly.

"Sorry," Meg mouthed.

Alisha just shook her head. Working alongside her best friend during the summer months didn't normally involve getting called out in front of the other employees. Though she couldn't blame Meg for overlooking Hank's presence. He was as permanent a fixture as the antique cash register out front.

Meg grabbed a foil pan full of ribs and backed out the door. "You go ahead with the coleslaw; I'm going to start loading the food into your car."

"No hurry," Alisha called after her. Maybe if they took long enough packing up lunch, the paleontologists would get tired of waiting and grab sandwiches from Stella's Deli instead.

Gnawing on her lip, Alisha scribbled "Brisket" on the lid of a foil tray. Equal parts mortified about her fumbling reintroduction to Quentin and petrified to face him again, she'd managed to avoid the crew entirely. Despite her curiosity about the excavation, she hadn't so much as peeked out the window all week for fear of being spotted.

"Awful nice of your grandpa to feed those geologists." Hank slid a foil pan off the wire rack and spooned steaming mac and cheese into it. "A big nuisance, if you ask me, them poking around."

They'd decided to tell everyone that the crew from CNU was doing a geological survey, not excavating dinosaur fossils. Less intrigue, hopefully less interest and potential for exposure.

"Yeah, well, they're so quiet we hardly know they're there." A total lie; she could think of nothing else. "Plus, he knows if he caters lunch today, they'll get hooked on our barbecue and be repeat customers all summer."

Hank chuckled. "Can't argue with that." He slid the sealed tray next to the others. "I'm gonna head on out and check the smoker."

"Thanks, Hank." She picked up the meat and carried it out the side door to the alley. Meg stood by the Geo, scrolling through her phone. Alisha set the food in the trunk and walked backward toward the door. "Care to help bring out the rest of the food, Marge, or am I interrupting your Tindering?"

"I've told you a million times, it's not Tinder." She hurried over and swung the door open, bracing her back against it to let Alisha through. "It's an app called Forever Love for people who are marriage minded."

Alisha snorted. *Marriage minded?* "Mm-hmm, and how's that going for you?"

"Okay, so I've dated a few duds. But I'm learning how to decode the profiles to weed out the guys who are just looking for a casual fling."

"Wait, I'm confused. I thought you said every man signed up to find a bride!" Alisha laughed and dodged her friend's slap.

"I don't know why you're so dead set against dating, Ali. That attitude might've been cute before, but in case you haven't noticed, we're not getting any younger. Aren't you worried about being single when you turn"—she hoisted up the stack of containers and whispered—"thirty?"

"Careful, someone might hear you!" Alisha feigned horror. "But no, I'm really not. And anyway, if I got into a relationship right now, it would only last a couple months. I'm leaving town, remember?"

"Don't remind me," Meg said with a pout. "But what if the guy you're dating left too?" Meg's eyes held a wicked gleam. "Don't tell me you haven't considered it. Like I haven't noticed the look you get on your face every time you text him."

"What look on my face?" She grabbed a bag of homemade rolls and opened the door for her friend. "And how do you know I've been texting Quentin?" Apparently she hadn't been as discreet as she thought.

"Alisha, you text him more than you text me. I'd be offended if we didn't see each other pretty much every day." Meg stacked the trays on top of the others. "I've kept my mouth shut about your texting spree because you're skittish as heck about men, and I figured asking about him would make you block his number or something else drastic."

Sadly, she had a point.

"So are you going to do something about it?" Meg prodded.

"What, like throw myself at him?"

"How about casually running into him on the daily and letting fate do the rest? Seems easier than avoiding someone who's going to be staked out in your yard all summer. And less stressful than bottling up all that tension you've built with two months of emotional foreplay."

Alisha groaned. "You're ridiculous."

"Yet you love me," she said in a singsong voice.

She tossed the rolls into the trunk and slammed it shut. Meg had a point. Pursuing a relationship with Quentin would be easier than avoiding him. For most people. But casual didn't work for her. She'd never learned the knack of separating head from heart. And though she yearned for a family of her own, commitment terrified her. More than never leaving town, more than opening a bakery in Chicago and failing.

The idea of relying on a man left her palms clammy, fighting for purchase on a rope above an abyss. And having a husband and kids who counted on her? Worse. What if she wasn't up for the long haul? Her grandparents had sacrificed so much to raise her and Simone, and she couldn't even commit to the family business. How could she ever stay true to a man? No one should sign up to be her family. No dating, then. Not for her.

"You're assuming Quentin is even remotely interested in me," she said, deflecting.

"He'd be a fool if he wasn't."

Meg had that one backward. He'd be a fool if he *was*.

"Where do you want these?" Alisha hovered near the kitchen island, peering over the stack of trays in her arms.

Fishing tea bags out of a crystal carafe, Granny sent a smile their way even warmer than the buttery yellow paint on the kitchen walls.

"Just set 'em down anywhere," she said. "Then you girls oughta go on out back and check out the dig."

"Naw, Margaret's not interested in the dinosaur." A baritone voice broke into the conversation. Alisha's grandpa strode in and tossed a sheaf of papers on the counter, leaning over to peck his wife on the cheek.

He pretended to do a double take at Meg's expression. "Wait, you're not, are you?"

Alisha laughed and poked her friend's shoulder. "After all these years, it's like you don't know him at all. You think Grandpa would let you leave without seeing the big show? You're one of the few people who knows what's really going on." And so far—she knocked on the wood cabinet under the countertop—no one else in town seemed to suspect anything out of the ordinary.

"My granddaughter's right." One corner of his mouth lifted in a grin underneath white stubble. "I'll meet you out there."

Meg wasted no time in rushing down the hall, but Alisha hung back, leaning against the counter. "Let me help you set up, Granny."

Head in the fridge, her grandma flapped a hand at her. "No, no. I can manage just fine. You go on and take a peek at all the hullabaloo." She emerged from the fridge with a jar of homemade pickles and padded over in the ratty pink slippers she wore in every season. "This is a once-in-a-lifetime thing, sweetie. Don't hide in here." She shooed Alisha toward the door with a playful swat on her butt. "Get on out there."

"Okay, Granny, jeez!" She danced away, wishing for the millionth time she had a set of docile grandparents. Sometimes she wasn't sure who was taking care of whom. But the memory of Granny's frail body, of her mom fading, of the razor's edge between *here* and *gone*, remained tattooed on her heart, inscribed on her mind. Every moment, she strove to outwit disaster with sheer dependability.

She swept through the screen door and caught up to Meg.

"You didn't tell me a Discovery Channel special had taken over your yard," her friend muttered, shielding her eyes with her hand.

Two pickups—one of them Quentin's—were parked by the edge of the pit, tailgates down, filled with a mishmash of tools. Strings crisscrossed the dig, breaking the area into sections. The giant bone wasn't visible, maybe hidden under one of the tarps.

Laughter drifted toward them, and eighties pop screeched out from a battered radio. Toward the back of the dig, Quentin stood scribbling in a battered yellow journal. He closed the book and looked toward the house. His eyes met hers, and a smile blazed across his face. A dazzlingly white, infectious grin.

Meg let out a low, long whistle. "Girl, forget what I said." For once, she didn't shout. "Please *do* throw yourself at that man. Hard, and as many times as it takes."

Alisha elbowed her and kept walking toward the pit.

"You know, violence only makes you look guilty." Meg grabbed her arm.

Speaking out of the side of her mouth, Alisha whispered, "Guilty of what, exactly?"

Eyes fixated on Quentin, an affliction Alisha understood all too well, Meg said, "Of crushing on a sexy paleontologist. Duh." She spoke in an undertone, gesturing toward the dig. "Just look, Ali. There's a movie set complete with a leading actor in your backyard. All it's missing is a heroine."

"In case you didn't notice, he's not an actor—he's a scientist!" she hissed.

Meg grinned like the Cheshire cat. She knew Alisha's weakness for men with big brains.

Grandpa walked up between them and slung an arm around her shoulders. "Well, whaddya think?" He lifted his chin toward the cluttered dig. "Nothin' this big has happened in Hawksburg for quite some time. More fun than a pool, though I reckon the dino docs wouldn't mind a nice cool dip right about now."

He crouched down on the lip of the pit. "Hiya, Dr. Harris. This is Meg Anderson. And I believe you've already met my granddaughter."

Tucking the notepad into the pocket of his cargo shorts, Quentin picked his way over to them. "Nice to meet you, Meg. I'd shake your hand, but . . ." He grinned, holding aloft dirt-encrusted fingers. "And yes, Alisha and I have met." The brief smile he sent her way held the secret of their conversations tucked at its edges. Heat buzzed through her veins, and it had nothing to do with the warmth radiating from the packed earth.

"Alisha, you've met Bridget."

One boot on her shovel, Bridget smiled up at them from under a tan baseball cap, the sleeves of her denim shirt rolled up to her elbows.

Quentin turned and motioned to the other three people crouched in the dirt, tools in hand. "And this is Caitlyn Hsu, Dev Mehra, and Forrest Abernathy."

They all waved equally dirty hands.

"Thanks again for allowing us to work on your land, Mr. Blake. You're doing a great thing here," said Bridget.

"More'n happy to do our part to advance science. Guess you never know what you might find when you start digging around."

"True, otherwise we'd be out of a job!" Caitlyn tossed her dusty black braid over one shoulder and laughed.

"Anyway, it's gettin' on toward noon." Grandpa rubbed a paisley hankie across his brow, then stuffed it into the back pocket of his jeans. "The girls brought over some lunch for everyone. Ready for a break?"

Dev used his forearm to hitch up the bill on his Cubs hat and wiped his forehead. "Is this the famous barbecue we've been hearing about?"

"Yup." Her grandpa stood up with a slight wobble, and Alisha caught his elbow. "C'mon in, and we can eat. Once you've washed up. My wife Ellie'd kill me if I didn't mention that." He winked. "Meg, you're more'n welcome to stay too."

"Thanks, Mr. Blake, but I need to run some errands. Nice meeting you all." She waved at the paleontologists. "Ali, I'll see you later."

"See ya," said Alisha. A full-out inquest was coming later, but thank goodness she'd be spared from any patented Meg Anderson outbursts during lunch.

Caitlyn climbed out of the pit, followed by Forrest, his chestnut hair twisted up into a sloppy bun held in place with a tie-dyed scrunchie. Dev hung back, recording something on a crumpled stack of papers on a clipboard.

"Dining room's straight through the back door on the right." Alisha pointed toward the house. "Can't miss it. But you'd better take off your boots on the porch, or it'll be hell to pay."

Forrest brushed dust off the front of his purple tee shirt, which read *Science: Like Magic, Only Real,* and gave her a lopsided smile. "You mean tracking dirt through your house isn't the appropriate thank-you for getting our hands on a once-in-a-lifetime discovery and free lunch?"

"Speaking of free . . ." Bridget stepped off the ladder into the grass, but Alisha waved her off.

"No worries. My grandpa would never let you pay. Feeding people is his passion. Plus, it's not entirely altruistic. He knows our barbecue is addictive." Alisha grinned.

Bridget returned her smile, then turned toward the dig. "Coming, y'all?"

Quentin held up a tape measure. "I need to finish these measurements. You guys go ahead. I'll be there in a minute."

"Suit yourself," Dev said. "We'll try and save you some." He climbed up the ladder and strode off toward the house. The others followed with a wave to Alisha.

She should go. But being so near Quentin again, her heart thrummed with the same yearning that had awoken the second she'd laid eyes on him back in March. Except now all the words they'd exchanged filled the pit, muddying the waters.

Flirting in the kitchen on a rainy afternoon felt like a lifetime ago. And chatting on a screen made her bold. But real-life Dr. Harris, in his element? Way out of her league.

Get in the house, Blake. None of this is for you. But she didn't budge. Instead, her eyes roamed over Quentin's long frame. Frowning in concentration, he used one knee as a prop for the notebook, his other leg stretched out in the dirt, measuring tape abandoned next to his boot. He paused, raised his pencil to his mouth, and bit down gently on the eraser.

A low noise escaped Alisha's lips, and she clapped a hand over her mouth. Quentin's head snapped up, surprise washing over his features. "Oh, you're still here?"

"Yeah, just, um . . ." She dropped her hand and crossed her arms. Crossed her ankles, too, for good measure. "Just checking things out."

His face broke into a wide and knowing grin.

Oh Lordy.

Yes, it was a *really* good thing she hadn't been able to see him during their chats. A flash of him hovering at the edge of the kitchen, rain drenched and adorably hesitant, sprang to mind with terrible timing. She unwound her legs like a newborn foal, rocking sideways in the process. "The dig. Checking the dig out. It looks so different already."

His face fell ever so slightly, but he nodded and pushed himself to stand, dusting off his hands. "We've been busy. There's so much here. It's remarkable any of this was preserved."

Alisha cleared her throat. "I can't believe no one ever discovered any dinosaurs in Illinois until now."

Quentin nodded, the wattage on his smile returning. "Wild, right?"

Goose bumps pricked her arms. "It really is!"

Arms crossed, he tilted his head.

"What?"

He pressed a thumb to his full lower lip, and Alisha willed herself not to melt.

"Sorry, it's just . . . I get that you're excited because we found these fossils on your grandparents' land. But most people aren't so interested in dinosaurs."

Should she do this? Too late—her mouth was already moving, coaxed into motion by Quentin's puzzled smile.

"So, full disclosure, I may or may not have founded a *Jurassic Park* fan club in my basement as a kid." Why-oh-why-oh-why had she volunteered that privileged information after keeping it under wraps for months?

In too deep, she blundered on. "I wasn't allowed to see *Jurassic Park* at the same age as most of my friends. My parents were worried I'd have nightmares. In their defense, I had a lot of nightmares, but not until later. And not because of scary movies."

Say less, say less.

"Anyway, I'd worked the movie up to such a big deal. Forbidden fruit, so to speak. When I finally saw *Jurassic Park* at a sleepover, I became low-key obsessed. I made my sister secretary of the club and everything." The fossilized skeleton in her closet, and she just word-vomited it to the hottest man she'd ever met. *Why? Why? Why?*

Flailing, she fought the dumpster fire with the gasoline of more words. "I always fantasized about marrying Dr. Grant someday, though Ian Malcolm was my dream guy in the looks department."

After her final insane confession, two facts slammed into her brain with the force of dual torpedoes:

(a) She'd confessed all this to a real-life doctor of paleontology.

(b) He was a perfect mix of Dr. Grant and Dr. Malcolm, a tall, dark, and handsome dinosaur nerd.

She prayed to all the saints for a second pit to open up and save her from this tragedy.

But Quentin's eyes shone. "Seriously, Alisha? That movie is my life," he said, gushing. "Well, okay, not literally, obviously. Well, kind of literally. That is, er . . ." He hooked a finger under the collar of his white tee and dragged it sideways to reveal a tantalizing view of his collarbone. "What I mean is, I don't deal with living dinosaurs. Obviously."

He palmed the back of his neck, face sheepish. "So yeah, I fell in love with *Jurassic Park* as a kid too." He bit his lip and dropped his elbow. "Though Ellie Sattler isn't my type."

Her cheeks ignited. So he *had* caught the end of her speech, after all. But wait, was he flirting with her? In spite of seeing her all sweaty and tongue-tied and clumsy on Monday?

But yeah, his eyes bore into her with a look she'd been half dreading, half dreaming of for weeks, and she was 95 percent sure he was into her.

Paralyzed, instinct kicked in.

Time to flee the scene.

"Well, I'll let you get back to your, um . . . your measurements. Didn't mean to keep you. I'm sure Granny could use my help." She turned around without waiting for an answer, a stifled groan escaping her lips.

Granny needs my help? Talk about a romance killer. Proof she was incapable of having a normal conversation without the benefit of autocorrect. Didn't matter, though. If she could just survive this one last Hawksburg summer, then by fall, all her dreams would be set in motion.

In the meantime, she needed to focus on paving the way for her move and keeping nosy neighbors at bay. Distractions hindered her focus, put her grandparents' security in harm's way. And Quentin, in all his work boot–clad sun-kissed glory, was one heck of a distraction.

CHAPTER 13

QUENTIN

"Who wants strawberry shortcake?" Alisha's grandmother looked around the table with a smile.

"I'm never going to turn down dessert," said Forrest, and a chorus of agreement went up from the other paleontologists.

Alisha hopped to her feet, reaching over to lift Cait's empty plate. "Here, lemme clear that out of the way for you."

The perfect opening. Quentin sent up a prayer of thanks for parents who'd drilled good manners into him and gathered up the rest of his colleagues' plates. Mrs. Blake put a hand on his arm. "You don't need to do that, dear." She lifted her chin to indicate the dirty dishes.

"It's no problem," he said, and meant it.

He found Alisha in the kitchen glugging heavy cream into a stand mixer. Laid out like the "After" picture from one of the home-reno shows Mercedes used to force him to sit through, counters ran along three walls of the airy room, anchored by a large center island. Bright white cabinets stretched to the ceiling, and a big picture window above the sink looked out into the side yard. A kitchen Ma would kill for, after making do with her cramped sixties model for years. He set the plates on the counter, and Alisha turned to him in surprise.

"Oh, you didn't need to do that!"

Quentin grinned. "That's what your grandma said."

She rolled her eyes but smiled. "You've heard the adage 'the customer's always right'? In this family we take it a step further: 'Guests should never lift a finger.'"

He laughed. "Good thing I'm not a guest, then. I work here." Her surprised laugh gave him life. "So the food's as good as you said. Although—dang it!" He snapped his fingers. "Should've taken a picture for Facebook."

"What else are smartphones for, right?"

"But really, it was kind of you to feed us. We usually camp out on digs. Smoked brisket and pulled chicken is a big step up from hot dogs and walking tacos."

Grinning, she popped the lid on a glass Tupperware dish, and the smell of fresh strawberries filled the kitchen. "Make sure you repeat that loudly for my grandpa's benefit."

He chuckled and turned on the faucet. "Got it."

Someone tapped his shoulder, and he twisted around to find Alisha at his elbow. "What are you doing?" She leaned around him and shut off the faucet.

"Washing the dishes." He turned it back on.

"You really don't have to." She angled between him and the sink and turned off the water again, daring him with an upturned chin and sparkling eyes, their hips a hairbreadth apart.

How easy would it be to frame her in with his hands on the counter and capture her lips in a kiss? Instead, fighting to control his wayward thoughts, he reached around, brushing her waist, and flicked on the water again.

"If I admit I'm doing the dishes just to hang out with you, will you let me stay?"

She swallowed, the sound loud in the stillness, and his gaze traced the long line of her neck. He snapped his eyes up and found hers hooded, dark.

"Yeah. Sure. I mean . . . yeah." Reaching behind herself again, she grabbed a bottle of dish soap and pushed it into his chest, a sly grin on her rosy lips. "As long as you can manage to stay dry today."

Warmth spread up Quentin's neck, and he clasped the bottle, a jolt slicing through him when their fingertips touched. "Still blaming me for the rain?"

Almost no space remained between them, and her eyes hadn't left his face. Caught in her sway, he stood frozen. The whirring of the stand mixer changed in tone, and Alisha sucked in a quick breath and slid away, clicked off the mixer.

"Didn't you compare yourself to Thor?" She took out a stack of small plates from the cupboard, her twists swinging along her shoulder blades. "Who else should I blame?"

"I specifically didn't. If I recall, *you* did." He lathered up the plates with suds, wishing he'd used cold water instead.

"Hmm, my memory of the day is a little fuzzy. Guess I'll have to take your word for it." Her curly lashes brushed her cheeks as she swirled a crescent of deep-magenta sauce onto the plates, a hint of a smile on her lips.

He liked this side of her, open and silly. Back in March, when she'd talked about her family, her life here, he'd sensed a heaviness. But today, playfulness reigned.

Scrubbing the dishes, he watched her out of the corner of his eye. She placed a halved biscuit on the center of each plate, topped by a spoonful of berries.

He turned on the tap to rinse the plates and looked her way again, to find her with a tub of sour cream, spoon poised over the bowl of what he'd assumed was whipped cream. She caught his eye. "I know what you're thinking, but don't knock it till you try it." She plopped in a big dollop of sour cream and cranked up the speed again.

Yuck. What would she add next, mayo? He cringed, setting the plates in the dish drainer. He leaned over to fetch the dish towel off the counter, but she intercepted him, boxing him out. Again with the closeness. It almost made him forgive her for ruining the whipped cream. Almost, but not quite.

He eyed the spoon in her hand. "You'd best keep that nasty concoction far away from me." Snatching up the towel, he held it up between them like a matador.

"Just try it." She ducked under the towel, between his arms, and he forgot to breathe. That is, until she raised the spoon to his lips. Nose scrunched, he tentatively darted out his tongue.

Wow. Okay, that was amazing. Tangy and sweet and super luscious.

At the look on his face, she mm-hmmed, low in her throat, and the vibration struck a tuning fork in Quentin, setting his whole body abuzz. She slipped the spoon in her mouth, finishing off the bite, and he bit back a raspy breath.

"Ali, need a hand?" Mrs. Blake's voice cut through the haze around his brain, and Quentin leaped back just as Alisha dropped the spoon into the sink. Soapy water splashed up all over his shirt.

He plucked the wet fabric away from his stomach and met Alisha's eyes. Deadpan, she licked a dab of cream off her pinkie. "Nope, all good here," she called. She let her eyes drift down his front and trace their way back up. Heat blazed through his body. "Quentin, you remember the way to the bathroom, right?"

With that, she picked up the tray of plates and flounced out of the kitchen.

A few hours later, he knelt in the scorching bed of his dad's pickup, rummaging around with more force than was strictly necessary for another bottle of superglue in the totes that held their tools. The mixed signals Alisha kept throwing out were leaving him dizzy. They'd spent an entire month texting pretty much every day, but she'd basically run away when he'd arrived in town. She hadn't come out to the dig, hadn't so much as shown her face until today.

But despite the air-conditioned chill, the temperature in the kitchen after lunch had reached a boiling point. Was this all just a game to her, or did he somehow not measure up to the guy he'd projected in all their conversations? He wrenched a stray roll of toilet paper out of the tote and tossed it into the corner.

"I may never eat again." Dev's voice came from down in the dirt, accompanied by a loud belch.

"Yeah, right. I saw you polish off a granola bar five minutes ago." Caitlyn this time, her tone playful.

Dev's hoarse laugh reached Quentin's ears. "Guilty. But hear me out, guys. Was that not the best food you've ever eaten?"

"I'm pretty sure you said the same thing about the ramen place you dragged me to last week." Cait, again.

"That was *ramen*," said Dev. "This was *barbecue*. A man is allowed to have favorites of multiple cuisines."

Cait's laughter sailed up out of the pit.

"As the only Texan in residence, I'm the only one here qualified to talk about barbecue." Bridget's drawl carried over from where Quentin had left her chiseling out a fragment of vertebra. "I *know* real barbecue." She paused, and the scrape of tools halted. "And that, y'all, was *barbecue*."

"See? Thank you," Dev said. "Why did no one mention the thick granddaughter, though?"

Quentin halted his search, ears pricked. Heels sliding up under him of their own volition, he peered down into the dig.

"Maybe because Dr. Harris called dibs," Caitlyn said, voice low.

What the heck? Quentin's fingers squeezed the side of the pickup, barely registering the searing heat of the metal.

Bridget's ball-capped head swiveled toward Cait, who had the grace to look shamefaced. "Just kidding." But she continued speaking under her breath, and Quentin crept forward another few feet to catch her words. "Whatever, good for him. I hear half the department's thrown themselves at him since his breakup, and it's like hitting a brick wall." She snickered. "He obviously needs to find someone to break him out of the rut he's been in."

"Dude!" Forrest's head jerked up, and he drew his hand across his throat in a slicing *Cut it out* motion.

Giving up on finding the glue, Quentin grabbed the nearest tool bag and slung it into a bare quadrant of dirt. Dev and Caitlyn snapped their heads up, eyes darting toward one another. He jumped out of the bed of the truck and went down the ladder, skipping the last few rungs. Did they think he was deaf?

"Bit careless with university property, huh?" Dev nodded toward the bag, cocky grin back in place, though a bit wobbly at the edges.

"Most of the tools are older than you, Dev." Quentin yanked out a pick. "I think they'll survive, and if they don't, it'll be a mercy killing." He knelt down next to Forrest and breathed deep to slow his heartbeat so he wouldn't damage any fragile fossils.

The intersection of his love life and work was leaving him off kilter. And for what? A woman who may or may not have been into him? Why couldn't he just be content with this excavation and forget about her?

Sitting back on his heels, Quentin thumbed a trail of sweat off his cheek. If he didn't pay attention, he was going to miss something crucial. No sense in proving his father right with a slipup on the discovery of a lifetime. He wiped his palm on the rough fabric of his shorts, then took a firm grip on the pick. "Why don't you run me through what you've found since this morning, Forrest?"

CHAPTER 14

ALISHA

Out of the corner of her eye, Alisha saw Meg's face pressed to the attic window like a dog in the back seat of a car, panting. *Sheesh.*

"You do realize how attractive your professor is, don't you?"

Opening her browser, she tried to tune out Meg and the nonstop newsreel of Quentin thoughts spinning through her head. He certainly wasn't "hers," and the sooner she made peace with that, the better.

She bit down on her fingernail and scrolled through the latest set of retail bakery listings. Several of the spaces showed promise, and she clicked through the details. Muffled words reached her ears. She hazarded a glance and found Meg still fogging up the glass octagon, forehead pressed to the windowpane.

"He's got all the bases covered. Sexy nerd. Check. Rough and dirty. Check, check." Meg sunk down onto the cushioned window seat. She lifted her hair off her shoulders and fanned herself. "And those boots. Hoo boy! What girl doesn't love a man in muddy work boots?"

Then she tipped her head between her knees and gathered all her hair into a ponytail. Alisha rubbed a hand on her own damp neck under the weighty warmth of her twists. Thanks to Grandpa's well-meaning thriftiness, the temperature in her attic bedroom had to be pushing eighty degrees.

Meg spoke around the elastic band clenched between her teeth. "All he's missing is Clark Kent glasses."

Alisha grunted, then turned back to the screen, clicking several photos to open them in new tabs. She wouldn't take the bait. But Meg had known her forever.

Like a shark sensing blood in the water, she yanked the ponytail holder out of her mouth and wound it around her hair. "What's that? Hmm? You're telling me the man wears glasses?" Her voice squeaked at the last syllable.

"Yes, okay? He has glasses." Alisha threw her arms up in defeat. "I saw him wearing them the other day." She got up from the desk and flopped down onto her embroidered quilt, goose bumps flooding her arms at the memory of him sitting on the pickup's tailgate in the morning sunlight. The big round frames combined with his grown-out curls gave his face a new dimension of intellectual hotness.

Meg collapsed backward against the wall, likewise stricken at her own mental picture, no doubt. Arms lifeless at her sides, she stared Alisha down.

"Your dino doctor checks all of my marriage boxes." She lifted fingers one at a time, starting with her thumb. "Steady job, polite, intelligent—'Hel-*lo*, Professor'—and he's a ten."

In response to her stoic gaze, Meg threw herself forward and strode over like a panther. She grabbed Alisha's knee, rocking it back and forth.

"A *lit-er-al* ten." She let go and looked down her thin nose at Alisha. "Stop lying to yourself, woman. I know you think he's the perfect package." The perfect, way-too-good-for-her, *Just kidding, we delivered it to the wrong house and can you please drop it off at your nearest post office?* package.

"If I admit I think he's cute, will you promise to never use the word 'package' again?"

Crossing her arms, Meg shook her head. "Absolutely not."

"Absolutely not as in you'll never say 'package' again?"

"Absolutely not as in you know I can't promise that."

Alisha laughed and scooted back against her headboard, the varnish sticky between her shoulder blades. Ridiculous, sure, but Meg's enthusiasm was contagious. For a moment she envisioned letting Quentin in for real, pursuing him instead of running scared.

Blowing out a breath, Alisha said, "Yes, he's obviously super cute."

"An understatement, but go on."

"There definitely aren't any guys like him in Hawksburg," Alisha conceded.

"Zero," said Meg.

"Or in the whole state, more likely." Alisha spoke quietly, eyes on the ceiling, a grin lifting her cheeks in spite of her efforts to keep her face impassive.

"Ah, the truth comes out! I *knew* it, Ali. You're head over heels for this guy."

She scowled. Trust Meg to make the leap from not interested to wedding bells in a single bound.

"Okay, but you do like him. In a more-than-just-friends kind of way," Meg said, to press the issue.

Letting her head fall back again, Alisha spoke in a monotone, like a child copying a scripted apology on a blackboard. "I admit I like him a little bit more than just friends." A lotta bit, and what did that mean for her future? For her grandparents' future?

Hands cupped around her mouth like a megaphone, Meg announced to the audience of one, "Ladies and gentlemen, you heard it here first!"

Jiminy Crickets, she never should've chosen a former cheer captain for a best friend.

Meg dropped her hands and sauntered over to the closet. "Ali, coming from you, that's basically a declaration of love. Should I call the church?" See, wedding bells.

"If I didn't like you so much, I'd hate you." Alisha glared up at the bare timbers of the peaked ceiling.

Meg laughed. "And since we've agreed you're going to pursue this guy . . ." They had *not* agreed on anything, but yeah, the idea seemed less terrible by the minute. "Because you like him and he likes you, and this fall you'll be sharing an area code, you know what this calls for." She opened both closet doors like a magician whipping a handkerchief off a cageful of doves.

Alisha closed her eyes and massaged her forehead. "I refuse to do a rom-com-style outfit montage for you, Marge."

"Who said anything about you? We're done discussing your love life for now. *I'm* going to do the obligatory outfit montage."

The screech of shifting hangers reached her ears. "I'm not even going to ask."

"I know, because you're selfish like that." She opened one eye and found Meg grinning over her shoulder. "I've got a date tonight, off Forever Love. And I know you're so blissed out over Dr. Sexy McDinoBones you'll let me borrow whatever I want."

"I *always* let you borrow whatever you want. But most of my stuff won't fit you." Alisha sat up and hugged her knees to her chest. Despite their difference in physique—Meg was thin with zero hips, the opposite of her muscular curves—their similarity in height sometimes allowed them to swap tops and dresses.

Holding a yellow sundress aloft, Meg asked, "What about this? Is it new? I've never seen you wear it."

"That's Simone's. You know she'd kill me if I let you borrow anything of hers."

True with regard to Alisha, too, if her sister ever discovered she'd taken the dress. Simone had rescinded Alisha's closet privileges years ago after an incident with a barbed wire fence and her favorite pair of jeans.

"Your sister never needs to know. Besides, I can take Simone."

Also true. Meg and Simone once had an all-out smackdown over the PlayStation remote. Meg reigned victorious as player one. But then again, she was thirteen at the time, and Simone a gangly nine-year-old.

"I dunno about that." Alisha crossed her arms over her chest. "She started going to a kickboxing gym."

Hand on her hip, Meg asked, "Excuse me, Ali, did you just flex on me?"

She blinked down at her biceps. "Not intentionally." Chuckling, she pointed to a dress. "Grab the polka dot one. I think the color will look great on you."

Pulling out the skirt of a flowing midnight-blue dress, Meg wrapped the material around her body. Alisha nodded. "That's the one. I might just give it to you. I bought it a few weeks ago because I loved the print, but I don't know if I can pull off the small polka dots with my bulkiness."

"But you're a bodybuilder. Isn't that the look you're going for?" Meg lifted the hanger off the rack and held the dress against her chest, checking herself out in the full-length mirror on the back of the door. "Big muscles on display and all that?"

Alisha pulled a pillow into her lap. "Meg, we've had this conversation. I am *not* a bodybuilder. Not that there's anything wrong with that. But I'm a powerlifter."

"Tomayto, tomahto." Meg went back to perusing the closet, but she kept the polka dot dress slung over her arm.

"No, not the same. Bodybuilders lift weights for aesthetics as well as strength. Bodybuilding competitions are about symmetry and well-developed muscles. They get onstage in bathing suits. But powerlifting has nothing to do with looks. When we compete, it's all about who can lift the most weight at the meet. How we look is a side effect, not the goal."

Meg pulled out another dress, and Alisha shrugged. "Sure, take it."

After squinting at the garment, Meg returned it to the closet.

"But I've noticed my upper body is a lot bigger than even a couple years ago." Alisha rubbed her hands up the outside of her arms, cupping her shoulders. "And most guys don't like girls with muscles. Or at least not big muscles."

"By 'most guys,' are you referring to Zachary, by any chance?"

Zachary Paxton was a guy she'd dated in college, for a whole month and a half, until he'd told her to choose him or powerlifting. No-brainer.

"Not just Whack Zach. I used to hear a lot of guys talk, back when I went to the gym, before I built my own setup."

Meg choked out a laugh. "I'm sorry, Ali. But we've been down this road. Do *not* take Hawksburg as representative of the population at large. Guys here may love a thigh gap, but I guarantee not everyone does."

Though she didn't want to spell out her reasons to Meg, she latched on to any reason to stay out of the dating game. Once before, she'd opened her heart. Fell in love with a guy she'd met in Econ 201—Cole. And he was great, amazing, wonderful. Then Granny got sick, and she'd fled campus and never looked back. Her relationship became another casualty of her devotion to family.

Now Alisha never allowed anyone to get close. Built up defenses, physical and emotional, heck, even environmental—no guy was interested in coming home to an attic above her grandparents. All the walls kept her safe. But not only her. The walls protected those around her too.

Whenever feelings arose, *real* feelings, she bailed. Opening her heart left her vulnerable to getting hurt. Or hurting someone else. Like Cole, who didn't deserve to be left, even though she hadn't had a choice. Like her grandparents, who needed her focus here, looking out for them.

Leaning into the depths of the closet, Meg said, "So, based on one jerk from undergrad and a handful of tools at the gym, you think Dr. Handsome Harris"—Alisha launched the pillow at her friend, but it bounced off the dresser, badly off target—"thinks you're too jacked?"

"All I'm saying is, he didn't seem interested Monday morning." Her plan to keep him away bearing fruit, and yet . . .

"Maybe because his colleague was right there, and your good ol' grandad could've stepped out at any moment! I highly doubt he would've sexted you for months if he didn't like what he saw back in March."

"Meg, seriously, yuck. We've just been chatting. About food, our hobbies, random GIFs." And okay, yes, a few totally G-rated pictures, which Meg did *not* need to know about.

"*Naked* GIFs." Meg spun around and leered like a perv, shaking her eyebrows.

"Gross! There's no such thing."

"Is too—look it up," said Meg.

"I will not." Alisha tried to channel the dignity of Violet Crawley.

"Double-dare you."

"Meg, we're adults."

In response, Meg pulled her phone out of her back pocket. She tapped a few times and tossed it onto the bed.

"Margaret Ophelia Anderson, I swear, if there's a penis on this screen . . ." Alisha picked up the phone like she would a venomous snake.

Peeking through one eye, Alisha spied the purple Forever Love logo and a short bio. *Thank goodness—no genitals.* She snorted out a laugh, then opened both eyes and pinched to zoom. "Oh, this is the guy you're meeting tonight? Eric, huh? Where's the picture?"

Meg sat on the foot of the bed. "There isn't one."

"What do you mean, 'There isn't one'?" Alisha asked.

"Like I said before, it's an app for people who want to get married. We don't use pictures because that's superficial. We connect on a personal and emotional level first." Meg sniffed and crossed her ankles like a charm school student.

"This from the girl who just grilled me about naked GIFs?" Alisha chuckled. "Awfully high and mighty, now, aren't you?"

"That was you. You've got a stake with a real guy. I'm still slumming it out in the cyberworld." Fine hairs, damp with sweat, curled around Meg's face, making her look young and vulnerable.

Leaning forward, Alisha caught her friend's eyes, imploring. "I wish you wouldn't pressure yourself so much. Marriage is not an end-all, be-all."

"Easy for you to say." Meg screwed up her face, gesturing with the hanger. "You've always been so independent. Guys love that, by the way." She glared at Alisha, then twisted her mouth sideways, chin puckered. "But you know I'm happiest in a relationship. And I'm a thirty-year-old teacher in the middle of nowhere. Men aren't exactly falling out of trees to ask me out." Her voice shrank to a fraction of its usual vibrancy. "Is it so wrong to want one long, lasting relationship? That happens to be called marriage?"

"No, silly goose." She leaned over and wrapped Meg in a hug. "It's not wrong at all."

And Alisha wanted those things, too—marriage, a family—oh, did she want them. Could she move past all the wreckage of her past? Maybe letting someone in, letting *Quentin* in, wouldn't be an earth-quake but an ice cube pressed to a burn. Healing. *Maybe.*

"And Eric sounds great." Alisha lifted her chin and read aloud over her friend's shoulder. "'Tech savvy, love n00b. Cheaters never prosper.' Heck of a bio."

Meg smiled and took back her phone. She peered at the screen as if it were a crystal ball. "I figured a sense of humor is a plus. Assuming it's tongue in cheek." Her eyes met Alisha's, uncertain. Behind all the boisterous bravado, her best friend was wholesome and sweet as banana bread: comfort food and sustenance, all in one. If happily ever after existed, no one deserved it more.

None of this was in her wheelhouse, but Meg didn't need doubts piled on. "I'm sure it is. And I'm also sure you're meeting in a well-lit area with plenty of witnesses, correct?"

"Yes, Aunt Alisha." Meg stuck out her tongue. "We're meeting at Applebee's. Big time, I know. And the code is the usual. 'I could use a latte.'"

The perfect bad-date code phrase for a woman who despised coffee.

"Okay. I'm rooting for you, girl, as always. Let me know how it goes." Alisha stood up and pulled open the bedroom door. Earthy notes of cumin and simmering stewed tomatoes wafted up from the kitchen. Granny's famous chili.

No doubt she'd made extra for the crew, especially since she hadn't been able to host anyone else since their arrival. Keeping the dig a secret was affecting all their lives, but Alisha couldn't imagine what a toll it would take if townsfolk guessed the real reason for the scientists' presence. Missed cookouts would be the least of their worries.

With a glint in her eyes, Meg gathered up her purse. "Is this you kicking me out so you can sit at the window and ogle your sexy scientist?"

"This is me kicking you out so I can plan next week's posts before I head in to work."

"And ogle that man," finished Meg.

Alisha snatched at the dress, but Meg laughed and danced out of reach.

"I'm going, I'm going." She paused at the top of the stairs. "But you're getting this dress back. It will look amazing on you, woman." Without waiting for a response, she clattered down the wooden stairs, calling out a goodbye to Alisha's grandparents.

Alisha padded over the cream shag rug to her desk, then paused by the window to check the progress on the dig. No other reason. At lunch yesterday, Forrest had told her they'd started with a process called "removing the overburden." Hard to see from up here, but the whole pit was deeper, and trenches marked the areas where they'd removed fossils. The string grid was gone, but they'd record the placement of bones and their position relative to each other on the map they'd made initially to reference throughout the dig.

Quentin's white T-shirt made him easy to spot. The mouthwatering way it stretched across his back as he bent to point at something in the dirt didn't hurt matters either. He noted something in the journal that never seemed to leave his side, then paused to shake his pen a few times. Caitlyn, digging nearby, pulled a pencil from behind her ear and tossed it toward him, laughing when he fumbled the catch.

The team made a cohesive unit, and their passion for their work shone through. Giving them permission to come and excavate was so clearly the right choice, despite any danger of exposure. Besides, even when the news broke, it wasn't as if America at large would be hitting refresh on their Twitter feed for midwestern dino news. Scientific interest she could handle. No one else would give a second's thought to the senior citizens and small-town baker who called this plot of land home.

Alisha sank into the Lucite desk chair and woke up her laptop. Typing in her password with rapid keystrokes, she made herself a promise. Next time she crossed paths with Quentin, she wouldn't hightail it in the other direction.

Baby steps.

CHAPTER 15

QUENTIN

Every muscle in Quentin's body ached, from the back of his neck to the soles of his feet. After this first week spent crouched in the dirt, his lower back spasmed like it'd been held in a vise. His fingers cramped, and his palms were blistered. A.k.a. . . . heaven.

Or it would've been, if not for his preoccupation with "the granddaughter."

At night he lay in the stuffy motel room, wrestling with why Alisha's texts had stopped cold the second he'd set foot in town. Why she'd flirted with him on Wednesday and hadn't even popped out to say hi since. But during the day, he blocked out all the uncertainty and focused his attention on the dig.

Besides the large exposed bone, they'd found several ribs and fragments of tail vertebrae. And this morning Cait had uncovered part of an ilium, which they'd carefully reburied. A hip bone could prove crucial in identifying the species, but the large fossils needed to stay covered until the time came to transport them back to the university.

They hypothesized that the bulk of the fossils belonged to a single theropod, the group of dinosaurs that included the infamous *Tyrannosaurus rex* and *Velociraptor* of cinematic fame. No way to positively identify the animal until they'd brought all the bones back to the lab and analyzed them.

Quitting time for now, though, before the blazing afternoon sun dried them out like the fossils sealed in meticulously labeled ziplock bags. He stood, and his knees cracked out a protest. Based on the wide grin Dev shot his way, he'd heard the creaky joints loud and clear.

Quentin shrugged with a *What can you do?* smile, then called out, "All right, everyone, let's call it a day."

"Woot, fine by me!" Caitlyn slowly unfolded herself from the ground. Forrest put up a finger, tongue poking out of the corner of his mouth as he worked a small fragment of bone free. Bridget was already topside, sorting specimen bags.

"There's a hot bath with my name on it." Hands on her hips, Cait twisted her torso side to side. "Or at least lukewarm. This morning's shower gave me frostbite. I'm not even sure our motel has a hot water heater."

Dev took off his sweat-soaked Cubs hat and sniffed at it with a grimace. "The rest of you wanna grab a beer at the bar in town? We can catch the game."

"Thanks, but I gotta go for a run. Work out the kinks." Quentin dug fists into his lower back.

Dev opened his mouth, probably to make a wisecrack, but at Quentin's glare he backed down, poking Forrest with the bill of his cap instead. "How 'bout you, Forrest, my man?"

Forrest swatted the hat away but nodded. "Sure, I could use a cold beer or three right about now."

After he hauled himself out of the dig, Quentin cast a glance at the house. He wished Alisha would show her face. Anything to give him a clue. But with the radio silence, it would be weird to march up and knock on the door. What would he say? *Hello. I like you. I miss you.* Talk about pitiful.

Instead, he climbed into the truck, wincing at the film of dust coating the leather seats. He'd need to detail it within an inch of his life if he didn't want Dad to disown him. Mirroring the truck, every inch of him itched under a fine layer of dirt. The grit had even worked its way into his eyelashes. A shower would wash away the dirt, but a run might chase away his stress over a certain MIA baker.

Back in his room, Quentin changed into shorts and a sleeveless performance tank. The chill of the air conditioner was such a relief that it took all his willpower not to collapse on the bed and pass out, dirt-encrusted socks and all. But he slid his Garmin around his wrist and hurried down the wooden staircase that hugged the ramshackle building.

Almost a full week without a run had left him jonesing for the adrenaline rush. A Google search this morning had turned up a lake with a bike path less than a mile from the motel. A muddy pond compared to Lake Michigan, but a nice change of scenery from corn, corn, and oh, look!—more corn. Also, running on an established exercise trail would leave him more at ease than braving the back roads around here.

He turned out of the parking lot and picked up an easy jog down the shoulder, the motion loosening his muscles and chasing away his tiredness. By the time he got to the gravel trail flanking the lake, there wasn't a soul around. Bird calls and the deep thrum of bullfrogs were the only sounds apart from his own breathing.

About a mile in, he picked up the pace. Without city noise to drown out his thoughts, his mind drifted to the rift between himself and his father. He hadn't told his family the significance of this dig, although his mom was happy he'd be staying relatively close to home this summer.

Why bother? Ma would've been proud whatever he and Hector chose to do with their lives, from janitor to president. He could discover a new species or putter away in anonymity his whole career, and it wouldn't make a bit of difference to her.

And Dad? Initially Quentin had been excited at the chance to use this dig to prove his father wrong. But he took issue with Quentin's entire profession, so a groundbreaking dinosaur discovery wouldn't earn him so much as a pat on the back. Prestige in the paleontological community would be like a whole lot of white noise to his dad, as unworthy of his attention as a gnat buzzing around his ears. Best keep the status quo than stir up a new bone of contention by sharing what made this excavation unique.

He spotted another runner rounding the bend. A familiar face, her twists piled up on her head and held in place with a fluorescent-yellow headband. His heart lifted. But with his luck, she might just keep on running right past him.

"Quentin?" She slowed to a walk, taking out her earbuds. Her chest rose and fell with exertion, and she drew her hands up high to rest them under her rib cage. A rivulet of sweat ran down her sternum, and he averted his gaze so he wouldn't track its slippery downward path.

"What are you doing here?" Alisha asked.

He grinned. "Running."

"Oh, duh." She mirrored his smile, then ducked her head and lifted a shoulder to wipe the sweat that dripped down her cheek.

In unison, Quentin drew up the hem of his shirt to scrub away his own sweat. He let it fall and caught her staring. She darted her eyes away, but his stomach tightened nonetheless. "Didn't know you were a runner."

She blew out a vibrating breath between her lips and squinted up at him. "Not sure I'd call myself a runner. I used to run track in high school, but now I just jog to stay in shape."

Quentin swept an appraising gaze down her body. She looked way more than just "in shape." For a second, he let his eyes wander like he hadn't back in the garage that first day. Muscle striations wrapped her shoulders, and her shorts were no match for the lush curve of her hips and thick, strong thighs.

He jerked his gaze up . . . straight into her eyes. *Rookie move.* But her eyes glimmered with mischief, not accusation. A jolt zapped through him, hard. Rubbing a thumb along his lips, he kicked the toe of his sneaker into the gravel. "Can I ask you a question? Did I do something wrong?"

Her eyebrows tipped inward. "No, why?"

"Well, is it my imagination, or have you been avoiding me all week?" Terrified of her answer, he rushed to clarify. "I mean, we were texting pretty much every day. I was counting down the days to come back here." He hesitated, realizing he was coming on strong, a Quentin Harris trait. "Because of the dig, of course. But also . . . I was really looking forward to seeing you again." He dropped his gaze to her bright pink-and-yellow shoes. Everything she wore was vibrant, like an exotic bird. Out of place in this faded, dusty town.

"You're not imagining things."

He brought his eyes to hers again, and this time a half smile caught at the corner of her mouth. She pressed her fingers to the sides of her face, then ran them down along her jaw, her expression sheepish. "What I'm trying to say is, I *was* looking forward to seeing you."

"*Was?*"

Her smile broadened. "Am." She puffed her cheeks out. "I guess I didn't trust it." Her voice raised at the end, almost a question.

Ah, trust. That, he understood. "How's this. I'm here, you're here."

"You are." She laughed and shot her eyes toward the lake and back. "I think that's the problem."

He raised a quizzical brow.

"Texting felt so much easier. You weren't here, and I could pretend the stakes were low. Then you showed up early on Monday, and I wasn't prepared and I kinda—"

"Freaked out?"

Alisha laughed, and Quentin joined in. "Thank God," he said. "Here I was feeling like I'd catfished you."

"Catfished me?"

"Yeah." Jamming his hands in his pockets, he wiggled his toe deeper into the gravel. "I thought we had a moment, back in March." Several moments. Really good moments. "And then everything was so fun and easy over the phone, but when I got here, you seemed . . . disappointed."

Alisha gawped at him. "Oh my gosh, no." She shook her head with a short laugh. "No. The opposite."

"The opposite?" He couldn't resist.

"Now you're fishing for compliments. Shameless." But she sunk her teeth into her luscious bottom lip, grinning. Had she been doing that during their texting sessions? Man, he'd been missing out, big time.

"Wanna finish the run together?"

Entranced by her lips, he almost missed her question. When she stopped speaking, he snapped out of it and found uncertainty clouding her eyes.

She clocked her gaze down his legs. "You know what? Never mind. No way I could keep up with you."

Reaching for her hand, he caught himself at the last second and raised it instead to halt her excuses. "Stop, Alisha. Yes, let's run together." He started jogging backward before she could change her mind and disappear on him again. "I don't always need to go fast."

"Oh ho, I see." She cocked one eyebrow with a smile.

Oops, walked right into that one. "What I meant was . . . Who says you couldn't keep up?"

"Nice save." She stayed put for a moment, the summer sun framing her in a golden glow, her shadow stretching along the path. "Okay, just promise not to make fun of my speed."

He held up three fingers, jogging in place. "Scout's honor."

Alisha caught up to him, and he let her set the pace. Below his norm, but not painfully so. And totally worth it for more time with her.

"Do you always run by the lake?" he asked after a moment.

"No, sometimes I stay closer to home. But with all the hills and blind curves? Let's just say I've wound up leaping into the weeds more than once to avoid being roadkill."

"I can see that." He frowned. "This is my first run since we arrived. I need to get some miles in, but do you think it's a good idea?"

She sniffed and shot him a look, perhaps mulling over what he was really asking. "Honestly? I'd stick to the jogging path if I were you. But the good news is, you're famous around here. Everyone knows you guys are working on Wayne Blake's land, even though they don't know about the dinosaur. So in that respect, you're good." She paused, breathing heavily. "Gosh, this sucks."

"It is what it is." A platitude he'd learned from his father.

"Which is shitty," she said.

What had it been like for her to grow up here? She was the Blakes' granddaughter, sure. But she was also one of the lone Black people—maybe the only one, without her sister—in a small town in the middle of nowhere. She'd never brought it up, but he wondered if she ever felt a sense of isolation.

Yet she'd come back to take care of her grandparents. Devotion to family, second-guessing their feelings, those things they shared. But he wanted to show her she didn't need to keep up her defenses with him.

The path led them back to the parking lot, and Quentin's mind raced for ways to draw out the evening. Their easy camaraderie was back, and he wanted to keep it going—*had* to keep it going, even if only for the summer. Even if only for *today*. Screw the consequences.

"Are you working tonight?" If she was, he'd take that as a sign, run straight back to the motel and get his head on strai—

"No, I'm on Saturday and Sunday." Panting, Alisha pushed her headband back farther. "Why?"

Halftime's up. Now or never. "Would you like to go grab a bite to eat? I'm not in the mood for cold cuts from my mini fridge."

There it was, stretched between them, tenuous as spider's silk: the first time he'd asked a woman out in over five years. Something shifted inside him, like a bone out of joint pressed back into alignment. Painful relief. But if she said no, he might have to become a monk, because he could not handle a flat-out rejection right now, not from Alisha.

She sniffed, nostrils flaring, then gave him another heart-stopping smile, the light in her eyes putting the sun to shame. "Yeah, I'd be up for that."

"Great!" His heart soared, orbiting somewhere in the upper atmosphere.

"Full disclosure—as you may have noticed, there's only two options here in town. My grandpa's restaurant and the Back Forty. You okay with a greasy burger and frozen fries?"

"Is this the competition talking?" He smiled.

"Caught me." She grinned. "Their burgers are dynamite. But trust me on the fries."

Quentin shrugged. "Who needs fries when you've got a great burger, anyway?"

Alisha cocked her head, eyes wide, and he laughed. "Okay, so fries are nonnegotiable. Noted. Is that a deal-breaker, or would you like to join me for dinner?"

She nodded, pulling her lip between her teeth again, then said, "Not a deal-breaker in this case." Did that mean what he thought it meant? "Just lemme get cleaned up, and I'll meet you there in an hour."

A yes? A yes!

She jimmied her car door, her back to him and his beaming face. "Want a ride back to the Hawk's Roost?"

He needed to hit pause and regain his cool before he did something insane, like try to kiss her, and ended up scaring her back into her shell for good. "Nah, gotta finish out my run."

"Knew I was slowing you down." She turned and shook a finger at him. He opened his mouth to deny it, but she smiled and got into the car. "See you in a jiffy."

Quentin waved, then picked up his jog, face alight. He could do this. Dating Alisha wouldn't mean putting the dig at risk, right? At this point, he might be willing to go for it anyway.

CHAPTER 16

ALISHA

Alisha stepped into the Back Forty, and at least half a dozen people waved. She winced. Jeez, it was like hillbilly *Cheers* in here. Life in a farm town meant you had twelve people on speed dial with pickups or tractors to dig you out when your car got stranded in a snowdrift. But if you wanted to go on a date without a live audience like a contestant on *The Bachelor*, tough luck.

Not that this was a date. Just two acquaintances getting to know each other better.

Over a meal.

Okay, so categorically a date.

Butterflies, dormant since she'd left Quentin by the lake, took flight again in her midsection. Even though she'd stubbornly resisted country music indoctrination, the nineties country that twanged from the jukebox enfolded her like a worn denim jacket to soothe her ragged nerves.

Running clammy palms down the back of her sundress, she double-checked that the hem wasn't tucked up into her panties. That had happened before. More than once. Alisha searched the familiar faces and found one that stuck out like a Nike ad in a sea of John Deere commercials.

Chelsea, Nicole, and Amber surrounded Quentin where he sat at the bar, hands on their hips, flipping their glossy hair and fluttering heavily mascaraed lashes, hawks circling fresh meat. Engulfed by a fierce urge to go stake her claim, she pressed a palm to her stomach, forcing herself to count her breaths instead.

Not like she was *jealous*. Not at all. Just eager to pick up where they'd left off. When Quentin asked her out, her yes had sprung from pure survival instinct. She couldn't take another second of the self-inflicted torture she'd lived through all week, with him closer than ever but out of reach.

What a waste those days of silence were, in retrospect. She hadn't imagined things, after all—he was into her. Grown-out twists, big arms, and all. And try as she might to ignore him, man, oh man was she into Dr. Quentin Harris. Crushing on him, hard core. And not in the mood to share his attention.

Land sakes, she sounded whiny. Hawksburg ladies couldn't be blamed for noticing him. The last single guy who'd shown up was old man Grady's long-lost son, who'd rolled into town with a drinking problem and a frazzled beard that brushed the top of his potbelly. And Quentin's tall, lean frame and movie-star smile would stop traffic on the Magnificent Mile, let alone the four corners of Hawksburg.

Just then, his eyes caught hers, and the butterflies combusted into fireworks in her chest. He nodded at the women and pushed back from the bar. His silver gaze remained trained on her, intoxicating in its intensity, and her reasons for avoiding him evaporated in a sizzle of steam. He wound his way through the maze of tables, a kelly-green polo hugging his chest, dark jeans slung low on his hips, a bottle in each hand.

Stopping in front of her, he held out the cider. "Bartender said this is the only drink you ever order."

Alisha looked toward Gracie, who was pouring drinks tonight. She winked and sauntered over to another patron. A fellow transplant,

Gracie had moved from California in high school and, like Alisha, still wasn't considered a local despite fifteen years in town. An ally. She accepted the cider and tapped it against the neck of his bottle.

He looked like he wanted to say something, but he took a drink first. "Is it always this crowded here?" Quentin palmed the back of his neck, glancing toward where the three women perched on barstools like crows on a power line, shooting daggers at Alisha.

With a shrug she said, "Nowhere else to go on Friday night. If you'd rather, we can skip it." She was aiming for nonchalance but worried she fell woefully short.

But Quentin shook his head. "No way, you promised me a greasy burger."

A gust of relief swept over her. *Play it cool, Blake.* But cool was miles outside her skill set. Still, he hadn't greeted her with a hug, or tossed out a tacky compliment. Perfect. Just two friends grabbing a burger. Not a date, after all.

A table opened up near the door, and she nabbed it. Quentin slid into the seat opposite her, his jeans grazing her knees under the table. The butterflies woke up and fluttered into Alisha's throat. She shifted to tuck the fabric of her skirt under her thighs, bare knees sliding along his, and he got an odd look on his face, scooting up and back so fast the chair lurched along the floor with a scrape.

Okay, point taken. Just friends. No need to make it any clearer. She picked up the menu to keep her trembling hands occupied, even though she could've recited it with her eyes closed—all ten pages' worth.

"So tell me more about this *Jurassic Park* fan club." Quentin's voice was rich and warm like Sunday-morning maple syrup, dripping with mirth. "How come I'm just now hearing about it?"

Alisha tilted her menu down. His elbows on the table, a wide and wicked grin was splashed across Quentin's face.

"No way you read the menu that fast." She brought it back up to hide her face.

His laugh sailed over the top of the laminated cardstock, hitting her burning ears. "Caught me. But you said the burgers are good here. So a burger it is." A long finger appeared over the top of her menu, dragging it down.

"There's like fifteen different burger choices, Quentin." She refused to give in.

His playful smile stretched wider. "Oh. In that case, I'll have what you're having."

She rolled her eyes, and he laughed, easing down deeper in his chair, bringing his knees back in contact with hers. This time he didn't move them. Did he notice? Right now that point of contact was *all* she noticed.

"So. *Jurassic Park* fan club," he said, charmingly relentless.

Defeated, she dropped the pretense of reading the menu.

Well, if she wanted to keep things safe and platonic, nothing would kill romance quite like the image of nerdy schoolgirl Alisha. "If I tell you, you're sworn to secrecy. I can't have all of you paleontologists out in our backyard laughing at the girl with a dinosaur tattoo."

His storm-gray eyes widened. "Wait a minute, you have a dinosaur tattoo?" His voice climbed a notch higher than usual. *Interesting*.

"Just the temporary kind." His face fell, and she filed that away. "But no more details until you swear."

Pressing his lips together, he held up his little finger. "Deal. Your dark dinosaur past is safe with me."

She locked her pinkie with his, catching his eyes over their clasped fingers. The world shifted into sharp focus in the stillness between heartbeats; then he dropped her hand and reached for his beer bottle. He tipped it toward her. "Spill."

"As for why I didn't whip out my *Jurassic Park* fan card earlier? Um, self-preservation?" She laughed, breathless. Also, she didn't want him to think she had some sort of creepy crush on him because of his profession. Maybe she harbored a slight, miniscule crush on him, but not because she had some sort of dinosaur fetish.

That and pure, unadulterated shame had prompted her decision to keep the dinosaur thing a secret. But now he sat across from her, so kind and open that she found herself reciprocating, going against pattern—which was becoming a pattern around Quentin, she realized. But right now she didn't want to think too hard about what that meant.

"Anyways, like I said, the film was off limits. So I think that made me like it even more. But that was just part of the intrigue. I was scared, sure, but also fascinated by the dinosaurs. And after I moved here, I watched it a lot because it reminded me of when things were better."

A small line formed between his brows at this tidbit, but she plowed on. "Thank goodness I met Meg. She was a huge dinosaur nerd too. We spent the summer plotting out our own *Jurassic Park* in her yard and blackmailed Simone into drawing up the plans." She smiled at the memory, twisting the sticky ketchup bottle in her hands. "We found dinosaur tattoos at the dollar store and gave ourselves half sleeves of *T. rex* skeletons. Granny wasn't too pleased with the result."

Quentin laughed. "And I thought *I* was the dino-obsessed one."

"Well, that was a long time ago. *I* grew out of it." Alisha raised her eyebrows at him and took a dainty sip of cider, then smiled to let him know she was teasing. She tugged the strap of her dress up on her shoulder.

Gracie appeared at the table in a flurry, pulling a notepad out of her back pocket. "Hey, Ali. You two ready to order? I gotta head back before a brawl breaks out." She gestured toward the bar, where Alisha spotted Forrest's tangled man bun. She caught Quentin following her gaze, and his eyes went wide.

Oh. *Oh.* She wasn't the only one worried about an audience here. Which meant maybe he really did kind of sort of *like* her? The idea shouldn't have sent a rush up her spine, but she found herself testing the waters nonetheless.

"I didn't realize the guys were here. We could've eaten with them," she told Quentin, watching his reaction. He tucked his chin, not quite meeting her eyes, and opened his mouth, but Gracie spoke up first.

"They've been holed up in the back room playing pool all night. Losing, mostly." Gracie grinned. "But after the Cubs scored that last run, they must've felt okay about showing their faces again."

"Nice hit!" She swiveled to see Dev give Forrest a high five. Across the bar, the regulars swore.

"Ah." Alisha understood the issue. Though they lived in Illinois, Hawksburg's proximity to Missouri meant locals rooted for the Saint Louis Cardinals, not Chicago's baseball teams.

Gracie nodded. "Yup. Bill and Dylan don't appreciate anyone cheering on the Cubs when we're down in the series two oh. Those boys are worse than my toddler." She pulled a pen out from behind her ear and clicked it open. "Anyways, what can I get for you two?"

Quentin raised his brows at Alisha.

"Two portobello burgers, please, on gluten-free buns. With sweet potato tots," she said.

"Got it." Gracie shot Alisha a questioning look, but another yell had her shoving the order pad in her apron. She scooped up the menus and strode off, calling out, "Gentlemen, next one's on the house if you can keep to your corners."

Watching the spectacle unfold, Alisha turned back to find Quentin slouched in his chair, arms crossed over his chest. His eyes narrowed. "Didn't realize you were a vegetarian, Alisha."

"I'm not."

"Gluten intolerant?"

"Nope." Alisha tucked her hands under her chin and beamed at him.

"Do you even like sweet potato tots?"

"Does anyone?" She took a long draw from the bottle.

"You set me up!" Quentin sat forward in a rush, hands on his thighs, and Alisha almost choked on her drink. Laughter bubbled up, dissolving the butterflies, and she barely kept herself from inhaling cider. His face was priceless. She swallowed carefully and then let herself go, laughter making her eyes water.

"Yes, I totally set you up, Mr. I'll Have What You're Having," she managed after a moment. "Payback for the *Jurassic Park* line of questioning."

"Hmm. I don't think the punishment fits the crime," he said. But a broad grin stretched Quentin's cheeks, no trace of rancor on his handsome face.

Their sense of humor was a perfect match. Another reason she'd come out tonight when she should've stayed home, keeping her eye on the prize or her feelings bottled up or whatever metaphor meant not going on a date with this way-too-sexy professor.

"We're even now."

Quentin shook his head and leaned forward to close the gap between them.

"Not in the slightest." She found herself watching his lips, mesmerized. "Although you do have to eat that mess you ordered, so I guess that helps."

Dragging her eyes back up to meet his, she smiled. "Nope, not a chance, bud. I'm gonna go talk to the kitchen staff about changing my order. But I can keep yours as is." Alisha pushed back her chair.

"Heck no. Anything with cow, dairy, and wheat works for me. But no olives," he added as she stood up.

"Got it. Be right back." She traipsed toward the kitchen, maybe letting her hips sway just a tad more than normal, and fought the impulse to check him out over her shoulder. *Silly.* He was just another man. A man she had no future with. So why did he suddenly feel so *important?*

A waiter backed out of the kitchen with three plates of deep-fried appetizers, and Alisha sidestepped him and passed through the double doors to talk with the cook, a short, round guy called Tommy.

Happy to change the orders, Tommy peeked through the pass-through, freckled cheeks gleaming with sweat above his sparse beard. "But, Ali, I gotta know. Who are these Chicago guys, really?" He leaned one elbow on the ledge, shot a glance over his shoulder. "Most people are going with land developers, looking to buy your grandpa out. Maybe put in a factory or subdivision."

Yeah, she'd heard that one too. "What about you?"

"With a crater-size hole in your yard?" A matching pit opened in her stomach at the mention of the dig. If he'd seen it, surely he must've guessed . . . "Forget developers. I'm going with aliens." He winked, and Alisha wheezed out a relieved laugh.

Straightening up, Tommy adjusted his beard net. "Anyway, enjoy your date with Mr. City Slicker."

Ugh, people really needed to get a hobby that didn't involve being up in everyone's business. "He's just a friend."

"If you say so. But either way, can you put in a good word for me? Tell him if it's condos, I want a ground-floor unit with pool access." He grinned, then pivoted to yell at one of the runners. Grateful to make her escape, she ducked back out through the swinging doors.

Now planted on a stool between the grad students, Bill wore Dev's Cubs hat backward, an arm slung across each paleontologist's shoulders, which would've been a change for the better, except she didn't need the crew getting all buddy-buddy with the locals. Not everyone would be as easy to put off as Tommy.

But confronting two tipsy dudes in the middle of the bar wouldn't do anything to squelch interest. And if land developers was the running bet, she'd take those odds. Dinosaurs were a lot more far fetched than real estate. Deciding to let it be, Alisha shot Quentin a double thumbs-up to show the order was fixed.

Except he wasn't sitting there anymore. In fact, he and the entire table had vanished, the two chairs left empty and forlorn. She made a circle of the bar and found Quentin carrying the table toward the corner, his forearms bunching with the strain.

"Just leave it there, man. Thanks." One of the bartenders, Matt, shoved another table against the wall next to it.

Quentin stepped back, and Alisha caught his eye. "Didn't like our spot by the door?"

"It's Friday," Matt said, clapping her on the shoulder.

She slapped a hand to her forehead. "Throwback night."

"You got it, Ali." Gracie appeared with their food, an apologetic smile on her face. "Sorry you guys got bumped, but we need the room. The Cardinals are one inning away from another loss, and I figured a diversion might go a long way to cool off hot tempers. You wanna eat over at the bar?"

Alisha looked toward Quentin, who gave a slight shake of his head. "No, we're good," she answered.

Gracie set their food down on one of the tables. "Suit yourselves."

All the chairs were stacked in a wonky mess, so Alisha scooted up onto the tabletop, tucking her dress under her thighs. Quentin followed suit, sliding up next to her, their hips nearly touching. He passed over her plate, and she set it on the table behind her. "So, welcome to Hawksburg. Consider this your baptism by fire."

He laughed and picked up his own burger. "This isn't so bad. It's like a reverse picnic."

She took in their position, perched on the table rather than seated on a blanket on the ground. "Not quite so idyllic."

"I've gotta disagree," he said. "This is way better than a regular picnic. Less ants, for one."

"I wouldn't be so sure about that." Alisha made a show of checking under the table, but she almost slid off, and Quentin grabbed her arm to steady her. His hand encircled her wrist, big and warm. "Careful, we can't have you falling again."

"Oh my gosh, just couldn't resist bringing that up, could you?"

"In my defense, if you could've seen yourself . . . I've never in my life seen someone so dirty." He let go of her arm. "Er . . ."

"It's okay. I *was* dirty. Filthy, in fact." Brazen in the tug of his magnetism, she held his gaze. "Good thing for showers."

"Yeah." His voice dipped low and husky. "Good thing."

Alisha swallowed, consumed by the sudden thought of what he would taste like. Crisp beer and salty fries. From the unfocused look on his face, his mind was tracing a similar path.

The music cut off abruptly, and Quentin cleared his throat. He bumped her shoe with his. "It's nice to see you laugh over it. Because if it was me"—he splayed his long fingers against his chest—"*I* would've been mortally embarrassed to face-plant in front of the most beautiful woman I've ever seen."

"Good thing I fell down in front of a dude, then." She smirked and dug her elbow into his ribs.

"You're the worst," he said, in a tone that implied the opposite.

She ducked her head and rolled the skirt of her dress between her fingers. "Takes one to know one." When she glanced up at him again, a look of intense concentration had replaced Quentin's smile. "What?"

"Just contemplating the many, many ways I could repay you for all your smack talk."

"Is that so?" She licked her lips and watched raw hunger consume Quentin's features, a match for the desire coursing through her.

"LISTEN UP, PARTY PEOPLE!" Gracie shouted into a microphone, and it screeched with feedback. Alisha jumped at the noise and nearly tumbled off the table again. This time when Quentin looped his arm around her waist, he didn't let go. A frisson tingled along her spine, warmth spreading in its wake.

Gracie tapped on the mike, and half the patrons covered their ears. "My main man Matt is coming around with Hula-Hoops. If you want one, raise your hand. You know the drill. Longest Hula-Hooper wins twenty bucks and a Back Forty T-shirt." She flapped a tie-dyed shirt like a starting flag.

"You couldn't pay me to wear one of those in public," someone at the bar mumbled.

Alisha leaned into Quentin with a wicked smile. "Speaking of payback . . ."

He straightened up like a kid caught passing notes in class. "Oh no. No, no, no."

"Oh yes. Yes, yes, yes." She sat up taller and waved her arm like a marooned Captain Jack Sparrow. "Yo, Gracie! Over here!" She pointed down at Quentin.

"Hey, guys, looks like we got our first victim. I mean, volunteer." Gracie grinned, then dug into a jar of glowsticks on the bar and flung one toward them, Frisbee-style. Alisha hopped down and picked it up, cracking the stick back and forth to activate it.

"C'mere, sir." She crooked a finger toward Quentin, and he slid down off the table with a beleaguered sigh, but his eyes were gleaming. She looped the glowstick around his neck, securing it with the clip. In the dim light, the faint pink glow illuminated the pulse at his throat, and her own heartbeat found a new rhythm, quick and light and heady. Her fingers lingered at his open collar. When she looked up, her gaze caught on his lips, parted and full.

Something collided into her butt and bounced back off, driving her forward into Quentin. His hands skimmed down her hips, steadying her, and the world fell away. His breath quickened against her temple. Nothing remained between his fingers and her skin except the pesky fabric of her dress. But still, she craved more of him.

If she stood on tiptoe . . .

"You two need a minute?"

The heckling roused Alisha from the trance, and she pushed away from Quentin's chest with a shaky hand. She glanced around to see what had hit her. An iridescent Hula-Hoop.

"Let's see your moves, Harris." Her voice came out low and throaty. What had gotten into her?

She passed him the Hula-Hoop, and he caught at her hand, thumb pressed into the center of her palm. A dart of exquisite longing arched through her. Holding her gaze, he slid the hoop over his head with a bad-boy grin that made her wonder just who was going to regret this.

Cheesy getup or not, Quentin swinging his hips in her vicinity was going to be a whole heck of a lot. And from the look on his face, he knew it.

So much for taking things slow.

CHAPTER 17

QUENTIN

Why hadn't he gone for it?

Quentin trudged down the aisle of the gas station, past shelves of granola bars and cellophane-wrapped muffins, his sights set on caffeinated salvation. He yanked the largest-size cup out of the dispenser and shoved it under the toffee cappuccino spigot. Maybe he could soothe his runaway desire with sugar therapy, topped off with a healthy dose of artificial flavor and a dash of preservatives. Despite a date filled with the best kind of tension, he and Alisha had parted ways with an awkward half hug in front of the bar.

Why? Because there wasn't a moment's privacy in this godforsaken town. Two nights ago Alisha's nearness had swept him away, but he'd plummeted back down to earth when Forrest and Dev cheered him on in the Hula-Hooping contest. How could he have forgotten they were headed to the bar? He couldn't care less about their seeing his dance moves, but his students finding out about his interest in the woman who lived at the field site? Less okay.

Growling under his breath, he pressed the little square button, and the machine fizzed to life. Chalky liquid spurted into the cup, splattering against the sides. Despite his minor freak-out when the bartender had pointed them out, the guys were so caught up in the game that they'd never even glanced their way until he'd gone and pulled the attention of the whole bar because his brain was all hazy and haywire over Alisha. Stupid.

Just like the stupid grin still splashed across his face two days later. He really should've been more concerned about the dig, about gossip, but the memory of the simmering look she'd sent him from under those dark curly lashes almost made his lack of caution worth it. Almost made him think he'd do it again, in a heartbeat.

He'd spent the last day and a half mulling over how to reach out to Alisha, but their bond had morphed into something different and new, and every time he'd flipped to her contact, his fingers couldn't find the right keys.

The machine whined and spat a last dose of frothy water into his cup, then subsided into silence. On his morning run, Quentin had passed the town's tea shop, Kettle Down. Nestled between Honey and Hickory and a run-down resale shop, pink-and-white awnings brightened the front of the café, the swirly-lettered sign beaming out an invitation. But he'd needed something stronger and sweeter to soften the sting of unrequited passion.

The bell over the door dinged, and he jerked his cup out from under the spigot. Boiling liquid splashed all over his hand. What were the odds? Actually, in a town of eleven hundred, pretty good. The door clanged shut behind Alisha, and she met his eyes. A huge smile broke out on her face. She immediately toned it down, though, a crying shame.

"Morning, Quentin." Her eyes fell on the cappuccino machine. "Pam doesn't serve coffee at the motel?"

"I wouldn't call what they serve at the motel 'coffee.' Caffeinated sludge is more like it." Shaking off his hand, he lifted the side of his finger to his mouth to soothe the sting.

Alisha stepped over and handed him some napkins as he tried to recalibrate and chase down the unraveled threads of his recent thoughts, tricky with her so close. "I don't doubt it. The Hawk's Roost is certainly not the Plaza."

He grinned. "At least we still have doors on our rooms."

"For now. But we'll see what happens if you keep trash-talking Pam's brew. She's pretty handy with power tools." She winked, and a snicker came from behind the register. Alisha half turned and waved a hand. "Oh, hey, Ryan."

The tips of Quentin's ears burned. He pitched his next words for her ears only. "Do you know *everyone* here?"

"Nope, they all know me." She sparkled at him, and he would've given anything to keep that going.

"Well, you do kind of stick out," he said in the same undertone.

"Is that a comment on my Blackness?"

"It's a comment on your sexiness."

Alisha's mouth dropped open just a bit, and he did a mental fist pump. Score one for Quentin. Nice to know he could throw her off her game too. Being around her reminded him of the time he'd joined some friends on their sailboat on Lake Michigan—the first and only time he'd been out on a boat—and a storm came up. Wonderful and worrisome, all at once.

She gave him a half smile and opened the doughnut case. Snapping the plastic tongs, she asked, "Want one?"

"Nah, I think I've already exceeded my daily sugar limit by about a hundred grams." He held the giant cappuccino aloft.

"Suit yourself." Alisha dropped a bear claw and a long john into a paper bag, and they headed over to the cash register. He reached for his wallet, but Alisha pulled hers out first. "I got this one."

The clerk cracked his knuckles on the counter, bouncing on the balls of his feet. "Hi, Ali. Since you're here—my boss wanted to ask you—we'd really like to start stocking your cookies."

Next to him, Alisha went rigid. She reached up to her necklace, tugging the gold crucifix back and forth on the chain.

Both men's eyes shifted to Alisha. She cleared her throat, ran a finger under her nose.

"Thanks for asking, Ryan. I'll definitely consider it." Her tone said otherwise. "Things are pretty busy right now at Honey and Hickory, but tell Joanne I'll be in touch." She fished out a ten.

Ryan accepted her cash with a reflexive flick of his long brown bangs and peered at Quentin from under the fringe, his frown reappearing. "Are you one of the geologists from Chicago?"

Another long pause. Quentin hadn't expected to be asked outright.

"He's with me," Alisha piped up, slipping her hand into his.

The register shot out and whacked Ryan in the stomach. Quentin winced in sympathy, trying to tamp down the blaze spreading through him at Alisha's touch. The clerk passed back her change without a word.

Letting the door swing closed after they'd stepped out into the humid air, he asked, "Still doubting your sexiness?"

Alisha frowned.

"That guy was practically drooling over you." He squeezed her hand. "And your cookies."

She dropped her eyes to their linked hands but didn't let go. "Yeah, well, Ryan drools all over anything female. And edible."

Quentin barked out a laugh. "Still, thanks for shutting him down. I appreciate you covering for us."

"It's pure self-interest. We don't want a bunch of spectators trampling the rosebushes." She stepped out from under the overhang into bright sunlight.

"Okay, first of all, how old are you?" He grinned. "Sometimes you sound like you're going on eighty-five."

At the end of their joined hands, she spun back toward him. "I hope that was a rhetorical question."

Ignoring her comment, he said, "And secondly, you don't take compliments well, do you?"

"I didn't think being called an octogenarian was a compliment." But she smiled and stepped closer again, into the shade.

Closing the distance between them, he swung her hand gently. "Anytime I say something nice, you brush it off."

Face to his, Alisha said quietly, "Try again."

"When you used to text me, I'd imagine your smile, and seeing it again in person, my memories didn't do it justice." He leaned closer, until they stood nearly chest to chest, and pitched his voice low. "This is where you say, 'Thank you, Quentin. You're so sweet and truthful.'" He batted his lashes.

Alisha laughed, just like he intended, but unfortunately she swung away again and dropped his hand, gesturing with the bag of doughnuts. "That *is* sweet of you. But not entirely tr—"

He shook his head. "Don't you dare try to tell me it isn't true. Your smile is easily the best part of my day."

"I think maybe you're in the wrong discipline, Professor." She twinkled at him, reaching a hand up over her head to brush her hair over her shoulder. "Are you sure you shouldn't be in the humanities?"

"Feelings over facts?" Quentin grimaced. "No thanks." Mercedes once told him he wouldn't know romance if it hit him over the head with a book of sonnets. "Are those both for you?"

"Hey, you had your chance!" She clutched the bag to her chest in mock possessiveness. "Sundays are my heavy lifting days. This is fuel for my workout." She crossed her arms and shrunk into herself, the posture she adopted whenever she talked about lifting weights.

Weird how someone so physically capable would act like her strength was a handicap.

"But hey, we can go back in if you've got buyer's remorse. Joanne and Clint make these fresh every morning. You really ought to try one while you're in town."

"Maybe another time. I just thought you might be meeting some-one. But since you're not . . . I, ah, actually . . ." He blew out through his lips. "Do you want to sit and talk awhile?"

"Oh." The word hung in the thick air between them.

Was it too soon to ask her out again? Probably way too soon. What was the cool thing, to wait a week? Two weeks? He should've checked with Tre. "Never mind. Sorry. I'm sure you have a whole plan for the day. Weight training, right?"

"Yeah." She hesitated a second more; then the mask slipped from her face, and her eyes shone up at him. "Really, my day's pretty open. I can lift later. But there's nowhere to sit here." She frowned at the dilap-idated parking lot, grass growing in the cracks, muddy water trapped in dips in the pavement. "I have an idea. But it requires getting in my car."

"That's an issue?"

She gestured to the Geo. "I dunno, you tell me."

He did, and grimaced. "I forgot. That's not a car; that's an abomination."

"I thought you might say that." Alisha smirked at him. "Being a car guy and all."

"Hold up." He pressed a hand to his chest. "*I* am not a car guy. But I do come from a family of car guys. And let me set the record straight—that thing is not street legal. Did it even pass emissions?"

Fiddling with her purse, Alisha pulled her keys out. "In case you hadn't noticed"—she spread her arms wide—"you're not in Cook County anymore, hotshot. No emissions tests here. But Geos are the OG of fuel-economy cars. She may not be pretty, but she's not a planet killer. At least, no more so than anything else running on fossil fuel," she amended.

"*Fossil* fuel?"

"Unintentional, I swear." She popped her lips. "But the next one might not be."

In spite of the corniness, Quentin found himself smiling. She was quirky, and fantastic, and he couldn't get enough. For better or for worse.

"So what's it going to be, Dr. Harris? Your principles or your . . ." She trailed off.

He gave her a huge grin over the roof of the car. "Definitely not my principles."

A plume of dust settled around the car. Alisha shifted into park on the gravel embankment alongside the road and tugged out her keys.

"This is it," she announced.

From what Quentin could tell, *it* was a cornfield. Or, more accurately, two cornfields, one on either side, stretching out into the distance.

Clutching the coffee he hadn't trusted to the sticky depths of the cup holder, he shifted on the torn fabric seat, wary. "You know, we could've just sat in your car at the gas station. Although this view is . . . greener."

A playful smile on her lips, she waggled her fingers at him. "Out."

"Don't have to tell me twice! This thing might spontaneously combust any second." He shoved against the door and stumbled out like he couldn't get away fast enough. Alisha stood by the hood with hands planted on her hips.

Eyeing him from under her brow, she cocked her head. "Are you done?"

"Almost." He walked around the car bent double, arms out, giving it a wide berth. He came to a stop in front of her, straightening up with a smile. "Now I'm done."

"Good. Prepare to be wowed," she said.

"I'm mostly prepared to become a Child of the Korn."

"Funny." She spoke flat, but a smile twitched at the corners of her lips.

He shot a last glance back at the car, the lone vehicle on the dirt road, then caught up to her. She smelled like sunshine and coconuts. Fruity and delicious. Quentin shoved his free hand in his pocket to keep himself from reaching out for her hand.

But the hairs prickled on the back of his neck, and he darted his eyes around. She'd brought him to a *cornfield*. In Podunkville, USA. The cornstalks rustled in the hot breeze, then subsided, the muggy stillness broken only by the buzz of insects and the crunch of their feet on gravel.

They followed the road for about a quarter mile, his concern growing, until out of nowhere the cornfield opened up to reveal a grassy lot, dotted with vehicles. At the far end of the field sat carnival rides, and beyond, rows of low-roofed white buildings.

Alisha stepped forward and spun around. "Ta-da! Welcome to the county fair."

Quentin tried for a convincing smile, aware the result was a lot of teeth and not much lips.

"I can see you're not appropriately wowed. Give it time. This is a hot attraction; that's why I parked way out in the boonies. By lunchtime this place will be crawling with people. And we picked the perfect day to come—they're showing pigs."

"Showing them what?"

Alisha coughed out a laugh and walked backward, eyes sparkling. Her purse dragged the V-neck of her T-shirt down, revealing a hot-pink bra strap. She reached for his hand. For the second time today. Not that he was counting. "C'mon, city boy."

All his objections dried on his lips. The softness of her hand in his had him willing his heart to slow down so he could catch his breath.

The carnival was quiet, all the games shuttered. Sleepy workers stepped over power cables and gathered in small groups in the shade. Alisha explained that the rides wouldn't start up until noon, but the barns were open to walk through. When he asked why anyone would want to tour a barn voluntarily, her grin told him she might agree with his logic. But he didn't push it, following her into the nearest building with way more gusto than a bunch of bunnies deserved, because if she was up for sacrificing in the name of time with him, well, then bring on the rodents.

They stepped into the gloom and peered into the rows of cages. Luxuriant, curly fur covered some rabbits, so thick it weighed the tips of their ears down. Other pens housed pink-eyed albinos, their jaws working furiously on bits of hay poking out of their mouths. Earth's biodiversity never ceased to amaze him.

One of the rabbits was easily the size of a dog. The label on its cage read FLEMISH GIANT. Giant was right. Quentin leaned close to one to snap a photo for his nieces, and the rabbit thumped its back feet on the metal cage. Next to the rabbit, Alisha jumped a mile, her sneakers skidding on the concrete as she danced away.

Not so eager for the bunnies, then. Fine by him.

The next barn housed horses. In one of the stalls, a huge horse regarded them through wise dark eyes, like a sentient Narnian beast. A black mane fell across its face, and feathery white hair fanned out around its hooves.

"A Budweiser horse!"

She laughed, pointing to the placard. "Clydesdale."

But she hung back in the center of the aisle, arms crossed. A gust of wind sent sawdust swirling around her purple high-tops in a small eddy.

"Hey, Alisha, you should see this guy." He peered into the next stall, waving her over. "So teeny."

On tiptoe, she stepped closer, craning her neck to see inside. Once she was next to him, he threaded his fingers through hers again and spoke low, eyes on the horse. "Why am I getting the vibe you're not into livestock?"

"Does it show?"

Laughing, he held up an index finger and thumb, meeting her eyes with a grin. "Just a little."

"Yeah, animals are not my thing." She bit her lip. "I mean, cats are okay."

Quentin screwed up his face. "Are cats even animals?"

To his delight, she grinned, relaxing. "Right? More like hell on four paws."

"Yes! When I think of pets, I picture dirt and mess and—"

"Biting, maiming?"

"I was going to say 'inconvenience,'" laughed Quentin. "But okay, yes, we could add bodily harm to the list. I prefer my animals extinct," he joked. "Although I wouldn't mind seeing a barnful of triceratops. Is that on the tour?"

Alisha smiled. "How is it that every time we talk, I like you even more?" Her eyes widened, and she captured her lip between her teeth.

Yeah, same. Her admission had him flat on the concrete floor, but he chose to play it off. "I'm very likable, that's why."

Tension broken, she swatted him gently on the arm and moved on.

"So if you're not an animal lover, why did you bring me here? Not that I'm complaining," he added. She was as skittish as the horses, and he didn't want to spook her into calling it quits.

She shrugged. "Because this is the only exciting thing to do today in the whole county, and it beats sitting on the hood of my car at a gas station?"

"I don't need exciting when I'm with you," he said, and the truth of his words hit him like a revelation.

Bumping their joined hands against his leg in an aw-shucks move, she squeezed his hand a little tighter, and his heart squeezed right along with it.

Nose pinched, she tried to steer them around the poultry barn, but he insisted on the full experience. There had to be at least twenty different breeds on display. He restrained himself from delivering a lecture about modern-day dinosaurs—just barely.

Exploring livestock barns at a run-down fairground? Hands down the weirdest date he'd ever been on. But here he was, grinning from ear to ear. Around Alisha, everything else faded away. So much so that he didn't see the crew until Alisha had pulled to a halt, dropping his hand like a red-hot poker.

Forrest, Bridget, Dev, and Caitlyn stood in the shadow of a barn. Eyes hidden behind mirrored plastic sunglasses, Dev was probably nursing a hangover from the alcohol-fueled euchre game Quentin had heard through the thin motel walls last night. Forrest's cheeks hollowed out as he sucked lemonade through a twisty straw.

"Hey, y'all!" Bridget looked back and forth between him and Alisha with a hint of a smile. "Didn't expect to see you here, Quentin. The guys said you'd gone for a run. I texted to see if you wanted to meet up with us, but when we didn't hear from you, we figured you were holed up in your room deciphering this week's notes."

He pulled out his phone. Sure enough, there were several new texts in the group thread. His phone had stayed in his pocket, forgotten ever since Alisha had shown up at the gas station. "Oh yeah, I was. Running, that is. And got some coffee." He stopped. Rambling only made him look guilty.

Caitlyn nabbed the cup from Forrest and slurped up the last of the liquid with a rattle.

White-knuckling her purse strap, Alisha backed up. "You know what? I'll leave you guys to it."

The carnival rides clanked into motion with a whirl of creepy accordion music and a burst of clanging bells.

"No, you stay." Cait tugged on Forrest's sleeve. "We'll go. I saw a sign for deep-fried butter, and this one bet me ten bucks it was a myth. And I plan to drag Dr. Reid onto the Ferris wheel."

Bridget groaned, but a good-natured smile lit up her face. "One ride. That's it. And then you owe me a deep-fried Oreo."

"Wait, that's a thing?" Forrest's eyes widened like he'd caught a glimpse of heaven.

"You'd better believe it. Have fun, you two." With a parting wave, Bridget motioned to Dev, who jerked to alertness and ambled after the others.

They stood in silence, Alisha twisting the strap of her purse like a boa constrictor asphyxiating its prey. The same strangulation seized his own gut. First Dev and Forrest had seen them at the Back Forty, and now the entire crew had caught him hand in hand with Alisha. Not as if they'd been spotted making out, but his personal life and work had never collided. If Bridget thought he wasn't pulling his weight or the grad students lost respect for him . . .

Alisha looked up at him, uncertainty painting her features, the same uncertainty scratching at his insides. The safe option would be to call it quits before things got messy.

Instead, he stepped closer, reassured by the flicker of relief that passed over her features. She wanted this, too, and that gave him the courage to push aside his fears, now that the immediate threat of discovery was gone. He would be more careful in the future, but as for today . . .

He held out his crooked elbow like a gallant gentleman and was rewarded by the sound of her laughter. "Lead on, Alisha. I hear the pigs are a can't-miss."

CHAPTER 18

QUENTIN

While the rest of the crew headed out for lunch on Friday, Quentin eased open the back door and padded down the hall, on alert for the clicking of Mrs. Blake's knitting needles, or the oldies station Mr. Blake usually cranked up while he worked in his study. But . . . nothing.

Ever since last weekend, he and Alisha had fallen into a new dynamic. On Tuesday morning she'd texted to ask if he could sneak over early and then met him on the front porch swing with a frozen caramel latte and a homemade blueberry streusel muffin. And two evenings in a row, he'd lingered after everyone else had left for the day, and he and Alisha had sat talking on the tailgate of his pickup until dusk. Today he'd packed a sandwich as an excuse not to join the crew in town for lunch.

He hesitated near the bathroom door, but he passed it up and came to a halt outside the cutaway to the kitchen. Alisha sat on a stool at the island, her braids held back by a purple bandana, wearing a ruffled apron and nothing else. His heart skipped a beat. Then she shifted, and the strap of her tank top slid out from under the apron. He heaved out a breath. *She lives with her grandparents—c'mon now.*

Her voluptuous lips were parted in concentration as she decorated rows of cookies. Quentin stood rapt, mesmerized by the hypnotic motion and the beauty of her calm competence. She picked up bag after pastel-hued bag of color, adding icing with steady, precise movements. Using a thin brush, she painted detail onto several of the cookies, leaning back now and again to scrutinize her work.

With a satisfied huff, she set down the paintbrush and used the inside of her wrist to push the bandana higher up on her head. She raised her eyes for the first time and let out a squeak, hand flying to her heart. "Lordy! How long have you been standing there?"

"Long enough to know I should recruit you to piece together some bone fragments."

Oof. Thank goodness Hector wasn't around. He needed some new pickup lines. Badly. "That is . . . your dexterity. It's impressive." He stepped into the kitchen, the wood floor cool under his stockinged feet. "May I?"

She nodded, and he came up next to her. Four different shapes of sugar cookies lay on parchment paper—sunglasses, beach balls, swim trunks, and flip-flops.

"A friend from church is hosting a pool party this weekend. I'm going to do some food-themed cookies too. Popsicles, ice cream cones . . ."

"Lemonade?"

"Good call. Maybe pink lemonade." She smiled and stretched, then caught him looking at the cell phone set up on a tripod.

"Recording tutorials for my social media." She clicked it off. "You'd be surprised how many people like to watch piping videos. It's really calming."

He actually wasn't surprised at all—he could've watched her all day, and he knew all too well the addictive nature of her baking tutorials. But he wouldn't call the effect she had on him "calming." The closer he got to Alisha Blake, the faster his heart beat.

Right now, inches from her, his senses were ratcheted up to hyper-alert. Her skin radiated a delectable mix of bright citrus and rich honey. His heart thudded loud in his eardrums, keeping pace with Alisha's inhales, her chest swelling against the apron with each breath.

To ease the sudden tension, he said, "Having your cookies at Honey and Hickory must've been a great launching-off point for your business."

A small frown appeared on her face, then vanished just as quickly. She gave him a close-lipped smile. "Actually, that's a recent thing. It wasn't until this spring that Grandpa let me have a say in our dessert menu."

"But you're a genius with sugar. What took him so long?"

"He's set in his ways." Alisha started spinning a piping bag on the slippery granite. "And most of our customers are locals. He didn't want to rock the boat, I guess."

"Is that why your cookies aren't at the gas station?" Her eyes flicked up, wary. "You just seemed so guarded when the guy asked you about it."

"Grandpa doesn't think I should sell out of other businesses. Wants to give people a reason to stop in at Honey and Hickory, which makes sense." The words rushed out, quick and slippery, like an oil slick.

"Makes sense for him. But what about you?"

"I've got this." She nudged one of the cookies, lifted her chin toward the tripod, to encompass social media and her online business, he guessed. But she had so much more to offer.

Quentin stepped closer, wanting to reach out and reassure her. "And soon you'll have a bakery of your own. Which is going to be amazing, I have zero doubt." She seemed tense today, on edge. Had something happened at the restaurant? "I wonder if your grandpa regrets not giving you more leeway."

She shivered. "How so?"

"You're leaving. Isn't his reluctance to share you part of it?"

Gaze averted, Alisha rubbed her hands down her thighs, pulling away. "Actually, my grandparents don't know I'm leaving."

Hold up. Had he heard her right? Her grandparents didn't know she planned to move *across the state* and open a bakery in one of the biggest cities in the country?

"Not like I'm hiding it. I just haven't told them yet." Her fingers moved to the apron string at her waist, picking at the knot. "I've spent the last few years building my cookie business, so I hoped when my grandpa saw my success, he'd realize I had bigger plans."

"Or you could just tell him and not expect him to play a guessing game." The retort seared his lips, but he didn't question its source. "When exactly *were* you planning to tell them?" He stepped back, arms crossed, aware he was looking down his nose at her but powerless to stop.

Alisha's eyes met his, flecks of sienna sparking like embers in the depths. "Well, I didn't expect a dinosaur to turn up in our backyard."

A boulder fell across Quentin, wedging his heart back in his chest, pressing his head firmly onto his shoulders. "So the fossil discovery threw off your plans?" He didn't buy it.

"That, and we lost one of our cooks. Then Grandpa asked me to revamp our dessert menu. I got the feeling he might need me more than he lets on. That's the real reason I put off the move." Alisha went back to spinning the bag, turquoise specks dripping off the tip as it whirled.

Alarm bells clanged in Quentin's mind. His heart dropped out of his chest and hit the floorboards. Lies of omission, hidden decisions . . . Mercedes all over again.

"I get putting off the move until we finish up," he said, gesturing toward the yard. "But why not tell your grandparents now and give them time to adjust? Don't you think they'd be happy to help you with planning? And don't they deserve some time to get used to the idea?"

All trace of warmth evaporated from Alisha's eyes, replaced by flint, hard and cold as a cliff's edge. "Wow, I can see you're used to giving lectures for a living." She sat up about three inches taller on her stool, reaching up to flick her twists back over her shoulders, one side, then the other, revealing angular collarbones and a long, ramrod-straight neck.

Quentin was simultaneously in awe of her regal beauty and wary of the steel in her backbone. Not intimidated enough to keep silent, though. "Yeah, well, sometimes it takes an outsider to see things clearly." He recognized the voice—his father's.

"An outsider?" she snapped, and he regretted his words, but not enough to take them back. "I guess you're right. Thank you for your expert and impartial opinion on my life choices. I'll be in touch if I need a follow-up psych eval, Dr. Harris." She savagely tore off her apron and threw it on the stool before striding out.

Once again, Quentin stood alone in Alisha's kitchen, but this time he knew exactly why. He couldn't be with someone who kept secrets from the people closest to them. He *wouldn't*.

The only problem? Convincing his foolish heart, which had fled the room alongside Alisha.

Stupid, worthless, irrational heart.

That evening, after he'd gotten out of the shower, a notification flashed on his phone where it sat on the sink basin. His traitorous heart pumped into overdrive. He wiped the towel down his chest, then rubbed his arms dry before curiosity got the best of him. He flipped the thin motel towel over his shoulder and picked up his cell.

Alisha:

I'm really sorry I stormed out on you earlier. I only got upset because you were telling me what I already know.

His eyebrows shot up. He hadn't expected an apology, and quite frankly he wasn't sure he deserved one. Where did he get off telling her how to live her life? Just because he felt a strong bond didn't mean they were on the same page. Didn't give him the right to weigh in on her choices. If they called whatever this was quits right now, then they'd both be better off. He drew the towel along his jaw.

Quentin:
I get it. Family is complicated. I'm sorry for speaking out of turn.

Alisha:
No need to apologize, really. But yes, family is A LOT.

Not wrong there—family was *everything*. Even though his father misunderstood him and berated his choices, Quentin couldn't imagine lying to those closest to him. A trait he'd thought he shared with Alisha. Another miscalculation, but at least this time he'd found out before it was too late.

He finished toweling off and grabbed his boxer briefs off the counter, then tugged gym shorts on. Unsure whether to respond or leave it at that, he stood with feet planted on the damp tiles, gnawing his lip. A drip of water rolled out of his hair and down his cheek. He lifted a shoulder to rub it off, and his phone pinged again.

Alisha:
Meg insists on throwing a bonfire for all of you. Apparently she feels like you need a proper Hawksburg welcome, whatever that means. I can tell her not to.

Quentin sucked his teeth. He picked the phone up and put it back down. Palms braced on the counter, he met his reflection in the mirror.

No denying he was developing feelings for this woman. But keeping her family in the dark about a huge change? Far too reminiscent of what Mercedes had done to him. He couldn't go through that again. *Could not.* His breathing sped up, fogging the mirror.

Don't cry. Do not *cry.* Inhales ragged, Quentin forced himself to think pragmatically. He and Bridget were running a once-in-a-lifetime dig, trapped out here in no-man's-land. A party would be good for morale, and it would be selfish to deny everyone else a chance to let loose. He would just have to keep his budding crush in check. Easier said than done, especially with Alisha's contrite attitude.

But an apology didn't mean she would tell her grandparents about her plans. And it didn't erase the fact she'd been keeping a secret for months, maybe years, from her whole family.

He sure as heck couldn't press the issue any further, that much was clear, but he *could* protect his own heart. Get over this misguided infatuation.

Quentin:
No, that's okay. I'm sure everyone would like that. What time?

Alisha:
8ish? I'll text you the address.

Quentin:
Sounds good.

Slipping on sandals, he pulled his T-shirt over his head and padded down the hallway to knock on Forrest and Dev's door.

"C'mon in!"

He stepped into the room and found them playing cards at the tiny table by the window, reading lamps on, a baseball game on at low volume.

"How's it going?" Dev tipped up his chair, cards at his chest.

Quentin sat down on one of the beds, with an eye on the TV. "Good," he lied.

A Sox batter struck out, and he clicked his tongue. "You guys got anything to drink?" Forrest nodded toward the mini fridge, and Quentin pulled out a Gatorade. He unscrewed it and took a big gulp to chase away the lump in his throat. "I came by to tell you guys Alisha's friend Meg invited us all to a bonfire tonight."

Both men perked up.

"Meg? The tall chick who brought us food the other day?" This from Forrest, who swiped a tendril of hair out of his eyes.

Quentin nodded and took another drink.

"Will Alisha be there too?" Dev asked, eyes on his cards.

"Since that's who told me about it, I'm assuming yes," said Quentin, voice level.

The guys shared a look.

"What?"

Forrest's eyebrows went up, but he kept his eyes on the table, discarding. "Nothing."

Dev remained silent for once.

"Anyway, it's gonna be another long week. We can blow off some steam tonight."

Forrest blushed beet red, and Dev coughed. Junior high all over again. Quentin took another swig of his Gatorade, then wiped off his mouth with the back of his hand. "I'm going to go ask the ladies if they're interested. How about I order some pizza, and we'll head over after dinner?"

Teeth flashing in a grin, Dev gave him a salute, then yelped and grabbed his shin, glaring at Forrest. Quentin shut the door on the snickers behind him. He sighed. Tonight should be an absolute blast.

CHAPTER 19

ALISHA

The bonfire crackled, sending sparks drifting into the twilight sky. Alisha sat on a log, turning a quickly warming hard cider in her hands and trying to look somewhere—anywhere!—other than at Quentin. He sat engrossed in conversation with Meg on the other side of the blaze, the sharp angles of his face lit up by flickering light. So achingly handsome her misguided heart turned into a molten puddle.

Meg caught her eye and raised her brows, tilting her head toward Quentin. Universal wingman code for *I'm telling him how awesome you are, but like in a totally subtle way.* Alisha pursed her lips and gave a small shake of her head. Misguided matchmaking schemes were probably half the reason Meg had thrown this awkward party anyway. They couldn't even invite friends for fear of people finding out the true reason for the dig.

The paleontologists' presence—okay, Quentin's presence—made everything complicated. Alisha tucked the bottle between her legs and untied her hoodie from her waist, then slipped her arms into the sleeves and zipped it to her neck. The night was warm, but she could use the extra armor as a shield against his invisible pull, a barrier between herself and the ring of truth in his words when he'd called her out in the kitchen earlier.

He'd probably known he wanted to be a paleontologist since age three, and every single one of his decisions had fallen into place like dominoes, landing him on an upward trajectory at a renowned university. And he obviously had no problem voicing his desires to his family. Sure, they weren't impressed, but he'd done it anyway, and then oh so clearly judged her for not doing the same.

But her situation wasn't so simple. His dad had another son to work the family business. Alisha filled that role, stepping up at Honey and Hickory so her sister could be free to pursue her own dreams. Not only that, he didn't have to shoulder the weight of guilt that came from single-handedly wrecking her grandparents' chance at having carefree golden years.

Quentin's laugh floated over the flames and pierced Alisha's chest, spreading a slow drip of fiery lava through her veins, down her arms, into her fingertips. Despite how he'd questioned her judgment, she still responded to him like a sugar rush. Yes, he'd climbed on his high horse over her choice to keep quiet, but until today, he'd been kind and funny and supportive.

Unfortunately.

Forrest plopped down next to her and swiped a lock of tangled hair back over his head. "Nice of your friend to invite us over."

"Meg loves a party." Alisha began peeling the label off her drink. "And we figured you guys needed a break."

He stretched feet clad in canvas slip-ons and striped crew socks toward the fire, rocking the log. "This *is* our break. Fieldwork. Best part of the job, if you ask me."

"Ditto." A rustle and clink of metal sounded over her shoulder, and Alisha turned to find Caitlyn dragging a camp chair across the grass. "Fieldwork is my happy place." She sank down onto the chair, setting a bag of marshmallows on her lap.

Forrest lunged for the bag, but Cait lifted it over her head.

"Not until I've had some, mister. If we let him have this bag, there'll be none left," she said.

"I've got plenty more. Be back in a sec." Meg stood up and walked off toward the house, trailed by her golden retriever.

Cait nudged Forrest's sneaker with the toe of her Teva sandal. "Why don't you make yourself useful, too, and go find some sticks?"

With an amicable sigh, he stood and curtsied. "As you wish, milady." When he straightened up, the firelight illuminated his graphic tee: *Paleontologist, Because Freakin' Awesome Isn't a Job Title.*

Caitlyn ripped the marshmallow bag open with her teeth. "Thanks for the invite, Alisha." She flicked a gaze toward where Quentin sat chatting with Bridget and Dev and lowered her voice. "Sorry we crashed your date with the professor the other day."

Alisha's cheeks flamed hotter than the fire. "It wasn't a date."

"Mm-hmm. Whatever you say."

Alisha stared into the flames, jaw tight.

"Just so you know, I think it's great you two hit it off. He's been in a funk for a while." Alisha darted her eyes sideways at Cait's words. "Nice to see something other than an intact fossil make him smile. Doc Harris is good people—he deserves it." Caitlyn popped a marshmallow in her mouth and spoke around it. "You seem like good people too. Especially since you're okay with us tearing up your backyard." Grinning, Cait tugged a flat bottle out of the pocket of her cargo capris and bent over to spritz mosquito repellent onto her legs, the citronella smell sharp against the smoke.

Meg reappeared with her arms full of a doomsday bunker's worth of marshmallows, graham crackers, and chocolate bars.

"S'mores!" Forrest materialized out of the darkness, a bunch of sticks in either fist.

He dug into Cait's bag of marshmallows and stole four, threading them onto a stick, one after the other. She shot Alisha an *I told you so* look.

Dev raised his beer toward the truckload of s'more fixings. "Did you buy all those for us, or were you expecting fifty more people?"

"No, but I can't escape my midwestern farm-girl roots." Meg chuckled. "Stockpiling is in my genes."

Headlights shone down the grass, then clicked off. Alisha sat up straight, on high alert.

"Thought you didn't invite anyone else." Quentin spoke from across the fire, his eyes an echo of the dusk-gray sky under his lowered brows.

They hadn't. Doubtful their flimsy geologist cover story would hold up after a few beers.

And Forrest's shirt . . . Cait must've realized the issue at the same time and nudged him, gesturing at the screen-printed stegosaurus skeleton. His eyes went wide, and he dropped his stick of flaming marshmallows.

Alisha snatched up the stick and pounded it on the ground to put out the fire. Gobs of gooey marshmallow smeared all over the grass. In a flash, Forrest yanked off his tee and flipped it inside out, just as Shawn strode into the circle gathered around the fire, in formfitting Wrangler jeans and cowboy boots, upper body obscured by five boxes of pizza. "Did someone order delivery?"

Meg shook her head, a Joker-esque smile plastered on her face. "Must have the wrong house."

Shawn lowered the pizzas, brow furrowed. "I was kidding. These are just rejects from tonight's orders. Saw your fire and figured I'd stop by." He blinked around at the unfamiliar faces and the half-dressed Forrest. "Heat getting to you, bud?"

"Oh, yeah . . . no." Forrest balled the fabric in his hands, red cheeks visible even in the firelight.

When it became clear he was done talking, Dev leaped in. "There was a spider. Big one. On his shirt. He's terrified of the suckers."

"Yep, total arachnophobe, this one." Cait elbowed him. "Right, Forrest?"

"Right. Yeah. Petrified. I'll just . . ." He tugged his shirt back on.

Nodding along like this whole interaction was normal, Shawn set the pizzas on an upturned log. "So, what's the occasion?"

Meg put the s'mores supplies on an empty chair by the fire, then pulled Shawn in for a quick hug, probably buying time. When she released him, she'd regained her poise. "The geologists can only stay cooped up in the Hawk's Roost for so long. Figured we'd show them a Hawksburg welcome."

"Well, I'll drink to that." Shawn took a step toward the cooler, and his grin changed to a frown. He lifted up his boot, peering at the sole. "Did your dog get into the marshmallows again, Meg?"

Preempting anyone's reply, Bridget got up and shoved a beer into Shawn's hands, clinking hers on it in a sloppy cheers. If he noticed the awkward vibes, he gave no sign, and soon everyone was chatting again, Shawn ensconced on a camp chair between a wary Bridget and Dev.

Meg and Alisha shared a helpless look. Shawn tended to take things at face value, so as long as he didn't ask too many questions . . .

"Why am I not surprised you're friends with the pizza guy?" Quentin appeared at her side, breaking into her anxious train of thought.

She looked up at him with a half smile. "Hazards of small-town life. And technically Shawn's also the grain elevator guy, the cross-country coach, and the baseball coach. He might also have a thing for my sister." Gosh, why did she respond to Quentin like he was truth serum? Or maybe it was the romantic flickers of firelight affecting her filter.

"Doesn't he know Simone lives in Chicago?"

"Yeah." She tipped the bottle of cider to her lips. "The heart wants what the heart wants, I guess."

Was he going to ask if she'd told Simone about her plan to move? She half wanted him to, because it would make it easier to stay mad. Half hoped he wouldn't, because the way the firelight caressed the planes of his face turned her insides gooier than Hershey's in a s'more.

After a beat, he exhaled and took a seat on the log. Close. "So is this pretty standard on summer nights?" He leaned back, resting his palms on the log, elbows locked.

"Bonfires? Definitely." She cradled the bottle to resist the urge to skim a hand down his arm, feel the smooth swell of muscle under her fingers. "What about you? I always wondered what it would be like to grow up in the city."

"Less stars, more concrete." He lifted a shoulder.

"Oh, c'mon. You gotta give me more than that." She bumped her knee to his, soft, and felt her heart pinch. "What did you do for fun growing up?"

"Basketball, baseball, video games. The usual stuff." He shifted his eyes to her, and flames danced in his shadowy pupils. "You?"

"Hayrides, barn dances, cow tipping. You know, country stuff," she joked. "Nah, I'm kidding. Pretty much like yours, minus video games, because bo-ring. That was Simone's thing." She hesitated. He clearly wasn't over their fight, and neither was she. Why not let him go? But her mouth betrayed her before she could weigh the consequences. "There is one thing you might not have done."

"Oh?"

"Yeah. C'mon." She stood up before her tenuous bravery deserted her and marched off into the night.

CHAPTER 20

QUENTIN

"Should I be afraid? I feel like this is how *Texas Chainsaw Massacre* begins." Goose bumps chased their way up Quentin's spine, and he cast a glance over his shoulder. "Or ends."

"Ooo-ooo," Alisha said and giggled, leading him off into the darkness.

He laughed, high-stepping over the uneven ground. "Way to put my mind at ease." Lengthening his strides, he caught up to her where she stood unlatching the door of a dilapidated barn in the moonlight. "Are you about to go full-blown country on me?"

Alisha blew out through her lips. "Hardly." She pulled at the door, but it stuck in the dirt. He gave her a hand, grabbing the splintered wood, and together they lifted it over the rut and swung it open. "You might have noticed I don't quite fit in around here."

"Because you're not white?" He followed her into the sheltered gloom.

"No." She grunted a laugh, scaling a ladder he could barely make out in the darkness. "Well, yeah. This town isn't very diverse, so of course there's been comments over the years. Ignorant ones. Rude ones. Most unintentional, though."

"Doesn't make it better."

"No. It does not." She reached the top and swung her leg over, disappearing from view. "But what I mean is, I don't fit in with the other women in town. I don't love canning vegetables or raising animals or knitting my own scarves."

With a last look out the door, where flickers from the bonfire broke the inky blackness, he stepped deeper into the barn. Musty air enveloped him, and he sneezed. "Is that why you want to leave?"

Alisha's head appeared over the edge, shadow against shadow. "Animal husbandry and domesticity?" She huffed another laugh. "No, not really."

She put a piece of straw in her mouth and drummed her heels against the bales. He smiled. Whether she'd admit it or not, she'd definitely gone country since they'd left the fireside.

"For one thing, I don't love the idea of raising kids in a small town." Her words came out garbled, and she plucked out the straw before continuing. "I want my children to have more opportunities at their fingertips. And I don't want them to feel like a token, like I did. I want my children to grow up surrounded by all different kinds of people."

Quentin tried not to add this to his list but failed. A small check mark went next to *Wants a family*. He almost missed out on what she said next.

"Mostly I just miss civilization." She laughed again, a lighter sound than before. "I was raised in the Chicago suburbs. So moving here was a bit of a culture shock. Growing up, we used to visit my grandparents in the city all the time, before they passed away. And we'd take the train into downtown to explore museums, the beach, festivals. Christkindlmarket at Christmastime. Taste of Chicago in the summer. I always told my mom I wanted to live in the city when I grew up."

Her voice hitched, and if not for the darkness, he would have dropped his eyes to give her a sense of privacy. "I'm about ten years late, but I'm finally making good on my promise."

During her speech, he'd remained standing on the wooden floorboards at the foot of the ladder, and now Alisha leaned farther out, teeth flashing in a wide smile. "Doing okay down there, city boy?"

Something skittered up his arm, and he slapped it off and danced away, knees high. Her cackle swooped out of the darkness.

"Just fine." A total lie.

Barn, country night . . . *nope.*

Great outdoors? Fine by him, especially with fossils nearby. But straight-up country? Outside his comfort zone by miles. He itched his neck where something with too many legs tickled his nape. But not to be outdone, he grabbed the rough edge and vaulted over, skipping the ladder. He stood up and found Alisha right in front of him, her teeth gleaming.

"Nice hops," she said.

Whatever they were standing on gave way unnervingly under his feet, like a trampoline. Hay? Straw? He didn't know the difference. She scampered higher, though, climbing the stack like a mountain goat. She reached the top and plopped down, kicking her heels against the bales.

Why had he come out here with her? After resolving to stay away, protect his heart, he'd fallen right back into her hypnotic pull. Grabbing on to the poky bales, he fought for purchase and scrabbled the rest of the way up, collapsing facedown next to her.

"Graceful." Her voice came from above his shoulder.

Quentin chuckled, inhaling dust. "That's why they pay me the big bucks." He coughed and rolled over, sitting up next to her, both of them facing out into the dim expanse. "This straw is really prickly."

"Hay."

"Yup. Hay. That's what I said." He shifted in search of a comfortable position. Impossible. "Other than that, though, super fun."

"You're teasing me." She reached over to poke him in his abs. His muscles tightened by reflex, everywhere, a bolt of lightning zooming through him at the touch. She dropped her hand, and he caught it, threading his fingers through hers.

"I *was* teasing you," he said, voice husky. "But I'm having fun. Being with you is becoming one of my favorite things." The cover of night and her hand in his left him dazed. His stubborn heart pounded in time with Alisha's, at war with a mind fighting to tame his desire by whispering, *Untrustworthy. Unsafe.*

But was she?

Her grandparents had been through a lot; he could understand Alisha's hesitation in wanting to spring more change on them. Waiting to share the news until the last minute didn't sit well with him at all. But moving across the state and away from home wasn't the same as breaking your engagement, was it?

And tonight she'd switched on, like a hundred-watt light bulb. She'd been candid and open and completely at ease. His plan to freeze her out left his chest tight, his blood cold. The opposite of the fire simmering through him now, smoldering between their clasped hands. He couldn't turn his back on her now. Not when maybe, just maybe, they had a real shot.

"I don't mind spending time with you, either, Quentin Harris," Alisha said softly, reaching up her other hand to press gently on his shoulder. Pushing, but he felt the pull instead. "Though I agree. The setting leaves a lot to be desired."

She dropped her fingertips from his shoulder and leaned back onto her arm. Even though their hands were still intertwined, he wanted more. Closer. His fuzzy brain couldn't seem to focus on her words.

"Meg loves this quiet life, but all I've ever wanted was the heartbeats of a thousand people around me. As funny as it sounds, I feel like I can breathe best when I'm surrounded by people. Out here, with the open expanses, things are too noisy." She tipped forward and pulled out a piece of hay, rolling it between her fingertips. "Doesn't make sense, I know."

"No, it does. I figured it was just because I grew up in the city, but when I'm on digs, I miss civilization so much." Her eyes swung in his direction, and he hastened to add, "Not just running water and flush toilets. But more so the sound of cars outside the window. The rattle of the L lately," he said, and one corner of his mouth lifted in a wry smile, thinking of the elevated Green Line train that ran right outside his apartment. "I feel most alive in the city." He brushed her thigh with their joined hands, forgetting it was bare until his knuckles skimmed the silky smoothness. "I guess we have that in common."

"That and dinosaurs," she said, a smile in her words.

"True." He grinned in return. "So, what did you used to do out here?"

"In haylofts? Well, Meg's grandparents had a rope swing in their barn across town, and we used to spend hours on it. I felt so free. But later . . . ," she said, then paused. "Later on, barns were a popular make-out spot."

Whoa, hold up. The banked fire between them combusted into a blaze. Did she mean . . . "So that's the, uh . . ." His voice broke, and he palmed his neck. "Making out in a barn is the activity you were thinking I might not have done, when you invited me out here?"

"What?" Her head swung up, and the whites of her wide eyes showed in the dim light. "Oh gosh. No. I just . . . I mean, I wasn't planning on *that*. I just . . ." She pulled up another handful of hay. "I guess I thought a trip to the country wouldn't be complete without a barn experience. Er, not *that* kind of a barn exp—"

"Alisha."

She stopped talking, and he swept a hungry gaze over the dip and curve of her lips. Then she leaned in, and he knew—*knew* that it was himself she was reaching for in the darkness. He let his elbow drop and dipped toward her, lifting his other hand to touch her cheek, but he paused just short, waiting.

In answer, she swayed forward and leaned into his palm. He caressed her temple, so soft, then swept his thumb down over her earlobe. Her breathing quickened, fingers grazing up his thigh, just below his hip.

"Alisha . . ." He breathed the next word, a wish, a prayer, and an invitation, all in one. "Please."

In the space of a skipped heartbeat, she erased the distance between them and pressed her lips to his. Thank the Lord above. Quentin cupped the other side of her face, and they melted into each other like ice cream dripping down a sugar cone, and every bit as sweet. Her lips parted under his, and he swallowed a groan as her fingers skated up his thigh to hook into his belt loop. A tug drew him closer, deeper.

The slickness of her tongue sent him plummeting, spiraling, and he surrendered. His hand dropped to her waist, gripping her tight. Light burst like a sparkler behind his eyelids—

Wait, no. Not sparks from the kiss. An actual light, beaming through the barn door. He and Alisha zapped apart like they'd touched an electric fence.

A disembodied voice spoke from below. "Dr. Harris?"

Quentin held up his arm, squinting. Next to him, Alisha shot to her feet and stumbled back, jostling the stack of hay. The light swept around the hayloft, then swung upward to reveal a face ghoulishly up-lit like an actor from *The Blair Witch Project*.

"Dev?"

The light bounced jerkily for another second as he fumbled to shut it off. "Sorry, guys. I just—dang." The light clicked off and left him silhouetted by firelight in the open door. "Um, how do I put this delicately . . ." He scratched at his beard, the sound loud in the sudden stillness. "Erm, so . . . Forrest is out front. Puking his guts out."

Behind him, Alisha burst into giggles. Her laughter sounded a little unhinged, and no wonder—Dev had just caught them making out like a couple of high schoolers. The sucky, sucky irony.

"Poor guy," she said, coughing the words out. "I'm not laughing at him, it's just—"

"His own fault? Oh yeah, one hundred percent." Dev cast a glance behind himself. "Might have been that second box of pizza he started in on. Or maybe the five s'mores. It's pretty unclear." He turned back around and hitched up a shoulder. "But since you're our DD . . ."

Alisha was already scrambling down, and Quentin slid down after her, straw pricking through his jeans at the back of his knees to join the pinpricks of regret needling his insides.

Their first kiss, interrupted by his grad student, of all people. Not how he pictured things going at all. And he *had* pictured it, dreamed of this kiss countless times. The moment their lips met felt like the most delicious confirmation of every bit of emotion that lay tangled up between them.

When he dropped down to the creaky floorboards next to her, Alisha raised her eyes to his for a second, a blatant longing in their depths that matched his own. Then she dropped her gaze, reaching down to brush hay off her shorts, and the moonlit sight of her bare legs sent his heart pounding out of his chest all over again.

Without another glance, she swept out the door. Dev trailed after her. Quentin took a second to collect himself in the semidarkness, wishing she'd stayed behind. He stepped out into the night and found the fire had died down. Cool air enveloped him, and he hurried his steps, hoping for a chance to get Alisha alone before he left. But when he reached the fire, she was nowhere to be seen.

Cait sat cross-legged on the ground, laughing with the pizza guy. "If you're looking for your lady"—she raised her piece of pizza over her shoulder, toward the house—"I think she went to give Bridget a hand with our drunken sailor."

"She's not my—" Quentin rubbed a hand across his forehead. "Okay, thanks."

Brows raised, Cait said nothing but took a huge bite, her eyes on his. Trusting Dev to bring her along, he left the fireside in search of the others. Meg materialized out of the darkness, a bottle of Gatorade and a towel in her hands.

Despite the turn of events, he smiled. "You weren't kidding about being stocked up."

"You don't even wanna know how many freezers I have."

He laughed. "I should probably be creeped out by that statement, but since I grew up with a bonus freezer in the basement, I get it."

Meg's grin flashed bright in the darkness, and she passed him the supplies, which he accepted with a shudder at the ordeal ahead.

"She's worth it, you know." Her eyes shone bright in the moonlight. "I know Alisha's not making this easy on you. But once she lets you in, it's for good."

For good? Quentin's grip on the bottle tightened as he walked away. One taste of Alisha, and he was a goner. The desperate way she'd tugged him closer had left him undone, tumbling, spinning around in a current too strong to resist. But she remained fixed, a beacon, drawing him onward toward an unknown shore that somehow promised refuge.

CHAPTER 21

ALISHA

Alisha tugged a piece of hay out of her hair and inhaled the lingering notes of woodsmoke, then tucked a bonnet over her twists. Their kiss in the barn replayed in her mind on an endless loop. Quentin's hands, rough with calluses but so gentle, caressing her face like a treasure. The firm hardness of his thigh under her hand when she yielded, finally, to the desires she'd fought to keep at bay.

His broken plea had roused something primal in her, chasing away her doubts until all that remained was Quentin and the solid reassurance of his body, the promise held in his kiss. The tantalizing slide into something new and lovely and absolutely perfect.

That is, until Dev barged in and killed the mood with a single sentence.

Alisha's groan ended in a chuckle. Meeting her reflection, she covered her flushed cheeks. How was she still giddy after such an anticlimactic end to the evening? Quentin, was how. Shaking her head, she opened the medicine cabinet to get out her face lotion. When she'd stopped in the house on her way out, Meg had tried to convince her to stay, but between the intoxicating cocktail of moonlight and Quentin, she didn't trust herself tonight.

Didn't trust herself not to close her eyes and dive, headfirst, into a relationship with Quentin.

She smoothed moisturizer onto her face. Twenty-nine and just now meeting a man who made her feel seen. Whole. Worthy.

At times like these she missed her mom most. The sharp pain of losing her had dulled over the years to an ache, but moments of indecision brought her loss to the forefront. She needed reassurance, a steadying hand on this swaying bridge toward happiness. To be sure in opening herself up to Quentin, she wouldn't be baring her neck for slaughter. Gulping, throat dry from the chilly night air and the campfire, Alisha padded downstairs to get water.

Lately all her emotions were simmering near the surface, threatening to erupt. Another reason she'd stayed away from men in the past. Otherwise, sentimentality bled into other areas of her life. Right now she needed to be clearheaded. She'd let her plans get pushed offtrack, or maybe she'd even been the one to pull the lever and divert the train herself.

And while she could point blame in a thousand directions, Quentin was right. She should've told her family about her bakery dream months ago, if not years. But leaving weighed heavy on her heart. Her grandparents had given her everything; was it so much to ask for her to stay here in Hawksburg, taking care of them and repaying the debt?

After reaching the bottom of the stairs, she turned and passed through the hallway, not needing light to know what memories filled the frames. Her smiling parents, beaming above baby Alisha in glamorous nineties splendor, her mom's curls pressed and hair sprayed, her dad with a dirty-blond mullet and bushy mustache. Their hands joined across Alisha's belly as she cried up at the photographer, in white leather booties and a yellow eyelet gown.

A few steps down, all four of them. Alisha, seated on her dad's lap, all elbows and knees in a checkered dress, her mom holding Simone—a chubby toddler with two bottom teeth poking out of her gums. Then the last family portrait—Simone and Alisha standing in front of their father, his hair now in an unkempt bowl cut, arms pressed against his sides. Stiff, posed. A formality.

The rest of the photos were of her and Simone—school portraits, basketball and track and field snapshots. One picture of Simone atop her horse, laughing down at the camera, her black velvet helmet tipped back jauntily. But no more family photos, no more mom and dad and daughters.

She switched on the light over the kitchen window, and the yellow glow illuminated her reflection against the darkness. Her mother's face stared back at her, Alisha's skin golden brown to her mother's deep-brown luster, but the same high cheekbones and wide, dark eyes. The pain swelled.

Alisha had spent years wondering whether seeing his wife's features reflected on his daughter's face was the reason he couldn't be their dad anymore. Now she knew better, but the root of the question still plagued her. What had she done to make him leave? Which of her flaws had driven him away?

Cancer stole her mother with unfathomable brutality. But losing her father to cowardice a year later, when he'd brought them here for a visit and then left without them, was an altogether different kind of devastation.

By the time Grandpa had tracked down his only child out in Oregon two years later, he had a new wife, a stepson, and a baby on the way.

One night, after her grandpa had returned home, raised voices had woken her up and drawn her downstairs, where she sat on the landing. Grandpa had confronted him, out in Portland. He told Granny her father had apologized and offered to pay any amount of child support, but he just couldn't see the girls. *His* girls.

"But, Ellie, I told him." Her grandfather's voice broke in a way she'd never heard before or since—the sound of a heart torn asunder. "I told

him we don't need your money. This isn't about that! I need my son
back. The girls need their father."

"And Kenny?" Granny's voice, small and quavering.

"He said no, said it was too much for any man to bear."

And they never heard from him again.

A tear rolled down her cheek, and she scrubbed the moisture away.
To cry over her worthless excuse of a father after all these years? Foolish.
Simone had done enough crying for both of them back then and, in the
time since, enough raging for the two of them combined.

More of a stream than a tsunami, Alisha's tears had trickled out
slowly over the years. She always wished the flow would run dry, but
it never did. *He* didn't deserve mourning, though. She saved it for her
mother, hoarding her pain until the hurt of losing her became overwhelming and she had to open the dam or drown.

But for her father, she had only anger and hurt. Rage, turned
inward, to doubt, and hopelessness, and fear.

Unwanted. Cast aside.

She filled up a glass and took a gasping drink. As she set it down
with an unsteady hand, the cup tipped, flooding the counter. She
reached for the dish towel, and the memory of Quentin standing at the
sink flashed into her mind. His deep voice drawing a laugh out of her,
a sudsy sponge in his hands. And what had he said?

Will you let me stay?

He wasn't searching for an exit. No hand on the doorknob, ready
to escape. Could she go all in with Quentin? Release her grip on her
parachute and fall, trusting him to catch her?

CHAPTER 22

QUENTIN

A trickle of sweat rolled between Quentin's collarbones. He climbed into the driver's side of the truck's cab and adjusted the mirror, shooting Alisha a shaky smile. "I haven't picked someone up from their parents' house for a date in a long time. Did I do okay?"

Only a half joke—showing up to the Blakes' with the intention of taking Alisha out felt wildly different from heading out to work in their yard.

When she didn't answer, Quentin glanced over and found Alisha's gaze fixed on the bouquet of sunset-hued flowers in her lap. She must've felt his eyes on her, because she looked up.

"What? Oh, yeah." She smiled. "The flowers for Granny were a nice touch."

"But . . ."

"No, it's nothing." She faced the window as he backed down the drive, her words hard to catch over the blasting AC. "It's just that you said 'date.' Which I'm guessing means you're okay with the fact Dev caught us canoodling?"

He grinned in spite of himself. *Canoodling*. Geriatric Alisha had made another appearance.

But yeah, the intersection of work and his personal life was uncharted water, tender and scary. Buying time, he spun the steering wheel and accelerated onto the dirt road, tires crunching on the gravel.

"I don't love the idea of my students speculating about us." Not that there was anything left to speculate about. "But ever since we met, I haven't been able to get you off my mind. And our kiss . . ." He darted his eyes toward her, then back to the road. "Our kiss felt like—" Like everything he ever wanted and exactly what he needed. Lightning and a gentle rain. Still waters and stardust.

"I really like spending time with you, Alisha." Feeling exposed, he pulled off onto the shoulder to let a rumbling tractor pass. "So if you're asking, 'Am I willing to give this a try?' Then the answer is yes. Very much, yes."

"You're up for giving this a try." She shot her eyes toward him, a familiar glint of mischief in their depths. "Even though our first date ended with you getting up close and personal with the business end of a Hula-Hoop and our last date nearly gave you hay fever?"

The seasick churning in his stomach eased, and he managed a grin. "I'll have you know I regret nothing about showcasing my Hula-Hooping skills. I plan to wear that undersize Back Forty T-shirt every chance I get." She chuckled, and he went on, bolder now. "And hay fever? Is that what the cool kids are calling it these days?" He winked. "Besides, that's not what I remember most about the barn."

"It isn't?" Her words ended in an adorable squeak, and her eyes dropped to his lips. "Me neither," she admitted. Her tongue flicked out and moistened her lips, and the memory of their delicious slide into one another had him biting down on his own tongue to keep himself in check.

"I'm willing to give it a try, Alisha, but are you?"

A flash of light glinted off the crucifix she slid back and forth along the gold chain. The pressure in the cab built under the weight of her indecision until he felt his ears would pop.

"I am." She leaned over and planted a quick kiss on his cheek. The ball of worry in his chest unknotted into gossamer threads of hope.

He shifted into drive and eased back onto the road. She picked up the bouquet, tracing a finger along the petals. "These gerbera daisies are gorgeous, by the way."

"Is that what those are called? They reminded me of you." The big, bold, beautiful Alisha he'd come to know behind the passive exterior she put on for the world.

"If this is our first official date, I feel like we should get some formalities out of the way. Name, occupation, pet peeves." Out of the corner of his eye, he caught her nod. Brisk and businesslike. He fought a grin at how cute she was.

"I'm Alisha Marianne Blake, a pastry chef who can bake an out-of-this-world chocolate chip cookie and an even better macaron. I think canned pie filling is the devil's work. And canned biscuits? Don't get me started. I'm a reluctant country girl who's moving to Chicago." She paused, and he ventured a glance and met those gorgeous dark eyes of hers. "And who are you, Man Who Picked Me Up in His Truck?"

"Quentin Cecilio Harris, your Uber driver. I hear you're on your way to an awesome date, so don't forget to tip."

"Cecilio, huh?"

"My grandfather's name," he said, nerves making him chatty.

But Alisha smiled. "I love family names. My middle name is my mother's." She bunched her dress in one fist, then turned to him, eyes shining. "Can you say it again?"

"Cecilio?"

"Yes. I like that." She repeated the name, rolling it on her tongue.

He bit his lip. "Sometimes you're surprising."

"Is that a good thing?"

Normally no, but for some reason he didn't mind being knocked off balance by Alisha. He regarded her out of the corner of his eye, beautiful and funny and strong and unexpected.

Was it a good thing? "Absolutely." He grinned. "And actually, this isn't strictly *my* truck."

"Is this your way of telling me I'm riding in a carjacked vehicle?" She reached for the door handle in mock horror.

"That would lend some excitement to the evening, right? But no, it's my dad's. I don't have much use for one, living so near campus."

"Ah, that explains the decor." Alisha waved her hand at the hula figurine on the dash and the small Virgin Mary medal hanging from the mirror.

"Mary is my mom's addition," Quentin said with a wry shrug.

"To balance out the hula girl?" Alisha chuckled. "Your family's Catholic?"

"Mom is, so Hector and I are. Dad's still on the fence."

"Me too! Mom converted when she married my father." She swept her eyes down him. "I had you pegged for a Catholic schoolboy."

"You did not."

"I did. You're so well mannered."

"That was more my mom's wrath than my Catholic school education."

She giggled. "Well, I'm glad. Now we don't need to argue over who's converting."

He licked his lips. Should he ignore the fact she basically brought up marriage? He sneaked a peek her way. Visibly paler, and her eyes were rimmed in white. Yes, definitely ignore.

"You missed a turn back there."

"Huh?"

"I figured we were going to the Back Forty."

Shuddering, he said, "I think I can do better than that for our first official date. This is a date, right? Just wanna make sure." He swung his gaze her way, and she rolled her eyes with a grin.

"Yes, a date."

"Okay, well, now that that's established . . . the lady who runs the tea shop said there's live music out at the fairgrounds tonight. I'm fully expecting a small-scale Lollapalooza."

She chuckled. "Oh yeah, the folk and art fest. Lollapalooza it is not. But it is a step up from pigs and chickens."

After a few minutes, he pulled up to a barricade, where a woman in a yellow vest was directing traffic. Quentin rolled down his window.

"Parking's five dollars."

He handed her a twenty and got his change, and they bumped over the grass to an open spot. He came over to the passenger side, and Alisha swung the door open. Between her short dress and the height of the truck, Quentin lost himself for a moment at the arresting sight of her bare bronze knees and the solid curve of her big thighs above them.

"Hey, beautiful." He recovered and extended his hand. She slid her hand into his grip without hesitation and scooted down onto the runner of the truck, then jumped to the ground.

Folk music rolled out from a stage at the far end of the field. They waded through the crowd and stopped at an art booth. Watercolor pictures filled the white tent. Mostly landscapes, with a few close-ups of farm animals thrown in for variety.

"Avant-garde stuff here," he whispered in Alisha's ear. She dug an elbow into his ribs.

"Shh."

The artist scowled at them, and Quentin offered a toothy smile, letting Alisha tug him out of the stall. He tripped over a cord on the ground, chuckling. She shook her head. "Serves you right."

"Sorry, that just wasn't my style." Maybe he should've censored himself, been more diplomatic.

But Alisha grinned. "You're not into drab watercolor paintings of livestock? How dare you."

A weight lifted off his chest at her reaction. "You weren't a fan either?"

"Ugh, no. But did you see the look on that guy's face? He totally heard you dissing his cow painting." Quentin opened his mouth to argue, but the man had come to the edge of the tent and stood glaring at them, arms crossed. Alisha dissolved into silent giggles. "Wonder what it was called. We should've checked. Maybe *A Cow, Interrupted*?"

More giggles. After four years of Mercedes's type-A edge, he found Alisha's silly side so refreshing. He could breathe with Alisha around. Except when she turned her earth-hued gaze toward him and sunk her teeth into her full bottom lip. Then suddenly there was no air in his lungs.

A group of elderly women in matching visors passed, forcing them to step aside into another tent. Quentin read the placard: HAND-CUT FRIES AND LEMONADE. "Hungry?"

"For french fries? Always," she said, and the guy manning the booth laughed.

He bought them an order of fries and two lemonades, and they resumed strolling. One of the booths sold photographs, and Alisha lingered over a picture of a shoreline, waves frothing on the rocks.

Quentin took the chance to drink in her features. Her berry-red lips were parted, the once-slick edges of her hair lifting from the humidity. Her skin glowed satiny in the afternoon sun. Unconsciously, he dipped his gaze down to the curves accentuated by her painted-on dress.

"Want a fry?"

He snapped his eyes up, but she'd caught him. Her smile slid off, replaced by an intense simmer, her own eyes clocking down his front. So it was like that, huh?

"I'm good." His stomach was too unsettled to eat. "But actually, if you don't mind, I wanted to stop in over there." He lifted his cup toward a tent selling doll clothes.

Alisha pursed her lips. "M'kay."

After wading their way through the crush of bodies, they arrived at the booth. She planted her hands on her hips, tilting her head up to him. "This is where you either tell me you have a daughter, a niece, or a creepy fetish."

Quentin barked out a laugh. "Two nieces, actually. Twins."

Wiping her brow exaggeratedly, Alisha said, "Thank the Lord. That it's not a fetish, that is. A daughter wouldn't have been a deal-breaker."

The second time she'd mentioned kids now, and he zeroed in on her words. *A daughter wouldn't have been a deal-breaker.* So she was serious about wanting children? Or at least okay with the idea.

Or maybe she just wasn't the kind of jerk who'd turn down a guy with a kid.

Sifting through the racks of dresses, Alisha said, "Twins, though. Yikes." Then she slapped a hand over her mouth. "I'm sorry, that was so rude! I didn't mean it that way. But I imagine raising twins must be difficult."

But Quentin laughed. "It's okay. It *is* scary. Toddlers are terrifying on their own, but when they come in pairs, there's no hope for the rest of us."

She pulled out a hanger with a sparkly tutu. "They're toddlers?"

"Oh no, they're five now," he said. "I'm just still scarred from their terrible twos. I feared for my brother's life on many occasions. Lauryn and Liliana were a handful."

"Pretty names! You sure they have American Girl dolls, though? These clothes can be pretty specific." She stopped and twisted her mouth sideways. "Not that I've kept my collection of dolls from childhood or anything. Definitely not."

He pulled down a frilly purple dress. "Nah, I'm sure." Face hot, he mumbled, "I know which kind of dolls they have because I took them to the American Girl store for their birthday."

She pushed his arm, and his pulse raced at the contact. "Of course you did, ya big softie. I can totally see it. You probably have a 'World's Best Uncle' shirt too." Underneath the razzing, her tone was warm.

"Now that you mention it, I bet I could find one here." He craned his neck and pretended to check for a T-shirt booth.

Pressing a palm to his cheek, she stilled him. "M-mm, nope, don't do that."

He laughed from deep in his belly, and she joined in.

Together they picked out a dress for each of the girls while he told her how they'd argued about what color to paint their bedroom, so his brother and sister-in-law had finally decided to tape a line down the middle and paint it half purple and half green.

"And the result is a nightmare. Like a Barney explosion. My eyes are still burning. I told Hector he owed me a case of beer for agreeing to help," he said, and Alisha chuckled.

After he paid for the doll clothes, they found an empty table near the band and sat down across from each other. Chin on her hand, Alisha put her lips around the straw and drew it into her mouth.

Concentrate, Quentin. He cleared his throat. "So why baking?"

She popped the lid off her lemonade and stirred the ice around, and it squeaked against the Styrofoam. "I originally went to college for accounting. But after I dropped out, I had a lot of time to think about what I wanted my future to look like, and I ended up deciding on pastry school. I grew up around food, in the Honey and Hickory kitchen. So I suppose a career in the culinary arts was inevitable. But I wanted something of my own," she said, then smiled. "Don't get me wrong: I can smoke a hog, and Grandpa taught me the secret to killer sauce, but that's his thing. Barbecue felt like reinventing the wheel. I wanted to fly."

"Wings, not wheels," he said.

Eyes alight, Alisha pointed the straw at him, and if he could capture the contagious joy in her smile, oh man . . .

"Yes, exactly. Wings." She poked the straw back into her cup. "I ultimately settled on cookies because they're straightforward. Cakes are pretentious and divisive. People either like the frosting or the cake itself.

Pastries are yummy, but fussy. They're a bit elitist. But cookies?" She plucked out a piece of ice and sucked on it, momentarily distracting him. Then she wedged it in her cheek and spoke.

"Cookies are like jeans—perfect for everyone. You never see someone picking chocolate out of chocolate chip cookies or scraping the filling out of a macaron. You can dress them up or down. And cookies are adaptable. Take chocolate chip cookies. So many possible add-ins. And don't get me started on sugar cookies—sweetened with brown sugar or powdered sugar or agave or honey. Plus, cookies are portable, no silverware required."

She took a breath and stopped with an embarrassed smile. "Sorry, I kinda nerded out right there."

Shaking his head, Quentin said, "Hello, professor here. Nerding out is my love language." Then he froze. Did he just use the l-word? He blinked and rushed on to cover. "Cookies! You were saying how much you love cookies."

Again? Why, why, why?

He rubbed at his sternum with his thumb. "Will that still be your, uh . . . the focus? When you open your bakery in the city? Cookies?"

Alisha nodded. "Yep. But I love to experiment . . ." Her eyes widened.

Okay, so this was catching. It didn't *mean* anything, right?

"I *enjoy* experimenting," she emphasized, "so the menu will constantly change, although I'll have signature cookies available year round. But I want to leave room for new flavors and new techniques."

"For someone who lives with their grandparents, you sure are big on new." If he was honest, that scared him.

"That's an odd thing to say." Alisha went back to sucking the ice, eyes narrowed.

Quentin puffed out his cheeks and slouched down, hand on his chin. "Sorry, just trying to get a full picture."

"I've lived in the same one-stoplight town for over half my life."
She screwed her mouth to the side. "All these years, I've been dying for
the freedom to go my own way, follow my passions, pursue my own
dreams. But I love my family, and I'd do anything for them. I'm trying
to reconcile those two things."

She raised her chin, daring him to speak. He kept his mouth shut,
and she went on, more hesitant. "But I know something's gotta change.
I just have to share my plans in the right way." She smiled. "Also, I need
a name."

He leaned forward again. "Wait, you haven't come up with a name
for your bakery?"

"I've tried! It's not easy, though. Have you ever named a dinosaur?"

"No, but I have a million ideas for when I do. And also, it's depen-
dent on the fossils." He took a sip of tart lemonade. "For instance, does
the skeleton resemble a Teenage Mutant Ninja Turtle? Then obviously
Michaelangeloasaurus."

Alisha laughed. "Okay, if you're so good at this, gimme a name for
my bakery."

"Cookies Galore," he said.

She covered her ears. "Eww."

"Cookies 'n' More."

"There is no 'more.' And is this a bakery or a twenty-four-hour
convenience store?"

Quentin grinned. He loved winding her up. "How about 'Cookies,
Cookies, Cookies'?"

"Wow, Quentin, you nailed it! That's perfect." She batted her eyelashes, then stuck out her tongue.

"Thanks. It's kind of my superpower, naming things." He brushed
off one shoulder. "Does this mean I'm a business partner?"

"Um, no, but you can be my dance partner." She jumped up and
held out a hand. He let her pull him up and over toward the makeshift
dance floor in the center of the tables, smiling like a slap-happy teen.

Alisha wasn't one of his calculated relationships. He responded to her on another level. Physically, emotionally. She slid her hands up onto his shoulders, and his heart chased the sensation, getting wedged in his throat. He threaded his arms around her waist and willed his hammering pulse to slow so it wouldn't drown out the band. When he dared, he stole a glance down at her, and she met his eyes.

"Hey, you," he said. Goose bumps tingled their way up his arms, despite the radiant heat.

"Hey." She smiled slow, red lips curving.

Everything else around them faded. There was only Alisha, her sweet orange blossom scent, the sway of her body under his hands . . .

"I've been dying to kiss you again."

"That makes two of us," she said.

He couldn't resist. "You want to kiss you too?" But a smile wasn't what he craved. He wanted, *needed*, her lips on his. Now. To tame her grin, he tightened his hands around her waist. Pressed his fingers around and down to the small of her back.

Her breath quickened, sharp and fast. He bent his head, capturing her mouth in a hungry kiss. She tightened her grip on his shoulder. Aching, he pulled her closer, slanting their mouths. Her lips were pliant and warm, tongue cool from the ice. He couldn't contain a soft moan and deepened the kiss. Tasting her, savoring her, drinking her in.

Dizzy and breathless, he pulled away, chest heaving like he'd just finished a sprint. He tipped his forehead to hers.

Alisha trailed her soft fingertips down his arm. "You good?"

"Very good," he said, then breathed out a small laugh. "Too good."

"No such thing, Quentin." She caressed the back of his neck, bringing him down for another kiss. This time she parted her lips from the start, slipping her tongue into his mouth, daring him, and he responded in turn, fitting her up tight against him. His hand swept up across her rib cage, and she gasped and sucked on his lower lip, like a reflex. Then she released it and sank back, panting.

Sucker punched, he drew in a shaky breath. She moved her hand to his chest, fingers splayed across his thundering heart, cherry lip locked between white teeth. "What?"

"You," said Quentin. "You're amazing, you know that?"

Alisha's curly lashes swept down against her cheek. Replacing her hand with her head, she nestled into the hollow of his chest. Their breathing settled into a shared rhythm.

When she spoke, her words slipped right into the heart of him. "You're not so bad yourself, Dr. Harris."

CHAPTER 23

ALISHA

They'd danced for a full set, then wandered off in search of more food. Walking backward, Alisha asked, "Funnel cake?"

"Definitely." Quentin caught up to her at the booth, and they placed their orders. She slotted her fingers through his, and at his answering squeeze, a shimmery tingle coursed through her.

A minute later a worker opened the window at the far end and slid two funnel cakes onto the ledge, one dusted with powdered sugar, the other laden with cherry topping. A fan blasted inside the stuffy booth, not doing much to push away the heat, and Alisha stuffed some extra cash into the Styrofoam cup by the window. She pulled her grease-soaked paper plate off the windowsill and stepped aside.

Quentin picked his up and drew the plate close to his face, inhaling.

"Knew you were a keeper."

His brows shot up.

Oh gosh, had she said that aloud? Her face heated, but she didn't shy away this time. "You're a sugar connoisseur. I should've seen the signs." They walked down the street toward a wooden footbridge, the asphalt beneath them radiating heat. "What made you go for the cherry topping?"

"Is this a quiz?"

"Absolutely not." Alisha traded hands, the heat seeping through the paper plate. "I just like picking people's brains about flavor."

He speared three glossy cherries on his fork, eyeing them, then quirked a brow. "It's delicious?"

"Okay, yeah. But why?" She put a hand on his arm to bring them to a halt, and the solid curve of his bicep sent a bolt of energy straight to her gut. Limbs shaky, she used her fork to pierce a cherry. "Take another bite, and this time, close your eyes." His lashes fluttered down, and she slid the fork into his mouth, waiting for him to chew. "What do you taste?"

"Tart. Sweet. Gooey." His eyes popped open—silver-gray shot through with green, precious metals and gemstones. When would she stop needing a defibrillator after that sight? "Sorry, gooey's not a flavor," he added.

"Actually it is. Well, not a flavor, but texture is an important component of what makes a great dessert. Take a cherry pie, for instance. With just the filling, you'd have a bowl of mush." She broke off a piece of funnel cake and held it up. "Tasty, sure, but add crust, and you get crunch, chew. Variety."

They stopped on the bridge and set their plates on the railing. Below them, the water idled along, sluggish in the heat of the day and dotted with water striders.

"So, what do you taste?" Quentin angled toward her, one elbow on the bridge.

Alisha tore off a small piece of funnel cake and went to put it in her mouth, but Quentin shook his head. "Close your eyes."

She twisted her lips but did as he said, letting her eyes drift closed before she popped it into her mouth. The bite melted on her tongue.

Golden oil and toasted flour. Powdered sugar clinging to the roof of her mouth like summer and sunshine. But all that faded away when Quentin stepped closer, cupped her elbows.

Her senses filled with him—earthy spices—cloves and cinnamon and the cleansing hit of ginger. Deep notes of molasses, unique unto itself. Her eyes opened.

"Alisha? What did you taste?" *You.*

"It's delicious," she said.

"Now you're messing with me."

"I'm not." Should she tell him this? "I just . . . I wasn't thinking so much of the funnel cake. I was thinking about you."

"Me?"

"Yeah . . . you know what? Never mind, it's weird."

"I like weird." He waited, one elbow on the railing, and something in his face made her uncurl her fists, open up the pieces of herself she kept hidden, as if Quentin were the moon and her heart a night-blooming flower.

"I kind of associate people with flavors. My grandpa? He's an acquired taste, but the closest I can get is crème brûlée. A caramelized shell on the outside. Burnt, bitter notes. But crack the surface, and you find nothing but sweet custard. And Granny? She's a lemon meringue pie. A classic. Pillowy, silken-sweet egg whites, tamed with a hint of sour lemon and a snap of rich, buttery crust."

Squinting at him, she stopped rambling, feeling naked under his smoldering gray gaze. She lifted her heavy twists off the spot between her shoulder blades and fanned her neck. "Told you it was weird."

"It's not. It's beautiful." He looked down at the water, then met her eyes. "Do you have one for me?"

"I didn't. Before. I tried to figure you out, but nothing ever fit. I think maybe because my doubts got in the way. But now . . ."

"Now?"

She traced her finger along the veins in his arm, watched his breath catch. "A ginger cookie. Not a gingersnap. Those are brittle and grate against your teeth. You're a chewy molasses cookie, the kind that gives when you bite into it, with exciting zings of crystallized ginger and pops of raw sugar." She dipped her chin, leaning on the railing again.

He moved behind her and slipped his arms around her waist, melting her to the core. He placed his mouth right by her ear, his breath tickling her neck. "What I'm hearing is, you like things a little spicy."

Laughing, she craned her neck around to catch the gleam in his eyes. "That's what you got out of that?"

"I heard what I heard."

She kissed him, quick and light; then her phone chimed. An all-caps, zero-punctuation telegram-style text from Hank.

Hank:

WHERE ARE THE POTATOES DID YOUR GRANDAD FORGET THE ORDER AGAIN

If she ever received a text from him with proper grammar, she might worry he'd suffered a stroke.

Alisha:

Check the bins along the back wall.

Hank:

ALREADY DID NO DICE.

She groaned. "Sorry, it looks like we've got to cut this short. I need to run to the grocery store and pick up some potatoes. Heaven forbid we run out of fries."

"Can't have anyone running off to the Back Forty to get their fry fix," Quentin teased. "Can I drive you, at least?" He rubbed his thumb along the inside of her elbow.

Scared to hear his answer, she asked, "Not tired of me yet?"

"Never."

Never. Always. Forever. Fairy tales. But she let herself be swept away in the fantasy. At least for now. At least for today. Never was a long way away.

CHAPTER 24

QUENTIN

Forrest walked backward between packages of toilet paper and bags of plaster, tugging the garden hose toward the pit. He hopped in, then pulled the hose in hand over hand.

"Go ahead and fill up that one first." Quentin pointed to the tall bucket nearest the femur.

Alisha appeared at the rim of the pit and dropped a cooler on the grass. "You guys do know you can use our bathroom, right?" She wrinkled her nose.

Laughing, Caitlyn dusted off her hands. "This isn't a field toilet . . . though, yeah, we'd normally have one of those. It's plaster-jacket day."

Bridget finished cutting open a bag of plaster and closed her pocketknife, squinting up at Alisha. "We're getting ready to prepare the big bones for transport back to Chicago," she explained.

They'd left the largest fossils mostly covered until now to protect them. Today they were digging all around the large fossils, exposing them. Now they would wrap the fossils in toilet paper, then coat that in burlap strips dipped in plaster, which would harden and protect the specimens during transport.

"Gotcha. Well, here's some lemonade, when you're ready for a break." Alisha patted the top of the cooler, then stood. "I'm headed out for a few hours."

Quentin limited himself to a brief nod, his eyes trained on the powdery swirl of water and plaster. Even though they'd agreed to make a go of it, they didn't need a repeat performance of the barn situation.

He ran a hand over curls long overdue for a trip to the barbershop. Good thing he and the crew were headed back home tomorrow for a holiday break. Alisha planned to spend the weekend with her sister, so they'd get time together outside Hawksburg, free from any run-ins with his colleagues or nosy townspeople.

Caught up in his musings, he didn't notice the shadows that fell across the dirt until a voice said, "Dr. Harris? Dr. Reid?"

The reporter shoved the huge microphone back into his face, and Quentin took a deep breath. Just another lecture, no biggie. Bridget's hair lifted in the hot breeze, tickling his neck, and she pulled it down to the other side, shooting him a smile.

"The fossils will need to be analyzed further before we know for sure. But based on our initial findings"—he lifted his chin toward the fossils awaiting plaster casting—"our preliminary guess is the bulk of the bones belong to a single dinosaur, from the Cretaceous period."

"And, Dr. Reid, how does this find impact the future of paleontology?"

"Fossils being discovered in this state offers up a whole new realm of possibilities. We'll be working with these findings for years to come, restructuring our view of the Cretaceous in this area."

"Excellent, thank you, Dr. Reid. Dr. Harris." The reporter turned to face the cameraman. "You heard it here first. Exciting possibilities being unearthed in the small town of Hawksburg, Illinois. And now, back to you in the studio, Liza."

The bright lights switched off, and Quentin stepped back, rubbing his forearm over his sweaty brow. Dang, it was brutal out today, and the heat was fanning the flames of his rising panic.

The reporter was already striding away, but the cameraman shifted the camera off his shoulder. "You guys did great. Really well. You can look out for the interview tonight on channel five."

As if they wanted to see an encore of the very publicity they'd been working to avoid. Teeth clenched, Quentin fished out his cell. He needed to get Dr. Yates on the phone.

"Quentin, we should call—" Bridget started to say, but he nodded and mouthed, "On it" and pointed to the phone at his ear. "Hi, yes. Lawrence?" He stepped a few paces away, toward the side of the house.

A dust plume approached, and Alisha's beat-up car turned into the driveway, swerving onto the grass to pass the van. It rolled to a stop in front of the garage. She jumped out and jogged their way, but he turned his back, refocusing on Lawrence's words.

"Was that a news crew who just left?" Alisha's voice carried on the wind.

He looked over his shoulder and caught Bridget nodding. "Sure was. They ambushed us. Said we could give them an interview, or they'd go ahead and run a story based on hearsay." She shoved her hands in her back pockets. "Do you have any idea who tipped them off?"

Quentin squinted toward Alisha, trying to catch her reply.

"Harris, are you listening?"

"I am, yes. Sorry." He walked farther off, toward the dig, ignoring the grad students huddled at the edge of the pit, where they'd climbed to after finishing their part in the interview—sitting hunched over the fossils, pretending to work.

"Yes, we're all set up to do the field jackets today and bring them back to the lab."

"All right, Harris. Frankly, I'm surprised you were able to keep it under wraps this long. It was bound to come out sooner or later. Let's meet after the holiday and talk next steps."

"Sounds good."

He rang off and strode back toward the house.

"Nothing we can do about it now." Bridget raked a hand through her hair and shook it out. "We won't know how bad it is until the segment airs."

"Not too bad, I don't think." Both women turned toward him, and he rocked back on his heels with a shrug. "At least, Lawrence is handling it well."

"Which was half the battle," said Bridget.

"Exactly. But I am concerned about your family," he told Alisha. "We really didn't want to turn your yard into some kind of sideshow."

Alisha frowned. "I was telling Bridget, I have a good idea who let the cat out of the bag."

"Well, doesn't make a difference now." Frustration clipped his words. Best-case scenario, public interest would blow over during their week away. But if people's curiosity escalated to trespassing on the Blakes' property or messing with the site . . . he dug his fingers into his temple.

Alisha pulled her phone out of her pocket and tapped it against her palm. "I know this is a huge headache for all of you, but I really need to head in and call my grandparents. Figure out a game plan."

As he watched her tense movements, Quentin's heart twisted at the worry they showed. All because of him. "Of course. Go ahead."

"Thanks." Alisha disappeared inside, the bang of the screen door against the frame like the shot of a starting pistol to his fears.

His mind raced with potential repercussions of the news segment, from neutral to devastating. He'd promised Alisha they'd fly under the radar, not bring press to her grandparents' doorstep. And now it was more crucial than ever to get the ilium and femur out of the ground and safely back to the university, just in case this tranquil patch of land turned into Grand Central Rubbernecking Station.

CHAPTER 25

ALISHA

"You don't have to stay here and babysit us." Granny frowned at her, face flushed from the scorching July sun, and pushed her wire-framed glasses higher up her nose.

Alisha ducked her head away from her grandmother's piercing gaze. After an hour spent kneeling in the dirt weeding the front garden, she regretted turning down Granny's offer of a foam mat.

The Hawksburg rumor mill had kicked into high gear after the segment aired on last night's evening news. Grandpa had spent this morning making the rounds of all his friends and local business owners, doing damage control on the dino situation. His biggest worry was people being mad about the story they'd fed them, but so far everyone's interest in the bones seemed to outweigh any grudges.

Ever the opportunist, he'd been talking about renaming their menu items to capitalize on the find, like Brontosaurus Brisket and Mosasaurus Mac and Cheese. The worst of the bunch? Cretaceous Coleslaw. Even Hank had told him to pump the brakes on that one. But Grandpa's reaction had confirmed Alisha's fears. He'd gone full steam ahead, not even considering how Granny might fare.

Gardening and canning tomatoes were supposed to be the biggest excitement in her life, not fending off news crews and the legions of townsfolk who'd stopped by "Just to say hi" and "Oh, by the way, mind if we go round back?"

All the buzz was building up behind a pressure valve inside Alisha, twisting so tight she thought she'd burst. "Now's a terrible time to leave, Granny."

A drone buzzed over the house, punctuating her statement, and she leaped up, but Granny moved quick as lightning, picking up a megaphone and then barking into it.

"Joshua Ames, don't make me call your mother!" At the edge of the tree line stood a figure on a four-wheeler.

"Sorry, Mrs. Blake." The drone zipped away, and a few moments later, the four-wheeler raced off toward the main road.

"See? This is why I can't leave you here on your own." Alisha knelt back down with a groan. She dug a spade into the mulch and uprooted a spiny weed from under the marigolds. "That might work with the neighbor kids, but what about if more reporters show up?"

Hand on the porch railing, Granny sank down on her stool, looking pleased with herself. She rested an elbow on her knee, catching her breath. "I think you overestimate the wow factor of a dinosaur bone. People in town are just excited 'cause it happened here. But it's not like Lady Gaga's camping out in our backyard."

Alisha chuckled, mostly at the idea of Granny playing host to the pop star. She poked her spade around another weed. "Still, I planned the visit before all this blew up. I can just as easily go another weekend."

"Worst-case scenario, what happens, Ali?"

Stomach roiling, she yanked out another weed and threw it into the bucket. "I dunno. I just feel better being here, just in case." She wouldn't say the words, let alone think them.

"I'm not gonna keel over dead because of a little excitement, Ali."

Her eyes snapped up.

"C'mon, child, you think I don't know what you're worried about?" Her grandma leaned forward on her stool to wrench out another weed and then shook off the dirt. "But I'm not fragile—a little fun won't break me."

"That's what this is? Fun?"

Hefting up the megaphone, Granny put it to her lips. "Heck yes, it's fun."

Laughing, Alisha covered her ears. "Okay, I get it."

"Not that I'm not upset my best friend couldn't keep her dang trap shut for once."

Last night Mrs. S had chugged over with a Bundt cake and admitted to spilling the beans in a Facebook post. She laid on the drama with a tearful apology as thick as the stodgy glaze on top of her lemon poppy seed confection. Not like Alisha hadn't guessed who'd let the cat out of the bag the moment she'd seen the news van peel out of the driveway.

Granny set the megaphone down. "Don't try and deny this dinosaur thing hasn't been a little fun, Ali. I haven't seen you this happy in a long time, sweetheart. Maybe since moving back." She brushed stray dirt off the yellow petals of the zinnias. "I think the dinosaur man might have a little something to do with it."

Dinosaur man. Alisha smiled in spite of her worry.

"Granny, he lives in Chicago."

"And? Who knows where your steps might lead you?" She yanked out a dandelion. "I just hate to see you hide away when things get a little rowdy."

"Hiding? I'm not hiding from anything. I'm keeping you safe."

"Keeping yourself safe, more like." Her grandma jammed her trowel into the earth. "It's high time you stopped using me as an excuse not to go after what you want."

Alisha jumped to her feet. Pins and needles shot through her legs, but she ignored them. "Everything I've done is for you and Grandpa.

Sometimes life doesn't work out how we plan, and I've made my peace with it."

Preparing for the worst and keeping up her defenses was the only thing protecting her modest sources of happiness. Love too big, and you get hurt big.

"If you think you're staying for me and your grandfather, you're lying to yourself. And I know you're not a liar. I raised you better'n that."

"Well, maybe you did, and maybe you didn't. After all, you raised my dad, and we all know how he turned out."

With that, Alisha tore off her gloves and stalked inside, slamming the door so hard the frame rattled. She kicked off her Crocs and charged up the steps, then cranked on the shower in the hall bathroom before running up the second flight of stairs to grab clean clothes. By the time she got back to the bathroom, steam billowed out of the doorway, and she couldn't see her reflection in the mirror. Good.

Once in the solitude of the shower, she let hot, salty tears fall. Here, where her weakness would be washed down the drain, she allowed herself to *feel*.

A liar. Worse than being a leaver. Maybe she hadn't lied outright, but she hadn't been truthful either. And the smart-aleck comment about her dad . . . where had that come from? They never talked about her dad. Ever.

But the truth remained: her father's blood coursed through her veins. She'd never deserted her family, but she sure *had* lied by omission to her grandparents and Simone. For years. She slammed off the water, not even sure if she'd finished washing or not.

Dragging a towel across her shoulders, Alisha stepped out of the shower. Tears threatened again, but a couple of deep breaths locked them down in the depths, where they belonged.

She smeared lotion all over her legs and threw on shorts and a tank. After grabbing an armful of toiletries, she took the stairs two at a time and dumped them into her duffel bag. A knock on her door halted her whirlwind of packing. Knowing who'd be on the other side, she opened it, guilt for lashing out nagging her insides. But Granny took one look at Alisha and gathered her in a tight hug. The scent of lavender wafted over Alisha like a calm breeze.

"I'm sorry. I didn't mean what I said about Dad," she said, lips moving against her grandma's hair.

Releasing her, Granny took a step back. "Oh no, I think maybe you did." Warm afternoon light flooded the room. "Ali, I know it's been many years since my son left you here in our care." She reached for Alisha's hands, then clasped them tightly. "But you need to know I've forgiven myself for how he turned out and the decisions he made. Parents are responsible for our children, yes. But once they're grown, they make their own choices."

Her eyelids dropped. "I'll always wonder if I did something wrong with Kenneth." She tightened her lips, and when she raised her eyes to Alisha's again, pain swam in their depths. "I *know* I did things wrong. But I wonder if I could have done more things *right*, to raise a son who wouldn't abandon his own children. But I can't blame myself for his actions, and I also can't hate him for it, because his selfishness gave me two of my greatest gifts." Granny stepped back, bringing their joined hands between them.

"But I need you to know something. Not only am *I* no longer responsible for my son's actions; most importantly, neither are *you*," she said, squeezing Alisha's fingers, hard. "You, little lady, were not and are not, *not ever*, responsible for your father's mistakes."

Alisha shifted her gaze to the side, where a shaft of sunlight lit up dust motes floating in the still air. She didn't believe she was responsible, not really. Just . . . culpable.

But Granny reached under her chin and dragged her back. "I mean it, Alisha Marianne."

Tears welled at the sound of her middle name, and Granny hugged her again, her platinum-crowned head pressed against her granddaughter's pounding heart.

"Oh, sweetheart, please. Please don't take his wretchedness on yourself." She rubbed Alisha's back between her shoulder blades. When she let go, her pale-green eyes were shimmering. "And, sweetie, I'm sorry I pushed you so hard. I guess maybe I thought the tough-love act might bring you out of this funk."

Shaking her head, Alisha said, "No, you didn't do anything wrong. I just . . ." She bit her thumbnail, but Granny tutted and touched her wrist. "Is that what you think of me? That I'm a—" Her throat swelled, and she swallowed hard, but the thickness remained. "A liar? A coward?"

Her grandma raised her eyebrows. "Pardon?"

"You . . . you think I'm scared to fight for my happiness. That I'm using you and Grandpa as an excuse."

"Oh no, honey. I don't think you're a coward at all. But I think maybe I am." A tear traced its way down Granny's cheek, and Alisha's heart clenched. "I saw how happy you've been since Quentin showed up. I saw the light in your eyes. And I got to thinking . . . maybe you've never been happy here, and I've been too blind to see it." Her grandmother heaved a sigh. "I love having you here, Ali. But I don't *need* you here."

"Even with the world turned upside down?"

"If you think one local news spot is enough to turn my world upside down, you must think I'm more of an old biddy than I imagined."

Alisha sniffed out a laugh, dabbing a fingertip to the corner of her eye. "Okay, I'll go, but I'm putting a Google Alert on my phone with our name."

"You'll do no such thing. Matter of fact, I think you ought to go dark for a week. Take a step back. What's it called? Unplug."

"I can't. I have to keep up with my posts."

"Half of them are scheduled anyway, right? Go visit your sister. Spend time with Quentin. Give yourself a chance to live in the moment, without distractions; figure out what it is *you* want. Can you do that for me?"

She could lie and say she would. Granny would never know. But she owed her this much. "Give me till tomorrow. I'll touch base with my followers, schedule a few more posts."

"All right, but then no Google, no Instabook, no nothing. Pretend that phone's got a cord attached. I don't want you obsessing over a little news broadcast all weekend."

"Fine, Granny. I'll give it a shot. Can I go now?"

"Nothing's stopping you."

🐾

Half an hour later, her bags were packed, though she wouldn't leave until morning. She sat on the couch, writing out a must-do list for the weekend staff at Honey and Hickory and trying not to peek over her shoulder out the window every second. But when she heard the rumble of a diesel engine out front, she leaped up.

She stopped at the front door and moved the gauzy curtain aside just in time to see Quentin climb down out of the pickup truck. The sight of a man stepping down out of a truck beat a man climbing out of a puny sports car any day. And *Quentin* hopping out of a truck? *Lordy.*

He reached back into the cab and came out with a pint of ice cream. She stepped out onto the porch, and Quentin shut the truck door, his eyes never leaving her face.

"Hi, beautiful."

Alisha reached a hand up to her necklace, twisting the chain. The midsummer sun cast shadows on the angular planes of his face, the clear depths of his eyes illuminated by the rays. He didn't look beautiful; he looked *gorgeous.* "Hi, handsome."

Grin blossoming into a smile, Quentin held up the ice cream. "Got any spoons?"

"I should've known you'd have homemade cones." Quentin and Alisha stood at the edge of the dig, his arm around her shoulder.

She nestled in closer, eyeing the waffle cone in her hand. "I figured if we're going to keep serving ice cream at Honey and Hickory, we need to step up our game. Commercial ice cream makers are pricey, but a waffle iron, not so much. It's good you brought some ice cream over, though, because I made these this morning, and I have to toss them tomorrow. They're best fresh."

He broke off a bit of cone and popped it into his mouth, then licked the ice cream off his thumb. "They're amazing, just like everything you make."

Ducking her head, she said, "You don't have to do that."

"What?"

"Compliment me all the time." His sweetness left her feeling like an overinflated balloon, and sooner or later someone would come along with a pin. But he pulled away and caught her eyes.

"You do know I'm just being honest, right?" He ran a finger along her knuckles, featherlight. "You think you have fifty thousand followers and a waiting list for your cookies because you're so-so?"

She shrugged. "Not so-so, but you act like I'm the best thing since sliced bread."

He shook his head. "Forget sliced bread. You're the best thing, period."

Searching his face, she found no trace of insincerity. His praise, poured out like a rich chocolate ganache, drenched her in velvet warmth. She dodged her eyes away.

"You make things seem so simple." And not just seem that way. Between her and Quentin, things *were* simple. Life had changed from a hard-edged puzzle piece to a slice of sponge cake. Airy and tender, awaiting icing. The problem? Everything else.

Her grandparents. Her future. Her past.

"How I feel about you is pretty much the only simple thing in my life," he said, and wow, yes. So much yes. Her jaw fell open a bit, pulse thudding in her ears. Then Quentin flicked his tongue at a drip of strawberry ice cream, and her pulse hammered somewhere else instead.

"You gotta stop with that." Alisha gripped his arm, and he went still, muscles bunched and taut under her fingers. His pupils darkened.

"What? Eating?" He licked the cone again, slow, eyes on hers.

"You know exactly what."

He backed up a step. Another. "Enlighten me."

Shaking her head, she followed, intent on showing him he wasn't the only one capable of teaching a lesson, but her flip-flop caught on something in the grass, and she fell forward, crashing into his chest. Quentin stumbled backward and hit the ground, cushioning her fall with his body.

She pressed one hand to the dry grass to leverage herself up, but he put a hand at the back of her neck, urging her down for a kiss. Ice cream forgotten, she pressed her mouth to his. He kissed her back, parting his mouth, his tongue a cool contrast from the warmth of his lips. A drip of something cold on the small of her back sent her upright, off his chest.

He pulled his arm away, revealing a cone dripping with pink rivulets.

One eyebrow quirked, he held up the intact cone. "Told you I had moves." She shoved at his chest playfully, and he grinned, licked at a drip that threatened to run over his fingers, then said, "Didn't even break the cone. Looks like my bad luck's finally on the upswing."

"*Your* bad luck?" Alisha inclined her head toward the chisel she'd tripped over. "I'm the one always falling down around you."

"Tripping isn't bad luck; it's clumsiness."

"Okay, then what's bad luck?"

"Being left at the altar," he said, without hesitation.

"Oh man . . . yes, that does qualify as bad luck. Although I'd have to actually have a fiancé for that to happen." Suddenly the shoe dropped. "You were engaged?"

"Yeah. About a year ago. She broke it off, though." He took his time sitting up, not meeting her eyes.

"So your fiancée . . . she left you." Alisha could hardly bring herself to say it. "She broke up with you at your *wedding*?"

"Rehearsal dinner." Quentin hunched forward, lat muscles flexing against his shirt like he was bracing for impact. "Though she never actually made it there. She, uh . . ." He cleared his throat. "Somewhere between the church and the restaurant, she decided to bail on me. On us. Our relationship. She did send me a text before the main course, though. So there's that."

"A *text*? What kind of heinous person does that?"

Quentin merely shrugged, picking at his ice cream cone.

"You're seriously not pissed about it?" she asked, incredulous.

"Oh, believe me, I've been pissed, and hurt, and angry."

"But . . ."

"But now . . ." He raised his head, squinting down into the prehistoric tableau laid out in front of them. "Now I think it's for the best. Obviously I wasn't what she wanted. At least we didn't wind up in a messy divorce." He swiped a drip of ice cream off the cone, wiped his thumb off in the grass. "I should've seen it coming."

"Are you kidding me, Quentin? You should've expected your fiancée to dump you the day before your wedding?" He flinched, and she instantly regretted her words. He wasn't the one she wanted to hurt. "I'm sorry, I didn't mean it like that." She blew out a breath and hugged her knees to her chest, searching for the right words.

"What I mean is—she said yes. No one gets engaged to someone they don't enjoy being around, to someone they're not in love with. Or if they do, they're the one with issues. I get that you're trying to be kind and noble." His shoulders hunched, and she continued, softer. "And succeeding, by the way. But I'd hate for you to believe this is somehow your fault, or something you had coming. You didn't deserve to be walked out on."

Rolling his shoulder blades down, he uncurled his spine. "You're right, and thank you." He flashed a small smile her way. "I thought justifying it would make it hurt less. Not true, really. The thing is, she and I are both career driven. But I also wanted a family. *Want* a family," he said, and she knew the words were meant for her. Which should terrify her. But it just . . . kind of . . . didn't.

"I think I pushed us toward marriage because we made sense on paper. She was steady and reliable. Or so I thought. Until she literally fled the country to be rid of me. Took a job in Spain." He laughed without humor. "But now I know there was something missing. Something *I* missed."

"Quentin, I'm so sorry."

He swept his gaze toward her, eyes darkening to a slate-gray smolder. "But hey, if Cedes and I would've gotten married, I never would've met you."

Mouth suddenly parched, she swallowed. "Technically you still would have, back in March."

"Mmm, but I would've been married when I met you," he said, voice husky and warm, like a furnace on full blast.

"And that would've been a bad thing?" There was a twisting in her core, painful and sweet.

"Definitely bad, Alisha Blake."

Letting his ice cream cone fall into the grass, Quentin tipped up her chin and kissed her, soft and slow.

Only themselves in the world, and everything made sense.

CHAPTER 26

QUENTIN

Quentin wrinkled his nose against the stink of nail polish and straightened his tiara. His size had saved him from the tutu his nieces had tried to add to his ensemble, but they'd subbed in the glittery blue Wonder Woman cape currently choking off his air supply. Resourceful little devils.

Fifteen or so Barbie dolls lay scattered on the rug, ignored. Candy Land had been kicked halfway under the couch, colorful cards spread in a wide swath. The twins faced off amid the wreckage of a smashed Duplo ice castle.

"I wanna be Elsa!" Liliana stomped her foot, right onto a LEGO brick. She howled and hopped sideways, making a grab for the doll.

"No, me!" Lauryn hid the princess behind her back.

Teetering on one foot, Liliana pointed at her sister. "You're always Elsa!"

"Am not!"

"Girls, girls, enough!" Quentin gingerly pinched the end of Elsa's blonde braid and plucked the doll out of Lauryn's grasp, careful not to smudge any of his pink nail polish. "Nobody gets to be Elsa tonight except me."

"But Uncle Q, I *never* get to be Elsa!" Lauryn balled her tiny hands into fists.

"You *always* do!" Lily argued.

Ready to yell, he chose to sing instead. His terrible falsetto filled the room as he sang out the only three words he knew. The girls instantly hushed. Committed now, Quentin tipped his head back and belted out Elsa's refrain. The bedazzled crown slipped off his head and fell to the carpet.

His nieces dissolved into giggles, rescuing him from further ad-libbing. He sat down cross-legged between them and held up the Barbie. "Now, do you guys wanna hear Elsa sing for real?" He spoke from behind the doll, high pitched, and his squeaky voice sent the girls into another fit of laughter. "I'll take that as a yes." He dropped out of the fake voice to save his vocal cords.

Lily ran over and grabbed the movie while he stood up and freed himself from the Velcro clutches of the cape. He clicked on the TV and popped the disc out of its case, slipping it into the player. By the time he turned around, both girls were settled on the sofa, ragged baby blankets over their legs, staring blankly at the screen. Creepy.

He padded off to the kitchen to get another slice of pizza and plopped down on the arm of the couch when he returned.

"Daddy says no food in the living room." Lily spoke without taking her eyes off the movie.

"And Mommy says no sitting on that part of the sofa," Lauryn chimed in.

"Well, Mommy and Daddy aren't paying Uncle Quentin to babysit, so Uncle Quentin is going to do what he likes," he said, though he slid down off the arm onto a cushion because Vanessa was a force to be reckoned with.

But Hector? Pah. Quentin shoved the greasy pizza into his mouth. Lily narrowed her eyes at him, and he shot her a sloppy grin. His phone chimed from the kitchen, and he leaped to his feet. Wiping pizza grease on his jeans, he tapped in his lock code with a knuckle.

Alisha:
So do you still wanna meet up tomorrow?

Quentin's cheeks lifted of their own volition. Grinning, he paced out into the living room and back, full of nervous energy. Alisha, here, in Chicago. This was beginning to feel real.

Quentin:
Are you asking me out?

No reply came. To distract himself, he grabbed a bottle of water out of the fridge and returned to the living room. Lauryn stood up and walked along the cushions to snuggle up against him. Lily climbed over her sister and onto his lap.

Dang, these girls were the sweetest. The familiar yearning for a family of his own resurfaced, but this time it didn't consume him. If things hadn't gone wrong with Mercedes, he might've become a father last year. For once, he acknowledged that fact without an answering stab of pain. They watched the movie for a few minutes, and then his phone beeped again.

He dragged his numb arm out from under Lauryn and held up his phone.

"Uncle Q, you're blocking the movie!"

"Sorry!" He pulled the screen closer until it was inches from his face and strained his neck backward to read the text.

Alisha:
Well, I have always wanted a curated tour of the dinosaur wing at the Field Museum.

Quentin:

Careful, you might regret it. I've been known to
go full Dr. Grant in the presence of fossils.

Alisha:

Is that a promise? 😳 😏

Quentin:

Excuse me, ma'am, but I don't appreciate being objectified. 😌

Alisha:

Maybe you should try not being so sexy, then.

Quentin's eyebrows shot up right along with his pulse. The phone slipped out of his hand and bonked Lily's head. "Oh, sorry, kid!" He pulled her close, kissing the top of her head.

"Ow! Owie!" Her wails were loud enough to wake the upstairs neighbors, if not the dead themselves. Quentin scooped her up and grabbed an ice pack out of the freezer.

"Sorry, sweetie." He tried to put the ice on her head, but she evaded him like Han Solo piloting the *Millennium Falcon*, so he tossed it on the counter.

Arms wrapped around his neck, Lily blinked up at him with puppy dog eyes. "Daddy always gives me an ice pop when I get an owie."

"Oh, he does, does he?" Quentin was skeptical; then again, his brother was a pushover. He opened the freezer and shoved cartons aside until he found a box of freezer pops. He set Lily on the counter so he could unwrap one and then handed it to her.

"What about my treat?" Lauryn had materialized at his side.

"Yeesh!" Startled, Quentin dutifully tore open another. "What the heck." He grabbed a third for himself and leaned against the counter.

The kitchen subsided into blissful silence, apart from the ticking of the wall clock.

Almost finished with his ice pop, Quentin looked down at Lauryn and gasped. Not the clock ticking, after all. His niece's freezer pop was melting faster than polar sea ice. A steady stream of purple drips slid off her elbow to splat onto the white tile floor.

She raised her arm to lick the trail of juice, and gravity sent the entire freezer pop sliding off the stick like a calving iceberg. It hit the floor, and purple droplets splattered in all directions. Lauryn tilted her head back and started to cry. A second plop signaled the demise of Lily's ice pop, and her howls were a good fifty decibels higher. He resisted the urge to duck and run for cover. Instead, he shoved the rest of his freezer pop into his mouth and bit down on the stick.

Mistake, mistake. Instant brain freeze.

Breathing through his nose, stick poking out of his mouth, Quentin stooped down and picked up both girls, one on either arm, and hustled into the bathroom. He murmured soothing nonsense to calm their tears while he cleaned their faces and hands with some baby wipes he found on the counter. Good enough.

By the time he'd found their pajamas, the twins' sobs had dwindled to sniffles, and Lauryn insisted on a giant stack of books for bedtime stories.

A thousand lifetimes later, the girls were tucked in bed. Quentin wiped up the evidence of the ice-pop meltdown, then tiptoed out to the living room and collapsed onto the couch. The *Frozen* title track played on repeat, but the remote sat on the TV stand, and he was too exhausted to bother getting up again.

Just as his eyes were closing, his phone pinged from under his butt, in the depths of the cushions.

Shoot . . . Alisha—he'd never answered!

Phone overhead, Quentin swiped away a text from his brother saying he and Vanessa would be home in an hour and opened Alisha's thread.

Quentin:
Hey sorry, I got caught up with my nieces.
How about tomorrow afternoon?

Alisha:
Simone and I are going to brunch, but I'm free later.
Wanna meet at the museum at 2?

Quentin:
Can't wait.

Quentin's feet hit the floor with a painful thud. He jolted out of his sleep and caught himself on an elbow just before his head followed suit. "What the heck?"

His brother loomed above him. "This is a new couch."

"You're welcome for watching your kids, jerk." He pushed himself up and peeled off the Candy Land card stuck to his elbow.

"Um, thank you?" Hector swept a hand to indicate the destruction, and Quentin winced. The living room looked like Toys "R" Us after Black Friday stampedes.

His sister-in-law appeared from the kitchen, twisting the cap off a bottle of water. "Thanks again for watching the girls, Q. We really appreciate it." Vanessa squinted at him. "What's that on your fingers?"

Huh? He lifted a hand to his face. "Oh. The girls and I did our nails."

Laughing, Vanessa said, "Hang on." She went to the bathroom and emerged with a bottle and a cotton ball. She caught up his hand and swabbed at the polish. "Did they give you any trouble? Other than making you play beautician."

He thought back to the minor sibling squabbles. Nothing compared to his knock-down, drag-out fights with Hector back in the day. "No, they were awesome. We watched a movie, and they fell asleep about ten."

Hector growled under his breath. "Ten? Their bedtime is eight!"

Fumes from the polish remover caught in Quentin's nose. He sneezed over his shoulder, then shrugged. "It's Saturday."

"Like my babies ever sleep in. Maybe they'll be up at four-thirty instead of four a.m., if we're lucky."

Vanessa swatted her husband's arm and capped the bottle. "You're all set. And what he means to say is 'Thank you.' We owe you one, Q."

"Seriously, no big deal." He held up his polish-free fingers. "You saved me from an embarrassing morning." After wrapping his sister-in-law in a hug, he reached over and gave Hector a noogie on his gelled hair. "I'll give you two lovebirds some privacy to finish your date."

Quentin escaped out the door before his brother could retaliate and jogged down the front steps with a smile. Having his own date set up for tomorrow had a little something to do with his buoyant mood.

CHAPTER 27

ALISHA

Simone leaned back under the scalloped maroon awning outside the brunch spot, one sandaled foot pressed to the brick wall, eyeing her with the unamused glare Momma used to save for their naughtiest antics. "I still can't believe this."

"I was gonna tell you." Alisha nudged a loose chunk of concrete with her sneaker.

"When? When you handed me a wedding program with my name listed as maid of honor?"

"Sim, come on."

"So you're saying I *wouldn't* be maid of honor?" Simone picked an invisible speck of lint off her white jumpsuit. "You know I will *end you* if you make Margaret Thatcher maid of honor."

"Oh my word, Simone. We all know Meg will get married before me. She'll be my *matron* of honor, so your title is safe."

Her sister's topaz eyes flashed dangerously, and Alisha relented. "Kidding, you know I'm kidding." She fanned her face with her palm; the morning sun was already fierce, filtering through the trees planted in the sidewalk. "But Quentin and I aren't even officially dating. Stop trying to marry me off."

Simone blew out through her lips. "'Officially dating.' What does that even mean? I'll never understand your generation and labels."

"*My* generation?" She stepped into the shade of the awning to make way for a couple exiting the restaurant. "You're four and a half years younger than me."

"Four years and ten months equals five years."

"Faulty math."

Simone ignored that. "So how does it feel to be *un*-officially dating your very own Ross Geller?"

A man wearing rolled-up khaki shorts and a muscle tank passed by, walking a terrier. He turned their way, and Simone fanned her fingers in a coy wave.

Alisha flicked her sister's elbow. "Ross who?"

As she rubbed at her arm, Simone's eyebrows twitched together. "You know, Rachel's Ross. From *Friends*. You do realize that dude was a paleontologist, right?"

"Oh my gosh." Alisha's mouth fell open.

"Girl." Simone hung her head like Alisha was an embarrassment. "How did you not make the connection?"

"It's been forever since we watched *Friends*. Besides, you're the one who made me sit through that show."

"Because if it was up to you, we would've watched *Bewitched* reruns every night."

"*I Love Lucy*," Alisha muttered.

"And you say you're not a boomer."

"Whatever. You're just bitter my mind is more sophisticated than yours and didn't immediately make the leap to pop culture when I met Quentin."

"Oh, okay." Simone crossed her arms, and the gold cuff on her wrist flashed in the sunlight. "You're gonna stand there and tell me you and your minion Meg haven't been dropping *Jurassic Park* references since he showed up?"

Tongue in her cheek, Alisha scowled. "I hate you so much."

"Behold, my sister the meganerd." Cackling, Simone struck a Vanna White pose. "But let's circle back to the fact that my chronically single sister is actually dating someone—"

The door opened again, and a twentysomething guy with green highlights and black gauges in his ears came out, propping the glass door open with his back, menus in hand. "Blake, party of two?" He snapped his gum.

"That's us." Alisha was already halfway inside.

"We're not finished, if that's what you're thinking." Simone bopped Alisha's butt with her clutch.

Swatting her away, Alisha hissed, "At least wait until we're sitting down."

Noisy chatter and the power duo of bacon and fresh coffee wafted over her. Her stomach growled.

Simone raised her voice above the din of silverware and conversation, turning sideways to edge past a table. "Why, so you can come up with ten excuses why you should've broken up with him already, before I found out?"

Alisha flinched. Her sister's accusation hit too close to home. If Simone hadn't gotten suspicious about her giddy grins over Quentin's texts last night, they wouldn't even be having this conversation.

But shockingly, talking about him didn't make her want to cut and run. Instead, it was like her heart was a balloon, and telling her sister about Quentin had cut the string. Now she was free but also alarmingly untethered. Could she trust herself with him, with a relationship?

They slid into a shiny red booth, and the host placed menus in front of them, dragging the mini placard with the daily specials to the center of the table. "Your server will be right over," he said, and whisked away.

"I would've told you," said Alisha.

"You wouldn't have." Simone disappeared behind her menu.

"But I'm glad you know." Alisha took off her purse and set it next to her against the wall.

Simone tipped her menu down. "Really?"

"Really." Alisha bit the inside of her cheek. "Quentin is different. I think he's the real deal."

With an eye roll suited for a Broadway stage, Simone said, "Okay, cut the middle-aged slang. What is the 'real deal'?"

Alisha wadded up a napkin and threw it toward her. "We spent like a whole month texting before any of this even started, and it always felt fresh and fun. When we talk, it's like we're the only two people in the world. I don't know how to describe it. He just . . . listens. Plus, he's hilarious." She paused, spinning her butter knife on the table with two fingers. "And, Simi, I think he really likes me."

"Why is that surprising?" Simone scrolled through her phone. "He's not the first guy to like you."

"Maybe not. But he's the first guy to see the real me. The *whole* me," she said. "That's a big deal. Not all of us are heartbreakers when we come out of the womb."

"A backhanded compliment, but yeah, I do have an innate talent." Simone pressed a flat hand to the ponytail she'd slicked back into a pouf. "So when do I get to meet this guy?"

Alisha stopped the knife with her index finger. "Never?"

"Come on, girl. It's time to try something new. Your old MO was *not* working." She reached across and jabbed Alisha's wrist with each word. "Let me meet him." Hiking up one shoulder, she said, "Who knows, maybe I'll hate him, and you'll have a reason to kick him to the curb."

Why didn't that sound appealing? By all rights, this was the point when she should've been begging for an out, not burrowing down deeper into what might be a deluded daydream.

"What happens if you decide to see this through?" Simone asked. "Planning to abandon your beloved Hawksburg for a man?"

The perfect opportunity to come clean. Air out her lie and tell her sister about her yearning to set up a life here, in the city.

Her phone buzzed. Once. Twice.

Simone lifted her palms. "You can get that."

Telling herself that particular conversation could wait—after all, it had waited seven years—she tugged her phone out of her purse. Opened the text.

A picture of Quentin with glasses on and an unbuttoned white dress shirt greeted her. The lenses accentuated the green flecks in his eyes, and a hint of a smile played at the corners of his parted lips. A flash of pecs and way-too-perfect six-pack was visible above the waistband of his jeans. She bit her lip.

"OMG, did he just sext you?"

Alisha clapped the phone to her chest, as good as clutching pearls. "No!"

"Yeah, right." Simone tilted her head sideways, gold hoops catching the light. "You're guilty as all get-out. What did he send you, a dick pic?"

The waitress sailed up to the table with a wide smile. Alisha slumped down in her seat, resisting the urge to continue the slide until she was hidden underneath the table. "What can I get for you ladies?"

How about two eggs with a side of mortification?

"I'll have an egg white spinach omelet," Simone said, holding loosely clasped hands by her cheek, her upturned face a ringer for a baroque saint. "But better bring my sister a smoothie, because she's so *thirsty*." She dropped the pose and planted her fingertips on the edge of the table, locking eyes with Alisha.

The waitress's lips quirked up, and Alisha shot daggers at her sister. "Um, actually, I'll have the raspberry cheesecake–stuffed french toast. Thanks." She kicked Simone's skinny shin.

"Sounds perfect—it'll be right out for you." The waitress grabbed the menus and departed.

"I don't know how we share the same genes."

Simone snickered. "Since the picture is supposedly PG . . ."

"How do you even know there *is* a picture?"

"Are you going to share it or leave it to my imagination?"

With a petty smirk, Alisha said, "I'll take door number two."

"Oh, girl, c'mon."

"Nuh-uh, nope. You took the wrong approach." Alisha kept the phone pressed to her chest. "Maybe one day you'll learn: shock and awe can't win every campaign."

"Fine, I won't push it, on the grounds you at least ask him if we can hang out tomorrow before you leave."

"Sure," Alisha mumbled absently, tipping her phone out for another peek.

Quentin:
Is this appropriate docent attire?

Alisha:
You're making me blush, Dr. Harris.

Another picture popped up: Quentin biting down on the earpiece of his frames. His teeth shone bright white, and . . . oh Lordy, his shirt was gone. Gosh, those round, muscular shoulders, and abs for days . . . she bit her lip against the impulse to run her hands down the smooth expanse of muscle.

Alisha:
Quentin Cecilio Harris, I didn't know you had it in you.

Quentin:
Alisha, there's a lot about me you'd be interested to learn. ☻

A phone inched across the table, propelled by Simone's finger: **Get a room.**

Caught out, Alisha put the phone in her lap, and her little sister shook her head. "Seriously? I'm *right here*. Can't you keep it in your pants for the next few hours?"

"Sorry, sis." She put the phone back into her purse.

Simone tucked her chin back, and her eyebrows shot up. "Wow, that was surprisingly easy."

"Yeah, well, I only get to see my baby sister once in a while." Alisha pulled the container of jelly packets over and started rearranging them by color. "I don't wanna be 'that girl.'"

"Alisha, you could never be 'that girl.' Honestly, I'm thrilled for you. I was beginning to worry." Simone inspected her flawless manicure, and Alisha resisted the urge to sit on her own hands to hide her raggedy cuticles. "Meg hasn't been doing her job."

"Excuse me?"

"You heard me. I counted on her to be my inside man. I was about to cut ties with that giantess if her performance kept plummeting." Simone delivered this perplexing news while leaning sideways halfway out of the booth, her eyes on a group of men seated near the front window. Talk about thirsty.

The waitress reappeared and cleared her throat, sending Simone upright in a rush. She set down two frothy lattes, and Alisha detected notes of hazelnut. *Mmm.* "When did you order these?"

"While you were drooling over your phone." Simone tore open a packet of Splenda and tapped it into her mug.

Alisha blew on the foam and took a tentative sip. "What's this about Meg? Who, by the way, is only like a half inch taller than you."

Stirring her latte with a bent wrist, Simone tapped the spoon and wiped it dry on a napkin. Ugh, so dainty. "You haven't noticed Meg steadily ramping up her efforts to fix you up?"

"Now that you mention it, yeah. That was you?" Alisha slurped down another mouthful of espresso.

She nodded. "Yup. But clearly she sucks at it. Wish I was closer so I could take the reins myself."

"Take the reins of *my* life?"

"Since you've had your foot on the brakes for . . . I dunno, *ten years*? Yeah." Alisha winced at the accuracy of her sister's assessment. "Who knows what would've happened if this prehistoric creature hadn't dumped the perfect guy in your lap."

Why did everyone think she was incapable of finding a man? She'd made a *choice* to stay single. A reasonable, well-thought-out, not-at-all-cowardly choice. But Simone rattled on.

"Jokes aside, you deserve a man in your life, Al, even if it's only for the summer. I may have just found out about him, and I'll reserve full judgment until I meet him, but I know you." Simone took a sip and let her head loll back in pleasure, then put her mug down. "You guard your heart so hard I'm surprised it hasn't turned to coal. But instead it sounds like you found a guy who sees you for the diamond you are. And whether you realize it or not, you're worth it. You deserve happiness, on your own terms."

Alisha sat back, mouth agape. "I don't know what to say."

"Because you've never been able to take a compliment, you ogre." But Simone smiled. "You're the best person I know, sis. And sooner or later, someone else was going to find out."

The best person she knew? What would Simone think when she found out the truth? Would it break her heart to know her sister had been lying all these years? Or would she see Alisha's intentions were pure?

Their food arrived, and talk turned to Simone's new coworker, who'd invited her out for mani-pedis and smuggled in a flask of bourbon to the high-end salon.

At the end of the meal, Alisha covered the check to assuage her conscience, and they walked out into the midday glare. Simone offered to drive her to the museum, but no way. Not until she'd prepared herself for the fallout of her sister getting a chance to see them together and draw conclusions.

And hey, Simone might forget about the whole thing by tomorrow. *Pssh*, yeah, right. Alisha said goodbye with a one-armed hug; then she and the butterfly convention fluttering in her stomach climbed into an Uber, eager to put family troubles aside for her second official very-much-definitely-a-date with Quentin.

CHAPTER 28

QUENTIN

"I see you found your shirt."

Quentin glanced down at his T-shirt, cheeks aflame. "Yeah, you know." He pinched the gray fabric and let it go. "No shoes, no shirt . . ."

"No service?" Alisha grinned up at him, eyes alight. She tipped her head against his shoulder, fingertips brushing the inside of his elbow. By some trick of physics, his face burned even hotter, the heat spreading to the tips of his ears.

"Maybe not the best attire for a museum visit; I'll give you that. But I had zero objections to the topless look." Alisha twined her fingers in his, and a deep tug coursed through his core.

What had gotten into him this morning? He'd never sent a woman a picture like that, not even Mercedes. And he sent Alisha *two*? But judging by the enthusiastic kiss she'd greeted him with on the front steps of the Field Museum a few minutes ago, and her current status, draped over his arm, his gamble had paid off.

"This is new." She pointed up at the towering skeleton of the long-necked titanosaur that stretched up toward the skylights. "And if I remember correctly, last time I visited, that *T. rex* had a lot less meat on its bones." She peeked over his shoulder at the full-scale model, complete with prey dangling from its jaws.

He laughed, seizing the chance to return to solid footing. "Yep. Pretty cool, right?" But nowhere near as amazing as their newfound ease with each other or Alisha's open affection, something he'd never expected. "Sue's skeleton got moved to a new exhibit upstairs. Wanna go check it out?"

Alisha nodded, and they headed toward the stairs. Families with kids of all ages crowded the expansive first floor. Hand in hand, he and Alisha navigated through the throng of couples and tourists wearing Nikons as necklaces, spinning in circles with unfurled maps of the museum like lost pirates.

Usually he came to the museum to work with the fossil collection or with a niece on his shoulders. But bringing a date? Yet another fragment of new pieced into his life. He watched her prance up the staircase in front of him, twists piled in an elaborate knot on top of her head, golden-brown fingers trailing on the carved banister. Bringing her here was a change he could get used to.

At the top of the stairs, a huge replica of the flying prehistoric reptile *Quetzalcoatlus* guarded the entrance to the dinosaur hall, and Alisha pulled him to a stop under its folded wings. "Yikes!"

A mom with a baby in a carrier bounced toward him with a smile. "Did you want a photo with your girlfriend?"

He opened his mouth, but before he could speak, Alisha had stepped around him and was handing the woman her cell. "Sure!" She draped one arm around his waist, then looked up at him. "If that's okay with you, Quentin?"

If that's okay? She just accepted the title of "girlfriend" without even a blink, let alone ducking and running for cover. *Okay?* More like fantastic! He pressed a kiss on her cheek, and the woman held up the phone.

"Aww, you two are so sweet!" She snapped a couple of pictures, then handed Alisha back her cell.

Moving over to the side so other visitors could access the photo op, she thanked the woman, then lifted the screen to flick through the photos, stopping on the last one of them beaming toward the camera. "That beak is no joke! We should've pretended to be scared."

But the first photo made the biggest impression on him: the one capturing his spontaneous kiss. Alisha's eyes were tipped toward the side, her sumptuous lips lifted in a wide smile, their hips glued together. Her fingers gripped his waist, bunching the fabric of his tee.

She so clearly *wanted* to be there, to be with *him*.

He trailed her through the exhibit, his light mood at odds with the dim, atmospheric surroundings and haunting music piped through hidden speakers. His mouth formed sentences on autopilot, leaving his mind free to bask in her nearness, her laugh, and the mischief dancing in her eyes when she mimicked the sinister leer of a small raptor.

"So, Dr. Harris, tell me more about you." She walked backward toward the hulking stegosaurus skeleton. "Your best friend is a White Sox fan." He nodded—he'd texted her once from a baseball game with Tre. "Good for him, because the Cubs suck. You've got a brother—just the one?" He nodded again. "Hector. Two nieces. You have a baseless aversion to sourdough—"

He laughed and interrupted her. "In cookies!"

She stuck out her tongue. "And you work at one of the most prestigious universities in the country. I've gotta say, I've been dying to know more about what you do on a daily basis when you're not messing up my yard. I really hope it has to do with prehistoric DNA trapped in amber and a dinosaur theme park."

Quentin grinned. "Well, I'm not authorized to say much. But you're on the right track." He checked over his shoulder furtively, then crooked a finger, and she leaned toward him, her perfume fresh and sweet, like a candied twist of orange peel.

"We purchased a large island off the coast of Cuba. The first crop of eggs is due to hatch anytime," he whispered, then froze, tongue wedged in his cheek when a boy stopped and shot them a weird look. He waited for the kid to move on, then continued the act of secrecy. "But I'm getting shifty vibes from the slob in charge of security."

With a soft laugh, Alisha brought her lips to his ear, and his abs tightened. "Maybe you oughta pay him more. I hear his currency of choice is Butterfingers and Barbasol," she whispered, then straightened up with a grin.

"Yeah, but he'd just blow it all on pie." He chuckled. "But really, what I do is much more boring."

"Nope, that line won't work on me. Remember, I've seen you in action."

He hesitated, his father's words reverberating in his skull, telling him no one really cared about dinosaurs or his stuffy world of academia. But Alisha stood in front of him, so expectant, like she really cared.

She already knew finding dinosaur fossils in Illinois was a huge deal. What she didn't know was digging up bones was just a small part of his job. He told her that his time in the lab, reconstructing fossils and sifting through data, reframing the way the past spoke to the present, fascinated him the most.

He kept waiting for her to check her phone, or stifle a yawn, but she never did. She asked questions to pull more out of him, rather than shut him up. Her face bore the same rapt expression as when she'd shown him their photos earlier. Earnest. Sincere. Joyful.

"You're so passionate about your work. It's inspiring," said Alisha. "And I'm sure, deep down, your dad is proud of you." She rubbed her thumb along the back of his hand.

That makes one of us.

To change the topic off his father, he said, "Hey, are you hungry? I know a good Mexican restaurant near here. We could go grab some lunch."

"Sounds great." They left the shadow of the looming *T. rex* skeleton, then passed through the Ice Age wing back out onto the balcony. A toddler darted past, chased by her harried dad, and Alisha scooted back, tripping over Quentin's feet.

"Whoops-a-daisy!" She recovered quickly and kept walking. Unable to let this one slide, he outpaced her, stopping in her path.

"Hold up, miss. Did you just say 'whoops-a-daisy'?"

Chin up, she tried to sweep past him. Quentin sidestepped. With a gleam in her eye, Alisha feinted right, then did a spin move, but he grabbed her waist and twirled her around, then set her down with a grin.

"I know, I'm ridiculous." She giggled. "But hey, when your grandparents raise you, kind of hard not to wind up with the vocabulary of an AARP member."

They started back down the marble staircase, worn smooth over the years by countless visitors. Alisha's white sneaker slipped on a step, and she flung a hand out. He grabbed her arm to steady her, loving the curve of her smooth muscles under his fingertips. A shiver went through him, and she looked his way.

"What?"

"It's just . . ." Ugh, he didn't know how to say this. "Your arms are so strong. All of you, really." So much for not sounding creepy. "I, uh . . . I just remember the first day of the dig . . . when Bridget and I showed up, we interrupted your workout. I saw how much weight you had on the bar. That's more than my brother dead lifts, and he hits the gym all the time. It seems like you're really into lifting, but you rarely mention it."

"You remember that?" She gripped her purse, wringing the thin strap in her fists.

"I remember everything about you." He reached out for her elbow, but she clamped it tight against her side.

"What's there to mention? I'm an amateur powerlifter." She shrugged. "Is that a problem?"

They'd reached the first floor, and Quentin turned to her as she descended the final step, her jaw set, eyes hooded.

"Are you serious?"

"Yes, I really like lifting big weights, and I don't intend to stop anytime soon." She dodged around him and continued toward the exit.

He paced alongside her. "No, I meant are you seriously asking if you being a weight lifter is a problem for me?"

"Powerlifter," she corrected.

"My bad, powerlifter. But why would I mind?" She stayed silent this time, and he jogged a couple of steps ahead to hold open the door, but she pushed out the other side. Once they were both outside, he touched her wrist. "Of course your strength isn't a problem for me. I can't believe you'd think that it would be."

She *did* turn toward him then, eyes shooting sparks. His words replayed in his mind, the shift in blame plain to see. "Not to put it on you. If you think that, I'm guessing it's because some loser had an issue with the size of your biceps." The idea was so ludicrous he had to stifle a laugh. "I think it's really cool you lift weights. And anyone who would make you feel bad for your size isn't worth your time."

In the bright sunlight, the dips and curves of her body glowed. Her flowy orange-and-yellow sundress showed off her muscles in a way that had him dying to run his fingertips across the hollow of her back. And whenever the round curves of her shoulder bumped into his arm today, electricity had danced through his body. "Not that my opinion matters, but I think your shape is extremely sexy."

The slow smile she gave him over her shoulder made him regret not saying something sooner. "Oh, it matters, Quentin." She stopped walking and leaned back against the brass banister, ankles crossed. He slipped a hand around her hip, dropping a kiss on her perfect, soft lips. When he pulled away, she said, "But I wasn't fishing for a compliment."

"Mm-hmm, sure you weren't." He winked. She pushed against his chest, grinning, then lifted a hand to shade her eyes. The full expanse of Lake Michigan, edged by city skyline, spread out in front of them.

"I never get tired of this view," said Alisha.

The sun had burned away the haze from earlier. Now there wasn't a cloud in the sky, and the surface of the lake echoed the azure blue above.

"Me either." But his eyes were fixed on her face. She rolled her own eyes and trotted down the first flight of stairs, her dress fluttering against her calves.

Quentin's ringtone sounded, and he pulled out his phone to check the caller ID. "Hey, Ma, what's up?" He slowed his pace, letting Alisha outdistance him while his mom explained the reason for her call. "Oh, okay. Yeah. I'll see what I can do, but it'll be a few hours." He stopped next to Alisha on the sidewalk, and she frowned slightly, head tilted.

"Why can't you come now?" Judgment filled his mom's next words. "Are you working on a Sunday, Quentin?"

"No, Ma. Not working, just busy." He rubbed his forehead. "I'll be over later, I promise."

"All right, *mijo*. I'll tell your dad. Love you."

"Love you too."

He puffed out his cheeks and hung up. "Sorry about that. I shouldn't have answered. Force of habit."

"No worries," said Alisha. "Everything okay?"

"Yep, all good." He rubbed a palm up his forearm. "She and Dad bought the twins a Nintendo Switch, and they're just having trouble setting it up."

"Aren't the girls kind of young for a gaming system?"

"Probably." He reached an arm across his chest, hugging one shoulder. "But they're my parents' only grandkids, and 'spoiled' doesn't begin to cover it."

She nodded in understanding. "Gotcha. Can't Hector help?"

Quentin raised both hands. "Right? You'd think. But my brother's about as technologically inept as the Neanderthal we just saw." He jerked a thumb over his shoulder toward the museum.

Alisha laughed. "You'd better go help them, then. I'll just see you when you get back to Hawksburg."

"No, there's no rush. We can still go eat." He caught her hands in his, stepping closer. "Actually, I have an idea. But remember, you can always say no. Got it?" She nodded, a small line appearing between her brows. "You're hungry, right?"

The line deepened, but she nodded again.

Was he nuts? Maybe, but he was going for it. "Wanna come with me to my parents'? Whatever my mom's making for Sunday dinner is bound to be even better than the place I had in mind."

She blinked at him, and he swung their hands between them, schooling his face into neutrality.

After a moment, the silence became too much. He squeezed her hands gently. "You can say no, Alisha. It was just an invitation."

This time she turned her face to the sparkling waves.

"You know what? Never mind, it was a crazy idea," he said, stomach bottoming out as he shifted his feet.

"Nooo . . ." Alisha spoke toward the horizon, the wind carrying her words away, and though his heart was sinking like a rock dropped into the watery depths, he kept his tone level.

"Cool. I'll just head over after you and I eat, then." He released one of her hands, intending to lead her down to the street, but she grabbed for his fingers and licked her lips.

"No, not crazy. I meant . . ." She stepped closer into his embrace and threaded his arms around the small of her back. The beat of his heart switched to a thudding hammer. "Yes. I'd love to go meet your family, Quentin."

CHAPTER 29

ALISHA

Alisha stuck her tongue out in concentration and snapped the puzzle piece into place on the hardwood floor. No easy task with a forty-pound child bouncing on her back, gripping the tendons of her neck like a sailor scaling the rigging of a ship.

"Over there, Miss Alisha! The rest of Maui's hook is right there, under Lily."

Liliana lifted up her bare foot, and a puzzle piece came with it. She giggled and tugged it off, then passed it to Alisha.

"Why don't you put it in?"

With a shy smile, Liliana took the piece back and snapped it into place. Despite the fact Lauryn was slowly asphyxiating her and she'd normally rather get a bikini wax than put together a jigsaw puzzle, Alisha had to admit she was enjoying herself. She hadn't been around kids much since babysitting gigs in high school, but these girls were precious.

With the puzzle complete, Lauryn finally released her grasp of Alisha's neck, and she took a gasping breath. That child had the grip of a honey badger.

"Your hair is so pretty." Her breath hit Alisha's nose, sharp with onion and garlic from the fresh salsa Quentin's mom had served with dinner. "Isn't her hair beautiful, Lil?"

Dark eyes serious, Liliana nodded.

"Thanks, girls." She swiveled around to smile at Lauryn. "Your hair is gorgeous too. And so is yours, Liliana."

Patting a small hand along her cornrows, Liliana dipped her chin with a shy smile.

"You can call her Lily. She likes it better." Lauryn knee-walked across the purple rug to sit down next to her sister. "Did your momma do your hair?" Lauryn flipped the end of one of her own curly pigtails, tiny nose wrinkled. "I hate sitting still for Mommy. But she lets me watch YouTube videos."

Alisha shook her head. "No, my mom didn't put these in, but I did have to sit in the chair for-ev-er," she confessed. "My butt even fell asleep."

Dissolving into giggles, Lauryn fell backward. "You said 'butt'!" Both girls erupted in howls of laughter.

Oops. The floorboards creaked behind her, and Alisha twisted around to see Quentin in the doorway, his face inscrutable.

"Girls, we got the Switch working. Why don't you go check it out?" He hooked a thumb over his shoulder. The twins shrieked and trampled over the puzzle, slipping in their rush.

"I get to go first!"

"No, me!"

Reggie's deep baritone reverberated down the hall, telling them to calm down. Quentin sighed. "Sorry for that."

Alisha flicked her hand. "*Pfff.* They're great. All kids are loud."

He stuck one hand in his pocket, leaning against the doorframe. "I meant, asking about your mom. Lauryn can be really pushy."

"Quentin, she's five. I get it."

He nodded, solemn.

239

"My mom did love to do my hair, though." Alisha played with the end of one of her twists. "She used those big plastic barrettes. Loud colors, you know? Neon green and bright yellow. And hair bands with big glittery balls on the end." She smiled, smoothing a hand along the sunburst fabric of her skirt, but pain pooled below her breastbone.

Quentin's eyebrows pinched together, and he ran fingers under his jaw. "Seeing the girls . . . I didn't think about how it might feel for you."

She held up her hand. "No, no, not at all. It was really great to meet them. To meet your family." Uncharacteristic tears welled under her eyelids, and she tucked her head, rolling the hem of her dress between her fingers, fighting to compose herself. Quentin sank down to the floor next to her, warm and solid, and one of his arms came around her shoulders.

The gesture undid her hard-won floodwall, sending tears crashing through the breach. They overflowed and ran down her cheeks. Face pricking with shame, she burrowed into his chest, and he wrapped his other arm around her, holding her tight.

No one spoke, and the room faded away, the pain thrumming but dull. Tears at bay, she trusted herself to talk again and wiped a palm down her face. Hiding in his arms reminded her of the shelter of her favorite maple tree. She inhaled a shaky breath. "I'm sorry. I really am fine. It's just . . ."

Tears built behind her eyes again, and she took a moment to breathe them away. "Talking to the girls reminded me. After Mom died, my dad had no idea how to do my hair. And he was so sad; I didn't want to keep asking him for help. I tried to braid it myself, but it looked a mess. I started wearing headbands to school every day, and when that wasn't enough, I tied on a scarf."

She paused, remembering how embarrassed she'd been to show up to class. "My teacher pulled me aside and told me I was violating dress code. No hats or hair coverings." She recalled the intense shame. How the teacher's reprimand had piled guilt on her humiliation.

"When I took off the scarf, my hair was a ratty disaster. All matted in some areas, fro-ed out in others. Of course, kids thought that was hilarious." She wiped her nose. "Anyway, didn't matter. I only stayed at that school for a year. I got a fresh start when I moved in with my grandparents." She didn't mention that the first thing her grandma did was cut her hair short.

And she couldn't blame Granny, faced with the mess her son had left behind. She didn't know what to do. And losing her hair? Just a drop in the bucket of Alisha's sorrows.

Hair grew back, but not parents.

"What about your dad?"

"What about him?" Hardness crept into Alisha's chest, tightened her vocal cords. "He took us to visit Granny and Grandpa the summer after Mom died, like always. He left to go back to the city for work on Monday, and he never came back."

There it was. The sob story she seldom sobbed over. The embarrassing, dysfunctional family history she kept under wraps. She'd watched enough friends' faces fall when they found out the whole truth to know how bad the situation made her look. The girl whom no one wanted.

Leaning back, she detached herself from Quentin's comfort. Good to get it out there, actually. Telling him would nip whatever this was between them in the bud. He would feel sorry for her and slowly distance himself, not wanting the stain of her past to mar his future.

The stark truth of her father's cowardice gave their relationship an expiration date. Saved her the pain of an inevitable future breakup. But Quentin spoke up before she could drag herself away. "Your dad is an asshole."

Running her fingers through the fibers of the shag carpet, Alisha shrugged.

"Seriously, Alisha." He scooted closer and rested a hand on her knee. "Anyone who'd walk out on his family, on his own daughters, who'd lost their mother? I've never beat anyone up, never thrown a punch and meant it. But if I ever meet your father, I'll gladly knock him out flat."

Alisha rubbed a finger along the erratic pulse at her wrist. His anger was the opposite of most people's unwanted pity. But perversely, she found herself rising to her dad's defense. "He was hurting. He lost his wife. The love of his life."

Squaring his body to hers, Quentin rubbed the pads of his thumbs along the front of her shoulders. The heat in his palms seared its way to her heart, cauterizing the pain.

"Which would give him all the more reason to keep the two people he loved most in life close."

She opened her mouth, but Quentin wasn't finished.

"He failed you, Alisha. He's a total, one hundred percent loser. And not only that: he lost out on a relationship with one of the most incredible people I've ever met. It's completely despicable."

Her face crumpled again. He wasn't wrong. In fact, he was 100 percent right. Which was why she had to keep her distance. Because her dad was a leaver. So *she* was a leaver. A loser, like Quentin said. Only a matter of time.

Seeing her face, he squeezed her tight against his solid chest, the steady beat of his heart slowing hers. They sat that way for a long time, until she became less aware of her pain than of his presence.

A deep voice shouted from the living room. "Q, what're you doing back there? I need your help with these stupid controllers!"

Alisha cocked an eyebrow at him. "Q?"

A corner of his lip turned up, and he pulled one shoulder to his ear. "That's what my family's always called me."

"Suits you," she said, voice scratchy. She cleared her throat, pressing the heel of her hand to her damp cheek. "Best get out there before they come looking."

"Nah, they can wait." Quentin stroked his thumb gently along her chin. "This is more important."

"No, I'm fine." She sniffed, unbearably, and gave him a close-lipped smile. "You go. I'll be right there."

"You sure?"

At her nod, he tipped up her chin and kissed one of the tear tracks on her cheek, whisper soft, then stood and walked out.

Alisha lingered, picking up the puzzle pieces and setting them in the cardboard box. She'd just crumbled to bits in front of a man, something she'd never once done in all of her twenty-nine years. And he'd been able to handle it, hadn't shied away. Her world shifted into focus, somehow intact, and flooded with light. The realization Quentin was behind the new perspective shook her to the core.

Before she could overthink the effect his response had had on her, she unfolded herself from the floor and walked out to the small front room, where Quentin and his brother were messing around with a TV housed in a sturdy oak entertainment center. The twins jumped around, controllers raised above their heads. Reggie sat in a corner of the tan sectional. He squinted at one of the video game cases under the benevolent gaze of Our Lady of Guadalupe, a ceramic dish of rosaries at her feet. The women were nowhere in sight, so Alisha peeked into the kitchen.

Isabel stood at the stove, one hand on her plump hip, a metal spatula in the other. She gestured with it as she spoke to Quentin's sister-in-law, a tiny woman with a huge smile, her hair cropped short at the sides, shiny coils longer at the top, styled with a deep side part. Vanessa was cutting open a bag of powdered sugar with kitchen shears. Her smile grew impossibly wider when Alisha walked in.

"I see my girls didn't destroy you yet."

Alisha laughed. "Nope, still in one piece."

Vanessa chuckled. "Thanks for playing with them. My sisters all live in Baltimore, so the girls soak up any female attention they can get."

"Oh, I had fun! I don't have any nieces or nephews, so it was a nice change of pace."

Pencil-thin eyebrows arched, Isabel regarded Alisha over her shoulder. "No brothers or sisters?"

"I do have a sister, actually. She lives in the city. Logan Square. But she's not looking to settle down anytime soon. She's only twenty-four."

With a sniff, Isabel turned back to the stove. "What about you?"

"Me?" Alisha's voice squeaked out.

Steam curling her bangs, Isabel turned her way again. "Any plans to settle down soon?"

Bunching her dress in her fists, Alisha swallowed. "I hadn't given it much thought, actually. Not until recently."

She hadn't admitted that to herself yet, and now she was spilling it aloud—to his mother, of all people? But Isabel's face relaxed, and she turned back to the stove. Just then Quentin strode in, his heather-gray tee hugging his chest, legs long in fitted olive shorts. He towered over his mom by nearly a foot, but he stooped down to plant a kiss on the top of her head.

"Mmm, sopapillas!" He rubbed his palms together, eyes alight. "Alisha, Ma must like you a lot. I haven't gotten these in almost a year!"

Isabel swatted at him with the spatula before using it to flip the puffy piece of dough. "I'm only making these because they're Lily's and Lauryn's favorite."

Hands cupped to his jaw, Quentin mouthed, "She likes you." Then he walked over and slipped an arm around Alisha's waist, tugging her close. She couldn't say she minded the PDA, not one bit. She felt affirmed, welcomed.

Despite Isabel's pointed questions, his whole family swallowed her up just like Quentin's comforting embrace. Dinner had been filled with overlapping chatter and good-natured ribbing, something Alisha missed. Ever since Simone had left for college, things at the farmhouse had been too quiet. The noise and energy in this house were contagious.

And the love swirling through his parents' home? Familiar, and every bit as welcome.

But thinking the l-word with Quentin's arms around her had sent her into a tailspin. She flailed around for something to say. "So did you see Quentin on the news the other day?"

"News?" Reggie entered the kitchen, and Quentin's arm tensed around her. He hadn't told them? His dad frowned at her, and Isabel tipped a golden-brown sopapilla onto a paper towel–lined plate, then turned, hands on her hips, to give Alisha her full attention. *Uh-oh.*

"Um, yeah." She glanced up at Quentin. A muscle in his jaw clenched, and worry shot through her limbs. "He and the other paleontologists were interviewed by a news crew about the find. It's pretty—" Reggie crossed his big arms, and she gulped. "It's pretty historic."

"Historic? More like *pre*historic." Hector walked in, snickering.

Oh gosh, Hector too? He joined his father at the doorjamb, and shoulder to bulky shoulder, the two men blocked out all light from the front room. The kitchen went dead silent.

Was it hot in here? Just the stove, right? Not because she'd somehow outed Quentin to his family. How did they not know this?

Reggie's gaze flicked from her to his son. "You mean to say the dig you're working on downstate is a big deal?" His voice rolled out like a freight train, and she wished she could see Quentin's reaction.

"No, not really a big deal." He spoke without emotion, but he gripped her tighter, as if for support. His shirt rucked up as he raised a too-casual shoulder. "Just unique."

No way could she let him downplay his achievement.

"It actually *is* a big deal." Addressing them from the shelter of his body gave her courage. He'd supported her dreams; she could do the same for his. "You guys do know there's never been a dinosaur discovered in Illinois, right?"

Isabel stared back at her, face impassive.

"Really? He hasn't told you?"

He let go of her then and stepped away, waving a hand to dismiss the magnitude. "There hasn't been. But we always thought there might be. Not a total shock."

Reggie was squinting now, pinning her under his iron gaze.

Hector spoke up. "Lemme get this straight. My little brother discovered the first-ever dinosaur bones in the whole state, on your land." He pointed at Alisha, and she nodded. "And he's now world famous. And we, his family, are the last to hear about it?"

Oh gosh. She hoped that was a rhetorical question. Quentin's jaw bunched, and her pulse skyrocketed straight up through the popcorn ceiling.

"Well, it's no cancer cure, but I guess my youngest son has finally done something right. 'Bout time!" Reggie punctuated this bizarre declaration by tugging his son in for a half hug, but Quentin's back was ramrod straight, his triceps tensed and rigid.

Hector pulled his phone out of the back pocket of his jeans. "Which news outlet ran the story?" he asked, typing with his thumbs.

"Um, all of them?" Alisha spoke quietly. Isabel's eyebrows disappeared into her wispy salt-and-pepper bangs.

A hiss and pop sounded from the hot oil. Alisha's nostrils flared, catching the acrid smell of burnt dough. The smoke alarm sounded, and the kitchen descended into chaos.

A while later, Alisha and Quentin stood out on the empty sidewalk in front of the house.

"I'm so sorry, Quentin. I had no idea your family didn't know about the dig."

"It's not your fault." He paced a few steps away, then swung around. "And my family *did* know about the dig, but I told them it was regular summer fieldwork. I didn't think they'd understand the significance."

"Of the only dinosaur discovered in the whole state, ever?" Anyone would understand the importance. His reasoning didn't add up.

"Not everyone's as obsessed with dinosaurs as you and I." Quentin kicked at a tuft of grass growing through the uneven concrete.

She held on to her elbow, scratching a spot where a mosquito had found her. "Granted, but I don't think you're giving them enough credit."

"Only because they give me *none*." He groaned and clasped his hands behind his head. She tried not to be distracted by the way his biceps bulged. "Look, Alisha, I know I have no cause to complain." His tone softened. "My parents are both still alive, and together, in my life."

Alisha shook her head. "That's not everything. I'm not naive enough to think just because they're here, everything's perfect. Tell me what's going on."

Dropping his elbows, he faced the street, lined with parked cars. "You know my dad's never approved of my decision to go into paleo. Since I was a gifted kid, he wanted me to be a doctor or a lawyer. Maybe an engineer. Not just for the money, though I call him out on that, but more so for the prestige. He wanted to know his son was successful."

"But you are successful!" She couldn't believe Quentin's father couldn't see his son's career excellence. Not just anyone was on tenure track at Chicago Northern University.

"Not to him."

"And you don't think the acclaim over this excavation will make him rethink things?"

"One interview isn't going to change his mind, Alisha."

Not knowing how to dispute that, she came up behind him and engulfed him in a hug, head pillowed between his shoulder blades. He inhaled sharply and stroked a hand up her arm to her wrist. Then he turned to face her, settling his hands on her hips.

Dusk faded into darkness around them, the hum of a lawn mower in a neighbor's backyard kicking up the uniquely summertime scents of fresh-cut grass and gasoline. Nostalgia and belonging. Home.

They remained face to face for a moment, gazes locked, before she lifted her mouth to his, and he captured her lips in a kiss full of yearning. A vibration pulsed against her hip, and she pulled back, chest heaving. Knowing there was no putting off Buzzkill Simone, she answered.

"Please tell me you invited your boy toy to the beach tomorrow," her sister said by way of greeting, and Alisha winced at the volume.

"As a matter of fact, I hadn't."

"You're still with him, aren't you?" She caught Quentin smiling down at her, half-shadowed in the glow of the streetlamp. "I expected you back like an hour ago."

"I know, I'm sorry." He ducked his head and nuzzled the hollow of her neck, sending delicious shivers down her spine. "I should've texted."

"Give him the phone," said Simone.

"I will not." She fisted her free hand in the soft fabric of his shirt and feebly pushed him away. "Your family's right inside!" She craned her neck to check over her shoulder, but he splayed his long fingers against the small of her back, drawing her close.

"Ma always closes the drapes at seven o'clock sharp," he murmured against her neck.

Her sister's snippy tone came over the airwaves. "Does Pops know the guy digging up his lawn has his tongue down your throat?"

"Simone, why is it always threats with you?"

"Because you don't respond to reason. Quit with the heavy breathing already and pass him the phone."

With a growl, Alisha handed the phone to a heavy-lidded Quentin.

He lifted it to his ear. Nodded. "Yeah, sure thing. Sounds good." He hung up. "Apparently I'm joining you at the beach tomorrow." He slid the phone into her purse without taking his eyes off her, hands drifting back up to cup her jaw. "She also says to put you in an Uber because I'm monopolizing you."

He dipped his head toward her again for a deep kiss, his tongue sweet from the honey he'd drizzled on his sopapilla. Alisha let her head fall back as he traced kisses down her neck to her collarbone, his arms gripping her, offering support when her knees turned to jelly.

Then he slid his hands under her thighs and lifted her, carrying her backward until tree bark bristled against her spine. She arched her back, shuddering at the firm pressure of his hips. "But I don't think a few more minutes will make a difference . . ."

CHAPTER 30

QUENTIN

As Quentin's shoes pounded the pavement, warm wind buffeted his chest, the concrete Lakefront Trail suffused with rosy predawn light. He relished the peace these morning runs brought him. The trail was relatively quiet at this time of day, though stalwart bikers and runners dotted the path.

Lake Michigan would be crowded with boats by midday, but for now the surface lay placid, the hulls of moored sailboats reflected on the mirrored surface. The slap of water against the wave breaks punctuated the quiet hum of traffic.

His watch lit up with a glow, displaying just under an eight-minute pace. Not bad for mile twelve. A few miles farther he slowed to a walk, recovering as the first rays of sun crept over the horizon. Once he'd cooled down, he stood by the edge of the water and reached into his pocket.

In the palm of his hand, sunbeams glinted off the engagement ring he'd gotten for Mercedes. He'd already told Hector to get rid of the wedding band back in March. Now, without the smallest trace of remorse, he cocked his arm back and hurled the diamond ring out into the lake.

Mercedes would always be a part of his past, but he no longer wanted her in his present.

Alisha now, and maybe, just maybe, Alisha always.

"Wait, she still hasn't told you?" Alisha's sister tipped her giant sunglasses down, revealing light-brown eyes and a smattering of freckles on her high, round cheekbones. In the past half hour since Quentin had arrived at the beach, heart in his throat at the prospect of meeting another member of Alisha's family, he still hadn't quite found his bearings among the sisterly dynamics.

"Simone, cut it out." Alisha sat on a towel across from him on the crowded beach, her cheeks flushed, but maybe just from the heat. The sand was blistering—it had to be at least ninety-five out here in the blinding sun.

Adjusting his aviators, Quentin asked, "Told me what?"

Simone hooted and slapped her knee. She was tall like her sister, but that's where the similarity ended. Unlike Alisha's soft curves, Simone was all angles and sharp edges, from her thin limbs to the pointed once-over she'd given him when he'd first arrived. Pushing her sunglasses back up with one finger, she shifted forward, spreading out her elbows and rubbing her hands together. "Oooh, this is good."

Daggers shot from Alisha's eyes. "Simone Eleanor Blake, I swear if you tell him, I will beat you back to your apartment and kidnap Mr. Flouncy."

"You wouldn't dare," said Simone. "You know his one good button eye is hanging on by a thread. He'd never make it."

"Try me." Alisha crossed her arms, and the effect it had on her bikini top caught Quentin's attention.

"Okay—but, Al, I feel like theft isn't something you should hide in a relationship." Simone's smile returned.

At the word "relationship," his heart kicked up a notch, but he was also a little concerned by another word. "Theft?"

Under Alisha's glare, her sister desisted and rooted around in her beach bag. She produced a can of sunscreen and unleashed a steady spray at her stomach until the coconut-scented mist had filled the air.

Coughing, Alisha waved a hand in front of her face. "Okay, okay. *Sim*-mer down."

"Girl, quit." She aimed the sunscreen like a canister of pepper spray, and Alisha lifted her arms in defense. Simone chuckled and slid it back into her bag. "I can't believe you'd play like that in front of your man."

"He likes it." She tipped up her chin and grinned at him. "You like my cheesiness, right?"

Quentin nodded. He did.

Simone poked a finger into her open mouth, miming puking. "That makes one of us. But you're not going to distract me that easy, sis. Tell the man what you've got in your closet."

What *did* she have in her closet? A wardrobe full of shoplifted items? Stolen antiquities? Quentin was—justifiably, right?—freaking out a little. "What's in your closet, Alisha?" He poked her sweat-slick knee with his finger.

She threw her arms up in defeat. "Jeez, fine." With a final scowl at her sister, she muttered, "Your hat, is all."

"My what, now?"

"Your beanie. From the day we first met." She shrugged one glistening shoulder. "You left it at the house after you came out to investigate the bone."

"And she kept it." Simone grinned. "Like a creep."

"I just forgot to give it back," Alisha protested, but her lowered gaze suggested otherwise.

A smile crept onto Quentin's cheeks. He leaned toward Simone. With his eyes on Alisha, he lifted a hand and spoke behind it in a stage whisper. "I gotta ask. Is this a pattern with your sister? Holding on to stuff from guys she doesn't even know? Does she have a shrine full of pilfered stuff from other men I should be worried about?"

Simone grinned. "Great question. As far as I know, you're the first. Though whether that's flattering or—"

Alisha grabbed the brim of Simone's hat and yanked it off. "You're a punk, you know that?"

Simone raised her voice, pretending like her sister wasn't even there. "You know, if I had to guess, I'd say she still wears your hat sometimes. Like at least once a week."

Quentin started laughing.

"I absolutely do not." Alisha threw the sun hat back at her sister, indignant. "I *do not* wear it once a week, or at all. Like she would even know. She doesn't even live near me!"

Quentin descended into spasms of laughter, and she whirled on him.

"You find this hilarious, don't you?" Her bikini string slipped, and she reached up to retie it. "Excuse me for thinking you smelled nice," she said, chin tucked to her chest.

Unable to catch his breath, he pounded the sand.

"Okay, dude, it's not *that* funny." Simone had stopped laughing. She frowned at him like he ought to be committed to a mental hospital.

He just laughed harder. "You didn't think *I* smelled good." Palm pressed to the burning sand, he coughed the words out between guffaws. "You thought my . . ." Quentin howled. "You thought my bro-bro-brother did." He collapsed onto his forearm, laughter overtaking him again.

"I don't follow," said Simone, but Alisha's eyes widened.

"It was *Hector's* hat?"

Abs cramped from laughing so hard, he nodded.

Alisha covered her face with her hands. "Oh my gosh. I feel like such a moron."

"Real talk," he said, "you've probably had that beanie longer than I did. I found it in the truck on the way over."

Behind her hands, Alisha groaned.

"Hey." Quentin's chuckles receded, and he sat up to close the distance between them. He splayed one hand on the sun-warmed skin of her thigh and tugged at her wrists until she dropped her hands. "Hey, I'm flattered you were into me from day one." He leaned in and pressed his lips to hers in reassurance. But midkiss, his stomach shook with laughter again, and she shoved him away with a shake of her head. He fell back, tugging her on top of him.

"Ahem . . . guys, I'm literally right here," Simone said, brushing sand off her straw hat.

"Anyway"—Quentin smirked up at Alisha from where he lay sprawled on the towel—"Hector will be happy to get his hat back. If you're done wearing it to bed, that is."

"Hey, no one ever said I wore it to bed!" Alisha lunged at him, and he crab-walked backward a few feet, then stood, kicking up sand as he tore off toward the lake. He whirled back around just before she slammed into him and tackled him down into the cold water.

When he came up, she smiled into his eyes. Their lips collided, her arms sliding up the back of his head, and he angled deeper, kissing her until they were both breathless.

Droplets of water glistened on her dark lashes. "Hector can have his stupid hat back, but you'd better not say a word about me wearing it."

Quentin raised a brow at her, slipping a hand up under her knees to cradle her, weightless in the chest-deep water. "Oh, so you did wear it?"

She bit her lip, toying with his earlobe. "I thought it was yours. And I didn't sleep in it so much as lie in bed wearing it."

"Oh yeah?" His heart beat faster.

"No, of course not, you weirdo!" She laughed and shook her head.

Then they were kissing again. He caressed her rib cage, reveling in the feeling of her body in his arms.

A lifeguard paddled by on a kayak, and Quentin glanced toward shore. The current had shifted them farther down the beach. He set her down and swam a short distance through the waves, then flipped onto his back, floating.

Alisha caught up, face serious. "So my grandparents said things have calmed down at home. Looks like it may blow over. Any word from Dr. Yates?"

"No. We're still on to meet tomorrow, and I figure no news is good news. The dig will make waves in the scientific community, but as long as the general public isn't overly interested in it, your family should be out of the spotlight."

"I appreciate you looking out for us."

"Of course." Quentin put his feet down and stood up, the water lapping at his waist. "Speaking of your family, did you tell Simone about your plan to move?" Shoot, where had that come from? But he couldn't well take it back.

"No." Alisha gazed out toward the horizon. "I found out this morning someone else leased the property I had my eye on."

"Do you have more options?"

"As of now, only one," she said.

"So lock it down! Then you can tell Simone."

"It's not that easy." Alisha pushed wet curls from her face. She must've taken her twists out last night. He loved her hair loose and natural, loved all her different looks, her vibrant clothes, her unabashed nerdiness. He loved everything about her.

Everything except this.

"Why? Why are you making it so hard?"

"I still haven't told my grandparents, for one." Her gaze flicked to the shore, and she ran her fingertips through the water.

"But you will, so what's the problem?"

"I dunno, Quentin. Maybe losing this property is a sign. Maybe I'm not meant to move."

Not meant to move? "Then what are we even doing here?" He ran a trembling hand up his arm, chest tight.

"What do you mean?"

"I mean, why did I even come here today?" Spots danced at the edge of his vision. "We have no future if you don't move."

Alisha's nostrils flared. "Are you serious right now?"

Was he?

"It's not like moving was my idea, Alisha." Why was she being so unreasonable? "Not like I'm trying to get you to alter the course of your life for me. You *want* to be here in the city. Listen, I'm up for a long-distance relationship. But I'd have to know, down the road, we could be together for real. Otherwise, what's the point?"

"Wow. Just wow, Quentin. Great to know you'd sacrifice for me. That you're not putting me on a timetable. How gracious of you." She pushed past him and churned through the water toward shore.

"Alisha, wait!" Desperate to talk without her sister around, Quentin hiked up his knees, splashing through the shallows. He angled in front of her to block her retreat.

"I'm sorry. I didn't mean to lay it out that way. It's just—" He ground his teeth together, fighting for the right words. "You don't really mean what you said about not moving, do you? So when are you going to tell Simone, if not now? You're this close to leasing a bakery." He pinched a thumb and forefinger together in the air, then brought his hand down to hers, winding their fingers together under the water. "How have you not told her, or your grandma?"

"Um, how had you not told your parents you were working on the biggest discovery in your profession in the state's history?" She yanked her hand away.

He narrowed his eyes. "Don't turn this on me. Not telling my parents about the find has no bearing on my future."

"Maybe not. But it's a hard discussion, and you dodged it." She stepped out of the way of a Frisbee, and he followed her into deeper water. She faced him again, her turquoise swimsuit visible through the clear water as she paddled her arms back and forth on the surface. "You didn't tell your family about the significance because paleontology is your dream, and they've made light of it your whole life. Am I right?"

Quentin couldn't bear to nod. Alisha peered toward shore, and he followed her gaze to where Simone sat, reading a book in the shade of her floppy hat. "My sister is the one who got to dream big. I never did. This is all new for me. It's going to take some time."

"Alisha, I get it, but you've been waiting *years*. There's no reason to wait another moment!" The current dragged at his calves, and he took a step sideways on the shifting sand. "Affordable properties in the city don't just grow on trees."

"You think I don't know that? That I don't feel my chances slipping away?"

"Then do something about it!"

Bobbing up with a set of waves kicked out by a speedboat far past the buoys, she pursed her lips. "But what if this is for the best? I still haven't told my grandparents. Haven't leased a property." She cupped water in her hands, then opened her fingers and let it drip out. "The money would go a lot further for a bakery in Hawksburg."

"Are you serious right now?" The current tugged him again, separating them by another meter, and he struggled to regain his footing, then came back to her, placing shaky hands on her shoulders. She didn't draw back, but under his fingers, her muscles went stiff. "One little setback and you give up?"

"It wouldn't be giving up. It would be reconfiguring." She planted her feet, jaw set.

"*Reconfiguring?* That's what you call staying in a town you can't stand, bored to death?" His head buzzed, blood leaving his face. "And doing it without me?"

She leveled a gaze at him. "Frankly, you're the least of my worries at this point."

He dropped his hands away from the slickness of her wet skin. Chilly water slipped through his fingers, and a searing bolt of ice tore through his chest. Hurt cascaded in a brutal, all-encompassing avalanche of anger.

"I don't think that's it at all. I think you're *scared*." He shot out the word like a poison-tipped tentacle. She drew her strong arms across her chest to protect her heart.

A small voice told him to stop, but he barreled over the warning, pain giving edge to his words. "You're scared to tell your family. Scared to open up to me. You're scared you might fall in love with me." He let the words flow, fast, before he could change his mind. "Life isn't always safe. Falling in love is never a sure thing. But if you don't take down your walls and be honest with people, no one will get in, and you'll end up alone."

Across the charged air between them, Alisha spoke, voice flat and calm as the water, her trembling chin the only giveaway. "It's not me who's scared of ending up alone, Quentin."

CHAPTER 31

ALISHA

"What're you doin' out here in the rain?"

Eye on the viewfinder, Alisha knelt on the porch and snapped another photo of the white porcelain plate piled with ginger-molasses cookies.

"Just social media stuff." She'd been back home since last night, with no word from Quentin since he'd stormed away from her on the beach. This morning she'd tried to call, then texted an apology, asking for an update about his meeting with Dr. Yates, and nothing. Not that she blamed him. She'd torn off the scab on the wound closest to his heart.

The crew would return by midweek to finish out the dig. Did he even want to see her again? And if so, what would she say to him about their future? She was still torn between staying and going. Caught between the status quo and the unknown.

She took a last photo, capturing the peeling gray paint of the porch floor—an eyesore according to Mrs. S, but shabby chic in Instagram aesthetics—and the individual sugar crystals on the cookies. Sitting back on her heels, she lowered the camera and smiled up to where

Grandpa stood at the open front door. "Finished." She picked up the plate and offered him one.

He bit into it and chewed with an appreciative murmur. "Tasty as always." He crossed over to the porch swing, and she joined him. They swung back and forth for a moment to the patter of rain on the roof.

"You know, you've really gone and knocked it outta the park with the dessert menu, Ali girl. Not that I had any doubts. But business is up since we started serving real desserts. I should've listened to you a long time ago."

At his praise, Alisha almost choked on her mouthful of spicy-sweet cookie.

"Although, whether that's thanks to your desserts or our fifteen minutes of fame remains to be seen." She slanted him a look and caught him grinning. "Teasing, Ali. And no, we didn't have any trouble from nosy newsmen while you were away, like I been telling ya since last night. All quiet, except half the town's on our case for not sharing the news ourselves. But they'll get over it."

The rain picked up, streaming down in a curtain, and he raised his voice over the racket. "I came out to ask a favor. I know you're busy with orders and whatnot, but I was hoping you could whip up a cake for my birthday party. Nothing fancy," he added.

She swallowed. "Sure! But I thought you were trying to fly under the radar this year."

He chuckled. "A man can hope. But Hank convinced me I oughta celebrate seventy-five in a big way. Figured we could have a little shindig at the restaurant." The metal chains creaked as they swung forward and back. "Already asked your sister, but she can't make it down on such short notice." He took another bite, and a small shower of crumbs bounced off his belly.

"Fine by me, though. Glad she's got her career all taken care of. Won't catch me complainin' about a steady job." He eyed the half-eaten cookie in his hand, tufts of white arm hair standing out around his leather wristwatch. "Which reminds me, with business at Honey and Hickory good as it is, and you having free rein with your desserts, maybe you wanna take a break from this?"

She pivoted toward him on the threadbare cushion. "Why would I want a break from it?"

"I'll never understand your generation, spinnin' out your energy in a thousand different directions," he said, more to the rain-soaked garden than her. Alisha kept her mouth shut, so he went on, louder. "As delicious as your cookies are, Ali—and they *are* mighty tasty, don't get me wrong—your side business is a distraction." He sniffed.

"From what, exactly?"

"From your *job*." He leaned heavy on the last word. "The one I'm paying ya for. In case you'd forgotten."

No. She had not, in fact, forgotten who signed her checks, or whose roof she lived under. Four months and an entirely revamped dessert menu, yet nothing had truly changed. Ribs tight, she sat paralyzed. The water sluicing out of the eaves made her ears ring.

After all she'd done to atone for the sins of her father, Grandpa *still* saw her as a burden?

She leveraged herself to her feet, and the swing jerked on its chains. "How could I forget?"

The short walk across the porch lengthened, swallowed her up. She made it to the door and eased it shut behind her—quiet, slow. Leaned her head against the doorframe. Granny called out something from the living room, but Alisha ignored her, blindsided.

Grandpa didn't want her here anymore. Granny didn't need her. The fence around her was built of self-doubt, not circumstance. Quentin was right. She couldn't stay in Hawksburg forever. But was she brave enough to leave?

CHAPTER 32

QUENTIN

Tre swung open the door of his condo. "Here he is, the man of the hour! Can I have an autograph, Dr. Harris?"

Instantly regretting his decision to come over, Quentin pushed past his friend into the spacious entryway and toed off his Nikes. He'd come straight from meeting with Lawrence, who'd reamed him out for not getting out ahead of the situation and anticipating the arrival of the reporters.

The chair of his department hated losing control, but with the dig public knowledge and no damage to the site thus far, the worst was behind them. They could control the narrative going forward, issue a press release once they'd definitively identified the fossils. As it stood, things were fine.

With the dig, at least. With Alisha? Right now, their future was murkier than the dregs of the creamy caramel latte he'd knocked back on his way over, a poor remedy for the root of a sleepless night.

He stalked through sunbeams slanting across the open-plan space and into the kitchen in search of something stronger than espresso.

"Hello to you too." Tre trailed after him. "Saw your ugly mug on the news, bragging about those old bones. You paleo guys get all the glory."

Tuning out his friend's rambling, Quentin yanked open the stainless steel french doors of the refrigerator and grabbed a bottle at random. He tugged out a few drawers until he found an opener and wrenched off the top.

Leaning against the island, Tre asked, "Can I get you anything else, Hulk? Maybe some bricks to smash?"

Quentin bumped the drawer closed with his hip and drained half the beer. "Nope, I'm good."

"Great. So long as *you're* set." Tre shook his head and pulled out a bottle of red wine from the rack in the corner. He unwrapped the top and twisted in the corkscrew. "Since you dropped by unannounced . . ." With a grunt, he worked the cork free. "I'm guessing either your AC is out again or it's lady trouble."

Spying a box of oatmeal cream pies on the counter, Quentin tore into one, finishing half in a single bite and washing it down with beer. On the second bite, his teeth sank into the cookie, and he remembered Alisha's words. *A ginger cookie.* Soft and sweet? Yeah, right. More like salty and sour.

He'd snapped at her, left her high and dry on the sandy beach. On the day he'd meant to offer her his heart, he'd bruised hers instead. The cookie stuck like paste in his throat, and he took another swig.

Tre raised his eyebrows. "Lady trouble it is. What happened between you and the farm girl?"

Fighting down the mouthful of cookie, Quentin said, "I don't date *girls*, since I'm an adult man."

"Again with this, Q? Can I trade you in for a less woke model?" Tre screwed a wine aerator into the top of the bottle and sighed like a martyr. "Whatever, my bad. Farm *woman*?" He scrunched up his face and tipped the bottle toward Quentin. "Gotta admit, not quite the same ring to it."

Tre opened a glass-front cabinet and slid out two wineglasses, but Quentin shook his head, so he put one back.

Under his breath, Tre said, "Too macho for merlot, but gets hung up over terminology . . ." At Quentin's slow blink, he desisted. "All right, are you gonna polish off the entire package of Little Debbies or tell me what's bothering you before Radhika gets home in, oh"—he checked his Apple Watch—"half an hour?"

After striding over to the leather couch, Quentin threw himself down into its plush depths.

"Door number one, I see. Cool." Tre settled into the tufted velvet armchair next to him and clicked on *SportsCenter*.

A smile tugged at Quentin's lips in spite of himself. He eyed the dregs of his beer. Shoot, he was becoming a lightweight.

"What?" Tre took a sip of wine, and Quentin's smile grew.

"You."

"Me?"

"Yes, you. Sitting there in your wingback chair, sipping overpriced wine. I'm getting a very 'Sherlock Holmes meets Frederick Douglass' vibe. Where's your ascot and pipe?" He pretended to glance around in search of the missing accessories.

"Shut up, man. You sound like Radhika." Tre sniffed and turned his attention back to the TV. "She says I've let this bougie new condo go to my head."

Quentin inhaled his sip of beer, pounding a fist to his sternum. "Amen to that," he finally managed.

"Yeah, yeah." Commercials came on, and Tre switched to a baseball game. "So what's going on, Q?"

"Alisha and I are over," Quentin said, then hissed when the Cubs player hit a homer.

"Wait. You were *dating* the farm woman?"

"Tre, come on. Quit with that crap." He leaned over the arm of the couch to put his empty bottle on the side table, noting the green marble coaster with a shake of his head. This place was a far cry from the crappy apartment he and Tre had shared in their twenties. "And yes, we *were* dating. You know we've been texting since March and hanging out all summer. Well, I finally convinced her to go out with me for real. Then this weekend, she met my family—"

"Rewind, pause. You've been holding out on me! I'm proud of you, brother. It's. About. Time!" Tre leaned forward and held out a fist, but Quentin glowered at him, so he sat back, crossing an ankle over his knee.

"So she met your family. That's the problem? Mama Isabel scared her off? Can't say I'm surprised." Tre opened his eyes wide, lips pulled back in horror.

"Is nothing sacred? That's my *mother* you're talking about." Quentin scowled at him. "But no, things went really well. And we saw each other the next day. I hung out with her and her sister." Tre opened his mouth, but Quentin kept going to stave off his friend's dirty mind. "We had a great time, went to North Ave Beach . . ."

"Dr. Harris chilling on the beach with two ladies?" Tre lifted up his glass, shaking both shoulders and circling his hips on the cushion. "Didn't think you had it in you, Q."

Quentin stood up and strode to the kitchen. Tre called after him, "Sorry. I'm done, I swear."

After snatching out another beer, he came back in, taking a seat at the far side of the couch this time. Tre flipped back to *SportsCenter*. Eyes on the TV, he asked, "So, pray tell, between the kissing and the bikinis and meeting the family, what exactly is the issue?"

He gulped down a mouthful of skunky beer. "I may have given her a lecture on how to live her life."

"Shocking."

"Seriously, Tre, I don't need this."

"Q, I'm just waiting to hear what the problem is. If she's known you since March, you've probably lectured her at least a dozen times by now."

Chewing the inside of his cheek, Quentin crossed his arms, the cold beer bottle resting against his elbow.

"You're really telling me this is the first time you've tried to point out the error of her ways?" Behind black wire frames, Tre aimed a skeptical look his way.

Quentin narrowed his eyes. Tre kept his face bland. Finally he conceded, "There may have been one or two other times."

"Ha. Knew it!" A thump sounded from where Tre smacked the arm of the chair.

"I can't help it, man." He set the bottle on his leg and pointed to the TV for Tre to switch back to the baseball game. "I just can't stand for her to make the same mistakes."

"As who?"

"As Mercedes."

Tre sat forward, hand on his knee. "Hold up, how so?"

"She's planning to move here, which should be great news. She wants to open up a bakery, and she can do it too. Has *been* doing it, for years. Her cookies are phenomenal, and cool looking too. That's going to be her shop—only cookies." At Tre's rapid blinks, he wrapped up the cookie endorsement.

"But the thing is, she works for her grandpa and lives with her grandparents too. And she hasn't told them."

"Maybe she's waiting for the right time?" The Cubs scored another run, and Tre swore.

"Like when she's already gone, over a text?" The bitter tinge to his words tasted rotten in his mouth, but he couldn't keep the image of the life-altering text out of his mind: You'll be out the tux money, but my dad will handle the rest. Wish you all the best.

Wish you all the best. Right. Like a tuxedo deposit was the only collateral damage of a broken engagement.

"Ah." Tre ran his fingers over his goatee like a wise wizard. "Dang, Q."

Vindicated, Quentin washed another swallow of beer down his throat. "You see the problem?"

"I see *a* problem, yeah."

He swallowed a burp, stomach gurgling. "What's that supposed to mean?"

Tre slung back the last of his wine. "It means, stay for dinner. Radhika's bringing Lou Malnati's."

🐾

"You'd better eat more than that, Q. You know this one won't touch leftovers." Radhika pointed her fork toward Tre, her wavy black hair piled on top of her head in a messy bun. A box of deep-dish sausage pizza sat in the middle of the circular turned-wood table, three thick slices missing.

Quentin smiled and put a hand on his overfull belly. He hadn't finished off the *entire* package of oatmeal cream pies during his sob-fest with Tre, but he'd come pretty close. "I'll do my best."

She nodded and went back to cutting up her slice. "So when do you head back down to . . . where is it again?"

"Hawksburg. We'll be going back tomorrow for another three weeks."

"Gotcha. Pretty cool. Tre's been keeping me updated, and I saw you on WGN." Tre groaned, but his wife ignored him. "How're things with the woman you met? Alisha, right?"

"They broke up," Tre chimed in from the peanut gallery. "He dumped her preemptively so she wouldn't leave him like Mercedes did."

Quentin nearly inhaled a bite of cheese. "What? No." He glared at his friend. "Tre, that is not what I said. And way to throw me under the bus."

Tre opened his mouth, but Radhika lifted a hand, and he closed it. *Amazing.* Quentin needed to learn that trick.

"I didn't break up with her; we had a fight. She plans to move here soon but hasn't told anyone in her family! Including her grandfather, and she manages his restaurant."

"So you're worried she's going to desert her family the way Mercedes deserted you?" Radhika took a sip of water.

"Okay, really, Radhika? I'm not one of your patients. I came to hang out with my friends, not be psychoanalyzed."

"Man, Q, will you listen to yourself?" Tre wiped his mouth with a paper napkin, but some crumbs remained in his mustache. "Defensive much? She's just trying to help. As your *friend.*"

"Yeah, well, it feels more like an ambush."

Radhika speared a bite of pizza and spoke around it. "It's just dinner."

Her attitude pissed him off. "Sorry. But come on. Is it so crazy that I don't want to see someone get hurt the way I did? Should I feel bad for wanting to protect her sister and her grandparents?"

"Are you sure it's them you're trying to protect?"

Quentin ground his teeth. "Okay, and what if it *is* me I'm trying to protect?" He pinched the bridge of his nose. "I can't go through that again. I . . ." His breath hitched.

Radhika put down her fork. "What you went through with your wedding? It sucked. And no one blames you for putting up your defenses. But does Alisha even know about Mercedes?"

He nodded hard, once. Reached across with his knuckle to wipe at the corner of his eye. His vision swam, stomach shifting at the sight of congealing cheese layered under a solid slab of sausage and thick, tomato-filled sauce.

"Have you told her how similar this situation feels to you?"

He raised his eyes then, regarding her through the blur. "No. But I don't think Alisha's anything like Mercedes; I really don't. What's between us is so much more, so much better. But what if I'm wrong?"

"If you're wrong, you'll wind up hurt." Radhika scrunched up her napkin in her fist. "But it sounds like you already are hurting. So let her in, Quentin. She might surprise you."

Alisha had surprised him since day one, in good and scary and wonderful ways. And here he sat, wanting more. Wanting all of her, forever.

Watching him, Tre said, "Shoot, Q. It's like that, huh?" He fetched the half-empty wine bottle off the counter.

"Like what?"

"I guess I should've known." He poured another glass, the deep-red liquid glugging out of the spout, and slid it toward Quentin. "You don't do anything by halves."

"What are you talking about?"

"You're in love with this farm woman."

Despite an involuntary groan, Quentin couldn't keep the smile off his face. "She'd kill you for calling her that. Alisha is not a fan of country life."

"The man does not even deny it." Tre clipped each word out, then chuckled. "Why am I not surprised?"

"Whatever. I owe you one for helping me get my head straight." Quentin lifted his glass, grinning, and yes, not denying his friend's assertion one iota.

"Yup, you sure do." Tre clinked his glass with Quentin's. "Just remember this when we call you asking for free babysitting."

"Mm-hmm, sure." Quentin lifted his wine. Then he paused, glass halfway to his lips. Flicked his eyes toward Radhika and her tumbler of ice water. "Babysitting?"

Coming around behind his wife's chair, Tre kissed her cheek.

"You're pregnant?"

Radhika and Tre nodded in unison.

"You didn't really think I asked you to stay for dinner just to figure out your love life, did you?" Tre beamed from ear to ear.

Quentin leaped up and went around to give Radhika a hug. Of course, mush-hearted guy that he was, Tre leaned over and grabbed him around the neck. He thumped his friend on the back. "I'm so happy for you two!"

Smoothing a hand down the front of her purple-and-white Northwestern tee, Radhika grinned. "Don't you dare tell me I'm showing yet, Quentin. Too early. This is just the pizza."

But Tre passed Quentin his phone and slid his hands around his wife's belly. "Here's the first sonogram."

"Already showing off pictures of your kid?" He grinned down at Radhika. "Your husband's in deep." Quentin made appreciative noises about the black-and-white blur, then passed the phone back. "You thought of names yet? Besides Quentin, of course."

Tre tossed out silly names, and Quentin waited for the familiar sting of resentment, but his chest expanded, filled with joy for his best friend. Tre had taken a few years of convincing, but it couldn't have been more obvious he wanted to be a dad. He was ready.

And Quentin? Kids were great and all, but what did he really want right now?

Alisha.

He wanted her and her trust issues and prickly defenses and old-lady slang and all. Together, their broken pieces fit together into symmetry. But what about her? Did she feel the bone-deep ache of being apart? Would it be enough to make her step out and take a chance on herself?

CHAPTER 33

ALISHA

The barbell dug into Alisha's shoulders, and sweat stung her eyes. The paleontologists were working in the backyard, so she kept the overhead doors down, in no mood for a repeat performance of the first day. But after she'd finished her set, she couldn't bear the heat and whipped off her T-shirt, panting in black leggings and white Converse.

This morning the crew had come back to work at the dig, but like a coward, she'd spent the night at Meg's, then hid out at the restaurant all day, burning browned butter and overworking tart dough. A wreck of a workday, but she wasn't about to mope around the house and make herself available. Not after Quentin had ghosted her. Lizzo blasted through her headphones, but she upped the volume even more.

It's not me who's scared of ending up alone. Hypocrite. As if that wasn't *all* she worried about, day and night. Like a gladiator pitted against a friend in the arena, she'd had the gall to take his deepest hurt and spin it on him. All because the truth of his words had left her reeling. He was right—she *was* inventing excuses to stay. But still, he couldn't waltz into her life and push her to change everything immediately on his terms.

Never mind that she wanted the change. Never mind that she wanted *him*, desperately.

Alisha turned back to the weight rack and finished another set of heavy squats, her thighs trembling at the last rep. After she'd reracked the bar, she ducked out, turned around, and froze. Quentin stood at the side door, black T-shirt covered in a dusting of dirt, a White Sox baseball hat tugged down over his brow. Pulse in her throat, she slid off her headphones but didn't bother to put on her shirt.

"Sorry. I didn't mean to interrupt you." He closed the door behind him, looking not at all sorry. His gaze consumed her, dark and hungry. "No one answered up at the house, but when I saw your car in the drive, I thought I might find you in here."

Twitchy under his scrutiny, she tightened her ponytail. "Found me."

Quentin took off his hat and ran a hand over his fresh-cut curls, the action sending a traitorous tug through her gut. "I've missed you so much. I've been dying to talk to you all day."

"No missed calls. No texts." She grabbed up her phone from the bench and shook it, hating herself for her catty tone.

"In person." His brow furrowed, and the intensity in his eyes faded. He walked up to the edge of the rubber mat, twisting his hat in his hands. "I shouldn't have reacted the way I did at the beach." He paused and rubbed a finger under his bottom lip.

"It's just, after Mercedes, I'm scared any woman I meet is going to pull something over on me. And the thought of you not telling your family you're leaving until the last minute didn't sit well with me. I guess . . ." He hesitated again. "I guess I imagined them waking up and you being gone."

A toxic brew of emotions shot through Alisha's veins, so potent she stumbled back and banged her head on the barbell. "Like my father?"

"What? No, Alisha, that's not what I meant."

"Yet it's exactly what you said." She unbuckled her weight belt and tossed it aside, needing space to breathe.

He strode over to where she stood at the squat rack, and she backed under the barbell, the steel bar a barrier between them.

"I'm sorry, Alisha. That's why I'm here, apologizing. I iced you out and blamed you for my own issues. That was wrong of me. I know you wouldn't do something like that."

"Do you? Because I would *never*." Her voice trembled. "I'd rather not go at all than leave my grandparents in a lurch."

"I know, and that worries me too." Quentin stepped under the barbell until he stood inches from her. She steeled herself to not back down. "You'd rather stay miserable than open up about your dreams."

He was so near she had to tilt back her head to meet his eyes. "Why even come in here to have this conversation if everything I do scares you?"

"Because you're important to me, Alisha. You matter. And it's worth it to talk about the hard stuff, even if opening up might hurt."

"Doesn't seem to be hurting you." She crossed her arms, regretting it when her forearms brushed against his solid abs.

"Stop trying to push me away." He brought up his arms to touch her, then dropped them by his sides, exhaling with a growl like a caged panther. "Every time I dredge up these feelings over what happened with my wedding, all I feel is pain. I don't want to repeat the same mistakes. But one of those mistakes was not talking to my ex when I was scared of what her answer might be. Pushing doubts under the rug. I know you and I are just starting out, but I want us to have a chance."

A chance.

A hope.

A future? The word bounced off the walls she'd built like the wallop of a sledgehammer, and she bunched her fists, wishing for the rigid steel of a barbell to anchor her. Shore up her resistance. But Quentin's eyes bore into hers, and the crack in her defenses widened.

"I care about you, Alisha. Way more than casual. But if you don't feel the same way . . ."

Doubt gathered in her chest, marshaling for a rebuttal. She inhaled, forcing herself to hold his gaze, and she found the whispers of her own fears reflected in his eyes, but something else too. Something brave. Something daring. Could she rise to the challenge?

"And if I do?"

"If you do, then I'm kind of hoping . . ." He cleared his throat. "I'm *very much* hoping we can give this a shot."

"Even though we might crash and burn." Her words landed heavy, a statement. But he answered the question, never wavering.

"Even then. You're worth the risk."

Worth the risk. *Worthy.*

Slowly, she unwound her arms, left her heart exposed. Then, like cannonballing into an ice-cold swimming pool, she threw herself forward and clasped him tight. In a heartbeat, he returned the hug, and she breathed out for the first time in days.

"Can we talk like this?" His damp T-shirt muffled her words. *How does he still smell so delicious under all this grime and sweat?* "It's easier."

His chest bounced under her cheek in a silent laugh. "Yeah, of course."

She shifted, searching for words to match her feelings, the process like breaking in new shoes. "Seven whole years I've been in limbo, Quentin." She swallowed to wash the rust down her throat. "I moved back to help my grandparents and ended up getting stuck in time. Turns out, my family doesn't need me here anymore, yet here I am, scared to leave." She breathed deep again, in and out, and he kneaded the knots in her back, staying silent.

The refuge of his arms brought out more words. "For years I haven't let anyone get close to me besides my family and Meg. Then suddenly you come along. And I like you so much." So much it scared the crap out of her. "I want to be with you; I want us to have a future. But I don't know if I can let that happen." She stopped talking and burrowed into his embrace.

"Let what happen?"

"You."

His hands stilled, and she ached for them to start up again. "Then how about you don't let it happen?" She drew away, a crease appearing on her forehead, but he pulled her back and rubbed two fingers down her spine. "Don't *let* it happen. *Make* it happen," he said, his voice the rumble of thunder rolling in after a drought.

"What does that even mean?" She went to look up at him, and he loosened his grip, sliding his clasped hands to her lower back.

"Fate brought us together, but if you make the choice to stay with me, it won't be happenstance. It will be your decision. Take back your power, Alisha." He stepped away and gently disentangled himself from her arms.

"I'm right here." He ducked under the racked barbell, stopping at the edge of the mat.

Longing pierced her chest, fierce and deep.

"If you want me, want *us*, then come and get me. I want to work through things with you. I want to work through *life* with you." He paused, eyes burning into hers, not shying away. "What do *you* want?"

The distance between them left her bereft. What did she want? *Him.* Wanted him so badly her chest burned. The coals he'd ignited back in March craved fresh tinder. And she wanted a real bakery of her own, wanted to grow past the borders of this small town and break the chains of insecurity and doubt.

She took one step and wrapped her fingers around the barbell. "I want to be with you, Quentin."

Swinging under the bar, she took another step toward him, and he waited, standing firm. His gray-green eyes darkened to black, the sky before a summer storm. She took another step, and an opportunity unwound itself in her mind like a scroll.

Still a pace away, she halted. "My grandpa's birthday party is tomorrow. After it's over, I'm going to tell him and Granny about my plans."

She uttered the words like an oath. "Will you come with me and stand by my side when I finally tell my grandparents I'm moving on?"

"I dunno, Alisha. A family function?" He grinned, but he stayed planted, steady and sure. "You're asking a lot—"

Closing the last inches between them, she cut him off by pulling his gorgeous face down for a kiss. Breathless moments later, they broke away, and his eyes crinkled under the force of his smile.

Alisha gazed up at him. "I'll take that as a yes."

He nodded. "Yes, Alisha. I'll gladly be your backup, just so long as you know you can do this, with or without me." His eyes roamed her face, and her breathing quickened. "But yeah, I'll stand in your corner. Always."

Unable to resist, she bunched his shirt in her hands, the grit in the fabric rough against her fingers, and tugged him down. She brushed her lips against his, the kiss tentative and exploring at first, then hot and insistent, their mouths melting together in a fiery alchemy.

🐾

Grandpa's seventy-fifth birthday party was in full swing, Honey and Hickory packed to overflowing. The setting sun cast an apricot glow on the crowded room through the front bank of windows. So much for a small friends-and-family affair. More than half the town had shown up and reduced Alisha's towering three-tiered devil's food cake, Grandpa's favorite, to scraps.

While she carved up the cake, Quentin fed her bites of his slice. The decadent richness of the dark chocolate combined with his attentiveness sanded down her rough edges. No longer tied up like a pretzel, tonight her spirit stretched free and unburdened.

After serving up the last piece of cake, she mingled hand in hand with Quentin, introducing him to old friends and frenemies. With an exit strategy in place, she could acknowledge the good parts of her life here. But she was ready to say farewell and carve out her own place in the city. Grandpa didn't need her here any more than she wanted to stay. And Granny never stopped nudging her toward the door with admonitions and encouragements.

Now or never, and she chose now.

"Listen up, everybody!" Grandpa clapped his hands, and a hush fell over the buzzing room. "I know half of ya are expectin' a speech, and the other half are hopin' I keep my trap shut. Well, some of ya are about to be sorely disappointed, and I think you know who ya are." He winked, and laughter rippled through the crowd.

Alisha tugged Quentin to the side, where she could get a better view, and pulled out her phone to record a video.

People parted, and Grandpa backslapped his way toward the center of the room. "I'm getting on in years. No need to specify just how far along—lookin' at you, Hank."

"Seventy-five!" he shouted, and Grandpa waved him off.

"As I said, old enough. Back when I first started out, I set up my smoker in an empty lot off Second Street. I was just a kid, with a wife, a toddler, and a half-decent recipe for barbecue sauce." Tears shining in his eyes, he pivoted in a slow quarter turn to face the propped-open front door, sidewalk full of celebrants holding food on paper plates.

"I'd say I've come a long way since then. Hope I got a ways yet still to go." Applause rang out, pierced by a drawn-out whistle. She wished Simone could've made the trip. "Still, I'm getting old."

"Naw, you aren't old. *I'm* old!" a voice rang out, and next to her, Quentin chuckled.

"All of you know my granddaughter Ali. She's been workin' at this place longer than she'd like to admit." He winked, and someone whooped. He beckoned to Alisha, and she passed Quentin the phone, then scooted through the crowd, expecting Grandpa to give her the floor for a toast.

Instead, he grabbed her shoulder and dug in his fingertips. "Sweetheart, I've come to rely on you more'n you know these past few years. Can't imagine this place without ya."

Clearing his throat, he swung away to address the crowd. "It should come as no surprise that from here on out, our own sweet Alisha will be runnin' the place. I'm steppin' down. Honey and Hickory is all hers now, and I have every confidence she'll be serving up world-class barbecue for decades to come!"

The room erupted in cheers. Alisha stood there, mouth open. Rooted to the spot.

CHAPTER 34

QUENTIN

"So that's it?" Quentin couldn't believe Alisha hadn't said a word to Wayne except, "Thank you."

Thank you? The man had slammed the lid on her box of hopes and dreams and threw away the key!

Now they faced off in the alley by her grandfather's—no, *her* restaurant—except they were on the same side, fighting for the same future, if only she could see that. Why wouldn't she speak up? Despite the oppressive stillness of the night air, Quentin ached to reach out and wrap Alisha in his arms. He wanted to hold her close and soothe away her distress. But he couldn't, not if she wouldn't let him.

"That's what?"

The front door of the restaurant dinged open, and laughter spilled out. He waited until the partygoers' conversation had faded away. "You're going to take over for your grandpa and stay in Hawksburg forever?"

"This was always how it was going to be." She spoke toneless and flat, but he knew her well enough by now; the lack of expression was a shield.

"That's not what you said yesterday!" Desperation charged his words, snapping like static between them. "Or last week. Or last month."

"Forget yesterday!" His words ignited a spark in her. Good. If she cared enough to fight, he had a shot; *they* had a shot. "I was living in a fantasy world. I thought . . ." Her strong shoulders slumped in defeat. "I thought they didn't need me anymore. But they do. Grandpa needs me here, and I'm not going to let him down like my father did."

"What about your own dreams?" Couldn't she see how miserable she'd be living the shadow of a life? She was a burst of Technicolor in a sepia town. Pain for her seized his lungs, stole his breath. He choked out the words. "You're letting *yourself* down, Alisha."

"Don't." She raised her voice and jabbed a finger toward him like a rapier, though it trembled. "Don't you *dare*. You're not sad I'm losing out on *my* dreams." She glared at him and balled her fists for a fight. "You're upset because I canceled your future again."

Throwing her arms up, she let them fall with a hard snort of laughter. "Well. You want a future with me? Kids and a picket fence? Then quit your job. Move down here. Live in Hawksburg."

He pressed his lips together so hard his jaw popped. He couldn't do that. He'd worked too hard for his whole life to get where he was. Burned bridges with his family that were only just now getting rebuilt. If he gave up his career, it would've all been for nothing.

Alisha waited, her chin up like a boxer in the ring, eyes hooded. "Yeah, that's what I thought."

"That's not fair." *Why couldn't she see?* He didn't want kids without her. He didn't want a life without her. Everything about this tore him up inside.

To his surprise, her defiant posture evaporated, and she sank in on herself. "You're right—it's *not* fair of me to ask. You have a real future. A fulfilling career. I'd never want you to give it up for me."

She pulled at the silver chain around her neck like she was fighting for air. "But, Quentin, you were wrong. I can't change things. My future is here. It's always been here. It's time for me to stop daydreaming and get used to it. I'll never be happy if I don't."

"Will you be happy here, *ever*?" A truck rattled down the road behind him, trailer hitch clanking, and its headlights cast a glare on Alisha's face, her dry eyes. It wrecked him to see her shut down when he'd witnessed the depth of her hurt.

"I'd be lying if I said I didn't want you to come to Chicago. To give this . . ." He swallowed thickly. "To give what's between us a shot." Her arms were stiff, pressed tight against her rib cage. Like a moth to flame, he reached out to cup her elbows, and she shivered at his touch.

"But I think it's more than that." He slid his palms up her rigid arms. Beneath his calloused fingers, her skin was smooth, her softness a balm to his tormented soul. "You've been hiding your true self for so long, Alisha. You tried to blend in in this small town and act like this restaurant is what you wanted." His eyes bore into her face, willing her to lift her downcast eyes. "But you have a choice," he said, pleading.

"You're right—I do have a choice. But if I choose to leave, I'll be just like my dad." She thrust out her elbows and drove his hands away. "You accused me of fabricating excuses, but this is real." She walked backward, the crunch of gravel grating in the stillness. "My grandpa passed his legacy on to me." She thumped her chest, hard. "Do you want me to choose the coward's way out? To run away and shirk my responsibilities?"

"Staying true to yourself isn't cowardly," he said. She'd reached the end of the alley, a lone light overhead casting her in a wan glow, darkened streets stretching behind her.

"You could never in a million years be like your father, Alisha. I've never seen anyone so devoted and loyal. Choosing not to run the family business doesn't compare to walking out on your own kids! And what about your sister?"

Alisha's eyes shot to his, wide in the moonlight. "What about her?"

"She's living in the city, has her own life. Do you think she abandoned you? Do your grandparents think so?"

"No, she's a grown woman. And she visits all the time." Her eyes narrowed. "Don't do that; it's not the same. She's my little sister. My responsibility."

Quentin wanted to tear out his hair, but he willed himself still. "And your grandparents? The restaurant? It's all your responsibility? You're holding up everything on your own?" The black of night engulfed her like she was drowning in a well. Why wouldn't she reach out for the rope to save herself?

"That's not fair."

His own words echoed back at him. The brutal irony hit him like a fist to the jaw: Alisha's putting family first was the thing keeping them apart.

A bell clanged in his mind, signaling the end of the round. She had him on the ropes, but he threw one last hook, hoping to bring her back and stave off defeat. "Everything shouldn't fall on your shoulders, Alisha. Whatever happens between us, I want you to know your happiness matters. And it matters to me."

"Whatever happened between us *happened*." Her chest rose and fell beneath the white fabric of her dress. "But it's over now."

No, no, no. "Please don't do this, Alisha. Give it some time." He lifted a hand toward her, but his knees were locked. "Maybe in a year or two, you can sell this place and move to Chicago, make good on your dreams. I'll wait for you."

"No!" Like saying the word exhausted her, she stood gasping. Then she continued, quiet but firm. "No. I don't want you to wait a year for me. I don't want you to waste another moment on me." She advanced toward him then, leaving the light behind, and shadows swallowed her face. "Go, please."

He finally broke the inertia holding him in place and stepped closer, but she raised a hand to stop him.

"I'm not going to change my mind on this, Quentin. I am *never* going to leave my family. You and I have no future. Now go, or I will."

Quentin's heart squeezed so hard inside him he couldn't breathe. Tears pooled, but he bit them back and turned away toward the deserted street. "All right. I'm gone."

CHAPTER 35

QUENTIN

One heel of Quentin's boots hammered a staccato rhythm on the linoleum. The astringent scent of industrial cleaner bombarded his senses. He brushed a hand against his nose, put it back in his lap. An urgent summons from the chair of his department had him rushing off the dig and racing back to Chicago without even stopping for gas.

After a frenzied attempt to find parking for the stupid souped-up truck, he'd wound up paying a hefty fee on one of the campus lots. He'd detoured to his own office just long enough to throw on a spare button-down over his tee.

Across the desk, Lawrence's scowl created deep canyons in his forehead. The late-afternoon sun fought a losing battle against the shuttered blinds behind him. "You're off the dig."

A pickax slammed down on Quentin's cranium and split it in two, though in a detached way he realized he'd seen this coming. Predicted the end before he'd ever set foot in Hawksburg.

"May I ask why?" He pushed the words past lips gone numb and clumsy.

"You really think I'm going to let the university's name get dragged through the mud?"

An absurd image sprang to mind, the brick sign at the entrance to campus being hauled up out of the dig by a winch, mud glopping off the masonry like it had off Alisha's braids in March . . .

Pain gripped his chest, deflating his lungs. "I don't see what's changed, sir. It was bound to get out sometime."

"I suppose that's true, but it never should've happened in the first place."

His eyebrows pinched together. "But if we hadn't excavated, those fossils would still be in the ground. What could possibly be gained from leaving them in situ?"

"The fossils?" Lawrence shook his head, thin lips pulled back over nicotine-stained teeth. "I couldn't care less about the fossils at this point, Harris. Your conduct is the issue here."

Did he just say he didn't care about the *fossils*? Quentin hadn't drunk any water since breakfast; maybe he was hallucinating. "My conduct? In the interview?" But he hadn't given away any important details, nothing to spark controversy or undue attention.

"The interview? You think I called you in because of the *interview*? We already hashed that out Monday. I'm talking about you turning the dig site into your own personal love nest."

Oh. Oh *no*. Quentin slumped down in his seat, worrying the skin at his cuticles. The timing stung like pressure on a fresh bruise. For Lawrence to find out about Alisha now . . .

Lawrence glowered at him. "Are you really going to play dumb?" He twisted his monitor around, and Quentin's stomach bottomed out like a plane in freefall.

A photo filled the entire screen. Alisha sprawled on top of him in the grass, their mouths pressed against each other in a grainy yet excruciatingly explicit lip-lock, the dig laid out behind them in a tableau of infamy. The headline read, **ANOTHER MASSIVE BONE IN HAWKSBURG?**

Quentin's foot shot out in a panic reflex and collided with the trash can under the desk. He bent down and yanked it toward his chair, because very likely he was going to puke. Or pass out. Or both. Nausea rolled over him like a wave. His hands and feet seemed miles away. The chair shifted under him, and he fumbled for a grip on the armrests.

This was a nightmare. Showing up to defend his dissertation naked would pale in comparison.

A quick and flirty kiss. Just a peck, really. But out of context, it looked like field-site foreplay. And the cherry on top of the crap sundae? In the foreground, his hoodie lay in the grass where he'd tossed it that morning, the distinctive forest-green and gold of the CNU logo in plain view.

Watching his face, Lawrence lifted a pencil with the whisper of a leer. "The university sweatshirt's a nice touch. In case no one knew you were one of ours, they do now."

"I didn't—"

"Didn't what?" Lawrence tossed the pencil on the desk and sat back, crossing his arms. "Invite a member of the public onto the dig site? Use your fifteen minutes of fame to get laid?"

"I didn't invite her there." The words escaped a jaw clenched tight. "She lives there. It's the homeowner's granddaughter."

Lawrence dug his middle fingers into his temples. "You have got to be kidding me. Just when I think this cannot get worse. Do you think they're going to take kindly to you seducing their granddaughter?"

He made it sound like some sort of lurid affair. "It wasn't a seduction. It was a kiss." And a whole lot more, but he didn't need to bare his soul to Lawrence.

"A kiss. On the dig site. With the homeowners' granddaughter." Lawrence shook his head, a lank lock of gray hair falling over his brow. "You're up for tenure next year. Almost six years you've been with us, and not so much as a negative student eval. Then you get handed the find of a lifetime, the perfect opportunity to distinguish yourself. And you blow it to pieces over a woman. Unbelievable, Harris. The level of moronic self-sabotage is frankly astounding."

Any defense he had dried in his throat. The stark assessment rang in his ears, pinging against his skull. He'd jeopardized everything, risked it all. For nothing.

"Who took this photo?"

"Like I know?" Lawrence shrugged like the question was irrelevant, and at this point, it was. "One of your grad students? Maybe Reid. Did you sleep with her too? Nothing quite like a woman scorned to light a fire under your—"

"That's enough." Quentin leaned forward, though his hands trembled. "I will not tolerate you speaking about a member of our faculty like that." And no way any of his students took the photo either. The whole crew had already been halfway back to Chicago by the time he'd gone over to bid Alisha goodbye.

Lawrence threw an elbow over the back of his chair, eyes narrow. "You need to step off that pedestal, Harris. You've always championed that equality-in-the-workplace garbage. Should've known you were just using it to get in with the ladies. No man cares about that nonsense without an ulterior motive."

Quentin ground his molars together. "If I can prove I didn't jeopardize our access to the dig, will you allow me to return to work?"

"Is that a joke?" He snatched up the pencil and jabbed it toward the screen again. Quentin flinched. "This is tabloid crap right here. Involving a member of my staff." Lawrence jammed a thumb into the center of his chest. "You're lucky you're not cleaning out your desk right now."

"But the incident didn't even occur during a workday. This is my private life, on private property." A weak excuse, considering their so-called private life had been splashed across the landing page of a national gossip site.

"News flash, Harris—privacy is dead. Your little fling put the whole department in jeopardy, and now we have to deal with the ramifications of your colossal screwup. If—and I highly doubt it, judging by the propensity for people to retweet, like, and share garbage like this—but *if* it blows over by the end of summer, you might have a shot at teaching fall term. But no way in hell you're sniffing those Hawksburg bones."

CHAPTER 36

ALISHA

Mint mocha, cinnamon butterscotch, vanilla bean, caramel toffee.

Which latte flavor went best with a destroyed relationship and tattered dreams? Alisha ripped the page out of her notebook, covered in scribbled notes of what was meant to be a new cookie recipe, inspired by Quentin's penchant for gas station cappuccinos.

Instead, all the flavors had muddled into the chalky taste of loss. She tore the paper in half, then in half again, shredding until all that remained was the rumpled confetti of failure.

Sure, she'd told Quentin to go, but he'd *gone*. Left her behind without a backward glance.

What else did she expect? For him to stay in Hawksburg? Take up farming? Maybe put his PhD to use as a high school science teacher? Yeah, right. Everything that had transpired was inevitable. But that knowledge didn't stop the anguish of loss. Didn't fill the emptiness where she'd just begun to feel whole again.

After smiling and nodding through Grandpa's plans for retirement at breakfast—most of which revolved around uninterrupted fishing trips and terrorizing Granny's plants with a plan for a greenhouse—she'd taken off for Honey and Hickory, intent on baking therapy before

Hank showed up. She unlocked the door of the office and shoved it open.

Forget new and fresh. Stalking around past the rolltop desk, she knelt down in front of a dinged-up foot locker in the corner. She pried open the lid. Bingo. Grandpa's secret snack stash. Pretzels, wavy potato chips, and bite-size candy bars. She pulled out bag after bag like a Viking raiding a treasure chest. She dumped her haul on the counter and took out the food processor.

These cookies would never appear on a menu, here or in her nonexistent bakery, but when life gave you a dumpster fire, may as well throw the kitchen sink in too.

Maybe she'd gone overboard in baking six dozen cookies. She'd sent the staff home with most of them, but Quentin's truck wasn't in the driveway when she pulled in, so Alisha headed out back to share the results of her stress-baking spree without worrying about bumping into him.

Melted chunks of chocolate offset the salty pretzels and potato chips to perfection, and if she didn't get rid of them, she might end up eating the rest in an attempt to erase the pain of losing Quentin. Plastering on a smile, she approached the edge of the dig. All the paleontologists' heads popped up like prairie dogs.

"Hey, girl," Bridget stood and pulled off one of her work gloves. "If those are for us, you came at the perfect time. We were about done for the day."

Forrest scampered up the ladder and snatched a cookie, chewing with his mouth open. Dev followed close on his heels and elbowed his ribs. "Manners, dude." He raised a brow at Alisha. "May I?"

She nodded. "Help yourselves. Did Quentin already leave, then?"

The paleontologists traded a look. This time, visions of a clan of meerkats sprang to mind, and she bit back a smile.

"Quentin?" Bridget shaded her eyes, head cocked.

"Yeah. His truck's not here." Another undercurrent passed between the paleontologists. "What?"

"Alisha, Dr. Harris isn't coming back." Forrest spoke around the entire cookie in his mouth. Dev shot him a glare.

"What do you mean?" She'd watched everyone arrive before her shift, right on time, like the world hadn't tipped off its axis last night.

"You really don't know?" Cait bared all her teeth in a solid impersonation of the Michael Scott GIF. "Have you not checked your socials?"

"No. I've been working . . ." And stress-baking, and ranting against the universe . . .

She patted her pocket, but her phone was in her room. Off.

Bridget rolled her lips together, her brow creased. "Okay, first of all, don't freak out."

"Prof, c'mon. Of course she's freaking out." Dev patted her shoulder with all the finesse of a sea lion.

This was bad. Very bad.

"I'm freaking out."

He quirked an eyebrow toward Bridget. "Told you so."

Cait stepped up and put her arms on Alisha's shoulders. "Deep breath in. Attagirl. And out." While Alisha exhaled, Cait went on, "Someone leaked a photo of you and Dr. Harris making out at the dig."

Alisha gagged on a lungful of air. "WHAT?"

"And Lawrence took him off the project for compromising the integrity of the university's image." Forrest reached for another cookie while he said this, but Dev smacked his hand.

"Quentin's been fired? Because of me?"

Cait shook her head. "He hasn't been fired. He just can't work on this find anymore."

"Because of me." Alisha shoved the tub of cookies into Forrest's hands so she wouldn't drop it. Her worst fears were coming true. She'd let someone in, and being with her had destroyed him. But maybe she could fix this. Issue a statement or something. Maybe the photo wasn't that bad.

"Have you seen it? The photo?"

Another look. "Seriously, stop it with the herd mentality, and will someone just pass over their phone?" Alisha swallowed. "Please."

Dev dug his phone out of his pocket and tapped at the screen. Handed it to her. She sat down, hard. "I—we . . ."

Bridget settled down next to her, cross-legged. "I think the words you're looking for are 'a gross invasion of privacy.'"

"Or possibly"—Forrest took another bite of cookie—"'coopting private behavior for public consumption.'"

"Voyeurism," added Cait.

"But . . . this isn't what it looks like. I mean—"

"No need to explain, Alisha. What happened between you and Quentin is y'all's business." Bridget raised golden-brown eyes to hers, earnest. "He never let it affect his work. If y'all found happiness with each other, more power to you."

Happiness? Yeah, for all of two minutes, before she'd pushed him away, the ashes of her involvement in his life still volatile enough to torch his career. Happiness? All she'd brought him was a walloping dose of misery.

"But how can Dr. Yates take him off the dig? You and Quentin ran point on this!"

"For one thing, he doesn't have tenure. And even if he did, it's not as rock solid as you might think. Misconduct could still be grounds for disciplinary action. He could even be let go for something like this."

"Which is why we're wondering, Who took this photo?" Dev's eyes turned cold in the shadow of his hat brim.

Alisha's mouth fell open. "Are you accusing *me*? I'm in it, for gosh sakes!"

"Yeah, but your follower count has grown by over ten thousand since last week." Cait's eyebrow went up. "What? You think I didn't follow you once I found out you were a low-key baking celeb?"

It had? Talk about bad timing for a social media hiatus. "No, Cait. I would never orchestrate something like this. For one thing, I know how much the dig meant to Quentin. For another, my grandparents . . . oh my gosh. My grandparents!" She stood up on shaky legs, but Bridget hopped up and grabbed her arm.

"Slow down there, hon. They're not going to expire from shock at the sight of their granddaughter kissing."

Grandpa might, but that wasn't the real issue. "You don't get it. My job was to protect them. Now there are strangers lurking on our property, taking photos. What if our address gets leaked?" She raised an elbow to her mouth, swallowing the bitter taste of bile.

"Well, if it wasn't you, who was it?"

Forrest's question got cut off by the high-pitched whirr of a motorized scooter.

"Yoo-hoo, Ali! I brought over some coconut pound cake to celebrate your newfound fame!"

As one, the group turned toward Mrs. Snyder, and she rolled to a halt. "Is this a bad time?"

"Janet, what were you thinking?" Alisha's grandma set down a sweating glass of iced tea on the table and took a seat.

"I thought he was just here to photograph my hydrangeas!"

"Your hydrangeas aren't even that nice."

"You take that back, Ellie."

"I will not. Your pride is what got us into this mess."

"Please, I'd hardly call it a mess. Alisha just took over Honey and Hickory, and now she's famous. Way I see it, use this to your advantage.

Keep stirring the pot, and you'll have people lining up around the block."

Alisha twisted her own glass of tea in her hands, letting their argument wash over her, silent. Silence was her shelter. But she'd stayed silent for years, and her grandparents were more exposed than ever. Her life was in shambles. And she'd brought Quentin down with her, just like she'd feared.

She cleared her throat. "I'm not interested in a publicity stunt, Mrs. S. Quentin lost out on the biggest find of his career. He might even lose his job because of this. Because of me." If they'd had a hope of getting back together, the leaked photo had sent that up in smoke.

"I'm sorry, Ali. I had no idea." Janet licked her pink-stained lips. "Well, maybe I had some idea—after all, my hydrangeas haven't been blooming like they used to. But I thought it could only do some good! How am I to know those university types would be so fuddy-duddy about a little romance? And on your property too. The nerve!"

Wait a minute . . . *on their property.* Alisha pushed back her chair, stood up, and looked out to where the paleontologists were finishing up for the day, tools strewn across the yard, tire tracks muddying the grass next to Granny's tomato plants.

"I really am sorry." Janet put a hand on her arm, and Alisha patted it. None of this was Mrs. Snyder's fault; she was just a pawn. But she refused to be a passive player in her own life a second longer. "What are you going to do?"

"Speak up. For Quentin."

CHAPTER 37

QUENTIN

"Good news is, now you can go into finance like Dad always wanted." Hector waved an arm in front of his face to waft away the smoke from the open grill. When Quentin didn't say anything, he turned toward him with a grin. "Too soon? Too soon."

"You're awfully glib for someone standing so close to an open flame."

"Like you'd harm a hair on this gorgeous face of mine. Besides, I'm not the one you want to hit, am I right? Now, this Yates guy . . ." Hector closed the grill and wiped sweat off his forehead with a thick forearm. "Him I wouldn't mind meeting in a dark alley."

All talk, but Quentin appreciated the vote of support behind his brother's bluster. He shook his head, squinting against the smoke. "It's not just him. I made the university look bad. They're not going to prioritize me over covering up a scandal."

"A scandal? Dude, you kissed a girl. You didn't tear off her panties at the dig site."

"Yeah, well, everyone assumes I did." The invasiveness of it freaked him out. A couple of years ago, he'd considered not even announcing his engagement at work to maintain his privacy. Fast-forward to now, and the entire department had seen him with his tongue in Alisha's mouth . . .

He scrubbed a hand down his face, wishing he could wipe the image from cyberspace as easily.

"And so what if you had?" Hector flipped the burgers with a scrape of the spatula, and a hiss sounded where grease hit the hot coils. "The dig's in her backyard, for goodness' sakes. If she wants to screw the pool boy . . ."

Quentin leaned back against the deck railing, crossed his arms. "How long have you had that one in the barrel?"

"Since I watched the interview." Hector closed the grill and flashed a grin. "Bro, you've been poking around all summer in their future *swimming pool?* It fell into my lap. Kind of like—"

"Don't."

Hector desisted, seriousness creeping into his dark eyes. "But, Q, you've got a right to do as you please in your private life."

"That's what I told Lawrence." To keep a lid on his emotions, he picked up the package of cheese slices and pried up the seal. It stuck.

"And?"

Quentin bit into the plastic and ripped it open. "And he told me I forfeited that right."

"Bullshit. There's gotta be a way to fight this."

"If there is, I can't see one." Finally nabbing a piece of cheese, Quentin said, "Maybe if I keep my head down and this all blows over, I'll escape with my job."

Hand on his hip, Hector raised the spatula, projecting like a Shakespearean actor onstage. "But this is the find of a lifetime!"

Unamused, Quentin asked, "Another gem from the interview?"

"No, this one came from your girlfriend."

"Not my girlfriend."

"Okay, woman friend."

"No, idiot. I mean we're not together."

Hector glanced both ways over his shoulders. "Am I on an episode of *WandaVision* right now? Why are you messing with my head? You brought home a woman last weekend—the first woman since Mercedes—and she's not even your girlfriend?"

"Anymore."

His brother whistled, long and low. "Forget the burgers—you need a drink."

"A drink's not going to bring Alisha back." Nothing could, not now. The dig had stolen her privacy. His carelessness had exposed her and her family to humiliation. Whatever hope he'd had of winning her back had evaporated, right along with his standing at work.

Hector snapped his fingers in front of his face, and he realized he'd zoned out. "I said, is she mad because you posterized her love life?"

"What? No. I didn't even tell her."

"Um, is she off the grid?"

"No." Probably wished she were, now.

"Then she knows."

"Yeah, obviously." Quentin bit into a second piece of cheese to quell the nauseating churning in his gut. "But that's not what ended things. We broke up before this whole kiss debacle."

"And don't you think she might want to hear from you now?" At his head shake, his brother whistled low. "Wow, you really know how to pick 'em."

"Hector, I swear—"

"Okay, that was low, even for me. But, Q, she seemed awesome. The girls have been asking about her, and you know they hated Mercedes."

"They were toddlers when I was with her."

"Intuitive toddlers. When we watched *Tangled* the other day, they pointed at Mother Gothel and said, 'Look, it's Tía Cedes!'"

Quentin smothered a laugh. "At least she made an impression."

"Yeah, a horrible one." Hector discreetly slid the cheese packet out of reach. "Straight up, Alisha is different. Better. Better for you, obviously. *TMZ* kiss aside."

"Hector . . ."

"All I'm saying is, you should fight for her."

"I did. And she dumped me." Dumped herself in the process. Losing the find had stung like salt on the still-raw wound of watching, powerless, as she gave up on him, and herself. His insides were knotted into a giant ball of pain, and he couldn't even drown his sorrows in work.

"So fight harder!" Hector opened the grill again, and smoke billowed out.

"No." Quentin held out a platter for his brother to load up with burgers. "She made her choice to stay. She didn't want to fight for her future or fight for me. I'm done pushing her. If she's not ready to be honest with herself or her family, then nothing I can say or do will change that. I need to let it go." His grip on the plate slipped, and he put his other hand underneath. "I need to let her go."

Once again, he'd put his heart on the line. And once again, he'd gotten burned. Only this time it wasn't just his personal life up in smoke; his professional life had gotten caught up in the blaze, charred beyond recognition.

But the fire between him and Alisha didn't compare to anything he'd ever experienced. When he'd lost Mercedes, what hurt the most was the pain of a lost future and shattered dreams. In losing Alisha, he'd lost a friend, a confidante, and—he shuddered as the word popped unbidden to his mind—a soul mate.

But forget all that. Forget meant to be and destiny. All that mattered was a person's choices, and Alisha hadn't chosen him.

CHAPTER 38

ALISHA

A block ahead, a slight, stooped man Alisha recognized as Dr. Yates from his staff photo sat at a wrought iron bistro table, checking his watch. She waited for the traffic light to change, clenching her purse strap in her hands. The shadows from nearby buildings hung over the sidewalk, blanking his face in a smudge of charcoal. Why had she insisted on doing this in person? Surely a phone call would've sufficed.

But the **WALK** sign flashed on and propelled her off the curb, across the street. One step, another.

Forward motion. Action. *No more hiding, Alisha.*

He'd spotted her. Her steps faltered, ankle turning in a misstep. Quagmire nipped at her heels, but she kept moving, out of the quicksand of doubt.

Forward. Action.

Dr. Yates stood up, shoved one hand in his pocket, careless, casual. But the other hand smoothed his tie, restless, and though his eyes were hidden behind sunglasses, the edges of his mouth pinched tight. "Ms. Blake?"

"Dr. Yates." They shook hands.

Stand tall, Alisha. But he'd taken his seat. Er, sit tall. She used the table to steady herself. Sank into the chair. Straightened her spine. Pushed aside that nagging, naked feeling of exposure. And used her voice.

"Thank you for meeting me." Okay, so baby steps.

"Of course." He inclined his head her way with a tight smile. "We're indebted to you and your family for your contribution."

"Indebted." The perfect word choice. She'd come to call up the debt, is all.

"Yes, well . . . actually, that's what I came here about. We're no longer comfortable with the university excavating on our land."

He swept off his sunglasses to reveal narrow-set blue eyes. "Ma'am, if this is about Dr. Harris—"

"It's absolutely about Dr. Harris." About using her voice when he needed her most. The last time they'd spoken, she'd used her words to build a wall and shove him off into the chasm below. But now her words could be a lifeline. "Your handling of the situation is unacceptable."

Dr. Yates dug his fingers back over his head, leaving tracks in his thinning gray hair. "Couldn't agree more. His conduct was inexcusable. He should've known better than to embroil you in this drama."

"This *drama*," Alisha said, channeling Grandpa's flair for meaningful emphasis, "has nothing to do with Quentin's ability to do his job. And he didn't drag me into anything. It was mutual. A relationship." Her voice caught. It *had been* a relationship. Now? More collateral damage from her inability to fight for what she wanted. "And the fact remains that Quentin's private life is no one's business."

"I would disagree." Leaning back, he tucked his sunglasses into the pocket of his shirt. "Clearly Harris lost focus."

"Really?" Alisha withdrew a manila envelope from her purse. Gripped it tightly to still her shaking hands. "Because I have a signed document here from his grad students saying Dr. Harris provided excellent guidance all summer. And another letter from Dr. Reid, stating that

Quentin was indispensable in every part of the excavation, including being the one to identify the first dinosaur fossils in our state."

She passed the envelope to Dr. Yates, then placed it next to his americano when he didn't reach for it. "In layman's terms, Quentin did excellent work this summer, and also happened to have a girlfriend. He didn't leak the photo, nor has he done anything personally to tarnish the reputation of the university. In fact, your treatment of him following this invasion of his privacy is the only disgrace."

The speech rattled out faster than she'd practiced, but she'd spoken nonetheless.

"I can't think what else we could've possibly done, under the circumstances." His voice was cool, his ice-blue eyes colder.

Offer support. Go on record to defend Quentin. "Here's what you can do now. Reinstate Quentin fully. Or the tyrannosaur skull the crew unearthed yesterday becomes the foundation for my grandparents' swimming pool."

His eyes flashed. Boom. Her ace in the hole, and he'd never seen it coming.

Shuttering the eagerness in his expression, Dr. Yates pushed up his cuffs, placed his elbows on the table, palms up. A phony gesture of supplication. "Ms. Blake, you must see how bad this makes us look. One of our scientists, caught in a compromising position in the field."

"He was kissing his girlfriend in her backyard." Alisha gripped the sides of her purse, willing the flashes of memory away. Steeling her resolve. "Are your staff not allowed to date? Do they need to submit their partner choices for peer review?"

"Ms. Blake—"

"I'm pretty sure the only thing that makes you look bad is how eager you were to invalidate a colleague's role in a groundbreaking discovery." She stood, scraping her chair against the concrete. Shouldered her purse and looked down at Dr. Yates, waiting for him to meet her eyes. Then she summoned her last reserve of courage and found her voice.

"The choice is yours, Dr. Yates. Lose out on access to the discovery of a lifetime, or give a deserving man his job back."

🐾🐾

Legs still wobbly after her confrontation with Quentin's boss, Alisha walked off the elevator and up to a familiar apartment door. She opened the lock with her spare key and stepped inside. Fingertips to the entry-way wall, she slid off one heel, then the other. She squatted down to stack the pumps neatly by the door. Arriving midday would give her a few hours to collect herself before launching into phase two of her mission.

"Ali?"

Or not.

Caught unawares like a cat burglar, she looked up to find her sister walking out of the hallway from the bedroom. "Sim! I didn't think you'd be home yet." She took in the dark circles under Simone's eyes, the silk wrap around her edges. A baggy Bulls tee and men's boxers dwarfed her slender frame. "What's going on? Are you sick?"

"Really with the interrogation? This is my place; I don't need to answer to you." Hands on her slim hips, Simone exuded the haughty authority of a deified cat in ancient Egypt. "But no, I'm not sick. I'm unemployed." She dropped the bombshell without emotion, typical Sim.

A car alarm went off somewhere below, breaking the silence that followed. Alisha straightened up, wary. "Unemployed?"

"Yep. Surprise." Simone made sarcastic jazz hands.

"Since when?"

"Yesterday." She slouched over to the couch and fell backward, tossing her stockinged feet up on the glass coffee table. "What I thought was a promotion was actually a 'Kindly pack up your things and go screw yourself.'"

Hesitant, Alisha hovered at the edge of the living room, but Simone pushed up onto her elbows, forestalling any consolation. "I don't want sisterly wisdom right now. What I do want to know is, Why the heck are you here?"

She gulped. Pressed her lips together. "I have news." If telling her sister was hard before, now, in the wake of Simone's awful announcement, it seemed downright disrespectful. And yet, what had Meg said? *There's always going to be a dinosaur . . .* "Good news, but it can wait."

"Obviously not, if you drove all this way and snuck into my place."

"It's not breaking in if I have a key."

Simone pursed her lips. "Debatable. Now, tell me. What's the big news?"

Alisha cleared her throat, mustered the courage to use her voice, for herself this time.

For her future.

"I'm moving to Chicago." All nerves, like a new baker rolling out fondant for a wedding cake, she stomped on her doubts and pushed forward. "Opening up a cookie shop, hopefully by fall."

Simone's eyebrows shot up, but she stayed as still as a submerged crocodile. "When were you going to tell me you wanted out?"

"Now. This is me telling you." Alisha willed iron into her spine.

"Is this because of Quentin? Because I liked him, but dang, sis, you don't need to sell out for a man."

Alisha shook her head. "Selling out is the opposite of what I'm doing. I'm finally following my dreams."

"But what about the noise? The crowds?"

She twisted a curl near her temple. "Yeah, so I haven't been the most honest with you."

"The most honest?" Simone leaped off the couch, her calm facade falling away in an instant. "The most *honest*? You've been lying through your little teeth."

She deserved that. "I have been, for a long time. Look, I'm sorry, Sim. I know this seems sudden, and I should've told you. I—" Alisha latched on to the back of one of the black leather barstools, scrambling for a foothold among seven years of half truths.

"What about Honey and Hickory?" Simone worked her jaw sideways. "Where does that leave Grandpa?"

"Not like I'm indispensable. He'll find someone else to take over. Maybe Hank."

"Hank? He's older than Pops, for gosh sakes!" Her sister pushed the heel of her hand up under her nose. Sniffed hard.

"Sim, it'll be all right. I won't leave until it's all taken care of." Shocked to see tears in Simone's eyes, Alisha felt her heart shattering, and the shards pierced her chest. Simone *never* cried, the one trait they shared. "Oh, Simi. C'mere." She crossed the room and wrapped Simone's willowy frame in a hug.

But her sister broke the embrace and wiped a hand carelessly under her dripping nose. "Get off me."

"Sim, I get that you're upset."

"Upset? Yeah, I'm upset! You've had everything handed to you your whole life, and you're just going to throw it all away?"

Flinching at the slice of her sister's words, Alisha tamped down the urge to spin and walk out the door. Flee confrontation. But she couldn't take back her words, and suddenly she didn't want to. She wanted to see this through, to show Simone how much she needed a fresh start.

"You were set. A stake in the family business. A *home*." Simone's voice broke on the last word. "And you're giving it all up? Why?"

Forget running away. The nerve of her entitled baby sister, calling *her* out?

"What do you mean, 'Everything handed to me'? I put all my dreams aside for you! I moved back home to take care of Granny so you could focus on school. I became Grandpa's right hand so you wouldn't have to." She leaned toward Simone, close enough to see the gold-dust flecks in her eyes swimming in tears, no longer moved by the demonstration. "You're the one who's had everything handed to you, *sis*. A life in the city and a career on your own terms!"

"My own terms? My *own terms*?" Simone jabbed Alisha's chest, and Alisha wanted to wrench her finger off. "You think I wanted to leave my friends and family? Sell my horse? Move hundreds of miles away from the only home I knew? You muscled me out."

"I *what*?" Too shocked to process the information, Alisha gaped at her sister.

"While you were off at college, who do you think stepped up? Me! I'm the one who turned down extracurriculars and hanging out with my friends so I could put in more hours at Honey and Hickory. And I was the one *right there* after Granny's diagnosis, taking care of her, holdin' it down. Until you rode in on your white horse like some kind of self-styled savior."

Tears streamed down Simone's face now, and she choked on her snot. "And after all that, after all *I'd* done, you waltzed back home for Christmas, and Pops handed it all over to you, like I was nothing."

Alisha pressed a hand to the stool, steadying herself. "But you wanted out. You said at your graduation you couldn't stand to be in Hawksburg anymore."

"And you said you loved it there." Simone grabbed a roll of paper towels off the counter, tore one off, and mopped her face. "Clearly we're a pair of liars."

Hand clutched to her roiling stomach, Alisha shook her head in horror. "Land sakes alive, Simone."

Tossing the wadded-up paper towel onto the coffee table, Simone dragged her palms hard against her cheek, the underside of her eyes showing. "But I'm happy for you. Wish I would've known years ago, but you've got what you wanted. We Blake girls always land on our feet, right? No matter what comes our way."

Alisha opened her mouth to reply, but the words wouldn't come. Briny tears dripped onto her lips, and she wiped them away with a trembling hand. All these years of disappointment heaped and piled into mountains of pain. All the unbearable, bone-deep heartache. For nothing.

For worse than nothing. To cause her sister pain.

"Simone." On numb legs, she walked over and sank down on the couch, wrung out. "I had no idea. If only I would've known." A sudden hiccupping laugh seized her, and she clutched her chest.

Through a veil of tears, she saw Simone recoil. "This funny to you?"

"No, Sim." She waved a hand and gulped air. "It's not funny. It's sad. It's awful. I feel sick."

"Glad I have your pity." Simone crossed her arms. "That's not what I wanted. I've never needed or wanted your compassion."

Pressing the heel of her hand to the corner of one eye, then the other, Alisha said, "That's not what I meant, Sim. I don't pity you. I just hate the whole situation. And it's so *epically* stupid, because I never even wanted it. All these years I kept my mouth shut because I'm the oldest, and when Granny needed me most, I wasn't there. And then I knew, I just *knew*, you were going to get roped into Honey and Hickory. Already had been, while I was off gallivanting at college. I stole almost four years from you, and I couldn't forgive myself. Especially since I'm the reason you lost Dad."

"Hold on, sis. You think *you're* the reason Dad left?" Her sister collapsed next to her on the sofa like her legs wouldn't hold her any longer, and Alisha saw the five-year-old girl who'd lost her mother.

"I was so sad. So needy. Always asking him for things, pestering him. If only I could've kept it together, we might still be a family." Alisha started sobbing again and gestured jerkily to herself. "I'm sure it didn't help that I look j-j-just like Momma. He couldn't handle it. He couldn't handle *me*. And so you lost out on him too."

Her sister flew across the cushions like a streak of lightning and squeezed her in a tight hug before she could finish. "I always knew you were crazy." Simone pulled away and cupped Alisha's cheeks. "You think our father left because you were too much to handle?" Through fresh tears, Alisha nodded, bringing her sister's hands along with her.

"You were a child, Alisha. A child who'd just lost her mom." Simone's forehead crumpled. "You weren't supposed to be a rock. Heck, neither was he. He just needed to be there. But he wasn't." Simone searched her face. "You are not the reason that man left. Our deadbeat, no-good, worthless father left because he was too cowardly to raise two young women on his own."

Alisha turned away, but Simone grabbed her damp chin and dragged her back. "Do you hear me? You were just a kid, Ali. And if you'd been a grown woman, it wouldn't have made a bit of difference. Him leaving us was not your fault, or mine. Got it?" Alisha dodged her eyes to the side, and Simone pinched her chin. "I said, you hear me?"

She broke away. "Jeez, Simone, yes. I hear you."

Simone grabbed her again, cradling Alisha's head on her shoulder. "You can always speak up when you need to, sis. Your desires are important. *You* are important."

Face burrowed into her sister's perpetually Chanel-scented neck, Alisha hiccupped. "I missed this."

"What, arguing?"

"No, hugs."

Simone's shoulder vibrated under her. "Well, don't get used to it. I'm still not big on lovey-dovey crap."

"But the honesty? Can we keep that up?" Alisha sat up, gnawing at her lip. "If I'm hearing you right, you've been hiding a lot from me too. For a long time."

Her sister's eyes narrowed, and Alisha rushed on. "I'm not blaming you. I get it. You were trying to protect me. And I was trying to protect you. But that's the whole problem. Neither of us need another parent; we need a sister." She kept on talking, the words like WD-40 to unused hinges. "I never wanted to move back home or run a restaurant. All I ever wanted was to finish my degree and move to Chicago. Maybe because of Mom. Maybe cuz our best memories were there, I dunno."

She picked up speed and rattled on, giving free rein to the truth that sped out of her mouth like a runaway horse. No putting it back in the barn now. "Hawksburg has never felt like home. I knew if I ran Honey and Hickory, I'd never be able to leave, but I gave up everything so you could get out. I thought you *wanted* out."

Simone shook her head. "All I ever wanted was to *stay*. I barely remember life in the suburbs. Hawksburg's always been my home. And Granny and Pops are more my parents than my own. No offense to Momma," she said, and she traced the sign of the cross over herself. "My whole life was there, until it wasn't."

"You know, maybe you should think about moving back," Alisha said.

"What?"

"Move back. You lost your job. You don't love it here, right?" Alisha's head was spinning, but one thing was clear. "Take the restaurant!"

Simone stared at her.

"It's mine to give now, right? But I know Grandpa would've given it to you anyway if he'd known." She felt like a hot air balloon with the ropes cut. Jubilation hit Alisha like helium, and her voice rose. "Haven't you been listening, Sim? I don't want the restaurant. I never have."

She fished the keys out of her back pocket and pressed them into Simone's hands, cutting the ropes on the last weight holding her down. "But you do. So take it. Honey and Hickory is yours." She slammed the words down like a gavel and delivered herself free.

CHAPTER 39

QUENTIN

A heavy knock thudded on Quentin's office door.

"Come in." His eyes flicked over, and he almost dropped the book in his hands. "Dad?"

His father hovered at the doorway, a polo stretched across his broad chest, wearing slacks and shined-up loafers, like he'd come for a job interview. "Is this a bad time?" He rubbed a palm over the top of his head, gleaming under the fluorescent lights. "I can go if you're busy."

Bad time, yes. Trust his father to show up at work at the very moment he stood to lose everything. But busy? Ha. What he wouldn't give to be busy right now.

"No, of course not." He closed the book, using his thumb to hold his place, and scooted around the desk. His knees knocked against the chair in the tight space and sent it clattering against the wall. "Have a seat." Quentin gestured to the other chair, noting its shabbiness with an internal wince. He suppressed the sudden urge to tidy his desk, muscle memory from eighteen years of his father hollering at him to clean up after himself.

His dad squeezed himself into the chair like a parent at kinder-garten teacher conferences, vulnerable and wary. Dad had never once visited campus, let alone set foot in his office. Why now? "Is everything all right? Ma? Is she okay?"

Reggie waved a hand. "Your mother's fine." Quentin opened his mouth, but his dad continued. "Hector and the girls too. Everyone's fine. That's not why I came by."

"Oh." At a loss, he sat.

His dad dropped his eyes. "My phone's been ringing off the hook since your interview came on." He leaned back, but the wall brought him up short. "Everyone and their dog calling to congratulate me on my genius son. Not like I didn't know I had a bright kid. But hearing about your success from other people . . ." His cheek bulged where he poked his tongue into it.

"Success? I got kicked off the dig, Dad. You know that."

Reggie looked up, his brown eyes earnest. "You getting kicked off the dig has no bearing on your success, Q. Fact is, you made a ground-breaking discovery. People are trying to take it away from you, but I'm the one who's been stealing your achievements all along." His dad pressed a knuckle to the corner of his eye. "Your own father, tearing you down. I'm ashamed, Q. Ashamed it took someone else knocking you down to make me realize I've been doing it all along."

His father stretched out one leg, and the chair creaked. "It's not about the money, Q. Never has been. I just had such high hopes for you. Not every day a man fathers a genius. No offense to your brother."

Quentin grinned at that, shaking his head.

Somewhere down the hall, behind the closed door, a conversa-tion started up. His dad continued, voice pitched low. "I guess what it comes down to is, I never understood your interest in dinosaurs. Ancient monsters? What's to be gained from studying them? But I've been a fool. Doesn't matter whether I understand or not. It doesn't matter if this"—he gestured around the cramped office—"is what I would've picked for my son. It's not my life, Q. It's yours."

Quentin's breathing picked up, and Dad brushed a finger under his nose, pressed a thumb to the corner of his eye. "Now I see you're exactly where you need to be, changing the world. I'm sorry I stood in your way for so long, Quentin. Will you forgive me?"

Tears in his eyes matching his father's, Quentin nodded.

"Now, about this nonsense about you being suspended—"

Another knock sounded on the door, and before Quentin could say anything, Tre poked his head in. "Oh . . . hi, Mr. Harris." His eyebrows shot up, and he sent Quentin a totally obvious wide-eyed look of amazement. "Sorry, Q, didn't realize you had a visitor."

"It's fine, Tre." Reggie leveraged himself out of the low seat. "I was just leaving."

"Why not stay and celebrate?"

"Celebrate?" The Harris men spoke in unison, voices rusty.

Tre grinned. "Check your email. Word is, Lawrence met with Alisha yesterday."

"Alisha?" Here? Talking to Lawrence? But Alisha didn't confront people, not even her own family. No way she'd schedule a meeting with the chair of his department.

But Tre nodded. "That's what I hear. Just got off the phone with Bridget. Apparently she's been trying to reach you all morning."

Yeah, his phone was persona non grata right now, along with the entire internet. After signing into his laptop, he navigated straight to his inbox. One new message, from Lawrence.

His finger hovered over the mouse. Tre could be wrong. This could be the final blow, terminating his employment with the university and tanking his career. In front of his best friend. In front of his *father*.

He closed one eye. Clicked open the email. And let out a whoop.

"I'm reinstated! Cleared to go back to Hawksburg and finish out the season."

Alisha. She'd saved him. Spoken up when he needed her most. But how?

Leaning against the doorframe, Tre pushed up his glasses, a lopsided grin on his face. "Looks like your farm woman went to bat for you after all."

CHAPTER 40

ALISHA

Alisha got out of the car and stretched, muscles tight after the long drive, but Simone jumped out and slammed her door, lithe and limber. She caught Alisha's eye with a shrug. "Yoga. You should try it, old woman."

"If your sister's old, what am I?" Granny, red faced and sweaty under her sun hat, walked over from spreading mulch in the garden and squeezed them both in a hug.

"Well preserved." Simone grinned and stooped to plant a kiss on her grandma's cheek.

Tilting up the brim of her hat, Granny raised her brows, swinging her eyes toward Simone in a silent question, and Alisha nodded. "I told her."

Simone stepped back and crossed her arms. "And I still can't believe I'm not the first to hear. But I'm glad you're okay with it, Gran."

"Okay with what?" Wayne walked around from the side yard, rubbing a hankie over his brow. He planted a kiss on Simone's forehead. "What'd I miss? Other than a heads-up Sim was coming to town."

She could do this. Speak up. "Actually, Grandpa, I was hoping to call a family meeting."

"What? No." Simone raised her arms in an X in front of her face. "A family meeting was not part of the plan, Al."

But Wayne grinned. "Lemme fetch the pyrite, and I'll meet you ladies out on the back porch."

"This is beyond cheesy." Simone slouched down in her chair, pouting like a preteen.

"Ah-ah." Grandpa shook his finger at her. He tossed a glittery rock up, then snatched it out of the air. "You're not holding the fool's gold, you don't get to speak."

"Really, Pops? We're not twelve anymore."

He smiled indulgently at Simone's petulance. "Your sister is the one who called the meeting; I'm merely enforcing the bylaws."

"'Bylaws,' he says." But Simone hushed up.

"All right, Ali. You called this meeting; I'll give you the floor." He tossed the hunk of pyrite toward her, and she caught it, barely. Maybe this hadn't been such a good idea. She'd forgotten the rule of only one voice allowed at a time.

Could she get this out all on her own? Telling Granny before she left for the city had been shockingly easy, and breaking the news to Simone was like ripping off a Band-Aid. But Grandpa? Forget Band-Aids. She was about to dump raw alcohol on an open wound.

Simone made a bid for the pyrite, lunging forward like a cobra, but Alisha clutched it in her fist. Just the incentive she needed. "Simone, please. Enough with this tough-girl front. I know you miss our family meetings."

"I legit do not."

"Nuh-uh-uh. No talking." Alisha made a snapping motion with her hand. "You'll get your turn. But first, I've got something to say."

She pivoted on the blue-and-white-checkered ottoman to face Grandpa. "I don't want Honey and Hickory."

The room went still, letting in the drone of cicadas in the trees. Smoke from the Snyders' grill wafted over, and her stomach clenched at the savory aroma of charred meat. Turning the hunk of fool's gold in her hand, she said, "I shouldn't have accepted the restaurant, Grandpa. I've had a plan, for quite some time, to move to Chicago and open up my own bakery."

Alisha glanced toward her grandma, who smiled encouragement. "But I didn't tell you, any of you, because I was scared to let you down. Scared following my dreams meant abandoning you. But it doesn't. I'm not my dad. I might leave town . . ." She caught herself. "I *am* leaving town, but I'm not leaving this family. I'll always be here for you, even if I'm living in the city."

Nobody moved. Nobody spoke.

She set the jagged piece of fool's gold on the floor and rolled it toward her grandfather. It skipped and bounced along the threadbare braided rag rug and came to rest against his grass-stained tennis shoe.

Tipping forward, he swept out a loose fist and scooped it up. Set it on his knee.

"You know why your father, my son, left? Know why he walked out on you?"

Heart shrinking, Alisha shook her head.

Her grandpa ran his palms down his khakis, caught up the piece of fool's gold, and squeezed it in his fist. "Me neither. But I've spent years asking myself why, and the only thing I can think of was because of me. I'm his dad, see? A son needs his father. Needs his father to be strong, sure. But he needs his father to make space for him. And I didn't. When he didn't seem interested in the restaurant business, I resented it. So much so I pushed him away. He was my only son. I—" Wayne's voice cracked. "Anyway, when he pulled what he did, all I wondered is, 'What if I'd given him roots? What if he had ground beneath him? Would he have left then?' Maybe so. And then again, maybe not."

He looked up at Alisha. "I've been trying to give you roots, Ali. Though you never seemed to need them. Heck, seems more like what you needed was wings."

Wings, not wheels. Alisha brushed a hand across her cheek, and it came off wet.

"But you seemed so stressed these past few years. Hardly smiling. Up late baking. Waking before dawn just to finish out an order. Always on your phone with that social media stuff you said was a pain in the butt half the time. I thought maybe if I gave you Honey and Hickory, an established business, it'd give you the freedom to stop struggling. Guess I was wrong. All I did was mess up another kid."

"Oh, phooey," Ellie said, and Alisha laughed in spite of herself.

"Granny's right. You didn't ruin me, Grandpa. We're just both terrible at saying what we mean."

"Well, let me try again, then." Her grandfather leaned forward, his blue eyes dry but warm as blueberries in a cobbler. "I never meant to tie you down, or make your dreams seem unworthy, Alisha. I love you."

She swiped at another tear. "I did a lot of assuming, too, Grandpa. It's not all on you. And I love you so much."

Clapping, Simone jumped to her feet. "Bravo! Well done, you two. Family meeting adjourned."

"Um, no." Alisha leaped up and blocked her sister's escape. "You've got some explaining of your own to do, missy."

Simone sat down. Kept her mouth closed.

"Are you not going to tell them, Sim?"

Hand to her chest, she looked around. "Oh, me? What, we're done with the rock nonsense now?" She leaned forward and rested her elbows on her knees, toying with the silver ring on her thumb. "I miss Hawksburg. I've been wanting to move back, but I don't know if I ever would've, except . . ." She took a deep breath. "I got fired. And then Alisha showed up and told me she was moving to the city and—"

"I offered her Honey and Hickory."

Simone looked toward their grandfather. "Is that okay?"

"Why are you asking me? It was your sister's place to do with as she liked." Simone set her jaw, and he relented. "'Course I'm okay with it, baby girl. Long as it's what you want?"

She nodded.

"About dang time." Everyone's eyes swiveled toward Granny. "I'm thrilled you made a decision without asking our permission first, Ali."

"You are?"

Both her grandparents nodded.

"Me too," Grandpa said. "All I wanted was to see you happy, Alisha. See you whole. I'm sorry if I ever got in your way."

"Speaking of happy, can we get to the part where our Ali gets her happily ever after with a certain someone?" Granny bobbed her eyebrows. "I'm dying to know how it went with Quentin's boss."

The screen door swung open, and Meg stomped in, wearing tall rubber boots and cutoffs, her hair twined into a fishtail braid. "Yeah, Ali. Is Dr. Hot Stuff reinstated or not?"

"Who invited her?" Simone slumped back in her chair, glowering at Meg.

"Hello to you, too, Sim. And no one invited me, but it looks like I showed up right on time. Unless I'm interrupting something?"

"Yes."

Granny shot Simone a glare. "'Course not, Meg. We're just all anxiously waiting to hear Alisha's plan to win Quentin back."

"I don't have one. This right here?" She looked around the room. "This is my happily ever after."

Meg blew a raspberry. "Two thumbs down."

"For once I concur with Margaret," said Simone. "Zero out of five stars. Would not recommend."

Her family needed to back off. Maybe they should've started this conversation with a refresher on boundaries. "It's not meant to be, okay?"

"Are you kidding me, Ali?" Meg crossed her long arms. "You're deserting me after all, and it's not even for a man?"

Alisha gave Meg a side-eye. "I thought you were okay with me leaving?"

"I am! Or I was, when I thought you were in full possession of your faculties. But you're giving up on a future with Quentin for what? Pride?"

Her family and best friend all stared at her, their faces identical, unamused masks. She wanted to roll back the rug and hide underneath. "You don't know the full picture. He's not just gone because he got kicked off the job. Before that, the night of the party, I broke up with him."

"Alisha Marianne Blake." Granny pursed her lips.

"I was going to stay here in Hawksburg! What would be the point of us dating any longer?"

"The future isn't set in stone, hon. The least you could've done was give it time."

Alisha hung her head. "That's what he said. He begged me to reconsider. Said he'd wait years for me to get the restaurant settled."

"And?" The word rang out in chorus, and Alisha groaned.

"And I sent him packing! Chased him off like a stray dog begging for scraps." Her stomach curdled at the memory. "I proved to him I'm not cut out for the long haul. I couldn't even last a month in a real relationship."

"Not cut out for the long haul?" Grandpa broke in. "Ali, girl, you're *only* cut out for the long haul. If I'm hearing you right, you've wanted out of Hawksburg for seven years and not once said a word. If that's not constancy, I don't know what is."

"But dating me almost cost Quentin his job. He's not going to want to jump back into a relationship."

"You also saved his job." Granny shook her head. "I'm not saying you two need to start necking on the dig site again . . ."

"Gran!" Simone reached over and pushed their grandma's knee, grinning gleefully.

"But at least call the man."

But Granny didn't know about his ex. About how Alisha had become yet another woman Quentin cared about who'd taken his faith in her and dashed it to pieces.

"What's done is done. I'm not going to put him in a position of feeling bad for turning me down. Of needing to explain why we won't work. It's better this way. Cleaner." The circle of loved ones around her looked ready to argue back, but she shook her head. "Really. I have more than I need right here. Any more would be greedy."

How could she expect Quentin to trust her after what she'd done? Why beg for a second chance? She'd proved herself unworthy of him. All she could hope now was that he'd forget about her and move on.

CHAPTER 41

ALISHA

November

The bell over the door tinkled, letting in the hum of the city street and the skitter of dry leaves along the sidewalk.

"Welcome to Vanilla Honey," Alisha sang out, sliding a tray of golden-brown scalloped madeleines onto a display shelf. Butterscotch notes of blond chocolate wafted toward her. The flaked sea salt on top balanced the sweetness and lent texture to the airy cookies. "I'll be right with you."

"No hurry. Are your macarons vegan?"

She leaned deeper into the case to straighten the label. "Not all of them, but we do have several varieties of vegan cookies. Anything marked with a *V*, and *GF* if you're looking for gluten-free." Satisfied, she straightened up and peeled off her gloves, beaming her best customer-service smile directly into Caitlyn's grinning face. "Cait?"

"How's it been, Al, gal?"

"Um, good?" Seeing Cait brought memories surging back. Memories of Quentin she'd spent the past three months suppressing. Her smile wobbled.

"Just messing with you about the vegan cookies, Ali. Bring on the butter." Cait eased down the display, squatting to take a closer look at the spiced pumpkin whoopie pies with toasted-marshmallow cream filling Alisha had created in a nod to autumn.

Every time she whipped up a fresh batch, she battled away memories of Quentin's eyes dark as dusk across the fire, the sweetness of their first kiss. But Caitlyn's voice brought her back to the present.

"You know I've been Insta-stalking you since the day you fed me those to-die-for snickerdoodles. Been meaning to stop in since your grand opening." Cait planted her hands on khaki-clad knees and straightened up. "I've got to be honest: I came for the cookies, but I also stopped in because—"

The door to the shop opened again, and a group of middle-aged ladies came in.

Stepping aside, Cait bowed at the waist and swept out her arm. The women gave her a weird look but placed their order. Alisha fetched their selections and rang them up, one eye on Cait, who sat down at one of the brushed-gold tables, following her movements like a cat with a mouse.

Jittery, she somehow managed the transaction without dropping anything and then thanked her lucky stars she only had to reswipe the credit card once.

Cait jumped up the moment the three women had left, unzipping her windbreaker like she planned to stay for a while. "Okay, you're low on apple-butter thumbprints, so best get me three of those before someone else comes in. When do you close? Soon, right?"

She checked the purple agate wall clock. "Five minutes."

Cait's dark-brown eyes lit up. "Perfect. I'm gonna clean you out. But before we get to that . . ." She bit into one of the cookies Alisha had handed her. "OMG, yesss." She hugged herself and danced in place on the quartz-tiled floor. "Have you tasted this? Duh, of course you have—you're the sugar maven who created it." She took another bite, speaking with her mouth full. "Okay, back to business. Why the heck are you ghosting Dr. Harris?"

The question caught her off guard. "It's not ghosting if the other person wants nothing to do with you." At the other woman's skeptical look, she threw up her hands. "I singlehandedly imploded his career, Cait."

"Jeez, God complex much? There were two people in that photo, lest you forget, and one behind the camera. Besides, you fixed everything, so it's water under the bridge." Caitlyn swallowed. "Got any milk?"

Alisha pointed to the refrigerator case on the far wall, wishing it housed bottles of liquor instead.

"Nice. Blake thought of everything." Cait grabbed a half pint of skim milk and knocked it back like a shot, then wiped her mouth with the back of her wrist. "Back to you and Doc Harris."

Alisha opened her mouth, but Cait raised a hand. "I know you think he hates you, but if that's the case, why's he been moping around campus like a broody Heathcliff?"

"I wouldn't know." She kept her tone level, braced her palms on the steel countertop.

"Right, because you've been staying away because of some misguided martyr complex. Look"—she used her pinkie and thumb to dig a paper out of her pocket and slapped it on the counter like exhibit A—"I don't wanna get up in your business."

Alisha's eyebrows went up, and Cait grinned.

"Okay, so that's a lie. But can you blame me? Thanks to you and your family, I got the chance to work on a dig that will change the future of paleontology, so I feel like it's my civic duty to make sure you don't make a huge mistake." She tapped the flyer with her fingernail. "Just come to this. And if you still wanna live your life Harris-free, at least you'll have all the facts."

She polished off the third cookie, licking her fingers. "On to business. I've got fifty bucks and three sugar-crazy roommates. Hit me with the good stuff."

Moving on autopilot, Alisha filled up a box with cookies, though her mind was racing. Quentin didn't blame her for almost costing him his job? But why hadn't he reached out? *Because you drove him away.* Used her words to evict him from her life, and never to make amends.

Cait dropped some bills on the counter. "Life's too short to wallow, Al, pal." She picked up the stacked boxes and backed out the glass door. "Nothing like working with bones from millions of years ago to lend a little perspective. Time is not on your side."

Shell shocked, Alisha scooted around the counter and locked the front door, then collapsed into one of the teal plastic chairs and rested her forehead against the brushed-gold tabletop, finally grasping the truth of her self-imposed misery.

She'd kept herself from Quentin. If Cait was telling the truth, he'd stayed away to respect her wishes, not because he couldn't bear to be around her. Once again, she'd let self-doubt take the wheel. There was no one but her own foolish self to blame.

Meg had told her, and she hadn't listened. Quentin had begged her to see the truth, and she'd banished him. But they were both right: abandoning wasn't in her DNA. Her dad had made a horrible mistake all on his own. And she'd kept her distance because she'd never fully evicted her fears, clinging to the lie she was tainted by an innate flaw.

But she could do better. She'd *done* better. Fixed her mistakes, stood up for herself and those she loved. Leaving wasn't in her genes. *Love* was in her genes, imprinted on her soul. Her mom's unconditional love, right up until cancer claimed her body. Granny's quiet support. Grandpa, pushing her to be the best. Simone keeping tabs on her even from hundreds of miles away.

Love radiated through her veins with every beat of her heart. Love and the power to do her best for those she loved, including herself.

Quentin's face appeared in her mind, storm-gray eyes locked on hers, a smile on his lips. *Home.*

She unfolded the flyer in her hands and smiled. Jumped up and strode back into the kitchen. Pacing, she pulled her cell phone from her back pocket and dialed Meg. "You'll never guess who stopped by."

"The hot doc?"

"I wish." Unable to tame her giddy grin, Alisha pulled down a stack of containers to fill with unsold cookies for a woman's shelter.

"Wait, you *do* wish Quentin stopped in?"

"Yup. Meg, I need to go get him."

"Well, duh." Meg never minced words. "Woman, I've been telling you that since March, but you're the most stubborn person I know."

A loud squawk came through the phone, and Meg said, "I swear to you, if you don't leave the hens alone . . . sorry, this rooster is about to make me lose my dang mind. Do you think he'll take you back?"

"The rooster?" Alisha grinned, then sobered up, quick. She'd wasted so much time. "I'm not sure. He might never want to see me again." The possibility gutted her. "But I've gotta know. I've gotta tell him how I feel."

"Attagirl." Meg's support warmed her through the phone. "So what's the plan, Ali? Gonna grand-gesture him? Sneak into one of his classes and profess undying love on a hijacked PowerPoint presentation? Propose in sky letters at a Bears football game?"

"Tempting." She smoothed out the flyer on the counter. "But I'm going to keep things simple and just show up."

CHAPTER 42

QUENTIN AND ALISHA

Quentin tapped the notecards on the podium. He wouldn't need them, but the feel of the cardstock—familiar as dry earth and ancient rock—kept him grounded. He searched the lecture hall for the face of someone who offered that same safe harbor, amplified.

Would she come? Two days ago, he'd texted Alisha a screenshot of the event announcement. Didn't want to push. Didn't want to spill his feelings over text, garbled by distance and gone cold in transcription.

If she didn't come, he'd find another way to reach out, because he couldn't walk away without giving it one last shot. But oh, how he hoped she'd be here to witness the depths of his love on display for everyone to see. No longer caged in by doubts or curtailed by hesitation. Needed her to see the depths of the shift inside him, all because of loving her.

Work used to be his foundation, a perfectly planned future the center of his universe. But Alisha eclipsed all that. She was his bedrock, his shelter from the storm, and all the future he needed. He wanted to spend forever learning the shape and height and breadth of her. To give himself to her without holding back.

Dev touched his elbow. "Ready?"

No more time to stall, and Quentin nodded. In the second row, his mom caught his eye and waved. He chuckled and pulled the microphone toward himself. "Hi, everyone. Hi, Mom." Isabel cocked her head, lips pursed, but next to her, Hector laughed, his arms encircling both twins, perched on his knees.

"Welcome. And thanks for coming out on this chilly morning. As you know, we're here to talk about a momentous find. The first dinosaur fossils ever discovered in Illinois."

Next to him, Caitlyn whooped, and laughter rippled through the crowd.

"Yes, I think we can all agree it's a pretty big deal. We are presented with an opportunity to study these fossils, existing where they ought not to, as well as the unique geological conditions which allowed for their preservation."

Behind him, Tre grunted approval. Mr. and Mrs. Blake had granted the geology team access to the dig after Quentin had gotten reinstated. Tre might've been more excited about the chance to get his hands dirty on the field site than the impending birth of his own child.

Smiling, Quentin continued. "None of this would've been possible if not for the generosity of the Blake family, who not only allowed us to excavate on their property, but donated the fossils to the university."

A smattering of claps followed this announcement. He wished Alisha's grandparents could've made the trip, but he'd promised to send a recording, courtesy of his mother's propensity to document every moment of his life.

Of course, there was one Blake in particular whose absence he felt acutely. But hang on . . .

The door of the hall slid open, letting in a slant of light. A woman in a tight leather jacket and flowy skirt backed in, tripping over an invisible obstacle on the carpet, and his heart soared. *Alisha.*

Bent double, she slunk into the last row and pulled down the bottom of a seat, collapsing into it. Their eyes met, held.

The smile that lifted his cheeks turned wobbly, and when he glanced down at the notecards to buy time, the letters blurred. She'd come. Strength surged through his veins. Strength and euphoria and an exuberant sense of peace, like smudged sidewalk chalk muddled by raindrops into a burst of color. Happiness.

He put down the notecards, gripped the edges of the podium. "We're here to share our preliminary findings from the Hawksburg excavation. And if you would've told me at the start of this year that we'd be pulling dinosaur remains out of the dirt in western Illinois, I would've pinched myself, because surely I'd be dreaming."

He glanced up at Alisha to assure himself her presence was indeed real, and he found her eyes on his, lips parted.

"But so much of life is that way, right? You start out your life with dreams that seem so real you could reach out and grab them. For some of us, that dream is a singular thing. Paleontology, for me."

"Rubik's Cube world champion," Forrest muttered.

Quentin shot him a grin over his shoulder. "Whatever that dream is, circumstances either propel us toward it, or hinder us. Sometimes it doesn't look like we're on a path at all, but rather wandering in the wilderness. Something which"—he glanced at Dev and Cait—"I happen to know a little about as well."

Cait laughed and held up a finger. "One word: GPS."

He chuckled. "But other times, moments like this year, like today." He locked eyes with Alisha. "In these moments, all the lost and disparate pieces of your journey pull together, much like a shattered vertebra held together by superglue and a prayer. And as you begin to piece it together, the backbone, the essence of that thing you've been chasing all along, takes shape before you. And maybe it looks like what you imagined, but other times it's completely unexpected. New, and staring back at you. Whole and real and complete before you ever came along.

"And all we're doing"—he leaned one elbow on the podium, and though he addressed the crowd, his words were for Alisha—"our whole role, in fact, is to let these bones speak for themselves. To not put words in their mouth or reshape them into what we want, what we expect."

A flash of red caught his eye—Alisha's fingers, toying with the fringe of her scarf.

With a deep breath, Quentin pushed on. "Paleontology has enriched my life in ways I never imagined. This dig reminded me of the sheer joy in asking questions, in seeking truth, in living one's life to the fullest in the pursuit of knowledge, yes. But also in the pursuit of joy."

He cleared his throat. "I can't take credit for this find. A man named Steve Snyder scraped the earth away. Eleanor, Wayne, and Alisha Blake offered up their land. Dr. Bridget Reid, and my students Forrest Abernathy, Caitlyn Hsu, and Dev Mehra, identified bones from at least three animals over the course of the summer, most notably the skull, ribs, ilium, and femur of a new species of tyrannosaurid."

Another whoop, from Forrest this time, and cheers from his family.

"All of us had a hand—or backhoe—in the process, but I've generously been afforded the honor of naming the dinosaur discovered in Hawksburg, Illinois. I can't lie and say I haven't been preparing for this moment since I was ten." Laughter rippled through the crowd.

"I could name this dinosaur based on where she was found. Or her physical characteristics. But after this summer of discovery, only one name fits. Without further ado, I'd like to introduce you to the new species unearthed on the Blakes' property, *Tyrannosaurus mariannae*. Strong, powerful, and determined not to stay hidden any longer."

🦕🦕

After the others had finished presenting, they'd ended with a short Q&A panel. Now Quentin stood off to the side and scanned the room. Alisha was nowhere in sight, but his mom stepped sideways down the stairs in heels and wool trousers.

"I got so many photos!" She held up her phone and scrolled down through what looked like an entire SD card's worth of pictures. Quentin barked out a laugh and squeezed her shoulder.

Dad stepped down after her and gave him a curt nod. "Good thing you kept it short; otherwise, people in the back row might've nodded off." But he winked, a gesture Quentin hadn't seen in years, and yanked him in for a bear hug.

"I pick up your slack for thirty-three years and don't even get a dinosaur named after me?" Hector appeared, trailed by Lauryn, so focused on the tablet in her hands she nearly tripped down the last stair. "This is some bull—" Lauryn swiveled her head to look up at her dad, and his eyes went wide. "—loney. Baloney."

Grinning at his brother's ridiculousness, Quentin scooped up his niece, and she wrapped spindly arms around his neck, cutting off his air supply. He peeled off her arms and sucked in a breath. "Thanks for coming to cheer me on, Laur. Where's your sister?"

"Right here."

Quentin whipped around, stumbling on noodle legs. Alisha stood behind him, holding Lily's hand.

Alisha Marianne.

Lily let go of Alisha's hand and launched herself at his leg, but all his attention was fixated on the woman in front of him.

"That was quite a speech, Dr. Harris. And don't worry . . ." She tipped sideways and grinned at his dad. "No one in the back row was even close to falling asleep."

Alisha messing around with his father? Was this the twilight zone?

"Glad to hear it." Chuckling, Reggie gently disentangled Lauryn from his arms. Ma grabbed Lily's hand and tugged her away from his leg.

"See ya later, Q." Hector's smile lit his eyes. "Glad you finally caught a break."

His family melted into the crowd. Heart fizzy like uncorked champagne, he gazed down at Alisha, her kinky curls full and big around her face, no trace of doubt or hesitation in her gorgeous dark eyes.

🐾🐾

"You came." Quentin rubbed a hand along his clean-shaven jaw, and Alisha instantly regretted not calling him months ago. Did he really think she'd stay away once she found out he wanted her here? A herd of stampeding hadrosaurs couldn't keep her away, not anymore.

"Of course I came." She darted a glance around the crowded lecture hall. "Can we meet up somewhere, after you're through?"

"I'm through." The ghost of a smile caught the edges of his full lips. She might swoon, for real. Quentin in a T-shirt and work boots was a lot, but Dr. Harris all dressed up? Like trying to look at an eclipse with the naked eye. He wore the heck out of a gray blazer and dark jeans, the collar of his sky-blue dress shirt open at his throat.

"You sure?" His chin jerked down in a quick nod. "Okay . . . well, in that case, follow me." She would've grabbed his hand, but Quentin didn't need any more workplace angst. Jogging up the stairs, she checked to see if he was following her and stumbled.

He caught her elbow. "No rush. I'm not going anywhere."

But there was a rush. A big freaking rush. She'd waited way too long for this, and now every moment without him felt like a waste. She led him through the pockets of students milling in the hallway, her sneakers squeaking on the tile, then out the double doors and onto the sidewalk.

One block down. Another. They passed the entrance to campus.

"Are you abducting me?" Laughter tinged his words. "Because if so, you might want to wait for cover of darkness."

"Almost there." She looped an arm through his and pulled him aside, onto a patch of grass, fallen leaves crunching under her sneakers. "Here. Now we're just two people in a park."

He smiled down at her. "I'm not a celebrity or anything, Alisha."

The daily influx of DMs from strangers asking what it was like to be with the sexy scientist from TV would beg to differ, but she let it slide. "I brought you out here because I need to tell you something important. And personal. And I don't want any of your colleagues listening in."

"Important? And personal?" A slow smile spread up his face, the sun's first rays over the horizon, and she fell for him all over again.

Shy in the face of his brilliance, she gripped the ends of her scarf. "First of all, my Latin's a little rusty, but I'm pretty sure you just named a new species of dinosaur after my mom."

"And you." Her brows tugged together, and Quentin stepped closer. "I named the dinosaur after your mom, yes. And you."

If she'd been about to faint earlier, now crying was a real possibility. "But why?"

"You know why."

"I do?" Tears pooled in her eyes, and she tilted up her chin to stem the flow.

"You're my Indy." He clasped her hands in his. "You thought it was me, fighting off the bad guys in khaki and a fedora."

She sniffed out a laugh.

"But it was you, Alisha. Fierce and powerful. Swooping in to save the day like an absolute hero. *My* hero." His eyes shone, crinkling at the edges with a smile, and she blinked away her tears, quick, because mascara.

"Dang it, Quentin, you're stealing my speech! Now all that's left is I love you!"

Whoops-a-daisy.

A slow smile spread on Quentin's face. "You love me?" He bit his lip, and at the sight of his white teeth sinking into the fullness, she had to yank her scarf away from her neck because, *dang* . . .

Focus, Blake.

"I love you, so much." Now that she'd said it, she couldn't imagine why she'd ever held back. "I only stayed away because I thought you'd want nothing to do with me after I almost cost you your job."

Quentin opened his mouth, but Alisha pressed a finger to his lips. "Stop. I know you're going to say something charming and sincere and make me lose it, so don't. Not yet. Okay?"

He nodded, lips warm and soft against her finger, and she moved her hand down to his lapel, gripping the fabric like a lifeboat.

"I've had my walls up since day one. And not just with you. I kept my defenses up for twenty years, with everyone." His heart thudded against her palm. "I wasted the last seven years of my life being too proud and too scared to speak up. But I'm done hiding."

She forced herself to meet his eyes, though sharing her feelings still felt brand new. "I've been so scared of what-ifs I never made space for joy. Until you."

Until she'd fallen madly, completely in love with Dr. Quentin Harris.

"I want you to know I'm here for you now, and I'll *be* here for you, as long as you'll have me. Our future isn't written in stone, but I want to be with you, Quentin. Even with all the uncertainty and the messiness and the what-ifs, I choose you."

During the last part of her declaration, his smile had faded. Eyes dark and intent, he trailed a finger down her scarf, twined the tassels around his finger. "You told me what you want. But you haven't asked what I want."

Hands shaking, she asked, "What do you want, Quentin?"

"You."

Before she could react, his lips were on hers. The heat of his embrace engulfed her, and his touch set her whole body ablaze. She threw her arms around his neck and pulled him into her, deepening the kiss. Her heart burst with happiness like a firework, and Quentin was the match.

He pulled away, just barely, and spoke, so close his breath brushed her lips, sending delicious tingles down her spine. "Real quick, can we rewind to the first part of your speech? I need to hear it again."

She blinked. "I spent my whole life being a scaredy-cat?"

He chuckled and skimmed his hands down her waist. "Further."

"You're too charming for your own good?"

He dug his fingertips into her hips and brought her closer. "Further."

"I love you?"

"That's the one." The green in his eyes shimmered like a lagoon at sunset, and the tenderness in his expression filled her heart to overflowing.

"I love you so much, Quentin."

He pressed his forehead to hers and smiled. "It feels so amazing to hear you say that." He kissed her again, long enough to leave her breathless. Pulling back the barest amount, he grinned against her lips. "Just so we're clear, I loved you first, Alisha Marianne. Details."

ACKNOWLEDGMENTS

A huge and heartfelt thank-you to my amazing agent, Rachel Brooks. You saw the potential in my sugar-laden, dino-centric love story, and I am forever grateful. Deepest thanks to my talented editor Lauren Plude, whose editorial chats helped me get to the heart of these characters and gave me a chance to talk dinosaurs and pop culture, two of my favorite things. Your incredible vision helped make this book shine. Thank you for being the best possible cheerleader for Alisha and Quentin's story. And to the entire Montlake team—thank you for all your hard work and for making my debut publishing experience wonderful. I know my book is in great hands.

Thank you to paleontologists Dr. Danita Brandt and graduate student Lynnea Jackson. Despite reading a gazillion (give or take) books about dinosaurs to my children over the years, I am by no means an expert, so I reached out to Danita, a paleontology professor from my alma mater, Michigan State University. She enthusiastically agreed to share her knowledge and also put me in touch with Lynnea, another paleontologist. Lynnea and Danita offered invaluable insight throughout the process, going above and beyond to provide background information, resources, and details about fossils and excavation procedure I never would've thought to ask about. I am indebted to them for their expertise. Thanks also to fellow author Denise Williams for answering my questions about what dating policies might look like for university faculty. Any errors are entirely my own.

I want to thank my stellar critique group for offering feedback on the early draft of my manuscript and for motivating me to sit down and write whenever a chapter swap loomed. Also, a big thank-you to my writers group, the starting point where I made the leap toward pursuing my writing goals in earnest. And a shout-out to all the members of the writing community I've connected with on Instagram and Twitter. Your support and encouragement mean the world.

To my best friend turned beta reader, Karsha, I'm so grateful to have you by my side on this next adventure. And thank you to Charlynn, who read the first draft in serial format, chapter by chapter. Your anticipation for the next installment gave me the boost to keep telling the story.

My mother, Cynthia, has earned the distinction of my best and biggest fan since my birth. You told me I could do anything I set my mind to often enough that eventually I began to believe it. My mom also deserves credit for taking me to a matinee showing of *Jurassic Park*, where I'm sure she bought us a giant tub of buttered popcorn, because she's wonderful like that.

Family, in particular grandparents, are an important part of this book, and my own are a big part of my life. My incomparable grandfather taught me to stay positive and not worry about things that are out of my control, lessons that served me well on the road to publication. And my lovely grandma has always been supportive of my goals, makes strawberry shortcake that tastes like summertime in a bowl, and picks up the phone anytime I call asking for a recipe or just to talk.

To the reader: Writing books has been my lifelong dream, and by reading this, you've made it come true. Thank you.

And finally, to my husband, Peter. Without him, I quite literally would never have found the time to finish this book. He cooked meals and took care of the kids so I could lock myself in the room and write or tackle revisions. On long walks he was my sounding board for sticky plot points, and he never once teased me for bringing up my characters at dinnertime like they were real people. Thank you for believing in my dreams and giving me the support to pursue them.

ABOUT THE AUTHOR

Chandra Blumberg is a Michigan native who loves writing funny, heart-warming love stories about characters that feel real and relatable. When it comes to her writing process, getting to that happily ever after is half the fun.

After majoring in English at Michigan State University, Blumberg moved to the Chicago area, where she enjoys exploring museums and the beauty of Lake Michigan in all seasons. When she's not writing, she's usually making a mess in the kitchen with her kids, lifting heavy barbells at the gym, or traveling with her family. *Digging Up Love* is her first novel.